THE END OF US

Also by Olivia Kiernan

Play Dead For Me
The Killer in Me
If Looks Could Kill
The Murder Box

THE
END OF US

Olivia Kiernan

riverrun

First published in Great Britain in 2023 by

riverrun

An imprint of
Quercus Editions Ltd
Carmelite House
50 Victoria Embankment
London EC4Y 0DZ

An Hachette UK company

A CIP catalogue record for this book is available
from the British Library

HB ISBN 978 1 52942 200 9
TPB ISBN 978 1 52942 201 6
EBOOK ISBN 978 1 52942 203 0

10 9 8 7 6 5 4 3 2 1

Typeset by CC Book Production
Printed and bound in Great Britain by Clays Ltd, Elcograf S.p.A.

For Matthew and Grace

PROLOGUE

I don't know if it all started with the murder.

I say that because surely there is a run-up to killing someone. Events that precede. Culminate.

So, before then, I think.

That night after dinner. The night the Wrights made us the offer. We were desperate, and although we could hardly take them seriously, I had the sense that they were throwing us a lifeline but of a preposterous sort where just as your head is slipping beneath the water, instead of a helping hand to pull you free, someone throws you a cruise liner.

At first, Lana laughed at their suggestion. However, I noticed that every time the conversation drifted on, she found a way to steer our chat back to the subject. She attempted to disguise her interest, kept it light, pairing the end of her questions with an easy laugh. She reclined in her chair and held herself with the relaxed pose of someone testing a hypothetical for entertainment's sake.

'No one would actually have to be killed?' she asked with

a half-smile, curling and uncurling a lock of her hair between thumb and forefinger.

But despite her playful tone, I could see the earnest fix in her wide dark eyes. How, as the idea was turned about, her questions became more pointed. And by the end of the evening, I knew the whole thing had taken root in her mind and already begun its corruption.

Maybe events were set in motion even earlier than that, on the morning Lana threw herself on the bed and showed me an advert in a Wimbledon lifestyle magazine.

'Look at these houses,' she said. 'Didn't you used to live near here?'

Belvedere Court. A new development. Six luxury houses in a closed court. Georgian style, Hampton chic. The Court, as we came to call it, was situated just outside Wimbledon Village, along the edge of West Side Common. And it had a price tag to match.

'Yes,' I said, looking over the glossy advert. 'Five or six bedrooms. For all our children?' I gave her a smirk. 'Could we use all that space?'

But that was the point of these houses, wasn't it? You didn't pay for capacity because you needed it, you paid because you could.

Lana and I were on the same page when it came to children. Not yet. Not for a while. If ever. Another reason her parents disliked me. We intended to enjoy our freedoms for a few years because that's what we equated children to, an end to fun. We'd no idea we could end it all on our own.

'Dog?' Lana offered with a raised brow.

'Dog,' I agreed.

We'd been married two months and were still living in my one-room flat in the village. We were happy as loved-up teens, pressed up against one another in that flat, but we were ready to move, if only to make a statement about where we were going, how our life was going to look. We were stupid enough to think that validation came in the shape of four thousand square feet of Georgian house.

The moment I saw those houses, it felt more than I belonged there but that it was owed. Financially, the repayments were a stretch. The one-foot-wrong-and-we-were-fucked kind of stretch, but how often does life give you the chance to take back something stolen from you? I'd spent my childhood in that area although our home had long been demolished. Some people want to move as far away from their history as possible but I had an overwhelming urge to press my face right up against it and whisper *Fuck you* into its ear. Within a couple of weeks of that morning, the banks had given us a mortgage, helped along with a more than sizeable payment from Lana's father, and within three we'd moved into our new home sans dog. But the house was new. Whatever issues unfurled within its walls were issues we brought in. And therefore, it couldn't have started there.

The more I think on it, the more I wonder whether there was any way things could have turned out differently. What would Lana call it? Determinism. The idea of choice is an illusion; we are all prisoners to our experience. I could have lived a hundred different endings but it's only after it has all unfolded that I can see the choices that were available to me. I could have started out in a thousand different directions, but I feel that somehow, all paths were pointing towards the same end.

And so, if Lana was right, perhaps fate began to play on a scorching day in 1981, the summer that Charles and Diana wed and the afternoon of my twelfth birthday. My friends had just left, my mother was clearing up the garden and I was sitting in our drawing room with my dad, Ambie. We were eating birthday cake and watching Wimbledon highlights. John McEnroe was shouting 'You cannot be serious!' at the umpire, which seemed, at the time, the most outrageous act of disorder. My dad muttered something about Americans, then beyond the large bay window that overlooked our garden a movement caught his eye. A man was approaching my mother.

I could just about make out 'Can I help you?' then the low rumble of the man's voice.

All the while my dad sat still as a dog on point; his head tilted; his breath held so he could hear.

'No. No,' finally from my mother. And whatever spell had held Ambie frozen was broken.

Slowly, he put down the cake, then murmured, 'I hoped they wouldn't come today.'

Life as I knew it dissolved like salt in water. Within hours, we'd been evicted from our home and were out on the street, squinting against the humiliating glare of our neighbours.

However, if I could draw a line from then to here, I could see that my need to create a future out of my past was not the sole reason for events to turn out like they did. If I were a man who looked for patterns in life, those little flags that, on reflection, indicated a change, I might notice that all the significant events

4

in my life were connected to either a departure or an arrival. The bailiffs arriving at our door on my twelfth birthday. My mother leaving for Spain a few weeks later. Lana and I moving to Belvedere Court.

And if I were to put my finger under any one occasion and name it as the day it all started to go wrong, I'd rest my hand beneath the day our new neighbours, the Wrights, moved in.

CHAPTER 1

I unfolded the letter with the same caution one might use to disarm an explosive. I laid it on the table in front of me, a fingertip on the top right corner, one on the bottom left and peered down at my fate. The flimsiness of the paper added to the insult. Here is your future and we couldn't be bothered announcing your demise on better stationery. No, you get an automated printout that hasn't passed through the hands of a human. *That is how little this matters to us. We neither care about nor need your money but we'll be taking it regardless.*

The sun was rising over Belvedere Court, pink and orange light spilled in through the window. I was sitting at the large island in our kitchen. Our kitchen could have been hand-plucked from one of those modern-day living glossy magazines. Light with punches of charcoal and grey. Marble floors. Snow-white cabinets next to a double-door stainless steel fridge and a twelve-hob cooker. The island itself was made of polished granite, a milky grey shade with dark veins of charcoal and black traversing the surface. The kitchen, living and dining areas were separated by a

7

wide hallway that led upstairs to the second floor. Beyond that, another spiral staircase ascended to a converted attic room, a home cinema, that spread under the pitched roof. We've never watched a movie there. But that wasn't the point. The house was more than bricks and mortar. It was the dream. A symbol of how far I'd come. That despite how much life tried to steal, take and claw from me, I'd made it.

I looked down at the letter. The words 'mortgage arrears' and 'repossession' rose up from the page. Our mortgage had always been a stretch. Nothing that my salary couldn't cover but it relied on those monthly earnings staying the same. And those earnings should have stayed the same, the promise was that they'd grow, but somewhere over the last year, they plateaued, then slowly began to decline. At first, I thought it was a minor dip that would, like a ship at sea, right itself. I had no idea of the invisible wave that was slowly consuming the world's economy. Those first few months, I was enviably naïve. I'd still believed that some of my investments would come good. One on a restaurant and another, suggested to me by my bank manager, on a block of flats in Dublin. Of course, it hadn't been my own money I'd invested, I'd tapped into what equity our home could offer, sure that, in time, I would see a return three-fold.

Overnight, it seemed, the money disappeared. Then over the next year, tied to a hefty mortgage I couldn't cover, my wages failing to pick up despite working more hours, having exhausted all my overdrafts and credit cards, the price of our house began to drop. Not significantly in the grand scheme of things, houses in Wimbledon tend to hold their value, but enough, enough for me to taste fear. There was no denying what was coming. That despite all my efforts, I was about to lose everything and there was little I could do to stop it.

The bleat of Lana's alarm clock droned through the ceiling. I listened for the click of the bathroom door. I felt like the word 'repossession' was slowly branding itself into my forehead and thought about whether I should leave for work before she came down. Was avoiding the issue the same as lying? Lately, these were the questions on which my marriage hinged. Surviving marriage 101: How to keep secrets?

I told myself, as I'd been telling myself for many months now, smoothing across the lie like I was running my hands over fresh bedsheets, that we weren't the kind of couple that needed to tell or know everything about each other.

In truth, from the off, it was as if we were connected by some invisible thread. Our meet-cute, as the moviemakers call it, was nauseatingly Hollywood. I'd never had trouble meeting women. My mother was Irish, my father second generation Italian. My share in their legacy came in the form of my mother's surname which I claimed as my own shortly after she left in a bid to win her back but from my father, I received an Italian heritage that placed me firmly in the box of tall, dark and handsome; attributes, I was once told, that were tempered with that boyish, vulnerable quality women supposedly found appealing. Even so, and even though the timing was right to think about settling down, I wasn't looking for romance, but one of my patients had coerced me into attending a charity speed-dating event.

There had been a mixer beforehand and the turnout had been pretty good. But from the moment of stepping into the room, I saw only Lana. Does that sound unbelievable? Maybe it's true that memory is not as reliable as we'd like to tell ourselves, that I've erased the trivial and turned the lights up on what I want to recall, dusting our first interaction in a warm glow. But this is what I remembered. Other people in the room became background noise, props on a stage. She'd been standing in the far corner, her body angled slightly towards the wall, her focus on a shelf of books. Although she'd been alone and most people at the event had already claimed someone to talk to, I'd noticed how the men kept track of her location, the women too but for different reasons. I'd plucked two fresh glasses of champagne from a passing tray and walked in her direction.

The books were heavy academic tomes on philosophy. Nietzsche. Old leather-bound editions that were more to assist the aesthetics of the décor rather than for reading.

'Staring into the abyss already?' I'd said, shamefully smug at being able to reference the philosopher. But later I wished I'd chosen a different opening to the story of our relationship rather than one suggestive of some darkness within, a shadow reflecting a shadow.

I'd held out a glass and she'd turned, smiled and accepted the champagne. 'Thank you.'

Up close she was even more beautiful. She had an unshakeable air, poised, like a ballet dancer. Delicate features. Honey-edged, liquid brown eyes beneath dark brows, gleaming hair swept back in a loose bun. Her mouth had hinted at a cool sense of humour, the left corner turned upwards, just a little; a real Mona Lisa smile.

'You know Nietzsche?' she'd asked. There was a subtle deepening of colour along the arch of her cheekbones.

'Not personally,' I'd said. That smile. Each flash of it felt like I'd won a race. 'Have you read his views on speed-dating?'

She'd sipped her champagne. 'I missed that paper.'

'He's not a fan,' I'd said. 'Too many questions.'

'Too many answers,' she'd finished. 'Lana.'

'Myles.' Her eyes had never left mine throughout the entire interchange. 'You're the doctor.'

'Let me guess.' I had a sudden rush of nerves. This one, I'd thought, this woman was important. Every cell in my body was dancing. 'Lawyer?'

'Lawyer?' she'd repeated. 'Interesting you'd choose that.' She'd replied as if my deduction of her answered more questions about me than her.

'Therapist.' I had grinned then, knowing I had it right.

She had touched her glass to mine. 'Here we all are. A collection of Rob's professionals.' She'd nodded over my shoulder. 'That's his vet.' Her voice dropped, her eyes moved along. '. . . His hairdresser. His priest.'

'I'm beginning to think not all of us are getting out of here alive.'

She'd laughed. 'It is like an Agatha Christie novel, only we appear on the right side of the murder.'

'I don't know. There's still time.'

I folded the letter closed, shoved it into the front of my work bag. Lana didn't know how bad things were. She watched her money. She drew her income. She contributed to bills. And every six months we had a brief check-in on our accounts. But she didn't *watch* her money. Not like I did. With the knowledge that it could, one day, all go away. She trusted the mechanical shift of numbers from one account to another would continue to

11

happen. She trusted that everything would be okay because she could. Because it had never not been okay. Lana's family had money, owned some giant company that manufactured something to do with lasers.

I wasn't stupid, I knew if she found out I ran a real risk of losing her for good. I'd hoped to restore our finances before she had to find out. Then when I told her, it would be a tale of how we'd swerved close to the edge but I'd pulled it back. Now it was only a matter of time before my failure and lies were exposed. They'd come for my car first, then the house, and somewhere in between divorce was waiting. If I talked to Eric, my bank manager, I could probably hold them off for another couple of months. I wasn't sure what solution I hoped would manifest in that time, and even though it had been months, no extra day, hour or minute seemed long enough to accept what was coming. I needed more time.

I got up, switched on the coffee machine, added some beans to the grinder. Lana walked into the kitchen shortly after, already dressed in her work clothes, a fitted cream suit, the trousers tapering in just above the ankle and a pair of low white pumps.

She slid onto one of the high stools along the island and I placed a coffee in front of her before dipping my head and kissing her on the lips.

'Morning,' she said with a smile, and pulled her bag onto her lap. 'You're up early.'

'I know, sorry if I woke you.'

'It's fine. Gave me a chance to look at this.' She held out her phone.

The thought she'd discovered my lies pulled across my throat.

I looked down at a picture. It was of a spa hotel in France. Five stars. All-inclusive luxury.

'I was looking into booking a holiday,' she said. 'For Mum and Dad's anniversary. Just a few days away to spoil them a bit. What do you think?'

I poured a glass of water, swallowed two mouthfuls, then threw the rest down the sink. 'I don't think they'd want you to do that, darling. Your parents like to look after these things themselves.'

'I know. But that's the point, isn't it? I think it would be a nice gesture. They've done so much for us.'

Lana's dad had forked out for the deposit on our house and, it still pains me to admit it, a portion of the price. An act to assert dominance rather than generosity.

I sighed. 'I doubt they'd expect so much. We could take them out or –' not particularly desiring this outcome either – 'have them over for dinner.'

She wrinkled her nose, then switched off the phone and looked up at me, her head tilted. 'I'm not trying to buy approval, if that's what you're thinking. I gave up on that at fifteen. But I'm their only daughter. I should get them something –' she paused here – 'special.'

I knew the gift served as a slightly passive-aggressive gesture to show that she was trying to be a good daughter, rather than one with any real thought or meaning behind it. A showy now-do-you-see-me gift. I thought of the unused lunch booking for the Ritz we bought them last year. I thought of the wasted money.

Lana liked to believe she'd had it hard growing up. Not everything's about money, she'd say, telling me she'd grown up in an emotional recession. Where her dad preferred the phrase

'I'm proud of you' over 'I love you'. And her mother, who saw Lana as a slightly less polished version of herself, loved proportionately. The more Lana acted like her, the more she loved her. I confess I liked that Lana viewed her past this way, that she saw her privileges as cold burdens. In ways, I shouldn't admit to, it made me feel superior. That the bald callousness with which my mother had left me was at least honest. It gave me a queer sense of pride that there was no pretence in my upbringing. Wrongly, it made me feel like my success, my money, was somehow purer. That everything it provided was real.

When I'd first met her parents, it was in a tiny French restaurant near Lana's home in West Sussex on an evening in October. Fred Grosvenor had stood from the table when we entered. Lana made the introductions. He'd smiled, lines deepened around his eyes, dimples appeared in his cheeks.

'Good to meet you, son.' He'd put out his hand and I'd put mine in his but he didn't shake it.

Instead, he'd pulled me close and said in a low voice next my ear, 'You hurt her, you leave. You mess up, you leave. You don't get to work it out. Or I'll make your life a misery. You understand?' This was more or less to be as good as our relationship would get.

I walked across the kitchen to my wife and cupped her face in my hands. 'It's a nice idea. Can we talk about it later?' Then swiftly changing the subject, 'Do we have plans this evening? I was going to catch up on some paperwork at the surgery.'

She finished her coffee, carried the cup to the dishwasher. 'Charlotte and Daniel's.'

'Ah, yes,' I said. 'You need me to pick something up?'

'No,' she said, distracted. She waved a hand at me. 'The moving vans are back.'

I joined her at the window. Outside, the sky was turning a light peach and a fog hung over the lawns on The Court. Beyond that, through the tall iron gates, the mist spread in a gauzy layer over the Commons and park.

Across the street, a lorry beeped while it reversed along the pavement. It drew up in front of the only unoccupied house on The Court, then shuddered to a stop. Two men jumped down from the cab and pulled on large gloves as they walked to the rear of the vehicle.

'They can't have much more stuff coming. This is the third load,' I said.

There were six houses in Belvedere Court. At the furthest end of the street were the Croziers, a retired MP and his partner. They owned two cats. Next up, the Foresters, a family of four, with a live-in au pair, who collectively contributed to ninety per cent of the noise in The Court and seemed to find it impossible to move through a day without some element of chaos. We had dinner with them at their house shortly after we moved in and had done our best to avoid them since. 'When you've escaped hell once, you don't go back to check whether it was, in fact, hell,' Lana had said at the time.

Then there were the Sheltons – a widow, in her seventies, named Sheila. She was a patient of mine with surprisingly high blood pressure for such a slight woman. She lived with her thirty-something-year-old daughter, Rachel – a quiet, mousy-looking woman who kept her head down every time she skirted by our house with their spaniel to power-walk the Common. Lana was fascinated by this woman, joked about whatever crime she'd committed in her past haunting her. She was an accountant. Worked freelance. I think.

The only couple we met up with regularly were in number three, Daniel and Charlotte Preston. I knew both of them. Had known them individually before they'd been a couple. An odd coincidence made awkward because I'd first met Charlotte when I was a young med student in Bristol. She was studying Law. We'd shared an embarrassing one-night fumble after drinking too much at the students' union bar. Something neither of us ever talked about, nor had we, as far as I knew from Daniel, ever mentioned it to our spouses.

Daniel I'd met when I moved to London to do my foundation training. I was more broke than I'd ever been. The owner of the NHS Camden surgery I'd been placed in provided digs in his family home, and to top up my earnings, I worked the odd shift at a local bar down near the canal. Daniel was a regular. Every evening, straight from some building site and still covered in plaster dust, he'd prop himself up along the bar and down five pints of strong lager before heading home. Even at that stage, he was already well into his construction career and, in his words, couldn't put the money he was making away. Now Charlotte was an esteemed divorce lawyer at a family law practice in central London, while Daniel built shopping malls and spa hotels.

It wasn't until Lana and I moved into Belvedere Court that I'd been reacquainted with both of them. Thrust back into each other's lives, we defaulted to a position of couple friends, alternating dinner dates once a month, sometimes more. Daniel and

I played golf on the mornings we found ourselves free, while Lana and Charlotte relaxed over coffee or went to yoga classes.

I watched as the two removal men guided what looked like a large painting out of the back of the van. As they turned I saw that it wasn't a painting but an artistic display, what looked like knives arranged on canvas; a collection of sharp edges that caught the early morning light, the deadly blades fanning outwards like rays from the sun.

Lana tucked her hair back behind her ear and leaned forward. 'Are they knives?'

Out of the houses on The Court, the one across the street was the last to be occupied. It was a six-bed with a garden double the size of ours. A generous driveway swooped round the left of the house, making the most of a curve in the road that led to the gates. Once a week, on a Sunday, a van of cleaners pulled up outside the house and proceeded to air rooms and wipe down the unused surfaces. Occasionally, the sound of a lawnmower came from the back or a gardener would be visible trimming the climbing roses that bloomed like pink baubles along the side of the house.

Then last weekend, the moving vans had begun to arrive.

'What do you think? Married couple?' Lana said after a bit, nodding in the direction of the house.

'What will I get if I'm right?'

She grinned at me. 'The knowledge you were right.'

'Could be single,' I said.

The men gathered at the back for the next item. A leather four-seater in bubble-gum pink. One thing I've noticed over the years is that taste depreciates in direct proportion to a person's wealth, and if so, this person or persons were very wealthy indeed.

'It's like the inside of a uterus,' Lana murmured, the sight making up her mind about the latest residents on our street. 'Married. Hetero. He's a gynaecologist. She's an artist.' She pointed towards the sofa. 'Clearly, both psychopaths.'

I thought about how we wouldn't be around long enough to get to know our new neighbours. How different my life would be now if that had turned out to be true?

CHAPTER 2

I drove the short distance to work. I felt haunted by the letter. I went over and back on whether and when to tell Lana. My hands tightened on the steering wheel. I wouldn't just lose the house, my reputation in the village, but there was a good chance I'd lose my wife too.

I waited in the queue at the traffic lights and looked out at the streets I'd come to know as home. The small boutique stores that lined Wimbledon Village were raising their shutters. I watched a barista as she carried a pavement sign outside the café door. Thomas Morrisey, the organic grocer was polishing apples and setting them in the front window alongside shining peppers and pale cauliflower heads. He caught my eye, waved. I lifted a hand from the steering wheel. I loved this place. The pastel fascias that adorned the shopfronts in icing-sugar hues, light blues, greys, greens and creams. The hanging baskets and window boxes stuffed with pink geraniums, the dusky red brick of the older buildings. The doll's house feel of it. A life-size collectible village.

A young couple, in dark green wax jackets and matching hiking boots, walked their two collies by the butcher's and then in the direction of the Common. The woman caught my eye, flashed me a shy smile as she passed. Catherine Phipps. Immediately, my mind offered the following: twenty-six. Mild mitral valve prolapse, ruptured ovarian cyst on left. No medication.

On the clock tower of the old fire station, a magpie perched on top of the weathervane. The decision to move back here hadn't been intentional. From the moment of my ejection from Wimbledon and its leafy suburbs, I hadn't red-ringed it as some future destination to reclaim. At least not in a conscious sense. They say success is when opportunity intersects with hard work. And no one could deny that I had worked hard. Done double my share. Looked after an alcoholic depressed father while my own mother sunned it up with her new family in Spain.

All through school, scrimping, teasing out every pound. Any memory of my teen years was coloured in greys and blues, gloomy and cold. Like someone had raised a hand and held it over the sun. Lean, sour, fetid damp scent of mould, stale alcohol and greasy fried food. Beans on toast or corned beef? Colouring in the heels of my school shoes with black marker. Trainers bought a size too big, the toes stuffed with newspaper so that they would fit and endure. Homework done in a hat and scarf in the evening in front of TV game shows.

When I got part-time work at a local garage, the extra bit of cash deepened father's – Ambie's – shame, sent him further into the bottle. Then, I was the only one feeding the heating, the electricity. Every other week, I found new hiding places for my wages; behind the wallpaper, where it had loosened at

20

my bedroom window due to damp. Under the lino at the back door. But Ambie hunted out his drink money better than any bloodhound.

Despite life's best efforts, I got into medical school. My grades didn't exactly blaze a trail, but I'd learned that even the smallest push moves you forward. Once I got through Bristol, I could shake free the shame of my past. Any time I was asked about my family, I told them my dad was a retired restaurateur who now spent his time enjoying the spoils of his labour. It was partially the truth.

The lights changed and I moved off down the high street, towards Willowhaven Surgery. I pulled up in the car park behind the clinic. Our – or rather Nathan's – surgery, was a beautiful building. Red brick, two storeys, vibrant purple wisteria drooped from the walls. In the centre of the car park there was a circle of lawn that was home to a large willow tree. We were a private surgery reliant on healthy pensions and good medical insurance, all of which, even in recession-immune Wimbledon, were showing symptoms of significant decline. I'd worked hard on my life here, stitched myself into the fabric of the community. Cut ribbons at charity picnics, attended garden parties and gallery openings. Washed clean the stains of my childhood until the sour tang of imposter syndrome was a distant memory.

For months I'd watched the funds in our accounts sift away like water down a drain but hadn't really let myself believe what was happening. Now the jitter of anxiety was building beneath my skin. There were options. We could downsize. Move or rent a flat somewhere less expensive. I could remain at the surgery, but the network of patients who sought care from Willowhaven moved in similar circles. They would talk. They would leave. The stigma of bankruptcy would infect their view of the surgery. Of my care. And Lana. Increasingly, I doubted she'd stay with me. The lie. Even if she overcame that, this wasn't the life she signed up for. Not what she was used to. She would be furious at me for even thinking this, I could hear her outrage: *You think I'm that shallow? Do you even know me at all?* But saying something and living something are two different things entirely.

I turned off the ignition, got out of the car and made my way inside. I didn't expect anyone in until 8 a.m., and lately, our receptionist, Sam, was slow to arrive and fast to leave. There was a time when he'd be in before any of us and coffee would already be on the practising doctors' desks, and in winter rooms heated and ready for patients. Now Sam had his wake-up and turn-up down to the second and slid through the doors at eight thirty, a full five minutes before the clinic owner, Nathan Kingston, arrived.

Our team was as small as we could afford to keep it. Sam worked reception, taking Wednesdays and Friday mornings off, when Beatrice, a retired English teacher, stepped in. Vera, our admin and practice manager, spent most of her time attempting to train the various agency staff Nathan hired to help her. Patient numbers had fallen over the last six months, and where we used to have three nurses who spread the weekly hours between them, now we had one agency nurse who came one day a week to do bloods and regular check-ups.

The tightening of the purse strings had cast a pall of apathy across the clinic, infecting motivation, and Sam appeared more affected than anyone. I tried not to let it get under my skin that we were losing a half-hour of patient calls to his morning ablutions. I'd brought the issue up with Nathan at each of our last three meetings, highlighting that times were tough, we were haemorrhaging patients, excusing the pun, but we couldn't afford to miss one potential appointment. But Nathan was shaking hands with sixty-five years, his retirement achingly close, and the changes he'd made already seemed to use up whatever ambition he had for the future of the clinic.

I made for the staff room and scanned the noticeboard for new messages as I waited for the coffee machine to heat up. The decor inside the surgery was simple and bright, softened somewhat by the oak beams that traversed the arched ceiling. Plenty of green plants that at one time had been real but gradually over the years had been swapped out by plastic.

The staff room was big enough to fit a tea-and-coffee station. A minifridge. There was a round table surrounded by four blue plastic chairs where clinic meetings were held. On the wall next to the door there was a white board where Nathan would occasionally put up a case for us to solve.

I'd long suspected these cases were not so much medical riddles he'd unearthed from the internet but, in fact, his own patients he'd failed to diagnose. I'd worked with Nathan for less than a year before I realised he was a terrible doctor. But he had that priestly air that stoked unwavering loyalty in his patients. Originally, I'd planned to set up my own practice once I'd built a reputation in the Village but Nathan had mentioned more than once that he'd planned for me to be his successor. Therefore, I'd put heart and soul into my work for him. Then, right before the recession began nibbling away at our client base, he'd taken on another associate. Madison. And like siblings vying for parental attention, suddenly I had competition.

I looked over the case on the whiteboard. He must have added it after Friday evening's clinic. I knew if I searched through the patients he saw that day, I'd find on a case file, the list of symptoms laid out on the board. Forty-eight-year-old female. Nine-month-old fracture of the right distal radius. Hyperalgesia. Discoloration of skin over the fracture site. Oedema. Atrophy of the small muscles on the dorsal surface of the right hand. Skin texture shiny with mild hirsutism.

My colleague, Dr Madison Lopez, had already got to the case. No surprise there. In the course of the year she'd worked with us, she'd never bypassed an opportunity to show me up in front of Nathan. Madison was somewhere in her late twenties or early thirties. When I first met her, I'd asked her age to which she'd replied, 'does it matter?'. She had not been long in practice. I'd known that much. She still had that keen, too shiny, self-righteous air that bathes every new graduate embarking on their career. She was pretty. Long black hair she wore in a low ponytail, smooth unlined skin and wide brown eyes. On her first day, in an effort to make her feel welcome, I'd informed her that if she needed help or advice on any of her cases, my door was always open, that I understood how the case load and the responsibility of primary care, could be overwhelming. In an effort to bond, I'd gone into detail about a particular patient who'd presented with classic Guillain-Barré. But I'd misinterpreted his symptoms. Easily done. And thankfully it all turned out okay. I told her how I'd beaten myself up about it to the detriment of my other patients but in time I'd come to see that mistakes happen. We are only human after all. And that it was normal, on occasion, to feel out of your depth.

'Even now, with so many years under my belt, I feel like that,' I'd said.

Madison had taken my attempt at humility as astounding condescension. 'You feel out of your depth?'

There had been a coolness in her eyes that surprised me. 'Well no. That's not what I meant.'

'Good,' she'd said. 'But if you do. Ever feel like that, Dr Butler. My door is always open.'

I read her notes on the whiteboard. *Diagnosis*, she'd written in her perfect slanted penmanship. *Osteomyelitis*. Bone infection. Obviously, Dr Google had been having a bad day. I picked up the pen and added the likely diagnosis of Complex Regional Pain Syndrome, then initialled it. For the first time in days, I felt a bounce in my step as I scooped up my coffee and headed to my consulting room.

My room was large enough, airy and had a wide window that looked out on the high street. I kept the blinds open in the morning as I worked through the day's prescriptions and insurance forms. When I finished, I drank down the rest of my coffee, not caring that it had gone cold, then leaned back in my chair, stretching my hands over the top of my head. I heard the front door of the surgery open and then the familiar jangle of Sam's keys as he threw them on the front desk. Then a few seconds later, he called through.

'Dr Butler,' he said, slightly breathless. I pictured him, phone pinned between shoulder and chin, trying to get out of his jacket. 'You're early,' he said. Accusation.

'Not particularly. Mr Barton here?'

'Not yet,' he said. 'Can I get you a coffee?'

'At eleven, please. If it's not too much trouble?'

'Eleven,' he repeated. 'No, no, not at all.'

'Nathan in yet?'

'He's not due until ten this morning. Something to do with their cat,' he said.

I heard the front desk computer beep. And pictured Sam drawing his thick black glasses from his red hair and perching them at the end of his nose.

'When Mr Barton arrives, send him straight in. I've to be off at one sharp today,' I said. 'Let Vera know that the completed insurance reports are on her desk.'

'Of course,' he said and hung up.

I reached down to my bag, removed my mobile from the front along with the bill. Returning to my desk, I spread out the letter, then, bracing myself, opened up an internet server and logged on to my bank accounts. In front of me, the phone on my desk blinked silently, patients booking or, as had been the pattern of late, cancelling appointments. People were pinching the pennies – or in Wimbledon, pinching the pounds. Health care should be recession proof and it was, if you were in the public sector. Here, we were singing for our supper and there'd been a gradual trickle of patients who were suddenly preferring the NHS song. Those with long-term insurance contracts remained. Thankfully, it made up eighty per cent of my patient base, but my salary was still taking a hit. I stared at the statements, a cold kind of despair passing over me like a shadow. I clenched my fingers, reached for my mobile. Nothing was irretrievable. There had to be a way to pull this back.

'Myles,' Eric Davison said. 'It's not a good time.'

'I need to see you.'

Silence. A sigh. 'I have meetings until two.'

'I can meet you then,' I said.

'If this is about the house, Myles, you know there's nothing I can do. It's out of my hands.'

'I just wanted to take the temperature on where we're at. Time wise,' I said, trying to keep the desperate note out of my voice.

'I thought the letter said it all,' he said. 'As I said, once it moves from my hands, there's little I can do.'

'Eric, come on.' I felt a stab of anger but forced a chuckle of camaraderie into my voice. 'It's me.'

Silence.

'Look, I have some money coming in,' I lied. 'You owe me that after the investment you suggested.'

'I never suggested anything,' he said.

My back teeth ground together. There was a twenty-grand hole in our joint account to show for his advice. I pictured him running a hand round the collar of his shirt, his thick finger pushing against the flesh before settling on the knot of his tie which he'd then adjust slightly. He sighed down the line. 'Meet me at two,' he said. 'Ten minutes, that's all I can give you.'

'See you then,' I said. I hung up, stared at my phone, anger curling in my stomach. Eric had practically stalked me when I opened an account with his bank. 'Don't worry. Health care,' he'd said, 'is unsinkable. Us banks love you. People are always going to get sick, right?' He'd been good to me when times looked good. Stretched out my money so that he could stamp our mortgage forms quickly. An overdraft here. Another credit

27

card there. A bridging loan. Made sure I was tied up good and proper with him and now he was ready to pull in his catch.

There was a tap at the door and Mr Barton stuck his head around the corner. I logged out of my account.

'Come in, Bob,' I said. He limped forward, pressing his left hand into his thigh as he moved.

He lowered himself into the chair with an oof and a wince.

'Thank God I got in to see you, Dr Butler,' he said. 'Another flare-up. Started yesterday morning. Terrible pain.'

'Are you still on the medication I gave you last time?'

'I started them again yesterday.'

'You remember they should be taken every day, Bob. Even when you're feeling all right. That's what keeps the crystals in your blood under control.'

'I'm sorry, Doc. I forget. I'll remember next time.' He gave another groan of pain.

I hooked my steth over my neck, drew the cuff of the sphyg across the desk. I nodded to his sleeve and he dutifully rolled it up.

'Might be on the higher side this morning,' he said. 'My son's back living with us. This crash has been hard on him. His wife has filed for divorce. I love my son, but having a thirty-eight-year-old back at home is a bit stressful.'

'And how are you?'

'Worried about him, I suppose. You never stop wanting to take away your kids' worries, no matter how old they are,' he said.

I pressed the cuff around his arm and inflated it quickly. 'No,' I said, feeling a pang of jealousy. I released the air from the cuff slowly, watched the needle beat downwards. Then removed it and checked my notes. 'Better than last time. Let's book you in for a review next week. I think we can do better with your diet, don't you?' I glanced at him.

'It seems so,' he said and flushed, then jolted in pain, grabbing his leg again.

'Okay. Let's have a look at this foot.'

The day went on like that. Low-maintenance standard fare. Nothing too challenging, which meant my dilemma continued to brew in the back of my mind all morning. The clock moved along towards 1 p.m. and shortly before I emerged from my consulting room, intending to refresh with a coffee and get through referral letters and slips for tomorrow morning, Sam called out to me.

'Nathan asked to see you,' he said. 'He's free now in the staff room.'

I checked my watch, then headed down the hall.

Nathan was standing by the window, both hands in his pockets and his back to the door when I entered. He was in his usual brown suit. It had a kind of woodgrain texture. He told me once he had three of these suits. Changed his white shirt daily and sported a range of brightly coloured socks that were supposed to express his personality. He passed a hand down his red tie when he turned.

'Myles,' he said.

'Nathan, I'm just about to step out.'

'Harold Rawlings has just passed. Bonnie has asked for one of us to oversee matters.'

The Rawlings were long-term patients who were part of every committee and society going in Wimbledon. But they were Nathan's patients.

'Our Georgie has just taken ill.'

I blinked.

'The cat,' he explained. 'Sofia would like me to accompany her to the vet. It's not looking good.'

I swallowed. Sofia, Nathan's wife, took a shine to me from the moment we met. Whatever fuck-ups, and there were a few I'd managed to get ensnared in, I knew it was Sofia who always reminded Nathan how far I'd come, reminded him that it was me he wanted to take over the surgery on his retirement. I lived with them on my first month on moving back to Wimbledon. They'd no children and I knew both Nathan and Sofia viewed me as more than just a protégé.

'Sofia shouldn't have to deal with that on her own,' I said. 'I'll go out to the Rawlings.'

He sighed. 'Thank you, Myles. I would have asked Dr Lopez, Madison, but you know how Bonnie Rawlings is.'

'It's important our loyal patients are supported by people they trust,' I said, not able to resist a dig at Madison.

'I thought so too,' he said. 'You might want to run your eyes over his notes. You've access, right?'

'Don't worry.'

'Right.' He took a deep breath, removed his mobile from his shirt pocket and looked at the screen. He gave me an apologetic look. 'That's Sofia now.'

'Let me know how Georgie fares.'

'I will.' He looked me in the eye and said, 'Thank you, Myles.'

I hurried back to my consulting room, wakened the computer, then logged on to Nathan's patient list. This was a privilege that had been bestowed on me eighteen months ago, in lieu of any other kind of promotion. I was a trusted associate. Should anything happen, I'd full access to the surgery's patient lists, files and accounts. I opened up Harold Rawlings's notes. He'd been ill for the last month. First hospitalised with pneumonia, steady list of antibiotics and painkillers. A little further back the hip fracture that likely instigated it all. He'd had an X-ray at one of our partners'. There were some unclaimed bills on his account that would need to be signed off by his next of kin. Bonnie, I presumed. I went about printing them off so that I could take them with me and at the same time phoned Eric.

'I can't make it. Something's come up,' I said. I continued to scroll through Harold Rawlings's notes.

'Look, Myles. As of this afternoon, my position here has become somewhat more precarious than when I spoke to you this morning.' He paused, I guess leaving space for sympathy. But it was difficult to feel any real sympathy for a man who'd, accidentally or not, seduced me into making an investment from our savings only to lose it all months later.

'I can hold off sending your account to debt collection for another couple of months. Tops. After that, someone else will be overseeing matters. Half of us got the warning today. Whatever pot you're planning on digging up to get a foothold, best get on it.'

I stared down at Harold Rawlings's notes, an idea forming. No one would notice if I were to add a few more appointments, print them off, then change the notes on our system back again. I'd heard of a few GPs adding fictitious complaints to their patients' histories in order to submit claims for payment. I swallowed. Harold Rawlings was dead, I told myself, and the Rawlings were

31

beyond wealthy. If there were any resultant hikes in their insurance fees, I doubt Bonnie would notice. There wouldn't be any real victims with this kind of crime. Morally, it was on the right side of bad. No one actually gets physically hurt, if you didn't count giant insurance conglomerates. And I think most would agree, they could do with the odd kicking. The money wouldn't be enough to clear my debts, but we had next to nothing in the bank, my earnings were being completely eaten up by our debts, our overdrafts maxed out. I couldn't get another credit card and I'd tried.

'Two months. I can do that,' I said. I pushed up the cuff of my shirt, checked the time. Logging out of the computer, I gathered up the necessary insurance forms and stuffed them into my bag. 'As before, I'd prefer you didn't mention this to Lana. I'm sure I'll be in a position to sort it out soon. I don't want to worry her unnecessarily.'

'Sure,' he said, not attempting to disguise the sarcasm in his voice.

CHAPTER 3

By the time I was halfway out to the Rawlings estate, I was sweating through my shirt. The idea that I was about to commit fraud loomed in my head. I pulled over at a gift shop, got out and went inside. There were no staff at the counter, which was packed with boxes of trinkets, nonsense, key rings, pens, fridge magnets, lip balms.

In times of stress, I've been inclined to take things. Items that don't belong to me. The objects I take are generally without purpose, to me anyway, and almost never have any real monetary value. The first time I took something, it was the day after I realised my mother wouldn't be returning. I stole a packet of football cards from our local newsagents. I didn't even like football that much. I don't need a psychologist to tell me the significance of when this habit started. There is a word for it. Kleptomania. But it sounds too heavy for what this is, a little swipe at the world. That is all. It feels restorative. Like I've reclaimed some small piece of ground and redressed a balance. I won't lie. It excites me. And then there's that contented calm that comes right after.

Not dissimilar to post-coital peace. It struck me that I hadn't succumbed to this little habit for some time. Four years perhaps. Right before I married Lana.

Voices were coming from a room at the back of the shop. I cleared my throat to alert the staff to my presence but no one materialised. I went to the card section, removed my phone and called Lana while I looked through the selection.

She answered promptly. I smiled at the sound of her voice.

'Rescue me from my couples therapy morning,' she said.

'I rather like your couples sessions.' A young woman appeared at the storeroom door. Her long hair was braided down over each shoulder. She saw me, clocked the phone, then disappeared again. 'You always return home incredibly grateful you married me.'

'Incredibly smug you mean, but with a mild twinge of lingering anxiety.'

'This does sound concerning. What can I do?'

'Just be wary of how you squeeze the toothpaste.'

'Is there a handbook or something I should read to help me avoid these marital faux pas?'

'Shelved right beside my thesis on "He doesn't think too deeply, she interprets that as he doesn't care".' A sigh. 'This is my signal that I need a break. Holiday soon?'

I swallowed. 'I can't. The surgery—'

'I know,' she said.

'Look, I've a lot on and wanted to see if we could skip dinner with Charlotte and Daniel tonight?' I experienced a sinking feeling in my chest. Lie after lie. They reproduced.

Daniel's construction business had been one of the first to fall into the recession black hole. The debt was slowly cannibalising his life. I wanted to be there for my friend but over the last few weeks, it seemed the only subject he could talk about. How Charlotte was the only one keeping the roof over their head. How she had no true idea of how much he actually owed. How he thought he might be depressed and could I prescribe something. His failure trailed after him like a shadow and resurrected in me a sick feeling of inevitability that all he was experiencing was ahead of me. But mostly, I wanted to keep our distance because I didn't want talk about recession and debt around Lana. Not when I couldn't answer her questions.

A pause. 'It's a little short notice,' she said. 'You know what Charlotte's like, she's likely bought out half the artisan shops in the village by now.' There was a hint of something bitter in her tone. Lana liked Charlotte, but intolerance always skirted the edges of their interactions.

I sighed. 'I could really do with a quiet one.'

'Okay. Sure. I'll call her. Chinese takeaway again? Or are you still scarred after last time?'

'The night of the empty fortune cookie,' I said.

I ran my fingers over the shelves of cards. Birthdays, Weddings, Thank You cards, until finally I found the selection of two that said *With Deepest Sympathy*. One had a silver cross on the front, the other a trio of lilies bound in a purple ribbon. I chose the lilies.

She laughed and asked playfully, 'Do you really believe your future is held in the palm of sugar and flour?'

'I thought we'd agreed you wouldn't psychoanalyse me?' I moved towards the counter with the card.

'I wouldn't dare,' she said. 'This, my friend, is what the layman refers to as common sense.'

'Oh, that oft absent quality of human nature. I'm reassured.'

'Besides, I couldn't begin to understand your mind, Myles Butler. Don't you know that—'

'It's impossible to psychoanalyse the Irish,' I finished for her.

'So says Freud.'

'Then so say all of us.'

'Lucky for me I have your Italian side to work on then,' she said. 'I love you.'

'Love you.' The words were heavy on my tongue, weighed down by guilt.

I hung up, cleared my throat loudly and put the card on the counter. In front of me, a box of souvenir pens. The top half of the pens were clear, an image of a tennis court printed on the back. I picked one up, tilted it and watched a miniature tennis ball float from one end to the other. I slipped the pen into my jacket pocket just as the young woman materialised from the storeroom.

'Sorry for the wait,' she said, as she stepped behind the counter.

'No problem.'

She looked down at the card. 'Just this?'

'Yes,' I said.

'Four ninety-nine.'

Daylight robbery without a please. I handed her a tenner and she counted out my change.

She closed the register drawer, then plucked at the end of her plait. 'Can I help you?' she said, looking over my shoulder.

'Thank you.' I took up the card and turned to leave.

Behind me stood a petite woman. Early forties, blonde hair in carefully crafted layers to just below her shoulders where the ends curved inwards towards the shallow dip at the base of her throat. Her eyes flicked to the breast pocket of my jacket and I felt the weight of the stolen pen like it was a rock.

'Excuse me,' she murmured. She met my eyes, then stepped round me, a trail of floral perfume in her wake. 'This please,' she said to the cashier and placed a candle on the counter.

'I love this scent,' the cashier said with more chirp than she'd bestowed on me. 'And it's on sale.'

The woman didn't turn when she answered but she raised her voice slightly so that I couldn't mistake what she said. 'It's a steal.'

That night, I lay in bed and stared into the darkness. The Court was silent. Lana was beside me, deep in sleep, her leg draped across my abdomen. I held it there with a palm, grateful and at the same time fighting a panic that these moments had been shifted into the realm of temporary. I lifted my head, folded the pillow and pushed it down into the crook of my neck. I forced my shoulders to relax and held my eyes closed. Lana groaned lightly in her sleep, let out a small sigh. I tightened my hold on her leg.

I tried to match my breathing to hers but instead of moving further towards sleep, each breath made me more tense. I slid out of bed, pulled on my jeans and a hoodie and made my way downstairs. The clock on the oven told me it was just before one in the morning.

I walked to the kitchen window, looked out on the street. It was quiet, the streetlights dimmed just enough to lend a peaceful ambience to The Court. Each of the houses looked on at each other as if mindful, watchful. I went to the drinks cupboard and drew out the bottle of brandy. I poured a glass and made my way to the living room. I pulled open the French doors that led onto the little slice of decking to the left of the front door. It had one of those American-style awnings, and when we first moved in, I had imagined evenings sitting out the front with Lana talking over our day. It hadn't quite worked out like that. In the daytime, it was a little too exposed, and a wave to one of the neighbours resulted in unexpected guests who would then drink our rosé and tell me about their ingrowing toenails. Now we sat out back if we wanted to take in the evening light and relax. But slowly, I had formed the habit of slipping out here when I couldn't sleep.

I watched the blinking light of a plane do its pre-landing round, swigged at the brandy and tried to relax. I didn't notice the shining black Mercedes that turned onto the street until it whined to a crawling roll, then stopped in front of the house across the road.

I leaned forward in the seat. The holly bushes that Lana had planted in the first week of moving in were thick enough that I knew, in the darkness, I would be obscured from view.

A woman appeared from the passenger side of the car, a slim elegant leg first, then an arm and finally a shimmer of blonde hair that appeared ashen in the darkness. I had a vague sense of recognition but couldn't place it. A man, her husband presumably, joined her, put his arm around her shoulder and gave a squeeze as if to comfort, as if to tell her that it's okay. His stance, the lift of his chest, said confidence. He walked to the front door of their home, opened it wide then he turned to the woman, gave a slight bow and swept his arm towards the door. The woman hooked her bag in the crook of her elbow. A tinkle of laughter drifted out across the street and she disappeared inside.

New neighbours. A light went on in the front of the house, and through the open blinds I could make out the shape of kitchen cupboards, a large vase of creamy flowers on the island. The woman appeared at the window and pulled the blinds closed. The husband stayed outside, moving round to the front of the car and sitting against the bonnet. He lit a cigarette and peered out over The Court.

CHAPTER 4

I wiped sweat from my eyes. My lungs burned. Even in the July morning warmth, my breath clouded the air but I pushed my body on, ran up the final trail from the Common, breaking free of the treeline and onto the street, but I didn't turn home yet. I ran until the strangling squeeze of my problems loosened from my neck. I could feel the inevitable coming as sure as a wild animal senses a storm. Every morning I woke, signalled a step closer to the end and yet, somehow, appeared to make it more impossible to confront the truth. I wavered between absolute belief that I'd lose Lana, the house and finally my career, to thinking that maybe I was underestimating my wife's ability for compassion. I reminded myself that she chose me, that she was my partner. My team. In moments of such optimism I thought about how if the roles were reversed, yes, the lying, the deceit was bad, and I would find that difficult too, but wasn't it also understandable?

By the time I turned down towards Hotel du Vin, and on towards Cannizaro Park, I'd made my decision. I was going to tell Lana. I wouldn't cram it into the moments we had together before or after work. I needed time, to let her anger rise and spread like smoke before it dispersed, then I would have a chance to explain. Tomorrow morning, I'd get up early, fetch her favourite pastries from the Village, make her breakfast. Let her read slowly through the papers. Then I'd tell her. I'd apologise for it all. Start at the beginning. Edit my way through the entire mess. Tell her how much I loved her and how sorry I was for not saying anything but how I'd thought I could protect her from the stress. And it had been agony not sharing it with her, to navigate this horror alone. But that I'd done it all for her.

In the back of my mind, I suppose I'd accepted that it was time to pull the safety cord and ask whether we could seek help from her dad. My motive in this wasn't solely financial, Fred Grosvenor was as likely to tell me to fuck off as a stranger on the street, but I knew Lana understood what it would cost me to put my hand out to her dad. How he'd make me squirm. How he'd never forget. And I also knew that there was a small but reliable part of Lana who had never raised the flag on her teen rebellion against her parents. It was a small gamble in my favour but I would take anything I could get.

I removed my phone. Six thirty. The sky was a watercolour blue, white clouds streaked across it like brushstrokes on canvas. Already there were plenty of people milling about the hill, dogs chasing each other in circles, their owners taking advantage of the slightly cooler air before the heat burned off the dew and mist and the temperature began to climb. I pushed up and down the hill until finally, I paused at a bench to stretch.

It had been four days since I'd begun altering a select group

41

of patient's notes. Adding a new ailment here, elaborating on a treatment there, submitting claims to their insurance companies. I wanted to get into work early, see if in the course of the night, payments had been made where I could then top up our joint account. Although there was a part of me that enjoyed the covert one-upmanship on Madison and, for how readily he succumbed to her brown-nosing, Nathan, the entire project made me feel a little grubby. It wasn't like when I stole from shops or pocketed small trinkets just because I could. When I did that, it was like letting out a long breath. This was different. The fact that it was out of need somehow made it seem more shameful. The process cracked open the lid on something. A well of possibility. I wasn't sure I wanted to know what was at the bottom of that well. What other darkness lurked down there.

I jogged back, slowing at the entrance of The Court and punching the code into the gate.

'Wait,' a woman's voice behind me.

The new neighbour. She ran towards me.

I put my hands on my waist. Blinked into the light. She was wearing black leggings, a bright purple vest. She stopped, caught her breath. Her hand pressed to just above her breasts.

'Thanks,' she said. 'I've forgotten that remote fob thing and can't remember the code.'

I recognised her as the woman who'd been behind me in the gift shop. *It's a steal.* She'd clearly seen what I'd done.

I entered the code and the gate pulled back slowly. 'No problem.'

'Nice to have another jogger as a neighbour,' she said, squinting up at me; blue gaze direct, pale eyebrows pulled down. She had a mild lisp when she spoke, her tongue lingering behind straight white teeth that had that evenness only achieved through braces. 'I'm Holly Wright.'

She lifted her hand from her chest and put it out in my direction.

I shook it, pulled the sweater from my back, returned her smile. 'Myles.'

We walked through the gates. I could feel her eyes on me, knew she was trying to place where she'd seen me before. 'Ah,' she said. 'I saw you in that gift shop.' She stopped walking.

'You did?' Heat crept up my face. I waited for her to mention the pen. I had an excuse ready on my tongue: I'd forgotten. I was on the way to do a miserable task, realised I needed a pen to sign the card and had clean forgotten to pay. Of course, I'd returned later when I realised I'd not paid. But when I looked at Holly Wright, her expression was not one of judgement, rather there was a spark of something in her eyes, one eyebrow pulled up into a high arch and a twitch of movement at the corners of her mouth.

'You were getting a condolence card,' she said.

'That's right. Sorry, I didn't recognise you.'

'I hope it wasn't someone close to you?'

'A patient. It wasn't unexpected.'

'You're the doctor?'

'That's right. I've a surgery in the Village.'

'We are looking for a good GP.' She waited a beat. 'I met one of the other couples on the street, they told me what you did. My husband's a surgeon, you see.'

'And you?'

43

She dug her fingers into her right side and bent forward slightly. 'Sorry, stitch. Haven't been running in a while and I'm afraid these beautiful surroundings carried me further than they should.' She let out a long, slow breath. 'I dabble in photography. Nothing so ambitious and consuming as my husband's career.' I thought I could hear the grate of bitterness in her voice. 'He'd love to meet you. We're having dinner this evening. We've invited another couple too. Trying to settle into a new area is . . . well, I find it nerve-racking, to be honest. It would be lovely to get to know some of you better. Jump in with both feet, in a way. Would you like to come?'

'That would be nice. Thank you.'

She beamed, pressed her palms together, like she might clap. 'Wonderful. Seven?'

I emerged from the consulting room shattered with tiredness. I walked down the hall, nodded at my last patient who was busy booking up some blood tests for the following week, in her hand the prescription for the urinary tract infection I'd just diagnosed.

'Thank you, Dr Butler,' she said.

'See you next week, Ms Sheridan.'

I carried two empty coffee mugs to the staff room and dropped them in the sink. Nathan was wiping clean the case board.

'Myles.' Nathan turned from the board. 'Heading off?'

'Yes. We've dinner plans,' I said.

'Lovely,' he said, rubbing a finger beneath his right eye, the skin moving like putty. 'I've another conundrum for you pair this week,' he said, putting down the cloth and picking up the marker.

'I'll look forward to it,' I said, tightening my grip on my bag.

'Hard luck for Madison on the last one.' I grinned. 'Good guess though.' I walked towards the door.

'What do you mean?' he said.

'Osteomyelitis?'

'She reached the same conclusion as you,' he said. 'Emailed a correction to me on Monday afternoon.'

My back teeth bumped together. Madison was not afraid of cheating for golden child status.

I forced a smile. 'I'm pleased she got there eventually.'

He patted the top of my shoulder, then returned to his office.

By the time I got home, it was coming up to 6 p.m. I loosened my tie as I climbed the stairs. Lana appeared in the doorway of our room. She was already dressed for dinner in a simple black number that clung to her hips and fell in soft folds to just above her knees. Her hair was down, shorter than it had been this morning. The loose waves coming to just above her shoulders, revealing the long elegant arch of her neck.

'Hello,' she said, replacing my fingers at my tie, pulling the knot free and looping the fabric over my head. She placed my face in her palms, stood on tiptoe and kissed me. 'Good day?'

'Better now,' I said. I cupped a handful of her hair. 'Nice haircut.'

'Only nice?' she said. She slid her hands down my chest, then wrapped her arms around my waist. I closed my eyes, laid my forehead against hers and tried not to think about how every moment I spent with her when I didn't tell her the truth was a betrayal. That's how she would see it. If you're not living in truth, you're not in your own reality at all.

A feeling of dread swelled in my chest, accompanied by a sinking nausea. I tried to force those feelings away. Kissed her, breathed in her warmth, the scent of her skin, the citrus bite of her perfume. She reached behind me, slid her hand down my back, over my buttocks. I caught the zip of her dress, drew it down, unhooked the straps from her shoulders and let the fabric flutter to a pool at her feet. Her fingers worked the belt at my waist. But it was panic, not desire that rose in me. My breath ragged for the wrong reasons. I tried to pull my thoughts back, made my mind follow the movement of her lips, the touch of her tongue. I turned her round, squeezed the flesh over her backside. She groaned, her hands moving back towards me. Then she paused. Hands stilled.

My throat tightened. 'I'm sorry.'

She pulled back, unsure what to do.

'Do you want to talk about it?' she asked, turning round to face me.

I tucked a lock of her hair behind her ear. 'I'm just conscious I need a shower. That's all.'

'Okay,' she said.

I turned to the en-suite, twisted on the water and shed the rest of my clothes. I stepped under the hot jets, tipped my face upwards and let the water sluice across my face, hoped it could wipe my mind clear of what had just happened. It didn't take much to ignite Lana's curiosity. Her husband, a man who never turned away from sex, suddenly unable to get it up. I squeezed my eyes shut. Not only was I in the shit financially, could lose my house, but I couldn't even fuck my wife. Lana was sexual. It was one of the things that drew us together like lit-up ions in the night. Our first few dates had consisted of entire weekends of sex. Even now, or at least up until a few weeks ago, all she

46

had to do was turn a certain way, or laugh, that tilt at the corner of her mouth, and the flame flared up as raw and bristling as when we first met.

I squeezed shampoo into my palm, scrubbed it across my head until my scalp was stinging. Then turned off the water and reached for a towel.

'I've left out your navy suit,' Lana called. I could hear the wardrobe door slide closed. 'See you downstairs?'

'I'll be ready in five,' I said.

I stood for a moment in the steamed-up bathroom. Reached out, wiped the mirror free of fog, told my reflection to pull himself together. Those that give up never come through and somehow there'll be a tipping point, I just had to push it in our favour. I took a deep breath, blew it out slowly, watched as the man in the mirror pulled himself upright, forced his chest high, blinked the water from dark eyelashes.

'Hello, hello. Come in,' Holly Wright ushered us inside No. 1 Belvedere Court. 'I'm Holly.' She put out her hand towards Lana.

'Lana,' Lana said. 'A little something for you both, and to say welcome to The Court.' She passed over a bottle of Krug.

'Very nice. Thank you,' Holly replied. She stepped back into the house, her heels clicked on the marble. She seemed nervous. Dwarfed by Lana's height. 'Come through to the kitchen area. I hope you like pasta. Gabe always makes enough to feed an army.'

She led us down the short, wide hallway. Above us a crystal chandelier cast tiny diamonds of light over the walls. From the direction of the kitchen came the sound of a cork being popped.

47

'The house looks great,' Lana said.

Holly turned. Flushed. 'Oh, I'm afraid I cheated a little and got in a designer. The only items we can really claim as ours are the books and the hideous art Gabe insists on buying.' She pointed down the hall where the framed knives were hanging. The work made more sense now that I knew he was a surgeon. There was a quiet aggression about the piece that intrigued and revolted at the same time.

'You bashing my tastes again, dear wife?' Gabe stepped out from behind the large kitchen island.

Holly's hand went to a pink band at her wrist; an elasticated hair tie or similar. The movement was swift, discreet, a quick snap against the skin. Then she went to him and he bent to her height so that she could press a fleeting kiss on his cheek. 'Would I ever?'

He raised an eyebrow at us. 'See how easy the lies slip from her tongue.' He passed us both a glass. 'Good of you to come to dinner. Welcome.'

He was dressed in dark chinos, a loose, long-sleeved crew neck in charcoal. He was slighter than I expected. Tall but lean. His hair, light brown with blonder streaks throughout, was swept back, Gatsby-style. Maybe there are those who would never have described him as good-looking, blue-grey eyes a little too deep-set, nose slightly deviated to the left – a historical sporting injury perhaps or a past moment of ill-judged violence – but I doubt there are many who'd have said he wasn't magnetic. There was an old-world feel to his look, his stance. An elegance. When his eyes landed on mine and he shook my hand, I'll admit I liked him immediately.

'Myles, lovely to meet you,' he said. 'I'm Gabriel. My friends call me Gabe. And you must be Lana,' he said, taking her hand in his and squeezing it gently. He didn't let go immediately.

Instead, he tilted his head. 'Hang on. Do we know each other?'

Lana gave a short laugh of surprise. 'You've barely changed.'

He pressed a hand to his chest, still not letting go of Lana's. 'I hope that's not true,' he laughed. 'Lana Grosvenor. I mean, it must be, what?'

'Twenty-five years?'

'God.' He drew a short, sharp breath. 'That's painful.'

I felt the first prick of jealousy. I didn't like getting glimpses of Lana's other lives. The lives before me, where I did not know her. I know I'm not supposed to admit such things. Not very modern of me, I get it. It's possessive and controlling, but I don't assign resentment to this feeling so I think that should count for something. It was a feeling of uncertainty. I could recognise that. The rug not quite whipped from beneath my feet, but a little tug on the fringes. I moved beside her, slid my arm round her waist.

Holly put her hand on her husband's arm and I could see my own emotions caught in her eyes. 'Well come on then,' she said. She looked between them. 'Were you both part of some secret cult or what?'

'We went to the same awful school together,' Lana said.

'Finley,' they both said in unison.

'*Audentes fortuna iuvat*,' Lana said and Gabe replied with a laugh.

'Fortune favours the brave,' he explained. 'Our school motto.'

'Gabe was a year ahead,' Lana added.

'Two,' he corrected.

'But everyone knew him,' she finished.

'I told you I was the life and soul,' Gabe said to Holly, then to us. 'May I offer you both some Chablis to start?'

'Please,' I said.

He poured the wine. 'I'm nearly ready to serve up here. Go on, make yourselves comfortable.'

We followed Holly into the dining room. The shape of the room was very similar to our own, a dining table at one end and a lounge at the other, only on the walls were numerous photographs of buildings. Everything from abandoned houses whose untended roofs sagged like old sofas, the doors and windows like missing teeth, to gleaming new-builds with glass fronts and sleek tarmac drives.

Soft Latin music trembled out into the room from hidden speakers. Standing by the window that looked out on the back garden, were Daniel and Charlotte Preston.

Holly said, 'I think you all know each other. Do feel free to sit anywhere.' She looked towards the dining table, which was simply dressed in white and silver, a bowl of white roses cut so that they formed a neat half-globe in the centre of the table. Nothing that would obscure an eyeline. 'I'll be back shortly.'

She returned to the kitchen and I watched as she approached Gabe, her hand going unconsciously to the small of his back as she stretched up and whispered something into his ear.

CHAPTER 5

We crossed the dining room.

'Hey,' I said to Daniel. He looked tired, soft around the jaw and middle. His eyes bloodshot, like he'd just woken up from sleeping off a hangover.

He pulled me close, bumped his shoulder against my chest as a way of greeting, his hand tightening on mine. 'Myles, mate. Good to see you.'

'You too,' I said. I leaned across him, kissed Charlotte's cheek. She pushed a strand of her red hair behind her ear and smiled at me, then turned to Lana.

'You look gorgeous,' she said, a little tightly, adding, 'As usual.'

Lana waved the compliment away. 'And you. How are you?' she said.

'I've not even had time to change after work,' Charlotte said, dusting down the front of her dress. She looked immaculate. Her red hair was poker straight, a burgundy suit dress that hugged her figure, large pearl earrings complemented the cream in her skin. 'We're okay.'

Daniel looked down at the beer he was holding; a rush of pink stained the top of his cheeks. 'Some stresses with work and that, but we're getting through it,' he said, giving Charlotte a smile. 'Aren't we?'

Daniel spent most nights in their upstairs game room on his PlayStation, downing beers and sleeping well into the afternoon. Charlotte was resentful. It wasn't that he'd lost his job, those were circumstances beyond his control, it was that he wasn't doing anything about it. And now, when she should be slowing down on work so they could think of having a family – Charlotte hungered after children like a plant seeking light – she was having to take on extra.

'Yes,' she replied, smiled a stiff smile and took a tiny step away from him.

How quickly love turned to revulsion.

'Please, everyone, sit down,' Holly said. Gabe placed two bowls of pasta in the centre of the table and a basket of garlic bread.

We sat, each selecting the seat next to our partners. Holly to the right of Gabe at the top of the table.

She scooped two large spoonfuls of pasta onto my plate, then nodded to the garlic bread. 'Help yourself,' she said.

I nodded to the photographs on the wall behind her head. 'They're really striking.'

'Thank you,' she said, a lift of pride in her voice.

'You're a photographer?' Lana asked.

She flushed, held up a palm. 'Hobbyist only. But I love to capture buildings. The places we make, where we leave pieces of ourselves.'

'Oh, you must take some photos of The Court,' Charlotte said, reaching for the bread. 'The Wimbledon rag would love it.'

Holly's mouth did a funny little twist at this but she covered her reaction with a wide smile. 'That would be special indeed. Good idea.'

I looked over at a photograph of a dark little cottage. The paint had worn off in patches around the exterior. A rusty wheelbarrow was perched along the side wall. There were still curtains in one of the downstairs windows; they hung limp as a dead body along the empty frame. A quote from Churchill ran through my mind: *We shape our buildings, thereafter they shape us.* I felt a finger of cold run across the back of my neck.

'So,' Lana said to Gabe. 'Do you see much of the old school crowd?'

'No,' Holly answered for him. 'We were meant to attend the reunion a year ago but – I can't recall why we didn't . . . Do you, darling?'

Gabe broke off a chunk of bread, laid it on the side of his plate. 'Those things are always so depressing.' He glanced at Lana. 'Sorry if you—'

'I went, and yes.' She laughed. 'It was depressing. Five of us dead.'

'Five?' Gabe said, eyebrows raised.

'Seems high, doesn't it?' Lana said with a short laugh.

'And how were the living?' Holly asked.

'Jaded, frankly,' Lana replied.

'Dead or half dead. Sounds about normal to me at our age,' Holly said.

Gabe lifted her hand from the table and kissed the inside of her wrist. 'Surely not us.'

'What hospital were you with before you moved?' I asked Gabe.

'York. The Merryfield. I ran the department there for a couple of years.'

'Before that we were in Manchester,' Holly said. 'Maybe third time's the charm.'

'The position at St Anne's is a real honour. I couldn't turn it down. It's going to be good here.' He grinned at his wife, then looked out at all of us as if we were already family. 'I know it.'

'I don't drink much wine, but when I do,' Daniel said, changing the subject, 'I reach for the best and this –' he raised his glass to the light and studied the ruby red glow of the wine – 'is pretty good.'

He brought the wine to his lips and I watched it disappear. Daniel was the loose cannon that threatened to crash through my evening. His usual outlook on life was irritatingly positive, but since the recession he switched between two moods, resentment and melancholy. I didn't want the conversation to tilt towards money and I knew that my last investment was also one he'd lost heavily on. Not that I intended to hide that from Lana forever, not that I could, it would come out, but I didn't want it to come out this evening.

'So, surgery,' Lana said to Gabe. She leaned back, her meal barely touched. 'Not the path I would have thought you'd go down.'

The statement unnerved me. The bluntness of it suggested past intimacy. Another person might be offended by the presumption but Gabe looked up. Smiled. A little flicker of something like pleasure in his eyes.

He laughed. 'Not clever enough?'

'I'd have thought politics or something corporate like banking.'

'Something without a soul, you mean?' He grinned.

She laughed. 'Not exactly.'

I felt something shift in my gut. A flashback to earlier when I couldn't get it up.

Heat gathered in my cheeks. 'No one escapes a couch session when Lana is around,' I said, then immediately felt bad for the bitterness in my tone.

She threw a quick frown in my direction, then turned back to Gabe. 'When I first met you, you were really intimidating. That incident in the school hall . . .' She shook her head. 'You were prefect and you took to that role like a general,' she said.

'I can well imagine,' Holly added.

'Hey!' Gabe said, but he lifted his glass, enjoying the attention. 'I was a responsible kid. What's wrong with that? From what I remember, you –' he raised his eyebrows at Lana – 'you were a . . . challenge, let's say.'

Lana pursed her lips, took up her fork, speared a piece of pasta and dropped it in her mouth. 'I was never one for rules.'

Holly dabbed at the corner of her mouth with a napkin. 'Gabe isn't either. Unless they are his own.'

'Prefects,' Daniel muttered. 'What bollocks.'

Charlotte placed her hand over his, gave it a warning squeeze.

'Sorry,' Daniel said, and helped himself to more wine.

'Sounds like there's more to this story in the school hall,' I said, wanting both to get a feel on exactly how well Gabe and Lana knew each other and take the conversation any direction other than Daniel's road of misery and how he got there.

Lana sipped her wine. 'Oh, it's nothing,' she said.

'My blazer, at the time, wouldn't have agreed,' Gabe said.

'He wouldn't let me clear, so I dumped my plate down his front,' Lana said.

'For those of us who didn't go to posh school . . .' Holly grinned. 'What is *clear*?'

'As Lana said, I was prefect. After meals, the other students had to ask if they'd permission to clear their plates. Lana had some vegetables on hers.'

'Three pieces of carrot,' she said.

'And quite a bit of gravy,' Gabe added, dusting down his front as if reliving the memory.

I felt Lana's hand on my leg, it slid up my thigh, her fingers squeezed. A quick glance between us, one of those looks that passed between couples, and heat built in my groin.

I hid my smile behind my wine glass. 'You didn't go to the same school?' I asked Holly.

She used her hands a lot when she spoke. She fluttered them before her, then swallowed her mouthful of food. 'Lord, no, I think I'd been to three different comps before I finally got settled in one just outside of Croydon.'

'Three?'

'Foster kid,' she said. Her hand drifted to her wrist again, then to her wine glass. 'I was lucky though, the last couple who looked after me were kind, generous, their home warm and inviting. I was lucky,' she repeated.

'Your parents, they—' Lana began, but Holly, anticipating her question, interrupted.

'I never knew them. They're dead,' she said, simply.

'Sorry,' Lana said.

'Oh, it's fine. I spent years in therapy trying to awaken some kind of grief about them.' She smiled at Lana. 'But there's nothing there. It's like scraping at an empty pot,' she finished with a tense laugh. 'I'm sure you'll have a diagnosis for that.' Another laugh. 'Anyway, tell us about your work, Charlotte. You mentioned something about law.'

'Family and divorce law, but lately the divorce part takes up most of my time,' Charlotte said. 'There's a lot of stresses on couples at the moment, and boy do people like to hurt those they loved the most.' She pushed her plate away, sat back. 'Honestly, I'd a client in today, who informed me she'd stayed awake for two days straight tracking her soon-to-be ex-husband's car, which it turns out did not move from his drive the entire time, so she could confront him with the relationship she thinks he's having with another woman. A relationship that's really none of her business.'

'Shouldn't you report that kind of thing?' I asked.

She sighed. 'I'd be reporting over half my clients. Honestly, most of them could have perfectly good careers in espionage once they're through divorce.'

Gabe laughed.

The tiny spike of jealousy I'd experienced in the hallway dissolved. As a couple, Gabe and Holly epitomised what I thought our life could be, should be and, in those few hours, was. In them, I saw what I hoped others perceived when they looked at

57

us, when they thought of us; hands firmly on the wheel of our lives and going places. Lana felt it too. The colour in her face was up, the smile lingered at the corners of her mouth all evening, her skin glowed under the candlelight. I'd almost forgotten about the lie, the pit of debt that threatened everything, that even as soon as tomorrow bailiffs could arrive on our doorstep.

The conversation settled on wine, then vineyards – the small town of Franschhoek where Daniel and Charlotte last took a holiday. Gabe chimed in that Holly and himself had taken their honeymoon there and stayed at an old chateau in the town that had been converted into a bespoke hotel. We've been there, Charlotte said, there'd been a cellar that ran the length of the restaurant. Then on to Lana's 'find yourself' pilgrimage along the Camino de Santiago in her late teens. A trek she valiantly tried for one day before being tempted away to travel the country instead.

'Tell me you found yourself,' Holly said. She leaned on the word 'tell' so it came out as playful pleading.

'At the bottom of a jug of sangria, sure,' Lana said. 'I think the searching you do at nineteen is only because you're young enough to be convinced there's another you out there.'

Charlotte drew in a swift breath. 'Gosh, it's depressing to think I'm the same person I was at nineteen. Some of my life choices were . . . questionable.'

Her gaze flitted briefly towards me. I deduced she was referring to our one-night stand. I liked Charlotte a lot. I understood her. She was a solid kind of person, a stick-by-you friend, but her intensity was off-putting for some. Her drive and controlling nature were often misinterpreted as overconfidence but I could see the fragility behind the mask. However, when she was hurting, she had a tendency to let her pain spill onto others. On those occasions, wherever there was an opportunity, no matter how slight, to deliver a cloaked insult, she'd take it. This, I thought, was a real skill of Charlotte's, to measure out just enough bile so that the jab was felt by her target but not so much that she couldn't withdraw, innocence intact, leaving her victim with only a faint residue of pain and bewilderment about what's just happened.

Daniel caught the look I shot her. He picked up his glass and finished his wine. 'So, heart surgery eh? What's that like? It must be rewarding?'

Gabe considered his question, 'I would say more satisfying. That feeling you get when the mechanics fall into place, where you see the problem. It's challenging enough to give you that little jolt of adrenaline but you have the exact right tool and, you're pretty sure, the right skills to fix it. You must feel that with your line of work too?'

'I work with buildings. Machinery,' Daniel said, with a laugh.

Gabe put down his cutlery. Lifted his glass. 'As do I,' he said, his tone one of mutual admiration. 'Of a biological nature, sure,' Gabe went on. 'When you're holding a human heart in your hand. And you feel that age-old beat, tick, tick, tick, of the muscle, the quiver of life, regulated by an electrical current, the shunt of blood up through the arteries and round the body. There seems to be nothing more mechanical, nothing more robust yet fragile, than this soft human machine. We are but complex engineering controlled by nothing more than chemistry and physics.'

Holly groaned.

Gabe smiled at her. 'Holly doesn't like it when I talk like this. She thinks others interpret it as cold.'

Holly gave a little shake of her shoulders, as if chasing off a shiver. 'A person is more than a muscle beating in their chest.'

Gabe laughed. 'A dose of potassium chloride would argue differently.'

'I've no idea what that means nor do I want to know,' Holly quipped.

I swallowed the last mouthful of pasta. It was a simple meal but packed with flavour. The pasta was al dente, the tomato sauce rich and herby, small cubes of 'nduja chorizo leaving a spicy note on my tongue. 'Who was it that believed the heart was the house of thought?' I asked.

Charlotte topped up her empty glass. 'I don't know, but my job would be a lot easier if people made decisions without it,' she said. 'I mean, all the better for my commission that my clients continuously go against sound advice and refuse a divorce settlement over trawling their ex through the court system, but there you have it.'

'Revenge must be sweet,' Daniel mumbled. The words ran into one another in a slur. He reached for the bottle of red and topped up his glass.

Holly looked at me. 'The Egyptians,' she said, answering my question.

'Thank you, Holly,' I replied.

Gabe grinned. 'Here I thought my fellow medic would back me up. If not check his neurology. Should that burden not be in the mind?'

I grinned back. 'The mind lies. It holds up an interpretation and tells us its reality,' I said. 'The rubber hand experiment?'

Lana *tsk*ed. 'I see we're reaching for high standard clinical trials here.'

'I'm lost,' Holly said with a laugh.

'Join the club,' Daniel added.

I put down my wine. 'Both hands are rested on a table in front of the subject. One hand, say the left, is covered with a box, a shoebox or something and a rubber hand is placed next to it, in line with the shoulder. The subject is asked to watch the fake hand while the examiner simultaneously strokes both the right hand and the fake left with a paintbrush. After a while, the subject is asked to point towards their hand. They will point to the fake one, not their own limb. The mind trusts what it sees, not what it feels.'

Daniel threw the rest of his wine down his throat. 'Everything's a fucking mirage.'

'Dan,' Charlotte warned.

Daniel shrugged. Then to me, 'You hear from Eric?'

My mouth went dry. 'Sorry, mate?'

'Eric,' he repeated. 'Our bank manager.'

Charlotte reached out to him. 'Not now, Dan.'

'I haven't spoken to him in months,' I said. 'Holly, if you're looking to get into the tennis club, you must let Lana help.'

'I heard there's an incredible waiting list.'

'The lady who validates members is a client. Probably shouldn't say that but,' Lana replied, then turned to me. 'I thought you mentioned something about seeing him last week?'

'Who?' I asked.

61

'Eric,' she said.

The room felt hot. The music pattered on in the background. I took a sip of water. 'I had to cancel. It wasn't urgent.'

Daniel let out a burst of air. 'He's been avoiding my calls for the last month. My emails. That investment was rotten to the core and he knew it.'

Charlotte went to stand up. 'I think we'd better go. Thank you for a delightful evening,' she said.

'But you must be wanting to talk to him,' Daniel continued to me. 'He said you went in on it too.'

I shook my head. 'No. I don't know what you're talking about. Sorry, Dan.'

'I'm sure it's all okay,' Lana said. She turned and smiled at me, but there was a flash of something in her eyes that made me nervous. Fuck you, Daniel.

Charlotte was gathering up her bag. 'We must return the favour. Have dinner at ours.'

Holly and Gabe stood. 'Are you sure you won't stay for coffee?'

'Yes,' Charlotte said, desperate to go. Daniel was already halfway down the hall; he waved a hand over his shoulder as he left. 'Sorry,' she said. 'He's struggling. The recession . . .' She trailed off.

'Totally understandable,' Gabe said. 'If there's anything we can do.'

'Short of having a million or so lying around.' Charlotte laughed a brittle laugh. Tears at the corner of her eyes. Something I knew she'd hate. She didn't like to look weak.

'We should be leaving too,' Lana added, her voice soft, regretful with a light ring to it like the trill of a cymbal.

This is the thing with marriage. So much can be said with so little. I tried to think of reasons, of excuses that would make her questions go away. Questions I knew would come the moment we crossed the threshold of our home. I stood, swallowing down a sigh, pressed a hand against my chest. The tightness there nothing to do with overindulgence at the dinner table. A dull ache; my heart, wanting me to spill our predicament like blood at her feet, a cry for mercy, but my mind . . .

You see, my mind could not be trusted at all.

CHAPTER 6

The sun flickered through the trees. Sweat rolled into my eyes. I blinked it away. Gabe was at my shoulder. He ran in that chest-out posture, head tilted back slightly like he was about to break into a sprint. I drew in ragged breaths. Tried to keep pace. The ground was pleasingly dry and dust rose up with each stride. Even though it was not yet seven, there were already groups of joggers and dog walkers cutting through the myriad of pathways that spread through the Common's woodlands like veins on the back of a hand. Some of the joggers were patients, who smiled or waved briefly as they passed their doctor, a man practising what he preached, taking his daily exercise when he could.

When you become a doctor, there's an immediate assumption that you do the right thing. For yourself and for others. Maybe Shipman made people wary for a while, but for the most part people are willing to believe you're more trustworthy than the average Joe on the street. This has always been a point of fascination to me, that that trust is completely unearned but in time its preservation becomes both a privilege and a burden. In the

Village, I was respected. I had integrity. There wasn't a local event where I didn't get an invite. Tickets were pressed into my hand during tennis season. Pimm's and champagne at garden parties.

There's a lot you can hide behind a status like that. People overlook the odd burst of bad behaviour. When I threw a punch at a surprise fortieth, the story became an amusing anecdote. The kind-hearted doctor who they'd assumed couldn't handle his drink one night. But when it came to debt, when you've lost everything, even though you've not committed a crime, I knew the stigma would cling to me like a pox. The hand of good fortune swipes at fates indiscriminately; where one person's bad decision leaves but a dent in the path, for the next it's the chasm that swallows them whole. Those that emerge unscathed naturally ask the question why it's happened to you. Not them. To them, the answer, no matter the truth, is always bathed in the scent of criminality, failure and, worse, impotence.

I gritted my teeth, edged slightly ahead of Gabe, aware that no matter how hard I pushed, I couldn't escape my problems. That the moment I stopped moving, the worry would be back, louder by the day, by the hour and pressing in on me until it had crushed me to nothing.

Gabe slowed. 'Listen, I wanted to check everything's okay after the other evening. I'm sorry if it ended on a bad note?' We stopped, crossed into The Court. He bent to catch his breath.

It had been a few days since the dinner with the Wrights and I'd managed to avoid both Daniel and Charlotte over that time. I wanted to avoid the entire mess.

'Daniel gets a few drinks in him and . . .' I trailed off. It wasn't entirely true. Daniel had always been more of a happy rather than belligerent drunk.

'Everything's okay with you though? It sounded like he was trying to start trouble between you and Lana?'

It was an oddly personal question from someone I didn't know all that well, but I shrugged it off. 'We lost a little in that investment, but who hasn't nowadays? We're great.'

He waited a beat as if he expected me to say more. 'Glad to hear it.'

When I'd got in from dinner that night, I'd waited for the questions I knew would come from Lana. Lana had a temper. If I was lucky, she blew up and ran out of steam quickly. She'd throw everything at me, insults, anger, frustration, in a wave of sharp but brief aggression and then it would be over. I preferred it that way. No lingering sulk. She said she couldn't abide emotional manipulation. She said she had a rule: you say what's bothering you or you decide that what's bothering you isn't all that important. But honestly, in time I grew to understand that this was a perfect example of do as I say, not as I do. In fact, Lana's preferred mode of punishment took the form of silent treatment, passive-aggressive hard stares and stonewalling. And that night, she'd exercised her right to stalk silently into the house, had dumped her bag on the sideboard and headed straight for our bedroom without so much as a backwards glance over her shoulder in my direction.

I had followed her slowly upstairs knowing that the longer her mood rumbled, the more questions would come firing my way. Questions I knew I wouldn't be able to answer and would therefore require me to add to the thick soup of lies that currently

66

threatened our marriage. She was in the bathroom, had already dressed in one of the plain white vests she wore to bed and was swirling her electric toothbrush furiously across her teeth.

I appeared in the mirror. 'We need to talk.'

There'd been a brief pause in the brushing. Then she'd rinsed her toothbrush, spat into the sink and dabbed at her mouth with the towel. I knew I'd caught her off guard. This wasn't our natural rhythm. Whatever the argument, I was never the one to confront the problem.

She'd stared at my reflection in the mirror for a moment, then turned. 'Tell me.'

I'd taken her hand, led her to the bed and sat her down.

'We lost some money,' I said. 'But we're fine. I've had to move some things around, and yes, on the surface it looks bad, but it's all under control now.'

There'd been some over and back. She'd never asked about the house, so I told myself I didn't really lie. As I said, Lana had never not had the safety-net of money. She'd kissed me. Relieved. Pulled my shirt over my head and drew me close. We'd made love. Not gentle. A clash of flesh, teeth and nails. She, energised by the swift rush of adrenaline our little brush with financial ruin had wrought. Me, charged up by some false sense of control.

Gabe clapped me on the shoulder. 'Remind me not to run with you again.'

'You were the one who took off in that last half-mile.' I pinched sweat from my eyes.

'I've a problem with competitiveness,' he said with a grin. 'Listen. No obligation but there's a dinner in Mayfair in a few weeks. The Fellowship of Surgeons and Physicians' annual event. I'm a member. I was thinking you and Lana might like to come. Might be dull but could be beneficial to you. Meet a few more consultants. Contacts for the practice?'

The FSP was a prestigious club of the UK's finest in health care, nicknamed The Toppers. Entry to which required passing a set of three gruelling exams. I'd attempted them shortly after completing my foundation training and an attempt is what they remained. But I may have been generous with the truth of my success when I'd first approached Nathan for work. One of those flourishes you add to your CV in the hopes that no one actually checks these things. And he never did. Whenever he brought the subject up, the gleam of paternal pride in his eye almost made me believe I'd passed. This would be the perfect opportunity to remind him how important I was to Willowhaven. How my credentials could carry me off at any time to work for a competitor. But mostly, the mention of the FSP annual dinner made me picture the sour look on Madison's face when she realised I was a member of the crème de la crème of British medics. Even if it wasn't true.

'That's generous of you,' I said. 'We'd love to go. Is it too much to ask if there were a spare couple of tickets? I'm sure Nathan would appreciate it.' There was nothing Nathan loved more than hobnobbing with people of importance.

Gabe shrugged. 'The more the merrier. I'll put down the surgery address, shall I?'

'Great.' I turned towards my house.

Willowhaven car park was jammed by the time I arrived for morning clinic. The run with Gabe had made me late. I stepped through the door to a full reception. It should have made me happy but I knew it was a backup in the diary rather than new business.

I swept by Sam's disapproving glare and headed for the staff room for coffee.

'You're late.' Dr Madison Lopez stood at the coffee machine, her slim hands around a mug. 'I've had to take on two of your patients.'

'Thank you,' I said. 'I've had a busy morning.'

'I've contacted Mrs Grimsby's consultant. She's booked in for hip surgery next week.'

I frowned. 'But she's already booked in for two months' time.'

'She's hypertensive and been on pain meds for five years, not the best mix.'

'I wanted to give her a chance to get her diet under control.'

'I made a judgement call. We're both happy with the outcome. Poor dear. She's in agony.'

Irritating. 'I'll give her a call.'

She looked down at her mug. 'She's switched to my books now. You shouldn't interfere. We want to avoid any confusion.' She tipped back the last of her coffee, touched her manicured nail to the corner of her mouth, then left the mug in the sink. 'Nathan is aware.'

Of course he fucking is.

She walked to the door but stopped before leaving. 'Also, Bonnie Rawlings called . . .' I stiffened, then turned to the coffee machine so that Madison couldn't see my face. 'She's expecting a call back. Something about an insurance claim for her late husband?'

69

'Thank you,' I said, turning. 'It will just be a minor paperwork issue, I'm sure.'

Madison's expression went from disinterest to intrigue. I'd said too much. But short of contacting each of the patients I'd put in claims for, she couldn't prove anything, and she couldn't do that without smearing my reputation, and even Madison wouldn't risk a defamation case against her. I hoped.

By the time I got home, all I wanted to do was trudge upstairs, pull the curtains and fall asleep. I turned off the ignition, got out of the car and looked out at the park. Beyond the gates, a couple of joggers in neon vests circled the park. A milky grey light stretched over the edges of the Common, the treeline punched out in black. Belvedere Court was quiet. Front-room lights were on in a few of the houses. Something about the uniformity of the houses, the glow of the eaves, the blue-grey slate on the roofs and the perfect lush green gardens made The Court appear slightly sinister. So much light but too many shadows.

The temperature had dropped since I'd left work; the breeze cool and teetering on cold. I hurried towards the house and pushed inside. I turned to close the door, then stopped. Across the street a woman was moving along the front of the Wright house. I couldn't make out her face, which was peering through the side of the front window, a phone to her ear. She was slim, tall, wearing dark, tight trousers and a long woollen coat, which even with the lower temperature seemed an odd choice of wardrobe for July. She straightened, pocketed the phone, then with a quick glance around the street hurried towards the exit of The Court. She didn't go through the gate, but instead pressed her

70

foot against the trunk of a silver birch and pushed over the wall. I took out my phone, intending to text Gabe about it, but as I moved further inside the house, I stumbled across something.

I steadied myself on the sideboard, then flicked on the light. On the floor, Lana's coat and bag. I stared down at the cream jacket and the soft leather Prada that I'd bought her last Christmas. I had sold the watch she'd gifted me for my birthday to pay for it. She'd yet to notice I no longer wore it.

I stared down at the discarded items. Lana liked order. Not to an obsessive level but I'd never known her to just drop her coat and bag where she stood. She'd usually take the jacket upstairs, put it away in the wardrobe. And the bag. Well, how often had I heard her say, 'Bag on the floor, money out the door.' There came a grating sound in the direction of the kitchen like a stool dragged across the floor. I reached out, pulled open a drawer on the hall sideboard, removed a heavy torch and made my way towards the sound.

'Lana?' I stepped through the doors.

The kitchen was dark apart from the light coming from the laptop. Lana sat on the far end of the island. The computer casting a glow on her face, a full glass of white wine to her right, the empty bottle on her left. Even in the dim light, I could tell she was upset.

'Did you think I wouldn't look?' Her voice had a stiffness to it, like it could take form, grab my throat.

Across the island, unfolded paper. Bills. So many bills. The paper trail I'd hidden beneath the Persian rug in my office upstairs. Had there been that many? I watched her fingers tighten around the stem of her wine glass.

'Our savings? All of them. Are gone?' she asked.

I stood still as stone. 'Yes.'

'We're completely broke. Worse than broke.' Voice rising. 'There's nothing here, Myles. Nothing. We're months behind on our mortgage.' Shouting now.

I almost felt relief that the anger was coming. I hoped it would pass quickly, like a wave that crashed on the shore, it would now thin out and retreat back to the sea. But I was wrong.

The wine glass flew across the room but didn't quite make its target. It crashed on the floor at my feet, wine spattered the legs of my trousers.

'Get out,' she said, voice low.

'Lana—'

She closed her eyes. Shutting me out.

'Can't we talk about this?' I asked.

Her eyes flicked open. 'You've had months to talk about it.' She snapped the laptop closed. 'Can you tell me how you've come home to this house every evening and acted as if everything was fine when we're fucking bankrupt?'

'I'm sorry,' I muttered. 'I didn't want to worry you. I guess I hoped that something would come around. That I could get us pointing in the right direction. I don't know what I was thinking.'

'I know what you were thinking.' She pushed back from the island. Stood up. 'You reacted to this like you do with everything. Fucking cowardly, Myles.' A blow that caught me right in the guts. 'You lied to me because it was easier and you wanted to avoid the confrontation. How's that going for you?'

'I never lied to you.'

'Seriously? Are you really going to try that argument?' Her

face flamed. 'If I fucked someone else and never told you about it, that would be okay, would it?'

'It's not really the same,' I said, stupidly.

She tipped her head to the side. 'Maybe I'll try it out. Maybe I'll have an affair. What you don't know doesn't exist, apparently.'

Lana had a skill for reminding you of your worst fears. Nothing would kill me quicker than her with another man.

I stepped forward, my feet crunching over the broken glass. If I could get to her, if I could put my arms around her, it would be okay. 'Lana, please,' I said. 'I thought I could sort it.'

She let out a bitter laugh, stepped out of my reach. 'Please leave. Right now.'

I hesitated, unsure what to do. Part of me wanted to avoid more conflict and worried that if I left her alone too long, I'd be greeted with divorce papers on my return, and another, more selfish part of me was aware of the faint scent of body odour that had begun to drift upwards from my armpits at around five, that feeling I had after a long day dealing with patients that I carried the residue of other human beings on my skin. I was desperate for a shower. I looked down at the broken fragments of the wine glass, then back at Lana. She glared at me, her right eyebrow arched to a fine point.

I nodded. 'I'll just grab a few things.' I said.

I returned the torch to the sideboard then went upstairs, pushed some fresh clothes into a bag, toothbrush and my phone charger, then made my way back to the hallway. I hovered outside the kitchen. I heard the fridge door open. The clink of another wine glass and the sound of a screw-top being opened. I walked to the front door, stepped outside and pulled it closed behind me. The first spits of rain were falling. I unlocked my car, got in and looked up at the kitchen window. The light was still off but I could feel Lana watching me. I had a hideous flashback of the red suitcase trundling after my mother as she hurried into the taxi on the day she left.

The rain turned from spittle to deluge with surprising swiftness. I put my hand on the ignition, started the car, then turned it off again. I could have driven to the surgery, slept on the examination table, pretended I'd come in early to catch up on admin. Or I could have spent the night at one of the boutique hotels in the Village, but some part of me was afraid to leave our home. I felt sure that if I left, I would never find my way back.

Some way into the night, the sound of voices woke me. I sat up, for a moment unsure about where I was. It was surprisingly cold. The rain was still falling. Heavy patter above my head. The interior of the windows had fogged up a little but in the rear-view, I could make out Gabe under the street lamp across the street. He was talking to someone. A woman. For a brief moment, I thought it was Lana, but something in the woman's posture didn't match; a slight curve of the shoulders, a hyperextension of her knees. And I recognised her as the woman I saw earlier, the one with the heavy coat who had levered herself over the wall of The Court so swiftly. Gabe had his hands on the tops of her shoulders. They moved out of view. And a few minutes later, I saw the red tail lights of his Mercedes light up. The gates to The Court slid open and the car disappeared into the night.

CHAPTER 7

I woke on the back seat, my overnight bag stuffed under my head. My neck stiff. Lana's car was gone already. I took out my phone and tried her number. It rang through to voicemail. I left a message; a simple apology and a plea for her to get in touch. Then I put the car in gear and drove to work.

It wasn't until I pulled back into my drive later that evening that I remembered the Wrights were due for dinner at 8 p.m. I pushed out of the car, determined not to let the argument between Lana and I fester any longer, and grabbed the bunch of deep pink peonies I'd picked up on the way home. They were her favourite. She loved their big busty blooms and concentrated colour and how when they were done flowering, they didn't hang around. There was no withering or turning brown along the petals like roses sometimes did. Instead, they disintegrated, fell apart, leaving large satin petals on the ground, as if they'd put everything they had into that one burst of life.

I let myself in, the scent of dinner greeted me in the hallway – sesame, onion, garlic and lime – and I knew she was cooking her favourite. Chicken shawarma that she'd dress up with shop-bought white pitta and made-from-scratch hummus in case anyone were to question her cooking creds and, on the side, couscous dotted with glistening pomegranate seed. Coldplay was playing from the kitchen and I took that as a poor sign.

'Hey,' I said.

She was already dressed for dinner. A figure-hugging black dress. The knot of her white apron rested at the nape of her neck. Her hair was loose. She hooked it behind her left ear. She was wearing a pair of jade drop earrings I'd bought her, for what I couldn't recall, only the sight of them brought about in me an intense twinge of guilt. It was the first time she'd worn them or it was the first time I'd noticed her wearing them. And I sensed I was to glean a significance to their presence now.

If, in a marriage, you can admit that there are habits you both retain which are tolerated but never loved by your partner, then of the habits Lana possessed, this was my least favourite. In moments of insecurity, or more often boredom, she liked to put to me past events we'd shared, sometimes fleeting, and occasionally those I'd worked hard to forget, to which she'd assigned an importance with regards to our relationship. When I say 'put to me', I don't mean she talked about them; she preferred symbolic nudges, the sudden appearance of a dress she wore on a night we made love after an argument, or a special brew of coffee we'd last had on our honeymoon. No matter the sentiment, it always felt like I'd just received notification of an IED somewhere beneath the floorboards. If I missed these subtle messages, she'd eventually point them out. *You never mentioned my dress.* On the surface, it seemed she didn't mind if I failed to get whatever coded message she was imparting, but I was under no illusion. These were tests of my worthiness, and I didn't pass many of them.

I swallowed, tried to remember when it was I gave her the earrings. It was over a year ago certainly. Likely more. They'd been expensive, but I knew from almost the moment I handed them over that she hadn't liked them. Diamonds. That was Lana's suit. But on the night I'd presented the earrings to her, she'd lifted the pair from the satin-lined box, held the clasps between thumb and forefinger, allowing the jade teardrops to settle on the cushion of her palm. 'They're stunning.' she'd said. To which I'd replied, 'You deserve them, and so much more.'

This was the message she intended to convey. A reminder of how she deserved more, probably more than me, a reminder of the bar I'd set myself and how I'd failed to cross it.

I held out the peonies. 'These are for you.'

She glanced at them. 'Would you mind putting them in a vase? Then you should probably clean up. They'll be here in an hour,' she said.

I took a breath. Not wanting to broach this subject, but at the same time needing to see some glimmer of light on the horizon. Finding a vase on the windowsill, I rinsed it out and filled it with water. 'We could ask your parents?'

She didn't turn but I saw the swift tightening of her spine, her shoulders coming up fractionally. She knew what I was asking. And I knew she understood what it took for me to ask. 'My dad gave a huge amount towards this house, and now you want him to bail us out of your debt?'

I bit my tongue. It wasn't solely my debt. 'We could pay him back over—'

'We can't,' she said. She tore open a packet of pitta, tipped them onto a roasting tin and slid them into the oven. The smell of the spice-covered chicken set my mouth to water.

'Lana—'

'We can't ask him.' She slammed the oven door, turned it off. 'Because he's not doing great himself. His business relied on construction, on engineering, new development. His income has practically dried up. He was going to ask us for a loan but that's out of the question now.'

I slid the peonies into the water, they drooped over the lip of the vase. A single waxy petal fell onto the counter.

'Can we not right now? I'm still angry,' Lana said. 'I need time to process it all. The house. Where we'll live . . .' She trailed off, already overwhelmed. 'I'm not leaving you. I know that's a worry . . .' She motioned in my direction, in the direction of my past trauma, of my mother leaving, like it was an irritating fly she couldn't shake off.

I lifted the flowers onto the window. 'Sure. Sorry. I'll get changed.' But she'd left the kitchen, had gone through to the dining-living area and was busy lighting the candles on the table and the small votives that she liked to dot round the shelves, along the sideboards.

When the Wrights arrived, like a switch being flicked, Lana's mood improved. She came to my side to greet them, her slim arm slid around my waist. A temporary truce. Both of us willing to live within that fictional realm all married couples must occupy

78

at some point; the stage play titled 'We Are Okay'. More than okay. We are happy. That we woke up every morning to love-making and soft words. We were united in the face of what could break us. We were the couple others wanted to be. We were the couple we wanted to be.

I kissed Holly's cool, rose-scented cheek and shook Gabe's hand. We moved to the kitchen.

'Oh my, that smells delicious,' Holly said, taking a deep appreciative lungful of air.

'All credit goes to my wife,' I said.

'And I'll take it,' Lana said, adding a smile and a soft laugh.

They stepped inside and we congregated around the kitchen island.

'Sorry we're a little late,' Gabe said. 'Holly couldn't find her shoes but after turning the entire house upside down, we finally found them. On her feet.'

'Shush, you.' Holly gave him a playful pat on the arm, and he flinched, leaning away with a short laugh. 'He was a good twenty minutes deciding what shirt to wear. I wouldn't mind, but they all look the same to me.'

He wore a loose white shirt tucked into light blue trousers. His nose and cheeks had that red hue like he'd been in the sun for too long. Holly was dressed in a soft white dress that came to just above her knees. The missing shoes, added another three inches to her petite stature, a glittering pair of silver stilettos. The band that had been on her wrist was absent; in its place three silver bangles that clinked when she moved her hand.

'You'd surgery today?' I asked Gabe.

'A couple of ablations is all. Was wrapped up by two p.m.,' he said. 'You?'

'I'm flat out,' I said, more for Lana's ears than my own. 'I'm taking all the patients I can at the moment.'

Lana picked up a plump red tomato, split it in two with a knife, then began dicing it into tiny pieces.

'You want help serving?' I asked Lana.

'No,' she said, too quickly, then catching herself. 'Thank you, darling. Everything's under control.' She scooped the diced tomato up and dropped it into the salad bowl, then turned to wash her hands.

'Let's get some music going in here,' I said. 'Come through.'

We went to the table. The curtains were drawn in the dining room, candles lit on the table. I took out my phone, selected a playlist of classical music, and the Chopin filtered out through the speakers hidden among the bookshelves.

I waited for Gabe and Holly to sit, then pulled out a chair and joined them, feeling redundant and guilty. I busied myself with the wine, uncorked a red.

Lana returned with the salad, a large bowl of beetroot, tomato, feta and spinach leaves, glistening with olive oil. She left it in the centre of the table. 'Wait,' she said to me, holding a hand out towards the wine I was about to pour. 'I have another.'

She went to the kitchen, collected four flutes from the island and a bottle of sparkling wine from the fridge. She sat, passed a glass round to each of us, then held the wine out towards Gabe. 'Maybe you'll do the honours, Mr Wright.'

'Sure,' he said, and took the bottle. He unwound the foil from the top, then paused, looked at the label. 'Ha. I remember this.

80

Thought it was outlawed by food standards a decade ago.' He laughed.

'Gabe!' Holly said, shocked.

'I thought you'd remember it,' Lana said. She looked between me and Holly, then explained. 'The last time we had this was at an end-of-year school party Gabe threw at his house.'

'Must have made quite the impact on your taste buds,' I said.

Gabe leaned towards me, lowered his voice. 'I thought it was the height of sophistication,' he said, wincing at the memory.

'Well, you were, until we were all ill the next morning,' Lana added. 'Although I think the amount we drank was much more the culprit over the quality.'

'My parents had words,' he said. 'You know, they'd no idea about the party. I genuinely believed I'd have the house cleaned up before they returned.' He shook his head. 'There were cigarette ends in the pool, someone had urinated – sorry – on one of the sofas in the drawing room.'

'That kid,' Lana added. 'Owen Hopkins-Crawley. Do you remember, had to have his stomach pumped?'

Gabe groaned. 'I have tried to bury some of these memories.' He wiped his eyes with his free hand, sighed. 'I'd really wanted to put on a good evening. It was a disaster. I was grounded for a full month after that stunt.'

Holly reached for the salad. 'Lord save us from posh-school nostalgia,' she mumbled. 'Where were you, Myles? Private?'

'Nowhere that wasn't best forgotten the moment I left,' I said.

'I knew I liked you,' Holly quipped.

'You may sneer,' Gabe replied with a grin. 'But it was life or death maintaining top dog status in that school.' He twisted the wire at the top of the bottle.

'Our hearts bleed,' Holly said, a glance in my direction. 'Cheap champagne and pool parties are almost the same as passing a litre bottle of White Lightning between your five friends in the local park, freezing your nips off, waiting for the alcohol to kick in.'

'Exactly,' I laughed, even though I'd never taken so much as a single swig of cider in my teens. At the time, the lack of control others sought from alcohol was something that had both terrified and disgusted me. And still does. I was halfway through the first year of my medical degree before I allowed myself my first drink, and then only because I was confident I would not be following in my dad's footsteps, that I would not wake up one day to discover that I'd lost everything. How naïve I was.

I poured a glass of sparkling water and took a long drink.

'Who's for some of the finest lighter fluid you'll ever drink?' Gabe said, pushing his thumb beneath the cork.

Lana held out her glass. 'For old times' sake.'

'Oh, go on then,' Holly said.

'You're not eager to try?' Gabe asked me.

'I want to be able to taste this lovely meal,' I said. 'Let's just have a palate cleanser ready.' I filled each of their glasses with the red wine.

By the time the main course arrived, they were already a foot into drunk. The laughter came too readily, the conversation bubbled around the table.

'Wait, I have one,' Gabe said, wiping his mouth with a napkin.

We were on the topic of embarrassing anecdotes. He gripped Holly's hand. 'Don't hate me.'

'Oh God. What?'

'So she rings me at work one day to say she's walked back from town and her car was missing from the drive and she's had to phone the police—'

'No, no. Shush,' Holly says, trying to cover his mouth.

He captured both her hands in his and pinned them to his lap. 'Don't worry, darling, I'm sure it happens to everyone. Anyway, the police come out and they're talking her through when she'd last seen it and it's only then she remembers she'd driven into town and her car was currently parked in the multi-storey at the shopping mall.'

I stood, filled everyone's glasses again, topped up my water. The evening was going better than I'd hoped. Lana sat, face propped on her cupped hand, a soft smile on her face. 'Myles has plenty of stories like that about me.'

Holly wiped a tear from the corner of her eye. Her fine blonde hair fell over the side of her face. 'Go on.'

'If I do,' I said. I genuinely couldn't think of one. 'I'd have to take them to my grave,' I said, then got up to clear the table.

I carried the dishes through to the kitchen. Outside, the sky had grown dark, heavy clouds churned beyond the window. The trees trembled. I slid another bottle of red from the rack and carried it through.

'I'm glad I've no work tomorrow,' Gabe said, scooping up his wine and taking a hearty gulp. 'How's the therapy going, Lana?'

'Oh, good. I had thought I'd cut back, there's a Psychology degree I've had my eye on but it never seems like the right time.'

Her chin came up. She didn't look in my direction but I sensed she was ready to spill my crimes out into the room. Could see the twitch at the corner of her mouth.

Lana worked three mornings a week, to keep her toe in, she'd said. She rented a small room off a dentist's office in the Village. She collected various quotes from her heroes, Jung and Freud, and framed them like prized paintings in her office. They stared down from the walls behind her desk which had, for the last two years, become the permanent home of a half-filled application for a degree in Clinical Psychology in City of London University. She was never able to muster the motivation to complete the form. It's not that she wasn't ambitious. Only, for her to get what she wanted, all she'd ever had to do was point her feet. The mountain came to her, not the other way around.

I knew it was somewhat unreasonable, but I felt a stab of resentment that she could blame me for not pursuing it now.

'Go for it,' Holly said. 'Life's short.' She put a palm to her mouth to catch a hiccup. 'Pardon me. You must be busy now right, with the recession? I mean, people are stressed, no? It's a fucking horror-show out there with people losing work, their homes.' She shuddered as if she were referring to a war taking place in some far-off country.

Lana sloshed more wine into her glass. 'It sure is. You can't trust anyone anymore.'

Gabe laughed. 'I hope this isn't qualified advice you're handing out, Lana.'

'Has anyone spoken to Daniel and Charlotte?' Holly said. 'I gathered it's hit them hard. So sad to see.'

'It only takes a mistake or two,' Gabe said.

'I think it's a little deeper than that,' Lana said.

Gabe shook his head. 'Maybe, but I believe there's always a solution to every problem. Just depends how far you're willing to go to find it.'

I didn't like the direction the conversation was going. I got up, went to the sideboard and produced a box of cigars.

'I forgot I had these.' I held the box up. I didn't care much for smoking them; in truth cigars made me feel nauseous. They'd been a gift from a patient a few years ago and had been sitting in a drawer ever since. 'Should we move to the sofas?'

Lana threw me a dark look from beneath her brows.

'Let's.' Holly collected up her glass and pushed back from the table. 'Whoa!' She laughed. 'I'm not sure my legs will be able to carry me across the room.'

She wobbled over to one of the tub chairs that looked towards the French doors, turned it round, then folded herself into the soft fabric and slipped off her shoes. 'That's better.'

Gabe dropped into a chair, set his wine on the coffee table, tugged at the knees of his trousers and crossed his legs. Lana sat into the two-seater facing them, pinning herself at the furthest end, away from where I'd be sitting.

I pushed open the curtains a little, then the doors so the smoke could escape. I handed a box of matches and a cigar to Gabe. Holly declined and Lana wrinkled her nose.

Gabe ran the cigar under his nose, inhaling the scent. He smiled appreciatively. 'It's been a while since I had one of these.' He held the cigar between thumb and fingers, struck a match which flared to life, and held the flame to the end of the cigar. Once it was lit, he waved the match through the air, drew on the cigar until blue-grey smoke poured from the corners of his mouth. I watched the ritual carefully and copied his movements. I inhaled the smoke before I remembered that wasn't a good idea. My throat closed; a burst of coughing sputtered from my mouth.

'Sorry,' I wheezed, eyes watering.

Lana edged even further from me, brought her wine to her lips and looked to Gabe. 'What would you do?' she asked, unable to let go of the subject. 'If you found yourself in Daniel's situation?'

Gabe shrugged a shoulder. 'Charlotte's on good money. He may end up divorced but he'll be okay eventually.'

'But you know what I mean.' Lana looked round at all of us, leaned forward, a playful smile on her lips. 'You're about to lose your home, every penny you've put away, your respect, your future. It's all gone. What do you do?'

'I don't know. Re-marry,' Holly replied with a laugh.

Gabe stretched back so he could look his wife in the eye. 'Good to know,' he said, in a good-natured tone. She gave a little shake of her shoulder in response.

I shifted in my seat. I didn't want to have this conversation. I knew it wouldn't end well. 'As Daniel and Charlotte are going through this, maybe this isn't the best time to . . .' I tried.

Gabe studied the cigar. 'Someone would have to die.'

Holly choked on her drink. 'Christ!' She cleared her throat, a flick of her fine blonde hair from her face. 'Sometimes I marvel at the fact that real-life people allow you to cut into their chests.' She shook her head. 'And how, pray tell, would this death go down?'

'I haven't thought of that bit yet. Hold on,' he said, a thought just occurring to him. 'I meant a fake death,' he paused. 'Obviously.'

'So, life insurance fraud.' She pursed her lips. 'Okay. Myles?'

I put out my cigar. The smoke was making me feel sick. The conversation was making me feel sick. The corners of the room stretched. The ground mush under my seat. I didn't answer quick enough.

Lana jumped in. 'Myles prefers to solve all his problems by pretending they're not happening.' There was no mistaking the sour note in her voice.

I attempted to laugh it off. 'Hey!' I said.

A look passed between Gabe and Holly. If they didn't know before, I felt certain they'd guessed now. Beside me Lana tensed, and I had the feeling that she'd told them already. My face grew hot. Gabe's eyes settled on mine and I could see the truth of our situation reflected back to me, along with something else. A drawing in of the eyebrows, a tilt of his head. Pity.

'Is this happening? To you?' he asked.

I allowed myself a quick glare at Lana.

'They'd find out eventually,' she said, defensive. She got up, fetched the wine from the table and filled her glass. When she came back to the two-seater, she sat closer.

'I suppose it is,' I answered Gabe.

Whatever joviality had peppered the evening was drowned out by the silence now spreading through the room. A dull pain began to beat at my temples. Gabe put the cigar on the side of the ashtray.

'It would be possible,' he said. 'We could do it?' His voice was calm, steady like the tone one might use to settle a nervous animal.

A laugh from Holly. 'What are you talking about?'

'You've life insurance?' he asked me.

Again Lana answered before me. 'I do,' she said, her eyes locked on his.

I put my hand on her knee. 'I think everyone's had a little too much to drink.'

She laid her hand over mine, met my eyes. 'No one would actually have to be killed, right?'

Gabe laughed. 'I mean no one's stopping you, but for this, no. That would be where the fraud part came in. No one dies. Otherwise, I think they call it murder.'

'How though?'

Gabe thought for second. 'You could go for a hike, a boat trip, never return, although you wouldn't get any money through for some time. Even years. We'd need a way to get a death cert quickly.'

Part of me thought I should get up then. Stand and begin to talk about early mornings. Start prompting to our guests that the dinner party was over and it was time to go. But there was a part of me, the part that was a desperate man clinging to the cliff-side by a fingernail, that wanted to hear what he had to say.

He was bent over his knees now, elbows pitched against his thighs, shirtsleeves rolled up his tanned forearms. His eyes moved across the rug beneath his feet as if the answers were inscribed there. 'You'd need a body,' he said.

'There's always some catch,' I said, adding a laugh. I went to stand but Lana's hand tightened on mine.

Holly clicked her fingers. 'You were telling me once about those unclaimed bodies in the hospital,' she said.

The curtains swelled and, like an invisible stranger, a cool breeze entered the room.

I felt it across the back of my neck. 'Bodies?'

'Sometimes bodies come through the hospital,' Gabe said. The candlelight picked out the hollows in his face, the highlights in his hair. You got the sense that however hard Gabe fell, he'd spring up again, like gravity could only half work at keeping him on the ground. I had a bizarre kind of longing then of wanting people to see in me what I saw in him. Or rather, I believed it was what people saw, and I wanted – no, needed – to keep hold of that belief. I knew it was a shallow motive or that I was succumbing to a sad kind of narcissism, but deep down I knew that, to me, that's what was really grating about this entire debt situation. But being in Gabe's presence made it feel possible that our problems could be worked out. That there was a solution, right there, and he would help us get to it. Even though we were speaking in hypotheticals, I tried to envision our way out of this predicament. What if it worked? Lana would have another name. Lana Butler would be dead.

He went on. 'These bodies are either unidentifiable or for whatever reason no one comes forward to claim them. It happens more often than you think, and if there's no foul play, those bodies go on to be cremated or buried.' He lifted his chin, looked across at me, eyes dark as ditchwater. 'It would be a matter of paperwork. A simple switch. Not even a switch really, but Lana's name in place of an unknown.'

I could feel Holly's pale gaze on my face. Lana's too. Waiting.

'You can't be serious? We're just playing here, right?' I turned to Lana, half expecting her to laugh this off. But there was a look in her eye that I recognised, not dissimilar to how she looked at me when we first met. A look that said she'd already made some decision, a decision that was going to change our lives forever.

Gabe shook his head, straightened, then stretched his arms over the back of the chair. The tension in the room dissolved. 'We could do it,' he said, quietly. 'We'd want a cut, of course.'

'Of course,' Holly said, in a high-pitched, jokey tone that attempted to bring the conversation back into the realm of 'what if' rather than 'what was going to be'.

Gabe picked up his cigar, lit it again and brought it to his mouth. 'But we could do it,' he stressed.

'Gabe!' Holly rolled her eyes.

'What?' He grinned at her quickly, but it was on Lana his gaze finally settled. 'The offer is there, just say the word.'

CHAPTER 8

The curtains were open and the blank night looked in on our room. I couldn't sleep. The evening played through my head over and again. The slow delivery of Gabe's plan. The steady bloom of excitement in Lana's eyes. If we did this, there would be an assessment by the insurance company, my thoughts ran on, possibly by police too. Or maybe there wouldn't be. Maybe they'd see the death certificate and the insurance company would pay out. I gave myself a moment, permission to indulge in the possibility that we could be debt-free. I pictured us somewhere on the Côte d'Azur, tanned and happy; Lana lounging at the end of a boat, a thin-stemmed glass in her hand, a large straw sunhat shielding her face where I could just make out the plump curve of her mouth which was pulled into a wide smile.

I turned onto my side, stuffed the pillow into the crook of my neck. Behind me, Lana pressed herself against my back.

Some time in my final year at school, I developed an unhealthy crush on my English teacher, Maggie Hartigan. She wasn't a great beauty, her chin, some might say, was not quite prominent

91

enough to balance the rest of her face, her eyes slightly too far apart, which gave her a slightly other-worldly appearance, but they were wide and expressive, and when she spoke, I held on to her every word. There was a quiet grace to her movements that turned even the toughest boys in my year to over-helpful servants. Opening a window for her when she complained of the heat, helping her rearrange desks, or carry in books. Her husband also worked at the school. He taught Science. Rumours were rife about how he abused her. How every weekend, he'd another woman on the go. And every so often, she'd turn up at the school with a fresh mark on her neck, or bruise along her temple. The result was that there was an air of protection around her. There were those of us, I'm certain, who would have killed her husband, if she'd asked.

At the time, home was a dark hovel of cold radiators, cold water and scraped-together meals. My father's descent into alcoholism was complete. My mother had stopped sending letters. I was working at a local garage at the weekends to top up our social allowance and faced the world rigid with anger about how difficult life had become. As far as I was concerned, there'd been an error in the system somewhere, and every day I felt that fault in the universe like sandpaper against my skin. It left me moody and defensive. I'd filled in my university choices. My means of escape, but many of them required references from teachers and people of standing in the community.

In all my scrambling to keep up with the pack, I realised I was running the wrong race altogether. I started to understand that it wasn't what I knew but who I knew that would be important. And the performance of it all became too much. I realised that while in school, grades might have been a great equaliser, but when it came to the real world, I'd be left behind. Eventually, my anger turned inwards, melted into a mulch of self-pity and futility. My grades fell quickly. But Maggie had a talent for drawing out students who were sullen and quiet. Concerned, she asked if I'd time to stay after school. I didn't, I told her. I had to get back for my dad.

I went home, made tea for myself and my dad, Ambie. The doorbell rang. I probably should have been more upset that she'd looked up my address and come to my house, but when I opened the door and saw her standing there, my first thought was how beautiful she looked. How stupid her fucking husband was for shagging around. She'd found a place that might take a scholarship, she'd said. She said she'd help me get there. All I needed was to submit a portfolio of work by the end of term. So, we met every Wednesday after school in the quiet of an empty classroom.

I can't remember who kissed who first.

I'm embarrassed now about how I stalked her through the school afterwards. My enduring memory is of the back of her neck, lined with the high collar of her blouse. Every time she saw me, she turned on her heel.

Finally, I managed to corner her in the staff canteen. She stood against the window, looking over my shoulder like a trapped animal about to leap.

'I wanted to talk to you,' I said.

'Myles, you're a nice boy, but what happened between us should never have happened. I'm very sorry.'

I reached out, rested my hand over hers. She tensed, a

movement that I interpreted as desire. 'I didn't mind. I like you. A lot.'

Her face flushed, cherry red to the tips of her ears. There were tears gathering on her bottom lashes.

I didn't hear the door open behind me and didn't have the time to register the hand at the back of my neck. Next thing I knew, I was on the other side of the room, on the floor, Mr Hartigan's wild eyes going from Maggie to me and back again. His fist flexed and unflexed.

That was the last time I saw Maggie at school. She called in sick the next day and never returned. Sometimes, I'd see her darting through the town as if something were pursuing her, but she never noticed me and I never spoke to her again. I graduated and got my place at Bristol University. Life went on for a while. But one weekend, returning home from a day-time binge with an old school mate, I found myself outside their house. I wasn't sure what I intended to do. There was no plan. All I knew was that I wanted him to taste a fraction of the fear his wife lived with daily.

Most drivers, when they get into a car, would notice something was wrong pretty quickly if their brake lines have been cut. The pedal feels soft, and the brakes don't fail immediately, but Hartigan was obviously as thick as his fists and didn't notice until his car was careening into the central reservation on the M5. He survived. Just. There was an investigation. A few of us students were interrogated by police and Maggie was under suspicion for a while, but nothing ever came of it.

This memory surfaced because, unlike then, through all the months of hiding from how bad our financial situation was, I realised, somewhere along the way, I'd accepted my fate. I had buried that part of myself that was capable of striking back and I knew what my future would look like, a reproduction of my childhood years. More depressing, considering all I'd done to get here. My position at the surgery would also become unstable once word got around. I'd be facing bankruptcy, the knowledge of which would spill out into the Village like an oil-slick on water. That kind of thing mattered. Especially here. We could move away, somewhere cheaper. I could get work in a practice there, but then as living costs go down so would my salary. I knew enough that once you were on that hamster wheel, you weren't getting off.

I felt Lana's hand on my shoulder. 'Are you awake?' she whispered.

'Yes,' I said. I stared out at the darkness through the pale smudge of my face reflected on the window across the room.

'I can't stop thinking about it.'

'Me neither.' I shuffled to my other side so that we were facing. I felt the warmth of her breath on my face. 'You think Gabe was serious?'

A movement from her that could have been a shrug of a shoulder. 'I think so.'

'It wouldn't be easy,' I said.

'We'd be careful. Plan it right.'

'It sounds like you've made up your mind,' I said. A car started up outside, the patter of voices in the street below. 'What about your parents?'

'They'd forgive me in time. In a couple of years, when we're clear of it all, I can get in touch with Mum and Dad. Dad first.

Explain. Once they knew I was all right, I'm sure they'd get over it,' she said, an unpleasant peevish tone to her voice.

I wasn't exactly Fred Grosvenor's number one fan, but even so I wasn't sure he deserved to grieve his daughter's death when she was still alive. And I was less sure he'd be ready to forgive the experience. I wouldn't.

But I said, 'Okay,' mentally checking off my list of questions. 'Where would we go? I'd have to sell up here, leave my job. You yours. Your clients, your friends . . .' She gave out a derisory laugh at this. Lana didn't seem to need many friends. She had plenty of casual mates she met for coffee or yoga classes, but she didn't appear to need anything deeper, apart from when it came to me. '. . . Your name, the life we've built here or wanted to build.'

'That life is gone. You know that. And where would we go? Anywhere. English speaking, of course. Spain, the South Coast, France. We could even go to Italy or Ireland if you wanted to explore your roots.' I didn't imagine the slight shudder in her body as she said this; Lana never had any intention of turning over the soil on my heritage and I knew she wouldn't begin now. 'You could continue practising,' she went on, giving it the hard sell. 'There'd be no need for you to change your name or what you do. I could begin my Psychology degree under a new identity.' She pushed upright to a sitting position. Adjusted the pillows behind her back. 'Look, we either accept the status quo and allow this debt to attach itself to us and pull us down, or we do something about it. Sometimes, for survival, you have to be selfish.' She rested her palm on the side of my face. 'I know it's not right but—'

'It's not about right or wrong,' I said, a sudden flare of irrational anger bursting in my chest. Her words suggested weakness, and pathetically I didn't want her to see me like that. 'Among other things, it's about what would happen if we're caught.'

I removed Lana's hand from my cheek and turned onto my back. The room was too hot. The air like warm soup. I got up, went to the window and pushed it open. The Wrights' house was in darkness apart from a halo of light cast down from the porch. I wondered were they awake. Were they having a similar conversation? Was Gabe thinking through the logistics of his plan? 'Fortune favours the brave'. Or was it 'Fortune favours those willing to do anything to grab at her skirts'? It bothered me that Lana never seemed to fully grasp the depths of my character, the shades of my personality. Or maybe she did. Maybe she knew my character better than myself and what really bothered me was that I mightn't fully understand hers.

Here was the solution to our problems and perhaps the solution to us. But at what cost? From time to time, I thought about my guilt around the Maggie Hartigan episode. Thought about how close I came to killing someone. And when you live with attempted murder as the threshold of your morality, it's easier to tell yourself that as long as you don't cross that line, you're okay. You're good. So, using some stranger's body to help us get free of our financial problems should have been an easy decision. The person was already dead.

I could see how it might work. If Gabe managed to alter the paperwork, the body would not even need to meet Lana's physical build or description. But it was a risk for him. And I couldn't understand why an esteemed surgeon with no need for extra cash would go in on this.

'We don't know them all that well,' I said to Lana, returning to bed.

'I know Gabe enough to believe he can pull this off.'

'Just because you went to the same school together,' I snapped. 'Regardless of what type of school it was, doesn't mean you know him.'

I felt rather than saw her pout.

Reaching for her hand in the darkness, I said, 'I'm not saying it isn't tempting. Although it would be a wrench to give up all we've built here, but I suppose we'd have to give up some of it regardless, and I would give it all up, for you, for us.' I experienced a strange twinge of conscience as I said that, coupled with the thought that it wasn't altogether true. And that thought was followed by a fleeting swoop of panic. It was true, I reassured myself. A breath. 'It's just not that simple. There's a reason people get caught for this kind of thing. And how would I explain your death to friends? To family?'

'I died in my sleep. An aneurysm. One of those sudden death syndrome things you told me about that happen to some people.'

'And where's the ambulance at the door? Where is the paramedic call-out report? In fact, where are the paramedics? Where's the transcript of my 999 call? Your admission record at hospital? Why, in an emergency, have the paramedics taken you to St Anne's over the Cavendish, which is closer? And you can bet Fred Grosvenor is going to want to speak to the doctor who saw you. I would.'

'Most of that would be a matter of changing records on a computer. As far as the doc that could speak to Dad, Gabe could do that, couldn't he? It would be his name on the paperwork after all,' she replied.

'Exactly,' I said. 'Why? Why are they helping us? What have they to gain? They have everything they need. Why is Gabriel Wright offering to risk his reputation to help us, a couple he barely knows?'

She lifted her hand. I could make out the movement of her fingers as they pushed against one eye then the other. There came brief sniffle, then a sigh. It struck me that I'd never seen Lana cry before. Even now, in the darkness, I couldn't be sure she actually was.

'I can't do that life, Myles,' she said. Her voice shook. 'Scraping away for nothing. I can't do it. This financial hole we're in will consume us and continue to consume us for years. I don't want that.'

After a moment, I heard a trembling breath as if she were bracing herself, then, 'But you're right.' A fractured laugh. 'You're right. It's a terrible idea. I guess I was desperate for . . . something.'

I kissed her forehead and she settled against me with a sigh. 'Why didn't you tell me about your life insurance policy?' I asked.

There was silence for a long moment and I thought she might have drifted off to sleep. Then, 'One never wants to give another the motive to kill them, do they?'

I turned onto my back and she slid her hand over my chest. I held her there. I felt like she might disappear; dissolve, fade

99

into mist and drift up and away with the morning. Sleep sank me into a hot soup of startling images, fragments of possible futures mixed with flashes of my past. Lana caught in a smile. The sun blinding against an endless baby-blue sky. Tears aching in my throat. Maggie Hartigan on my doorstep. Her voice, floating to me; gentle, coaxing, confused: 'What happened?'

CHAPTER 9

'I saw you in A&E last week.' Brian Lovett rolled up his sleeve and held out his arm like a pro.

I wrapped the cuff around his thin arm and he checked that the Velcro was secure. I put the diaphragm against the crease of his elbow. The skin soft as a baby's. Brian was a weekly regular. Would be daily if he had his way. Almost all of his illnesses could be put down to his extreme hypochondria. Prior to booking, he studied all conditions related to his symptoms which were always non-specific and mysteriously non-reproducible in a clinical setting. We had a few patients like that. Some were a version of socially accepted drug addicts, reliant on codeine and desperate for another opiate fix. They spent their days in their middle-class homes on the edge of cold sweats dreaming up ailments that would justify another prescription. I seemed to accumulate more of these patients than my colleagues. I reasoned this was because one day they wouldn't be crying wolf and I would be there when other medics would have eye-rolled. Sometimes, I thought they preferred to see me because I did have a tendency to give them what they wanted. Need is need. Whatever way you examine it.

Brian was not like that. Brian was a twenty-eight-year-old addicted to medical attention not drugs. And I'd never succeeded in diagnosing him with anything other than perfect health. I smiled tightly at him. I was desperate to get through my case load. Desperate to get some headspace to think about our situation. We'd more or less shelved the Wrights' offer, but still it played on the fringes of my mind and occasionally I found myself imagining what would happen if we went through with it.

'What were you doing at A&E?' I asked Brian. Hoping to distract him so I could get through the exam quickly.

'I had some strange bruising on my wrist,' he said. He pointed down at the completely normal blue vessels running beneath his skin. 'Were you ill?' he asked, pale grey eyes looking up at me.

Releasing the pressure in the cuff, I watched the needle on the gauge tick downwards, then unhooked the stethoscope from my ears. 'I was taking a patient.'

Eyes widened. Imagining himself in that scenario. Or fantasising.

'A patient? What happened?'

'Nothing serious,' I said, knowing that if I wasn't careful, he'd present with the same condition as Mrs Edwards within days. 'A minor fracture.'

I turned, made a note of his blood pressure, picked up my pen light. He was familiar with this dance and dutifully covered one eye while I flashed the light into the other three times before we switched sides like a well-choreographed dance.

I straightened, pocketed the pen light. 'It all looks good, Brian.'

I sat down at my computer. Added to his notes. A signal for him to leave.

He placed his finger against his throat, just over his carotid. 'Can't you feel that? It thrums against my ear. A whooshing sound.'

I grit my teeth. 'Have you had a cold recently?'

He frowned. 'I have been feeling a little run-down over the last few months. Why? I hear sometimes viruses get into the heart. The valves? Would that cause it?'

'Your valves are fine.'

'Can you know that for sure?'

'You had an echo only three weeks ago, remember?' A note appeared on my screen. A message from reception. Staff meeting midday.

'What if something has happened since then? I've only had this whooshing problem this past week. I read that it could be a bruit? That my arteries are likely furred up. It creates a turbulence in the blood, you know. Then that can result in clots. Strokes. Do you think that's what's happening?'

He was breathing a little fast now. The stark white skin over the top of his chest turning pink. I thought of Gabe – probably in the hospital right now, a sea of blue and greens, a bright halo of light illuminating his work; man versus God; and mercifully, his patient out cold – and felt a pang of pure liquid envy.

'Dr Butler?'

Stethoscope back in, I listened at his throat briefly, then pulled back. 'You only get this sound at night?'

'Yes.'

'How about nausea?'

He checked himself, pressed his hand against his abdomen. 'I don't think so.'

I could sit him down. Talk him through his anxiety. Tell him that sometimes the body makes noises. Sometimes we get pains, aches, fizzing sensations. That Dr Internet will always diagnose you with something when sometimes there's nothing.

In the end, I offered Brian what I always offered him: another appointment. 'Everything looks good for the moment. Would you like to check in again in a few weeks?'

'Thank you, Doctor,' he said. 'I do feel better already.'

I nodded. He left.

I sat for a moment and stared at the note on my screen. I felt I more than knew what was coming. I searched the drawer on my desk. The invites for The Toppers dinner in Mayfair had arrived a few days ago and I'd had the instinct to keep them hidden from Nathan until a situation arose where they might be useful. I found them at the back of the drawer. The card was high quality, embossed along the edges in gold. I slipped one invite into my diary which I then tucked under my arm and headed for the staff room.

I could hear the sing-song tinkle of Madison's voice as I approached. No doubt shoving as many knives into my back as possible while I wasn't there. I hurried to the door and pushed it open. Madison fell silent, a generous flush crept up her face. She looked down at her open notebook. Nathan pushed up from the table, flicked back the edges of his tired brown suit jacket. At one point, he used to look smart. Now he looked jaded and rumpled. Sloping mounds of skin beneath his eyes pulled along his lower lid so that the flesh never quite touched the thread-veined surface of his eye, reminiscent of a bloodhound's.

'Myles,' he said. 'Why don't you take a seat.' He pointed to a chair at the end of the table.

I sat. Madison closed her notebook, kept her place with a pencil.

'Coffee?' Nathan asked. He lifted the pot and poured me a cup. He offered the same to Madison, who shook her head with a sharp little jerk.

Opening up my files, I began, wanting to take control. 'So how is everyone? Sam put together the month's numbers. Up on June which is great. But I think we can do—'

Nathan held up a hand. 'Sorry, Myles, we didn't call the meeting to talk figures, although I agree it's nice to see an upwards trajectory for the first time in a year, I think.' He raised an eyebrow at Madison, who nodded, her lips bunching in a self-congratulatory manner.

No doubt Madison had, in her greasy grasp, a number of errors I had made on the few patients of mine that she'd had to see. Nathan was an easy win for anyone. He didn't care about details. Or justifications. He never went deep. Nathan wanted an easy life, lived on the surface. The hypocrisy was enough to make me spit my coffee. If I were to comb through any of his files, I knew I'd find any number of horrific clinical decisions.

'We're concerned, Myles,' he said. 'Concerned for you.'

This wasn't good.

'And for the clinic,' Madison added, meeting Nathan's eyes. It was clear this was a rehearsed conversation starter.

'Yes, yes. We're concerned for the clinic too,' Nathan added. He pulled a chair out, and sat down, but leaned his body away.

I gathered myself. Nathan would want this over quickly. Either me gone or this meeting ended.

'You're concerned for the clinic?' I addressed Madison.

She drew in her chin. 'Namely, you. We are at a financial precipice. With some of the changes I've made over the last six months, we're turning a corner. With the new evening clinic sessions I'm offering, along with new lab fast-track pathways and of course our upgraded membership programme, there's a good chance we'll be able to continue in this vein. Excuse the pun,' she said, an annoying twitch of a grin at the corner of her mouth. 'What we can't afford are complaints. Not in a place like Wimbledon where we rely on word of mouth,' she said.

'Complaints?' I asked.

'Yes,' Nathan said.

I leaned back in the chair. 'Has someone made a complaint against me?'

Madison went back to picking at the corner of her notebook. 'Not yet.'

I looked to Nathan. He looked down at his hands.

'As you know, I saw a couple of your patients the other morning,' Madison continued. 'When you were late.'

'I had a problem at home,' I said. 'It was unavoidable. Happy to return the favour, any time.'

'It's unlikely that will be necessary,' she said. 'I'm sure you understand that patients get attached to their doctor. They don't like to have to see someone else. In private practice, having that consistency is key to success.'

Madison had pushed her toe into the sand, drawn out a line between us. We would never be comrades. Enemies only. And now, as much as I wanted to get rid of her, a little perverse part of myself thought what would be the fun in that? She needed to stick around, so I could rub her nose in it when she inevitably failed.

She glanced up briefly. 'Is there a reason you're smiling?'

'Nerves,' I said.

'Mr Lambert.' Checking her notes. 'You prescribed an opiate-based painkiller.'

'No. No, I didn't.' Lambert was an ex-addict.

'Pethidine,' she said.

Silence. I didn't answer because as she said it, I saw my own hand curve round the 'p' and scratch across the surface of my prescription pad. It was the morning I'd spoken to my bank manager about the repossession notice on the house. Right before Nathan asked me to go out to the Rawlings' place. My head was a screech of panic. Lambert had been experiencing trigeminal neuralgia. And was in excruciating pain. He'd not slept in four days. He was begging for relief and, distracted, I'd forgotten about his past – what, twenty-odd years before? Or maybe that detail had tried to push through, and all I could think of was my own pain. My own problems.

'I did?' I asked.

She passed me a photocopy of the prescription. 'Luckily, the pharmacist caught it when he went to collect his medication.'

'So no harm then.'

She cocked an eyebrow at me. 'And Mr Vander? When was the last time you assessed his blood pressure?'

It went on like that, her beating me down with my failures which, yes, when listed out were questionable, but none were very grievous. I wasn't drinking on the job or anything, something I suspected Nathan indulged in from time to time.

'In short, we were thinking, considering you said there were some problems at home—' Nathan chimed in.

'Problems that are resolved now,' I said. I pulled out the performance sheet from my diary and let the Toppers invite fall out onto the table. I pushed it to one side as if it were nothing and picked up the performance sheet. 'Here are my numbers for the past month,' I said. 'They are the highest in the surgery.'

Nathan's gaze slid to the invite. I saw the flame of interest light in his eyes. He pulled in a little closer, cleared his throat and reached for the performance sheet. Madison shot me a glare. I was playing dirty. But once the bank took our home, there was a good chance my work would be the only good thing I had left. After our talk the other night, I wasn't all that confident Lana would stay by my side. And maybe I'd been harsh on how my patients would judge me once word got out. Sure, I was no wet-behind-the ears graduate lumbered with student debt, which had a kind of noble altruism attached to it. I sported the kind of debt that spoke of greed, arrogance and a need for luxury. But, perhaps, they'd admire my stick-with-it attitude, my get-up-and-go spirit. I liked to think so.

'If there's not actually been a complaint,' I said, 'I don't understand what this is about. Only –' I took a deep breath – 'it feels like an attempt to fire me. If anyone's uncomfortable with me working here, I'd prefer you just said it.'

'I thought he just did,' Madison said.

I gathered up my papers, scooped the invite from the table. 'I have a full clinic this afternoon.'

'Let's not get carried away,' Nathan said. 'We just wanted

to give you a chance to explain the findings that Madison has gathered. And now you have.'

I stood. 'I have. Mr Vander has a home blood-pressure monitor. He submits his readings weekly. I review them. His blood pressure fluctuates dramatically. Something that if he was your patient you'd likely have grasped too. Or maybe you wouldn't. The reason he takes his readings at home is because he has quite severe health anxieties and his BP goes up when taken by a doctor. If you'd care to look at my notes, you'll find that his home readings, although borderline, are not significant enough to start him on medication,' I said. 'You see,' I levelled with her, 'I believe in treating the whole patient, not just what we see on the day. You'll understand how important that is as you gain experience. There's a course coming up in London on this very subject. I recommend it to you.'

Madison flushed again. This time with anger.

Nathan glanced between us. 'Yes, yes,' he said. 'That sounds helpful.'

She opened her mouth to answer but closed it again.

'If that's all?' I asked.

'That's all,' Nathan answered.

Madison pushed back from the table and left, taking her notebook with her. I waited for the door to close.

I turned to Nathan. 'I don't appreciate being ambushed in the midst of clinic with this sort of peer jealousy because, let's face it, that's what it appears to be. I don't think any of us would continue to work where they felt like someone was looking over our shoulder all the time. Frankly,' I said, pushing the point home, 'I'm not sure a tribunal would look on this too kindly.'

'I'm sorry. You're right,' he said. He pushed a hand over the thin hair on his head. 'She insisted there was a concern, but I can see now that, yes, it could be jealousy or insecurity on her part. I'll talk to her.'

I reached down, finished my coffee, tried not to smile. 'Nathan, you and I have worked with each other a long time. I've given all I can to this surgery and will continue to do so. It's as important to me as it is to you. You must know that?'

He nodded slowly. 'I do,' he said. 'Let's see how we go, shall we?' He nodded at my hand. 'You're going to the Fellowship dinner?'

I frowned at him. Pretended not to know what he was asking, even though the invite burned in my palm like I was holding a piece of hot coal.

'Oh, this,' I said, eventually. 'Yes. I wasn't sure whether to go, but it might be beneficial to the surgery.' I paused. 'I hear the food is always good, if you and Sofia are free?'

His eyes widened, skin pulling downwards from the bottom, eyebrows pulling up until it seemed like his eyes might roll out onto his cheeks. 'I don't think we've anything on that weekend, if you can spare the tickets.'

'I'm sure we can work something out,' I said. 'Leave it with me.'

CHAPTER 10

Lana stepped out of the cab in a cloud of bergamot and verbena perfume. Her hair was pinned off to the side, revealing a series of three black stars just behind her right ear. Over the last two weeks, we'd circled each other like planets in orbit. We spoke, but never about what really occupied our minds. We were counting down but we weren't sure to what. Or rather, we couldn't bring ourselves to confront it. The tattoo was new. A week old. An impulsive decision on her lunch break, she'd said, followed by something along the lines of only living once. It was pretty. A linear constellation like the three sisters of Orion's belt. But Lana never liked tattoos. And the sudden change in this attitude made me nervous. As Lana told me often when talking about her couples therapy, people may want their partners to change, but changes in behaviour in the closed microclimate of a marriage aren't always for the better.

The sun was sinking behind London city's skyline and the evening burned, turning the streets of Mayfair orange. Lana tucked her purse under her right arm and strode into the hotel ahead of me. I resisted the urge to run my finger down the long line of her spine. I'd no right to feel happy. But I did. I possessed a giddy sort of smugness not dissimilar to when I stole. We may not be as we were, but there was a relief in knowing the secret was out.

This evening was the evening when I'd get us back on track. Where, away from our home, and out from beneath the shadow of our debt, I could remind Lana how good we were together, to make her see me again. The man she'd wanted from our first meeting. The man who loved her.

The Toppers dinner was being held in an event room on the ground floor of the Radisson. The room was beautifully decorated. Long swathes of white silk over the walls, lit up with deep blue neon lights, round tables also dressed white, the chairs covered in white linen, wide bows on the back. At the centre of each table, tall vases crowned with clusters of violet lilies and bright pink carnations. At the top of the room was the wide-screen projector left over from the day of lectures. The last slide said *Neuroscience and the Origin of Consciousness*.

Lana turned to me. 'Let's try and enjoy the night.'

I nodded, kissed the back of her hand and escorted her through the tables, casting out the odd smile to no one in particular. Gabe stood and shook my hand when we got to him, then leaned in to drop a kiss on Lana's cheek. I watched a pink flush rise behind her make-up, a few blotches appearing over the skin on her throat. Something dipped in my abdomen.

'This is nice,' I said, and pulled out a chair for Lana. I sat next to her.

'Renovated just a few months ago,' Holly said. She waved

a hand around the room, a glass of champagne clutched in her fingers. 'Without the fabric frippery they've drowned it in tonight, it's actually quite chic.'

There was another couple at the table. A man and woman. Older. The man's greying hair was a thin fuzz combed to the left. His face was that particular shade of puce that implied a heart attack was imminent, and he reclined in his chair with a rigidity that suggested if he leaned in at all, he'd roll away. The woman was the opposite. Cheekbones pointing through wrinkled skin, her teeth too big for her mouth. She wore a cream dress, a shawl of white organza around her narrow shoulders, the sheer fabric giving her an ethereal quality.

'Myles, Mr Henry and Sarah Reid,' Gabe said in their direction.

Henry made a signal to move.

I stood. 'Don't get up,' I said quickly. Reached across the table and met his outstretched fingers, shook his hand. 'Good to meet you, Mr Reid,' I said, then gave a nod to his wife, who sent me a brief smile.

'Henry,' Gabe said to the table, 'recently published a very good paper on emotional dysregulation and the heart.'

The man's colour deepened. 'You've been out of the loop a little too long, Wright. It was nothing groundbreaking, a lit review is all.' At this he gave a short laugh, which descended quickly into a series of rattling coughs.

Gabe looked flustered, only for a second, but I caught his reaction and wondered what Reid had meant by being out of the loop for too long.

'Important work all the same,' Gabe said quickly selecting a bread roll and splitting it with his thumb. 'What was the word the Greeks used? I read it one of your papers once and thought it revealed the ecstasy and agony of love perfectly.' He picked up his knife and scooped up a corner of butter.

Henry, not looking up from his plate: 'The origin of the word *artér*.' It came out with a sharp huff of exhalation. 'For artery.'

'That's right,' Gabe said; his smile widened. 'Meaning something by which a burden is carried.'

Holly lifted her wine glass. 'Not sure which of us he's saying is a burden,' she said with a laugh, her gaze flitting briefly to Lana.

'Never you, darling,' Gabe replied.

'Has Nathan arrived?' I asked.

'Ah yes, sorry, I had to seat him to the right of the room,' Gabe answered. 'He's enjoying himself though.'

I looked over. Nathan was in full conversation with an older, serious-looking man who was sitting across from him. Even from where I sat, I could tell he was in his element. His wife, Sofia, flicked the edge of a shawl over her shoulder. She caught my eye, lifted a hand and fluttered her fingers at me. I nodded.

The courses arrived swiftly. When the main came, I looked down at the steak. The water from the vegetables had mixed with the juices from the meat, with the result that my fillet sat in a pool of pale pink fluid. The effect made me feel queasy. The waitress held out a jug.

'Béarnaise?'

'Thank you,' I replied.

She anointed the meat with a dollop of thick sauce.

After – or, if I'd bothered to stress myself about it at the time, during – the meal, I noticed Lana growing unhappy. I sensed rather than understood that her unhappiness was down to me. It irked. I had hoped we could enjoy the evening together. So, instead of indulging her bad humour and asking if there was anything I could do, I ignored it. I turned towards Gabe, asked him if he'd caught any of the lectures, even if I didn't have the knowledge to grasp most of what he said about them, and I felt the slow growth of her mood as real as a hot duvet across my back.

I lowered my voice and said to Gabe, 'Listen, between fellow medics who know how competitive this job is, if Nathan asks—'

'Ah yes, your membership,' he laughed. 'He told me. Don't worry. Besides –' he put an arm around my shoulder – 'you should take those exams again. It took me ages to pass them. They'd be no trouble for you now.'

And because arrogance was something I took to naturally, I replied, 'Maybe I should.'

He pulled me close, a squeeze, shoulder to shoulder. Like we were players on a team. 'Anyway, you're as good as anyone in this room. Not that you need me to tell you.'

The evening moved on and the further Lana went into her sulk, the more determined I was to enjoy myself. I was drinking more than I would normally and no doubt the numerous glasses of champagne, then wine, then sweet wine, influenced my mood, but I felt like I were being given a glimpse of the life I'd always wanted. And I was going to take it. Even if it was for one night only.

When we were asked to stand so tables could be pushed back for dancing, Lana took this as the signal to leave.

'Lovely to meet you all.' She smiled down at the Reids, who

had shuffled their chairs round to watch the band and the empty dancefloor.

Henry, without the restraining support of the table, had pushed his backside into the chair and was leaning forward on a walking stick.

'We're not leaving yet?' I asked her. 'It's not even ten.'

She opened her clutch, checked the items in her bag, then clicked it closed again. 'You should stay. Get the most out of it.'

'If you want to leave, then we go together.' I stood, unhooked my jacket from the back of my chair, then I leaned in to kiss her.

She drew back; not much, just an inhale's worth, but she might as well have carved up a canyon between us. 'Don't,' she said, quietly.

I felt my face redden. 'Okay,' I said slowly.

Holly gave her a hug. 'Gabe's around somewhere. I'll let him know you had to leave.'

'Thank you for a lovely evening,' Lana said.

And with that she stalked away, the elegant line of her spine straight, head high. I contemplated staying. I hadn't had a chance to talk to Nathan. But Lana . . . It was like I was bound by an invisible thread and she held the other end. I hurried after her, catching up just as she broke out into the reception area.

'I'll get them to call a cab,' I said.

'Myles.' Nathan's voice from behind me.

I turned, Lana at the same time, stringing a wide smile across her face.

'Nathan,' I said.

'You know my wife Sofia, of course.' Sofia liked to dress

loudly. And with age, the brighter her clothes got. Tonight, it was a turquoise corseted gown that gathered skin, fat and cleavage into a mass on her chest. Her décolletage was spotted with age and wrinkled, and in the folds of flesh were her usual collection of resin necklaces. Large beads, that wouldn't look out of place on a Christmas tree, with earrings to match. Her auburn hair was swept into a chignon and looked crisp to touch.

I leaned forward and kissed her cheek, which was soft as folded silk. 'Lovely to see you again, Sofia. You look beautiful.'

'Good to see you, Myles,' she said, then as an afterthought, 'And you too, Lana.' She threw a dismissive glance at her.

I derived a sour little pleasure from the fact that Sofia adored me but had never warmed to my wife. In Sofia's company, I felt like some balance was restored from Fred Grosvenor's obvious distaste every time he had to spend time in my company.

'You're not leaving?' Nathan asked.

'We are,' Lana said. 'A headache.'

'What a shame,' he replied, then turned to me. 'I guess we'll meet at the clinic on Monday. You've caught up with Madison, Myles? She's about here somewhere.'

Madison.

'Here she is now,' Sofia said, and extended a hand out to her right, where Madison was approaching.

'Hello, Myles,' Madison smiled. I could almost feel the poison darts flying from her eyes.

'I didn't know you'd be here,' I said.

'My wife is head of the board.' She tilted her head. A smug expression on her face telling me she knew all about my little lie to Nathan.

'There'd been some mix-up with the tables,' Nathan said. 'Madison was kind enough to offer me her seat, so I could be closer to the front of the room. I have to say, we had the most fascinating group of consultants to dine with, many of whom are very keen to work with our referral system.'

Madison grinned. There's no way I could leave yet.

'I see a taxi outside,' Lana said then to me. 'You coming?'

I hesitated. She nodded goodbye and strode towards the door.

'Excuse me,' I said to Nathan and Sofia.

I ran after Lana and caught up with her just as she reached the taxi.

'I can't go just yet. I have to talk to Nathan and Sofia. It was part of the reason we came out tonight, remember?' I said. 'Tell me what's wrong.'

'I said I have a headache.'

'You've been in a mood for hours.'

'Oh you noticed, did you?' She lowered her voice. 'I've been in a mood for weeks, Myles. Not that you care. Blithely going along as if everything is fine.' Her voice was rising now, people on the street stepped around us.

'Lana, let's discuss this inside. Please,' I said.

'There is nothing to discuss.' She waved a hand towards the hotel. 'I thought I could accept what you did. What you let happen to our future, but I . . . I can't. I just can't. And you're not even trying. You behave as if we're not going to be turfed out in a couple of weeks. Is this how it goes? Is this the Butler trait I've missed all these years?'

A low blow that I felt right in the gut. But one I deserved.

'We've lost everything, Myles. Don't you get that?' she said through gritted teeth, then, saving the best for last, 'You should. It's not like you haven't been here before.'

She reached for the door of the taxi, opened it, dropped into the seat, then promptly grabbed the door and shut it.

I watched the car pull away, stunned.

'Everything okay?'

Holly was behind me, her arms wrapped around herself to guard against the evening chill.

'Fine,' I said. I turned, went back into the hotel and headed straight for the bar.

CHAPTER 11

I woke drenched in sweat, still wearing my clothes from the night before. There was a vague stinging at the back of my hand where the fingernails of my other hand were digging into the flesh, and fading into the darkness were the remnants of a dream. Lana's face, slowly changing colour. Her eyes fixed on mine, wide, almost bulging, desperate to tell me something. Her lips, dark and covered in spittle, made fish-mouth shapes up at me. Her hands clawed at her throat. It was then that I saw my own, spread like the wings of a bird around her neck, weight pushing down.

There was a buzzing noise vibrating through my head and it took me a moment to realise it was the doorbell. I sat up, gulped down the half-glass of water next to the bed, then looked across to Lana. She wasn't there. The doorbell went again. I switched on the lamp. Looked at my phone. It was 5.30 a.m. I tried to massage some feeling into my face. The bell went again and I stumbled downstairs in the semi-darkness towards the front door. I could still feel the alcohol churning through my veins, the haze of drunkenness not quite lifted.

I turned the lock and tugged the door open. There were two men on my doorstep. One tall, approaching six five, and wearing a grey suit and tie. The other, a policeman, was a slighter build. He adjusted his hat, swept a finger along the bright red hair just above his temple, as I took in their presence, blinking sleep and confusion from my eyes. Had I done something last night? What I could recall was patchy. Shots of tequila in the hotel bar. I couldn't remember getting home. I was aware of the low pungent notes of sweat, stale alcohol and the sulphurous heat coming from my mouth.

'Dr Butler?' The taller one said.

'Yes.' I cleared my throat. 'Yes, I'm Dr Butler.'

'Would you mind if we came inside?'

I didn't like this. I wanted to shut the door, get back into bed and restart the morning. And I didn't want whatever horror was circling in this man's eyes to enter my home. 'I'd prefer if you didn't,' I said.

A flicker of a frown. The red-haired policeman watched his colleague, waiting to see what he'd do next.

'Okay,' the taller man said. 'I'm Detective Sergeant Hunter,' he said, in a soft Bristolian accent. His grim tone made me uneasy. 'And this is PC Davies. I'm very sorry to wake you. I'm afraid we have some bad news. Does your wife, Lana, drive a red Mini Cooper?'

The pulse in my head thumped against my ears. I heard myself say, 'Yes.'

'We believe she was involved in an accident last night.'

I put my hand out to the frame of the door. I felt like I'd been punched. Or no, bigger than that, like someone had sliced away

121

part of my middle and I was folding in on myself. 'You believe? What do you mean? What type of accident?' And I made myself ask it, although I didn't want to know the answer because there could only be one answer if this man was standing in front of me. 'She's okay?'

From some way away, I heard him apologise, then something about emergency services. *Nothing to be done.* I swallowed. Flashes of last night's dream flickered through my mind. Had I made this happen?

'I'm very sorry, Dr Butler,' Hunter said again. Davies gave a small nod of his chin in response.

I was aware I wasn't taking in much of what he was saying. His words slipped around in my brain like greased ball bearings. I stared at him. Fixed on his appearance. He was my age, perhaps slightly younger. There was the beginning of a beard across his jaw, his dark hair was slicked to the side, the parting white and clear as a line of chalk. A collection of spittle sat at the corners of his mouth. His lips remained stiff, parting only at the centre when he spoke, reminding me of a bad ventriloquist I had seen as a child. Davies stood behind him, still and impassive as a shadow.

' . . . dead,' Hunter said, his voice laced with that whining compassion.

What was he saying? Lana was dead? She couldn't be. She couldn't just end. The Court stood out behind him, bathed in the blue ethereal light that manifests before proper sunrise, making the neighbourhood look like some strange manufactured hologram.

I saw her again, her getting into the taxi last night, her swift goodbye.

'Dr Butler? Is there anyone we can call for you? If not, we can have someone come here . . . after.'

Finally, Davies spoke up. 'Someone who can answer any more questions you might have.'

No. No. No. 'How? I'm sorry. What are you saying?' I asked.

'Your wife, she was—'

I held up a hand. 'I think you've made a mistake. My wife is – she's . . .' I half turned, pointed to the stairs. 'She's sleeping. We were at an event last night in town. She had a headache. Just last night. A few hours ago.'

I suddenly felt very hot. Clammy. I waited for Hunter to apologise for disturbing us, to be on his way and take his shadow with him. But his expression was stuck on that forced sympathy and it was beginning to make me angry.

'Look,' I said, firmly. 'I'll get her now.'

I left the door open, hurried back up the stairs taking them two at a time, pausing briefly at the top to let the spinning in my head slow. I staggered to our bedroom, even though I'd just come from there. Looked through the items in the bathroom. Her electric toothbrush dry and still plugged in next to the sink. Make-up brushes on the sink counter, her hairbrush. Then down the hall, to my study. Empty. Through the guest rooms. And finally the home cinema that we never got round to using. Empty. I went back downstairs. Stood in the middle of the hallway, between kitchen and living room. I heard the hot water click on.

I returned to the front door where only Hunter was waiting. I shook my head at him.

'I'm sorry,' he said again. 'We retrieved her bag from the vehicle with her driving licence but it would help us greatly if you felt able to . . . take a look at the remains for a formal identification.'

I tried to take in this information. Tried to believe what he was saying. They had it wrong. They had to have it wrong.

'Okay,' I said, slowly. They had it wrong. I'd go with them. And I'd see for myself that they had it wrong. 'Give me a minute,' I said, wanting this man off my doorstep. Wanting to erase him, his colleague and everything they were saying from existence.

'I'll wait in the car.' He turned, made his way quickly across our front lawn to the pavement where a squad car was parked up on the kerb. PC Davies was already in the driver's seat.

I closed the door. What had happened? My eyes landed on her phone, charging at a socket just below the sideboard. They did have it wrong. If she had decided to go somewhere in the car, she wouldn't have left without her phone. Not at night. A little voice in my head said maybe she hadn't wanted to be contacted. By me. Maybe she'd had enough. I pressed my fingers against my temples. No. If that had been the case, she would definitely have taken her phone. She'd need it to send me messages listing all the things I'd done wrong over the last few weeks. All the ways this was my fault. Then to back up her point, because Lana liked to seal off all possibilities of a counter argument, she'd follow up with numerous links to psychology articles. Homework for me to study so that I could 'understand my behaviour', as if our marriage were a thesis to be proved. She wasn't one for slipping away. She believed in finishing things. In drawing lines. In crushing opponents. If she was about to leave me, there wouldn't have been any lingering doubt. If she was going to go anywhere, in the middle of the night, to take a break, to leave

124

me, whatever – she'd want me to know about it. She'd have taken her phone. So, I thought, with what I knew, even then, to be an absurd shot of relief, Lana could not be dead.

I pulled upright, hands on hips. I let out a sigh, holding on to this one piece of evidence that, yes, they were wrong and Lana was okay. The car might have been stolen. I thought of that woman hanging around the Wright property some weeks back. Could there have been a break-in, and she's already at a police station right now? I went to the French doors in the living room, checked the latch. Then to the back door. Everything was secure. Or gone to a friends? My mind tripped on the mobile. No. She would have left a note. And again, she'd have taken her phone. Or the hospital? I didn't like that thought either. She could have gone into work. On a Sunday? An emergency call to see a troubled client. And she'd taken a taxi. But even as these thoughts came, I knew I was holding on to that maddening hope that comes with denial.

I returned to the hallway. I opened the front door a crack, cool air poured in on my hot skin. I peered out, a desperate part of me hoping that the police car would not be there. But it was. Beads of sweat formed along my hairline. The thought squeezed into my mind, like fingers prying open a crack in a wall. She was gone. I unplugged her phone. Swiped a shaking finger across the screen. I tried her passcode. It didn't work. I tried her birth date. Then thought a moment before trying our anniversary.

The screen lit up. I searched through her messages. The last three sent to me were short, terse texts that conveyed her anger at my lying. The lower-case 'x' that she normally left at the end of her messages was notably absent. I scrolled through the deleted folder. There was nothing that told me where she was or about what had happened. Then I looked through her call lists. Again, nothing. I waited, hoped that there was a message for me somewhere in the digital ether waiting to pick up the signal from her phone, but none came. Feeling like I was walking through treacle, I made my way back upstairs. I changed into a fresh shirt, my fingers clumsy on the buttons, then dragged my legs through a pair of jeans. I turned her phone off and slid it into my back pocket.

Detective Hunter got out of the passenger's side when he saw me approach.

'Thank you, Dr Butler. Are you sure there's no one we can call for you?'

I got into the back of the car and looked out at our home as if the answers might be written across the front. When I didn't answer, Davies started up the ignition, pulled jerkily away from the kerb and turned the car away from Belvedere Court.

At the hospital, I followed Hunter, Davies and some orderly down a warren of corridors. I caught my reflection on the gloss-covered walls. I barely recognised the slumped figure moving in tandem with me. I could almost convince myself I wasn't there at all. That I was still in bed, in Belvedere Court, and Lana was pressed along my side. It was bizarre that I felt suddenly ashamed of my appearance. I wished I hadn't skipped my shave. There was dark stubble along my jaw. My shirt was lopsided. I'd done the buttons up wrong. As we walked, I fixed them, combed fingers through my hair and swept it to the side. There was nothing I could do about the flip-flops.

A nurse appeared at a door, waved us inside. I was asked a few questions, then passed a clipboard to sign my name.

'Dr Butler, we'll need you to stay behind the screen,' the nurse said. 'When we go into the room, just indicate when you're ready. You may leave any time you wish. Okay?'

The room was overly neutral and divided in two by a perspex screen. I felt an immediate need to both get as far away from that screen as possible and to confront what was on the trolley on the other side: the shape of a body, draped in a white sheet.

'Whenever you're ready,' the nurse prompted.

A whirring began in my ears. I looked to the nurse and she stepped towards the trolley. She pulled the sheet back. I felt my bladder wanting to release.

The nurse watched my face.

I couldn't move. Couldn't speak. I don't know how long I stood staring at her but eventually Hunter's voice came from behind me.

'Dr Butler?'

Severe oedema around both orbital regions pressed her eyes closed. More oedema over the left maxilla, suggesting fracture, filled out any hollows that would have heightened the facial features. A deep gash ran from the hairline to the nasal region, which was also swollen. Another likely fracture, disfiguring the nose. There were moderate burns too on the other side of her face. The car must have caught fire somehow. But the more I dared look, the more I saw that beneath the superficial injuries, the shape was all wrong. Her hair, matted as it was, was straight and held none of the gentle waves I was familiar with. The shade of the hair was fractionally too dark, more black than brown, the length of the body on the table not quite tall enough. It wasn't Lana.

I stepped closer to the screen.

'We removed some items,' the nurse said quietly. She passed me a clear bag containing a pair a jade drop earrings. I examined them closely. Remembering how they stood out against her skin. I looked at the body again. Unsure. Perhaps I'd made a mistake. The disfigurement and my want, my need, for this not to be Lana convincing me that this was the body of another woman.

'Are they your wife's?'

I nodded. 'Yes.'

I wanted to get out of that room but I couldn't make myself move.

The nurse shifted uncomfortably. 'Dr Butler, is this your wife?'

I swallowed. Looked again. It wasn't. The bone structure of her face was all wrong, the width of her shoulders, but the more I looked, the more I thought my mind was playing tricks, that where I was seeing differences, there was only swelling, tissue damage, broken bones.

'I think so. Wait. I'm not sure,' I said.

'Did she have any distinguishing features? Birthmarks?'

I felt tears gather in my eyes for the first time that morning. My nose began to run. I shook my head, sniffed. Then, 'Yes. A tattoo,' I said. I traced a finger behind my ear. 'Here.'

The nurse moved forward, gently tilted the dead woman's head, and my stomach clenched. She pushed the right ear forward. And there, where the skin was unmarked, protected from the worst of the burns, was a tattoo. Three stars. Three sisters. A miniature constellation. I staggered back, put my hand out to

128

the wall, but was unable to lift my eyes from the tattoo. Flashes of Lana being driven away in the taxi. The jade green earrings against her neck. Gabe, that night in our home, after dinner. The cigar in his hand as the conversation slowly turned to how we'd deal if facing financial ruin. And his conclusion. *Someone would have to die.*

I looked again over the body, unsure about the direction of my thoughts. Unsure about what I was seeing. Who I was seeing. But the more I looked, the more I recognised all the differences between this woman and my wife. This wasn't what we had discussed. We had talked about a change in paperwork. My mouth turned to dust, then a flood of bile. I swallowed. Is this why Lana had got that tattoo? Was it intended as a signal to me about what was really happening? Lana, knowing I knew every curve and angle of her body, wanted to make sure I gave the right answer when they asked if this was indeed my wife.

'Dr Butler, is this your wife, Lana?' the nurse asked again quietly.

I turned away from the screen, as I replied. 'Yes,' I said. 'Yes, that's my wife. That's Lana Butler.'

CHAPTER 12

I had a desperate sense of falling. Something had clicked, switched, tripped, but I understood there was no going back. This woman who would take Lana's name to the grave. I was now on a trajectory where the path ahead dropped away from the horizon and I was shooting down a slide into God knows what.

The nurse reached forward and pulled the sheet back over the body, then she wrote something on the clipboard and passed it to me again.

'Could you sign here, please, Dr Butler?'

I signed my name and passed the clipboard back. She held out the sealed plastic bag. 'Your wife's personal belongings, Mr Butler. I'm sorry for your loss.'

Had Lana really done this? I found myself asking whether I trusted my wife. Then realised that really, this all fell on me. All she had to do was remain dead. It would be me that would field the questions. It would be me who would have to keep up the pretence. I'd have to inform her parents. Tell her clients she was dead. Clean out her rented office. Organise her funeral.

Persuade the insurance company that I was a man racked with grief and would gladly refuse any amount of money if I could have her back for just one more day.

I took the bag. The earrings clinked together and I had a moment of doubt about whether I was mistaken. That in my desire to know that Lana was alive, I was seeing what I wanted to see. I needed to speak to Gabe. To Holly. To Lana. I rubbed a hand down my face. There were more tears. I wiped them away. Searched my pocket for a tissue. Detective Hunter pulled a handful of tissue from a nearby dispenser and handed them to me.

'Thanks,' I mumbled, then blew my nose. 'May I go now?'

Hunter nodded. Davies held the door as I was guided back out into the corridor.

We walked in silence for a bit, then Hunter asked, 'You never asked how it happened?' I detected the note of suspicion in his voice.

I slowed. 'I'm sorry, Detective. I guess I was hoping –' I paused here to take a long breath – 'you were wrong.'

He nodded. 'Of course.'

'Where?' I asked. 'Where did it happen?'

'She hit a tree. South of Wimbledon,' he replied. The statement was blunt, which made me somewhat nervous.

'I don't know why she was out there. I don't understand.'

'Don't worry yourself about that right now, Dr Butler,' he said, the suspicion I saw in his eyes melting away to compassion.

'Her parents, perhaps,' I said. 'They live south. She might have been going there. I don't know.'

'Would you like me to call them?'

131

'No,' I said quickly.

'You sure?' Hunter studied my face. I rubbed the heel of my hand into my eye.

'I'll tell them.' The last thing I wanted was to tell Fred Grosvenor that his daughter was dead, but I knew that if the police contacted him, he'd push by them and demand to see her body.

I shook my head. Sighed. 'She's generally a careful driver.'

'The airbags never deployed,' he said. 'Very unusual for the driver's side. When was the last time she'd had the car serviced?'

'I don't know. It's probably in the logbook?'

'Did your wife smoke?'

Lana didn't smoke, but on occasion, if she was out, she'd beg or borrow a cigarette. Then I remembered that I wasn't answering for my wife. I was answering for whoever was lying cold on that table. 'Sometimes. What has that got to do with this?'

'The fire department reckoned from her burns, sorry, that she'd been lighting a cigarette, missed the turn and . . .' He trailed off, looking apologetic. Then more questions. 'We couldn't find her phone,' he said. 'Have you seen it?'

'I haven't,' I said, feeling the weight of the phone in my back pocket as I moved. He was asking a lot of questions and I thought then that it might be unusual for a detective sergeant to be delivering news of a death. 'I didn't think detectives did this,' I said, not quite able to finish my question but knowing he'd understand what I meant. It wasn't difficult to keep my voice on the right side of bewilderment.

His pace slowed a little and he glanced at me. 'It was early. I was around. It's best if there's two. For support.'

132

'Oh,' I said.

'Dr Butler, your wife didn't appear to be wearing—'

'Detective, I'm really sorry. I've just learned Lana is . . . .' I still couldn't say it. 'Can we do this later?'

He took a long breath, pulled himself upright. 'Of course, Doctor. Of course. I'm sorry,' he said returning to the role of compassionate companion. 'Are you sure we can't send someone out to you? It's not good to be alone after a shock like this.'

'No. Thank you. I . . . would rather be by myself,' I replied. Hoping that I sounded convincing. 'If you don't mind, I'll take a taxi back.'

He put his hand in his back pocket and removed a card. 'This is the number of a grief counsellor. She's very good. And she can speak to you whenever you want. Even visit if you need it.'

I took the card, smiled my thanks, then turned away from both men. Daylight was ahead and I walked slowly towards it. I felt their eyes on my back, hot as beams of sunlight, as I walked through the hospital doors, into the car park and towards the taxi rank. As soon as I was out of their eyeline, I removed my phone from my shirt pocket and dialled Gabe's number. The call rang out and his voicemail kicked in. I opened my mouth to leave a message, then thought better of it and hung up. If I already had one foot in life insurance fraud then it was probably best not to leave the questions I wanted to ask Gabe on his phone. I'd watched enough crime documentaries to know that police had ways of retrieving all sorts of information from mobiles. If I was going to speak to Gabe and Holly, it had to be face to face.

I pocketed my phone. Ahead, a bus dumped a load of passengers onto the pavement. They swelled out around me, adjusting

133

clothing, checking phones. A nurse in blue scrubs hooked a backpack onto his shoulders and rushed back towards the hospital. I thought of the woman lying on the trolley. The sweep of her hair from her forehead. I felt like I'd escaped something. A delayed wave of adrenaline crept through my blood. Sweat ran down my back. Then a cool, sickening shiver raised goosebumps on my skin. It was as if I'd seen some giant crevasse open up in the road ahead of me and had just managed to swerve it. I was itching to speak to Lana. To hear for myself that she was okay. Did she know what she'd just put me through? Of course she did.

The taxi dropped me off at the front of my house. I got out, half expecting, half hoping the front door would open and Lana would be standing there, arms folded, irritated that I'd left without discussing last night. At the end of the road, Mrs Shelton was shuffling around her garden, a soft wide-rimmed hat clutched in her hand. The sun wasn't quite high enough to justify its use, so she hooked it on the pillar of their low garden gate. Every now and then, she'd take the secateurs from her apron pocket and clip a dying bloom from a rose bush. One of the Foresters' rugrats was screaming in their front yard. The air had that damp quality, a hazy mist that cast me back to childhood days waking in the depths of summer holidays and knowing instinctively from the dew on the grass that it was going to be a scorcher of a day.

I opened my front door. Stepped into the hallway and stood inside. I listened for sounds that signalled Lana was home. But other than a quiet hum coming from the kitchen which I recognised to be the fridge, there was nothing. Behind me, I heard the taxi pull away. I took Lana's phone from my pocket, turned it on, looked down into the screen and willed a message from her.

'Myles?'

I put the phone down on the sideboard and turned around.

Charlotte. She was standing before me, dressed in her work armour – shoulder-padded navy suit. Her briefcase in one hand, a reusable coffee mug in the other. When she saw my face, her brow creased in concern.

'Are you okay?' she asked. 'You don't look well.'

'Not exactly. I think I'm coming down with something,' I said. I didn't want to tell her about Lana until I'd spoken to the Wrights. There could be a way to rewind this whole thing. Also, I couldn't face the reality of it all. Couldn't face the long trudge through the incoming wave of sympathy. Charlotte would insist on coming inside. She wouldn't be pushed away like the police. She would not leave me alone.

She moved her eyes over my face.

'I'm not drunk,' I said, a little too defensively, and I saw the flash of hurt cross her face.

'I hadn't thought so,' she said, but my tone made her linger. 'Can I get you something?' She took a step forward. 'Make you a tea?' She flicked a glance at her watch, then her gaze drifted beyond my shoulder into the still dark hallway.

'I'll be fine. I just need some more sleep.'

'Is Lana in?'

'She's at work.'

'On a Sunday? This early?'

This was Charlotte through and through. No one could work as hard as she did. No one else could possibly be up as early as her, on a Sunday, to put their nose to the grindstone.

'Yes,' I said. 'No. I'm not sure.' I drew the door over. 'Thank you,' I said again.

She nodded slowly.

I closed the door, then followed with the deadlock.

I went to the front of the house. The curtains were still closed and I peered out between the parting. Charlotte walked down the path but stopped at the end of our drive, turned, tipped her head back and looked over the front of the house. Finally, she checked her watch again, then hurried back across the street. Just before she got into her car, she removed her mobile from her case. As she got into the driver's seat, she brought the phone to her ear.

I pulled the curtains closed tightly. I should have told her that Lana was dead. Started the ball rolling. Now I'll have to explain myself later. But people behave strangely in grief, don't they? I looked over the living room, towards the dining table and the chairs we'd sat in a couple of weeks ago, where this plan had been laid out. The offer of help from the Wrights. My eye caught on a small object on the table. A small, shiny item. I knew what it was before I'd crossed the room. Lana's wedding band. I held it up and the walls of our home blurred against the simple gold ring.

I searched through all the drawers and cupboards in the house, looking for a note. A message. Then her coat pockets. A receipt for Pret, a clubcard to our local Waitrose. The business card of a beauty salon in town, three loyalty stamps on the back. I stood in the hallway in a state of stunned stupor. We'd discussed

Gabe's offer but we'd decided it was ridiculous. Crazy even. I tried Gabe's phone again but again there was no answer.

There had to be some clue. Some message she'd left behind. She didn't expect me to navigate this on my own. There had to be a contact number at least. I went back upstairs. Looked through her wardrobe. Her clothes were untouched. Her suitcase was still under our bed. Her shoes. In the en-suite, cosmetics lined the shelf above the sink. Her make-up and make-up brushes as they were early this morning, strewn across the bathroom counter – something that was unlike her; she preferred to keep them neat and organised in baskets beneath the sink. I picked up the lid of a tub of powder and screwed it back on. The rest I left as it was – again, part of me expecting her to return.

I went to the study at the end of the hall. The desk, which was always a mess of paper, was actually pretty tidy. Every envelope, every bill that came through the door, was usually unceremoniously dumped here, waiting for either of us to look through the pile and file them away. That was until I started taking those bills for myself. Hiding them. There was nothing on the desk from Lana. I woke the desktop. Looked for an email, searched through folders, but could find nothing.

Sometimes, if I was working late, on a patient's case, Lana would pour a glass of red wine, take a book from the shelves and curl up in the Chesterfield in the corner. She'd read quietly, the rasp of a page turning or the tap of my keyboard the only sounds breaking the silence. The book she had been reading was open and lying across the armrest. I recognised it as a copy she'd read many times. *Mystic River* by Dennis Lehane. Now I went to the chair, picked up the book. Silly of me to think there'd be some message there. I closed it, left it carefully on the side of the desk, then returned my attention to the chair, pushing my hands down the sides, but I came away with nothing apart from an old bunched-up lump of tissue.

I sat. The image of the woman's body in the hospital floated before my mind's eye; the nurse standing by, and Hunter's breath on my neck as he looked over my shoulder. Gabe said it would be an unclaimed body at the hospital. But Lana, she would have known about the tattoo. And the facial oedema, the swelling, that could only be caused if the victim was still alive when they'd hit that tree. Her heart would have been pumping. I pressed fingertips to my temples, rolled them over the skin. A dull ache swelled through my brain as I tried to unwind, to retrace what had happened. The police were called out to an accident. That would mean an ambulance. The victim's body had been burned. And the fire department had been there. More people involved. More witnesses.

Shaking out my shoulders, I stood. Reached for the drawers under the desk, rifled through them until I found the papers Lana had shown me weeks before.

'Just in case something does happen,' she'd said. 'The details are all here. You are named beneficiary.'

'That leaves me prime suspect in your murder investigation,' I'd replied with a laugh.

She'd put her wine glass on the desk. Pushed the chair I was sitting on back, and straddled me. Her arms hooked around my shoulders, her mouth so close to mine that her breath tickled my lips when she spoke. 'We'll have to make sure you look innocent then.'

I left the papers on the desk. The ache in my temple was growing. The wedding ring burned a hole in my pocket. This wasn't how we'd planned it. Or at least what was discussed, because I certainly hadn't planned anything. Why was it so complicated? It wouldn't be difficult to extricate myself from the situation. It's not too late to go back. Anyone in a state of trauma could positively identify the wrong body.

I looked out of the study window, down on The Court. Mrs Shelton was still working her way around the garden. Someone was moving in the upstairs window of the Wright home. From this angle, I could make out the right half of their back garden. Holly was sitting on a blanket in the lawn, a laptop open in front of her. She lifted a hand, pushed a finger beneath her sunglasses and rubbed at her face. I wondered whether she was searching for news of the accident.

I took up my phone, went to the window and looked across to the Wrights' house. After three rings, the call went to voicemail again, suggesting that Gabe had declined the call rather than couldn't get to the phone. Clutching the phone in my hand, I rushed downstairs, grabbed my keys from the side and crossed the street to their house. I pushed the doorbell, then, getting more impatient by the second, banged on the white gloss panels with my fist.

CHAPTER 13

'Just a minute.' Holly's voice on the other side of the door. Some mumbling and murmurings.

I beat my fist against the door again.

She pulled it open. The breeze from the movement lifted the fine blonde strands of her hair.

'Myles,' she said, a false kind of surprise in her expression.

She was dressed in a velour tracksuit, champagne colour, pearls in her ears, round her throat. She was barefoot, her toenails painted a sugary pink, a light layer of cream and powder over her face, a dusting of rose on her cheeks, but her eyes were red-rimmed, the skin on her lower lid stained with mascara.

'Where is she?' I asked, trying to keep my voice level.

She sighed, her shoulders dropping. 'You'd best come in.'

'Gabe?' I shouted, pushing by her.

Holly followed me down the hall into the kitchen. 'He's just finishing some work stuff in his office. He'll be down shortly.'

I ignored her. 'Gabe!'

A creak from the top of the stairs. 'Hey, hey,' he said. 'I'm here. What's with all the shouting?'

He came slowly down the stairs, hair damp and swept back from his face. A strip of tissue stuck to a shaving cut on his jaw. He turned one sleeve of his white shirt up to the elbow, then did the same the other side, tucking the cuff into itself to keep it in place. Then he took a chunky silver watch from his pocket, slid it onto his wrist and adjusted the clasp until it clicked closed.

'Where is she?' I asked.

He came to stand in front of me, hands now in pockets. 'We should probably talk,' he said.

He walked through to the kitchen and I noticed, as he moved, a limp in his right leg that he was attempting to disguise. Just inside the door there was a set of three suitcases.

'Drink?' he called out.

'No thanks. You going somewhere?' I pointed back at the cases.

'I think you need one,' he said. He reached into a cupboard below the white granite-topped island and produced a bottle of brandy and three glasses. 'Holly?'

She nodded. White-lipped. Her response to this disaster added to my concern for Lana.

Gabe poured the brandy. I held on to the side of the granite worktop. 'We're heading off for a few days,' he said. 'We're borrowing a place down by the coast. At Sandbanks, on the Dorset coast. The weather is supposed to be good this week. I've a few days off and I thought we should really take advantage. You should join us.'

I couldn't take in what I was hearing. How could he be

141

thinking I could go away and leave the mess they had landed me in? 'Where is Lana? Is she okay?'

He slid the glass towards me. I raised it to my mouth then put it down. I needed to keep a clear head.

Gabe took a slow sip of his drink. 'Lana is fine,' he said.

I hadn't realised how much I needed to hear those words. It felt like someone had driven a fist into my middle. I gripped my side.

'You went to the hospital this morning?' he went on.

'Yes. I woke or should I say was woken by police on my doorstep.'

He nodded, patiently, as if things were how they should be, like I'd just described how, when I vacated my house this morning, the sun was in the sky.

'I went with them,' I continued. 'They showed me a body. It wasn't Lana.'

A look passed between them. Holly rubbed a knuckle beneath her nose.

'And?' he asked.

'And what?' I snapped. 'I fucking told them it was her, didn't I?'

He glanced at the brandy in front of me and, taking his cue, I lifted the glass to my lips, only a sip. 'Her phone is still in the house. Her clothes. Her things.'

'This was a bad idea,' Holly hissed at him.

I looked at her in alarm. 'What do you mean?'

Gabe interjected. Lifted both his hands and patted the air. 'Relax. Everyone relax. It's not a problem. It's hardly a "body in the trunk of a car".' A flicker of a grin on his face. 'It's off, right? Her phone?'

142

'Yes.' I flinched, realising what he was asking. Could it have hit cell towers in the moments I'd turned it on? I ran my hand through my hair. There was already too much to remember.

'She should've taken it with her,' he said. 'Who doesn't take their phone with them? It's not a biggie, but if we're asking that question, then . . .' He shrugged. The implication being that the police might do too. 'Don't worry. You've a solid alibi.' As he spoke, I had a feeling that he'd been here before. That they had done this before. Which made Holly's anxiety about it all the more ominous.

The alibi was true though. I didn't get home from the Fellowship dinner until close to 4 a.m. 'People do pay others to get rid of their spouses,' I replied. 'Especially when they are in heaps of debt and that partner has significant life insurance.' Angry now. 'Didn't any of you think I had a right to know?'

Gabe frowned. Holly came to his side, her eyes widened. 'You didn't know?'

'Of course I didn't fucking know.'

'She said you'd both discussed it at length,' he said. 'She assured us you were on board. Just that you mustn't know when, or any details, in case you gave yourself away. If we'd thought you weren't in agreement, well, we would never have gone through with it.'

I pushed a hand through my hair. 'You've just helped my wife commit fraud.'

Gabe approached me, rested a hand on my shoulder. 'What do you want to do?'

'There's nothing I can do? I've already lied to the police.'

Gabe looked down into my face. 'You were in shock. It

143

wouldn't be the first time someone's identified remains incorrectly. We can take all of this back,' he said, echoing my thoughts from earlier. 'Lana could come home. You tell the police there's been a mistake. Someone had stolen her car, and the worse was assumed.'

I looked down, away from the intensity of his gaze. It might work. We could go back. Lana could come back, and after some uncomfortable questions, no doubt, from Hunter, we'd be as we were. But Lana's voice came back to from that night: *You're not even trying . . . Is this how it goes? Is this the Butler trait I've missed all these years?*

I straightened. 'No. No, it's done now.'

He gave my shoulder a squeeze, then dropped his hand. 'We're going to do everything to make sure this works. That it's worth it for you. You both needed a solution to a dilemma. A quick one. You've both worked hard. You work hard. You deserve the best. Lana knew your conscience would not allow you to take the steps needed, that's all. She did this for you. It's going to be okay.'

My conscience. Lana knew better than most that it wasn't conscience that drove people. But fear. It was fear of repercussions. Fears so deeply engraved in our psyches we rarely overcame them. I could almost feel her next to me, her hand on the cap of my skull, her fingers tracing my scalp. After all, she was fascinated by what fears lived inside a person's head, and she believed she had mine figured out a long time ago.

'I need to speak with her,' I said, steadily and quietly.

'I don't think that's wise,' Gabe said. 'Not yet.'

'Gabe, maybe—' Holly said.

He glanced quickly at his wife. 'This is the safest way, Holly.'

144

Holly sighed, 'Lana said she didn't want to be contacted. It's to protect you. To protect us. The less we know . . .' She gave a delicate little shrug of her shoulder.

I pulled out a seat, sat down. 'Is anyone in touch with her?'

'She's safe. I can relay any messages or questions you have, but really we should try not to contact her too much. Until after the funeral at least,' Gabe said.

I was suddenly exhausted.

'When we discussed this, you said it would be in hospital only,' I said. 'You made it sound like it was a simple matter of switching paperwork. I don't get it. There was a crash. The tattoo? There was a tattoo on that woman this morning. Behind her ear. Lana had one too. She got it a couple of weeks ago. Is this why she got one? How did she know about that? And the bruising on the woman's face? The swelling?'

Gabe reached for the brandy bottle again, topped up his glass, then Holly's. 'Myles, you need to trust us. No one's crossed any real lines here. I knew the body we'd chosen had the tattoo and had also died in a car accident. It was a stroke of luck, if you'll pardon the crudeness. But we had the opportunity to make this convincing. And for your sake, we took it. We didn't want to go to all this trouble to have any kind of in-depth investigation by the insurance company. Lana needed to die – sorry – in a convincing manner. We really wanted to have as swift a resolution as possible for your sake, and to do that we needed witnesses – police, paramedics – to verify her death. You've done the hard part. No one is here questioning you.'

He took another mouthful of his drink. 'Guys.' He looked to each of us; Holly's brow was becoming more creased by the second. Her eyes watering. 'Everything is how it should be. Myles, you'll get to talk to Lana. Soon. Just not yet, and surely you can see that's best. You don't want to be forced to lie to the wrong people. For now, play the grieving husband for a while, submit the insurance forms once we're through the funeral, and watch all your problems drift away.'

I went to remind him there'd be a post-mortem examination, that surely a pathologist would discover that the victim had already been dead. I tried to remember my post-mortem training. How many hours was it before time of death became questionable? A day? Not a couple of weeks. But he got there before me.

'The paramedics recorded a DOA. They, like us, look at a clinical picture, Myles. They attended a car accident. It was fatal for the single driver inside. There were fresh burns. They wouldn't have concerned themselves with looking at time of death which they will assume occurred at or soon after the accident. A pathologist might but by then the remains will have been refrigerated for some time,' he said, as if reading my mind. 'That's what you're thinking, isn't it?'

I nodded. I still couldn't quite get my head around the logistics of it, but he looked so sure. Somewhere in the back of my mind it registered that he knew quite a lot about the car accident. Of course he would have been there. No way could Lana have done this by herself. Even Holly was nodding, drawing in long breaths and rolling out her shoulders, but before I could throw the next series of questions at him the doorbell rang.

Holly glanced at Gabe as the bell trilled again then she turned and padded down the hall.

We waited, listened. A male voice. Then a voice I recognised.

146

'Yes, Detective,' Holly's reply.

Panic began to fizz beneath my skin. Why were the police here?

Gabe scooped up the glasses and dropped them in the sink, then returned the brandy to the cupboard below the island. 'He'll just want to know how your marriage was. Why Lana had left late at night. Just stick to the story and it will be okay.'

'Darling, this is Detective Sergeant Hunter,' Holly said, leading Hunter into the kitchen.

I slumped a little in the stool, trying and not succeeding, to affect the air of grieving widower rather than deceived husband.

If Hunter had a reaction to me being in the Wrights' house, he didn't show it. He walked up to the island, put out a hand to Gabe.

'Mr Wright?'

'Yes,' Gabe said. 'What can I do for you?'

'No need to unsettle yourself,' he said. 'Just a few simple questions.' He looked at me then. 'How are you doing, Dr Butler?'

I brought my hand up, rubbed the side of my face and shook my head. 'I . . . I don't know,' I said, surprising myself with the truth.

Again, that long pause as he studied my face. 'Tragic,' he said eventually. 'I'm so sorry.'

I swallowed, tongue sticky. 'Thank you.' I stood. 'I'll leave you to it.' I walked out of the kitchen towards the hall. Behind me I heard Holly fill the kettle.

'Tea?' she asked.

I stopped at the front door, waited for Hunter's answer.

He didn't need to think about it. He was planning on getting comfortable. 'A brew would be lovely. One sugar,' he said. 'The missus has me down from two spoons. Can't see it's making much difference myself, but then the doc tells me the changes should be on the inside.'

'You'd hope so,' Gabe replied.

I walked slowly back to the house. There was another car parked in my drive. I hurried towards the door, then caught a glimpse of the bumper sticker: *Life is like a box of chocolates: over-priced and never enough.* Linda, our cleaner. I forgot we had moved her day to when we'd normally be out.

I let myself in. I could hear the vacuum going upstairs. The hallway smelled of polish. I ran my finger along the hall sideboard. Squeaky clean. She will have seen Lana's phone. I picked it up from the sideboard. There wasn't much point in getting rid of it now. Linda, who lived for gossip, preferably gossip about other people's lives. She was just the sort to be a good citizen and take herself to the local police station.

There was a safe in the dining room, hidden behind a collection of fake encyclopaedias on the bottom shelf near the back corner of the room. I went to it, kneeled down, moved the books to one side, then opened the heavy metal box. I placed the phone inside. The vacuuming stopped. I could hear Linda making her way back across the landing. I closed the safe, replaced the books and stood just as she came around the corner.

'Dr Butler,' she said.

'Hello, Linda,' I said.

'You look terrible,' she said.

'I haven't had a good morning,' I replied.

'Mrs Butler said she'd have a new bleach for me today. She was meant to leave it out on the kitchen counter, if she wasn't in. But she's obviously forgotten,' she said with an irritated sigh. 'I was going to nip down to the shops to pick one up.'

I pinched the bridge of my nose, wanting nothing else but to be alone.

She stood, arms folded, a polishing rag dangling like a dead thing from her fingertips, and looked at me expectantly. I realised she was waiting for money.

'Yes, sorry.' I searched my pockets for change, finding a fiver and a few coins in one. When I opened my hand to count out the change, Lana's wedding ring was sitting among the change and pocket fluff.

I plucked the fiver from the debris and handed it to her.

'Thank you,' she said, unfolding her arms and taking the money from me.

'I thought she'd be here this morning,' she said.

'Who?'

'Your wife,' she said. Her eyes strayed in the direction of my back pocket.

I couldn't bring myself to say it. Even though I knew it was the perfect time to practise the grieving husband. The words formed on my tongue but I choked them down. Linda would ask questions, she'd wheedle every drop of information around Lana's death out of me, better than any detective hungry for a conviction. And then she'd come back for more. She was the sort to come around with casseroles, under the guise of concern, just so she could stick her beak in.

'Actually, Linda, I've got a lot to do today. I know we agreed to change the day but it won't work for me. Don't worry, you'll be paid in full.'

She frowned. 'But I've only just started upstairs and today's fridge and oven day. If I leave that for a whole week, it will be twice as much work next time.'

'We'll manage,' I said. I put my hand on her shoulder and guided her towards the front door.

She took a few steps to the door, then put the brakes on. I tried to keep my patience. 'I think I should talk to Mrs Butler about this,' she said. 'I have good word-of-mouth reputation, Doctor, I don't want it getting around that I do half-jobs.'

'I'll make sure I let Lana know that it was all my doing,' I said.

She stepped away from me, reached for her coat from the hooks on the hallstand and looped it over her arm. She gave the sideboard a pointed look. Then, putting the polishing cloth down, she turned and pulled the door open with a jolt of annoyance.

'Goodbye, Dr Butler,' she said.

Shortly after, I heard the rattle of her car starting up and the drone of the engine as she left The Court.

CHAPTER 14

I lay on the sofa, a half bottle of wine down. The TV in the corner was on mute, the only light in the room. It had been just over twelve hours since Hunter had woken me with news of Lana's death. The evening appeared shapeless without Lana, a dull lump of confusion and darkness. After I'd sent the cleaner on her way, I'd ordered pizza and begun to drink. An attempt to gain some courage to phone Lana's parents. I'd already avoided two calls from them. Obviously, they'd tried their daughter's phone and hadn't got an answer. If I didn't call them soon, they'd call round. Or worse, phone the police.

I picked up my mobile, searched for their house number. Yes, Lana's parents still preferred their landline over any other form of communication in the evening. This was so they could screen their calls. It rang four times before their answering machine kicked in. I waited for the beep.

'Julie, Fred, it's . . . Myles . . . if you're there, please pick up.' I waited. Nothing. Then added. 'It's about . . . Lana.'

'Myles?' Julie's mother's voice rolled down the line like a smooth pearl. 'What is it?'

'Julie, hello,' I said. I shuffled to the edge of the sofa, tried to get the words straight in my head. Perhaps it hadn't been a good idea to drink the wine prior to phoning them. I felt the burn of indigestion. 'Excuse me,' I said.

'Myles?'

'Sorry, Julie,' I said. 'It seems there was an accident last night. Lana's car hit a tree and . . . she's . . . she's . . .'

Silence, then, 'Is she okay?' There was a high-pitched lean to her voice.

'She died,' I said. More silence. Then I whispered. 'I'm sorry.'

'She can't be,' she said, and I knew what she meant. Lana couldn't be contained. Couldn't be snuffed out. Not by a mere car accident.

'I know,' I said, emotion thickening my voice. I felt the pain of guilt in my chest and blinked hard.

'Where is she?'

'She's at the mortuary. At the Cavendish.'

'There's been a mistake,' she said quickly. 'We need to see her.'

I tipped my head back. I couldn't risk Fred turning up at the hospital and demanding to view Lana's body. It shouldn't be allowed, I'd made sure to sign all the paperwork and had insisted her remains were dealt with swiftly and with the dignity she wanted. But Fred was one of those you didn't refuse. 'I'm afraid you can't. It's too late.'

Silence, where I could hear her breathing shift, change, speed up. But Julie was of the stiff-upper-lip sort and not even the death of her own daughter would allow others to see a crack of emotion.

'Should I try to get in touch with Fred?' I asked.

'No. No. He's off somewhere with work. I'll tell him.' Then another awful silence.

'I'm so sorry,' I said again, not sure if she heard me. Shortly afterwards there was a click and the line went dead.

I half expected Gabe to call round to fill me in on what Hunter wanted with them but in the end I was glad he didn't. I wanted the whole day to be over. If the detective thought there was foul play, everyone knew who they'd come for first. Me. It would be my life that was turned upside down. After a shower, I put on a fresh T-shirt. I took my clothes down to the utility room, put them in the washing machine, then removed the jeans, remembering that the ring was in the back pocket. I held it up to the light. I'd wanted to get her a flashier wedding band. There had been one in the jeweller's that had small diamonds embedded in platinum all the way round, but at the time Lana had said I was sufficient.

'Timeless,' she said. 'Why would you want anything different?'

I had a rush of anger at her that she could do this to me. I shoved the jeans in the wash, turned the machine on, then I went upstairs to our ensuite, unravelled a handful of toilet paper from the roll and buried the ring at the centre. I dropped the lot in the toilet and without a moment's thought, flushed our married life away.

I drew the curtains. Turned my phone on silent and fell asleep on top of the covers, my last thoughts a desperate wish that when I woke up, I'd discover that all of this had simply been a nightmare.

★

'Good morning, Dr Butler,' Sam said the next morning at the clinic. 'Mrs Dorsley is running a couple of minutes late.'

'Thanks, Sam.' I walked round the front desk, headed for the staff room.

I had hesitated about whether to go into the surgery or not, but the idea of sitting at home waiting for Hunter or Charlotte to knock on the door and interrogate me propelled me out of the house. I felt better. The path out of this was through, as they say. I didn't like to think too much about what would happen when the money came through from the insurance. The idea of giving up our home seemed as repulsive to me as when our true financial situation became apparent. As Gabe said, I'd worked hard, I'd done the right things. Mostly. I wasn't ready to give it all up. I hadn't worked out exactly how we could return to our status quo and I knew, deep down, that it was impossible, but just in case, I needed to keep things running along at work.

As I neared the staff room, I heard a familiar low-toned conversation. Madison's nasal whine and Nathan's mumbling return. I slowed. Eavesdroppers never hear good about themselves but forewarned is forearmed.

'He's a pathological liar,' Madison was saying.

'That's going a little far,' Nathan said.

'It doesn't concern you that he lied on his CV?'

I felt the colour leave my face. What was she doing looking up my CV?

'He's been a great asset to this surgery, Madison. What's in the past is in the past.'

'Nathan, he said he'd completed and passed The Toppers.

154

You yourself said that was the reason you gave him the position over other applicants.'

'Madison, really, it hardly matters now, does it?' I didn't know how long she'd been in there pulling me to pieces in front of Nathan but I could tell Nathan was getting uncomfortable. Not because he didn't agree with her really, just that agreeing with her would mean change. And Nathan would rather coast a car into a wall than turn the steering wheel. Luckily, for me, he was true to character.

'You have to be careful with these things, Madison. The surgery has picked up recently, thanks to you, but the last thing I'd want is an unfair dismissal case. Let me look after this, I'll do a review in time and we can go from there.'

'I'm not sure we've time for that,' she said. I didn't like the tartness in her voice.

I held my breath, glanced back up the corridor. Heat gathered down my back.

'Here,' she said. 'Look at this. I opened it in error this morning.'

The sound of a paper being unfolded.

'What is it? Looks like an insurance payment,' he said.

Fuck. I waited for him to see what Madison had seen.

'Oh,' he said.

'The payment is going to him.'

'That can't be right. Myles is a lot of things but he wouldn't steal from the surgery. Besides, we're computerised, any appointments, payments, go straight into our system.'

A sigh of frustration from Madison.

'I wouldn't have noticed anything was off with it either but I saw this patient last week when he was late. See here,' she said.

155

'This claim is with our orthopaedic partners for a consultation and MRI of the left knee for meniscus damage after a recent football injury.'

'So?'

'So? This patient is an eighty-nine-year-old woman who had both knees replaced ten years ago. Doubtful she's attending the weekly five-a-side.'

'Oh,' he said again.

'He's copied these notes from another case and filled in her details to claim money off her insurance for a treatment she's never had done.'

When she put it like that, it did sound bad.

'That's fraud,' Nathan said, stupidly.

'It's a criminal offence,' she said.

'It must be a mistake. Why would Myles risk his career for few thousand pounds?'

'I've heard there might be some financial difficulty,' she said. 'I know his bank manager. He's a patient.'

Fuck you, Eric. I searched for an excuse, a simple error in admin. It wouldn't explain the fact that the money was coming to me instead of the surgery, but I might have to choose the lesser of two lies. I didn't know if Nathan would go for it. I wouldn't. But I had to rely on Nathan's tendency to look the other way when things got rough. Given any kind of explanation, he might just take it. Then Madison drove the final nail into my coffin.

'We do need to keep this quiet,' she said. 'If it got out that there were false insurance claims being made out of the surgery, we'd all suffer. You do see he can't continue to work here,

Nathan. This is the only fraudulent claim we know of. I've tried to look through his notes but he has a lock on most of them.'

'Why would he do that?'

I'd heard enough and turned back down the hall. Sam was coming towards me.

'Dr Butler, your first patient is here,' he chirped.

I froze, smiled stiffly at him. 'Thank you.' I continued walking.

'Myles?' Nathan's voice.

I turned. 'Yes,' I said. 'Good morning, Nathan.'

He cleared his throat. 'Do you have time for a quick word?'

I raised my hand, pointed my thumb over my shoulder. 'I'm afraid I've a patient. Don't want to be late.'

He stepped forward. His brow furrowing. 'Are you okay?'

'Of course,' I said. I rounded the corner into the waiting room. 'Mrs Dorsley, come in.'

She grinned her false-teeth grin, then got up quicker than a thirty-year-old and followed me into the treatment room.

'Just a minute,' I said when we were inside. 'I have to turn the computer on and find your notes.'

She sat down on the chair near my desk and folded her skirt across her knees. 'Busy this morning?' she asked.

I opened up the file where I'd kept a record of those patients from whom I'd claimed insurance, then found the relevant notes and clicked through, deleting each one, then ensuring they were gone from trash and archives. Mrs Dorsley sat quietly. She couldn't see the screen but I knew she was taking in the frantic movement of my fingers on the keyboard.

'Sorry to keep you waiting,' I said, turning to her with a smile. 'I had a few things to take care of.'

She tilted her head. 'You look tired, Doctor.'

'Just missed my coffee is all. It's been a stressful couple of days.'

'How's Lana?'

I stiffened.

'Doctor?'

I took a breath in, let it out through my nose slowly, rolled a fragment of paper over and back on the desk. I don't know where the emotion came from but it welled up. Whether it was tiredness, shock or fear that flooded my body I don't know, but suddenly I couldn't open my mouth because I knew if I spoke I wouldn't be able to hold in all the horrors of the last twenty-four hours.

I swallowed hard. 'I'm sorry, Mrs Dorsley.'

My eyes and face grew hot. I stood up, paced over and back.

She snapped open her handbag and extracted a neatly pressed silk handkerchief, held it out in my direction.

I took it, smiled my thanks but still didn't feel ready to speak.

She waited patiently for a few seconds, then: 'Would you like me to get someone?'

I shook my head. 'No. No. I'll be okay,' I said, turning away. 'Lana is dead.' Surprisingly, it was becoming easier to say. It came out flat and toneless.

She was silent for a moment, then I felt her palm on my back. 'Oh my, Myles, I'm sorry. What a shock.'

'It is,' I said, lifting my head and dabbing my eyes with her handkerchief. 'This is very unprofessional of me,' I said.

'You should be at home. Why on earth did you come into work?'

158

I shook my head again. 'I don't know. I guess this was . . .'

'One thing you could control?' she offered.

'Sorry,' I said again. 'Only, it looks like on top of it all, I might be fired.'

She pulled back. 'That can't be right.'

I allowed myself to indulge in all the self-pity I'd been saving up.

'But you're the best doctor here,' she said. 'I'll have a word with Nathan.'

I held up a hand. 'No. No, please. Maybe I need some time off to process things.'

'He'll hardly fire you now. You've just lost your wife,' she said.

'Perhaps I could've tried harder. I've probably been a little lazy on paperwork et cetera but I'm always there for my patients.' I gave her a fierce look and she nodded on cue.

'Absolutely right. Well,' she said, lifting her bag off her lap slightly and dropping it down again with an air of finality. 'I won't be seeing anyone else. You know all my preferences and history. I used to see Nathan long ago. What a wet week he was. So humourless. You know I've never once seen him out of the same suit. That can't be hygienic.'

'I suppose not,' I agreed.

She got up. 'Come on,' she said. 'Let's get you sorted. Turn off that thingy.' She tipped her head towards the computer. 'Sam will reschedule your patients. You should be at home resting. Grieving.' She held up a finger to the objection she could see on my lips. I knew when I left the surgery, my chances of returning again were slim. 'I went through it all with our Jack. Dreadful time, but you will get through it. Shame though,' she said.

I did what I was told, only because leaving now, with Mrs Dorsley at my side, would prevent the inevitable post-mortem from Madison and Nathan on my shortcomings and deceit. They were undoubtedly circling over reception ready to swoop down as soon as my morning clinic ended.

'You'll have to reschedule Dr Butler's patients today. In fact, for at least a week,' she said to Sam.

Nathan, who was lingering in the doorway of the staff room up the hall, appeared and walked towards us.

I cleared my throat. 'I'm sorry for the short notice. There's been a death,' my voice shook again. I didn't know where this emotion was coming from. 'Lana's passed away,' I said stiffly.

Nathan's eyes widened. 'Oh, my goodness. Myles.'

'I think I should take some leave,' I said.

'Yes, yes, of course. We'll look after your patients. No need to worry about anything,' he said.

'Okay. Thank you,' I turned to Mrs Dorsley. Took the hand-kerchief from my pocket. 'Thank you.'

She took the square of silk with her fingertips and slotted it into her bag. 'If you need anything . . . I wouldn't say I can cook but if you need to talk,' she said.

I walked out of the clinic into a blinding sunshine, sat in my car and watched the cascade of wisteria that draped the walls of Willowhaven sway in the light summer breeze. I didn't want to let this go. My knuckles turned white on the steering wheel, palms sweaty. It was infuriating that Lana had done this to me and I was aware of a bitter kind of resentment growing in the pit of my stomach. I thought about the options available for our future, now that Lana had decided our life on my behalf. It was fair to say that our choices had been limited. And there had been a decent chance I'd have had to leave the Village anyway. But we hadn't even tried.

Now I'd have to move if I wanted to be with her. I looked out at the surgery and thought about the money that was set to come our way – or more accurately, my way – and I recognised that old feeling of begrudging stubbornness that had powered me through the grim, grey tones of my teen years. I would have found another way. Given time, I'd have pulled myself – ourselves – up, and out of this mess. But life had taught me to play the cards dealt and to play them on my terms, and as I looked out at Willowhaven Surgery, the symbol of all I had become, I had to acknowledge there was a small part of me that never intended to give this up.

CHAPTER 15

The week would give me time to wrap my head around things. Nathan's wife, Sofia. She could be the key. She'd vouch to Nathan for me. If I had to leave the Village, I'd need a good reference from Nathan and I knew if Madison was given free rein, she'd have me struck from the register too. I couldn't let that happen.

I drove slowly through the village streets. People were enjoying the good weather, a woman paused at a shop window to admire a yellow summer dress. The child at her side adjusted the hat on her doll's head, then lifted the doll onto her shoulder. A group of tourists in matching red baseball caps followed a guide towards the Dog and Fox pub. As I passed, I heard the guide say the date, 1776, and immediately my mind offered up, the first map created of Wimbledon, the Hill Hotel, the novelist Thackeray, and Lana and Myles, third date, champagne, a creamy mushroom risotto, parmesan shavings and truffle oil.

When I arrived at The Court, a text appeared on my phone from Gabe. An address in Sandbanks. *Come down if you can. G.* It wouldn't look good to leave so soon after my wife's death, but I needed to escape. People dealt with grief differently, didn't they? There were more missed calls on my phone. Every one from Fred Grosvenor. I could see there were two voicemails and knew they'd be from him too. Demanding answers. Wanting to know how this was all my fault. I knew he'd come here. And I felt certain he'd trip me up somewhere.

I opened my messages and typed out a text:

Fred, I'm sorry. I'm devastated. I don't feel able to talk right now. I'm going to take a break for a few days to let all of this sink in. I'll be in touch soon. M.

I took a breath, hit SEND, then turned my phone off. I was so absorbed in my thoughts I didn't notice the red Escort parked close to my house until I stepped out of the driver's seat and heard another car door slam behind me.

'Dr Butler,' Hunter announced as he strode across the lawn. 'I wasn't expecting you to be working today.' He looked at my briefcase.

'I wasn't,' I said, then started again. 'I went in. I don't know why. I didn't know what else to do.'

He rubbed a hand across the back of his neck. 'I could imagine I might be the same.'

I wasn't sure how to respond to that. 'Was there something you needed, Detective?'

'We require a few items from your house, Doctor.'

I looked back at our home. There was a van up the street; two people were waiting on my porch.

'I don't understand,' I said, panicking. 'Lana died in a car accident. Why do you need to search the house?'

He held up his hands. 'Not a search. A few of your wife's personal items is all. DNA samples to confirm her identity, that the remains are hers.'

I frowned. 'Identity? But I already did that.'

He nodded. 'We're aware.'

'What sort of items?'

'Hairbrush, make-up, that kind of thing usually works best.'

I swallowed. 'Our cleaner, she came round yesterday.'

'Don't worry, Dr Butler. This isn't TV, we'll get what we need.' He passed me a sheet of paper. A warrant or something like it, I supposed. 'We won't be long.' I looked over the paperwork and he pointed at where I was to sign, then handed me a pen. 'Actually, I'm glad you're here and I apologise if this isn't the right time, but there were a few more questions I wanted to ask you.'

'Questions?'

'You argued the last time you saw your wife?'

I blinked. Who had told him that? 'Not really an argument. A minor misunderstanding.'

'She left ahead of you on Saturday night. When you were both –' he flicked through the pages of his notebook – 'at this event in London? Is that right?'

'She had a headache.'

'And that's the last time you spoke to her?'

'Yes.'

'You didn't call her? Text her? She didn't text you to say she'd got home safely?'

'No,' I said. 'I wish I had now. The last time I spoke or inter-acted with her was outside the hotel in Mayfair. I didn't return home until four a.m.'

A tight smile. 'You got in at four?'

'Yes,' I said.

'Can you be more specific?'

'I don't know. Four fifteen, I think. I was pretty drunk, to be honest. I went straight to bed. I didn't even remove my clothing.'

'And when you got into bed, it didn't worry you that your wife was not there?'

'It would have if I'd noticed. But I didn't.'

'You sleep in the same room?'

I flushed. 'Yes. Look, as you've pointed out, we had a bit of an argument. I must have assumed she was in one of the guest rooms.'

He closed his notebook. 'You're saying this argument mightn't have been that minor, then? If you believed she'd sleep elsewhere because of it?' He didn't give me a chance to answer. Which I was grateful for because I had no more answers to give. Instead, he smiled at me like one smiles at an idiot.

'It was a small misunderstanding. I'm just trying to put things together like you are, Detective,' I said.

'Yes, I'm sorry,' he said. 'Is there anyone that might have wanted to harm your wife?'

I shook my head. 'She never mentioned anyone. Or any problems like that.'

'How about you?'

'Me?'

Another pause. 'Is there anyone who might want to get at you?'

I made a show of thinking about this for a moment, then gave him another shake of my head. 'I can't think of anyone.'

'How about her phone?' Hunter continued. There was a slight shift in the tone of his voice, his eyes fixed on my face with renewed intensity. Either Hunter had run whatever police ran to locate phones or he'd spoken to Linda already.

I cleared my throat. 'Yes. I found it yesterday.'

'We'll be needing that too,' he said.

I nodded. There hadn't been anything on the phone that hinted at the truth. At least, not that I had seen. And it struck me that this might be why Lana had left it behind. She wanted to make sure it was found and not damaged in the accident because she suspected the police would want to study her messages. All the police would see were the normal ups and downs of a man and wife. A man and wife who occasionally bickered but otherwise had a stable marriage despite the financial struggles they were facing. 'How long will it take? How long will you be in the house?'

'Less than an hour, if that,' he said.

I could feel the colour drop from my face. 'May I go inside? To pack a bag? I've a train to catch. Since Lana's . . . accident, I don't feel up to driving for long periods,' I said. Although I said this for his benefit, to convince him I was deeply traumatised after my wife's death, there was some truth in it.

'It's your home,' he said.

I walked up to the front door, opened it. I thought the two officers working with Hunter would wait, but no, they followed me in, treading carefully. I went upstairs and in our bedroom reached under the bed for my suitcase, then began to fill it with clothes. My trainers, sandals, a couple of pairs of light trousers, jeans and a few shirts.

166

When I straightened I saw that one of the officers was in the doorway. She pointed to the bathroom. 'Do you mind?'

Through the open door, I could see Lana's make-up laid out. Her electric toothbrush was still plugged in to the side of the sink. The woman didn't wait for me to reply. She entered the en-suite, removed a clear plastic bag from her pocket, then pulled the bin towards her. She grabbed a few fistfuls of tissue, pushed them into the bag and sealed it; set that to the side, then finding Lana's hairbrush in a drawer, gathered the dark strands captured in the teeth of the brush and pushed them into another bag. Then one by one she took each of the items of make-up and dropped them into another bag. I watched her with growing panic. But there was nothing I could do.

I picked up the suitcase and left the room. Sweat ran down my back and into the waistband of my trousers. I crept along to the study and opened the door. It let out a familiar squeak. I paused. Waited to make sure there were no footsteps following me. Then I went to the desk. The insurance details were as I'd left them yesterday. I put down the suitcase, folded the papers into an envelope, tucking the whole lot inside my jacket, then made my way back downstairs to remove Lana's mobile from the safe.

Hunter was waiting outside the door.

'Here's her phone,' I said.

'Thank you.' He glanced at the screen. 'You know her passcode by any chance?'

'It's our anniversary.' I gave him what I hoped was a sad expression, then told him the digits to enter.

He noted them down. 'We'll need the address you're staying at. In case we need to contact you.' A tightening in my chest.

I gave him the address, then fished about in my pocket. Handed him a card. 'This has my mobile number on it.'

'Sandbanks?' Hunter said. 'Very nice. You don't have family nearby?'

'I only have my father, but he's in Bristol.'

He raised his eyebrows at this. 'You're from there? For some reason, I thought you were from here.'

I shook my head, unsure why I was telling him this but, Hunter being a Bristolian, I thought I could win him over. 'I lived here for a few years. We moved to Bristol when I was twelve. Went to uni there too. It's a beautiful city.'

'It is,' he sighed. 'I miss it, but the missus wanted a change and so here I am.' He tapped the card in his hand. 'You know, your neighbours mentioned they were also taking a break in Sandbanks.'

I was beginning to work out Hunter. The man let on only half of what he knew. And from the way he was looking at me, there was no point in trying to hide the fact that I would be staying with the Wrights.

'Yes,' I said. 'They asked me along yesterday. I'm . . .' I sighed. 'Quite honestly, I don't trust myself to be alone at the moment, so I decided to take them up on their offer.'

He smiled. 'It's a blessing to have good neighbours in times such as these.'

'Yes,' I said. 'It is.'

CHAPTER 16

I sat at a café on the seafront, nursing a double espresso. The entire journey here, I worried about Hunter and what he was retrieving from our home. I'd tried Gabe's phone numerous times but there was no answer. Instead, I got a one-line text telling me to meet him here and he'd take me back to the house. I was desperate to speak with him. Right now, items that held Lana's DNA were on their way to some lab and it would be a matter of days before this dreadful plan blew up in our faces. My stomach clenched. I rolled out my shoulders, thought through what I could say when Hunter eventually discovered my lies. Lana would have to say she left me, that this was all some strange coincidence. And, as Gabe had initially suggested, we'd have to say that her car had been stolen. That I'd known none of it. I was innocent.

The terrace was full of people. Most sipped at glasses of chilled rosé or white wine. Salads and moules marinières appeared to be the popular order. I was still dressed in the suit I'd worn to the surgery that morning and the heat was beginning to get to me.

The train down had been packed, stuffy, and had left me feeling grubby. I felt self-conscious, out of place, my suitcase beside me marking me out as a new arrival. The waiter had already asked me twice if I was ready to order. I edged my seat a little further under the awning and flicked through my phone so I looked busy. More calls from Fred. A reply to my text to him demanding I phone him immediately. I deleted it. Then opened an internet browser.

On the Sussex news website there was a small piece showing the wreckage of Lana's car, a paragraph, *Woman Killed in Car Accident*. The wreckage – it was the first time I'd seen it – was not all that bad. The driver's side had taken all of the impact, it appeared. But even so, the force had not been enough to destroy the front of the car. However, I could make out the white disc of fractured glass on the windscreen, and given that Hunter had said the airbag didn't deploy, if there'd been no seatbelt, then clearly it had appeared convincing. I told myself that I was looking at things with the perspective of knowing it was all lies, smoke and mirrors, and that if I didn't know what I knew, I'd come to the same conclusion as those paramedics who turned up at the scene. Or Hunter. I scanned the article, my eyes catching on one phrase. *No other casualties*. That line lingered in my mind. *No other casualties*. I thought of the tattoo. The woman now lying in the mortuary. The woman I'd soon cremate as my wife. *No other casualties*. I thought of the burns on her body. The swelling on her face, the fresh-looking gash down her forehead. The bruising, bleeding under the skin that had required internal pressure in order to build. A pulse. A heartbeat. A life.

Since identifying the body at the hospital, I'd not been able to shake the feeling that I was now involved in something infinitely darker than what had been proposed that night at dinner. I didn't want to study my thoughts too closely. I didn't want to admit to where they pointed. But the more I attempted not to dwell on it, the more I was convinced that the victim in that crash had not been dead already. And if that were the case, who had we murdered?

'Hello, stranger.' Gabe. He grabbed hold of my suitcase. He was barefoot, in soft linen shorts, and had somehow, in the short time he'd been here, acquired a golden tan to his skin.

'Thanks for picking me up,' I said into the mirror sheen of his sunglasses.

'We're just a little way up the coast. Come on. There's air con in the car, it's sweltering out here,' he said.

I followed him to the Mercedes. Once he settled into the driver's seat, I told him about Hunter and that they were looking for a more formal identification of the body.

Gabe listened intently, staring ahead and guiding the Merc through a series of turns along the harbour road. When I finished, he nodded. 'I understand your concern, but Myles, I need you to relax, please. I knew this would happen. We've staged some items in the house.' He gave a shrug of his shoulder. 'Make-up brushes, tissues in the bathroom toilet, hairbrush, the head of her toothbrush. They'll all match with the correct DNA,' he said. I blinked and he grinned at me.

Again, I tried to get my head around how much Lana plotted this behind my back. Had they dragged that toothbrush across the teeth of a dead woman? Her hairbrush? Or had the make-up brushes actually belonged to this victim?

The question rose inside me like bile in the throat. 'What if they don't take those items to test?' I asked.

His chin pulled down as he grimaced. 'They will. They always do.'

I had that feeling again that they were well practised at this. I wasn't sure if that was reassuring or worrying. 'But if they don't?'

He shrugged again. 'I don't know.'

He pulled into the shade of a double garage at the back of a large two-storey house that overlooked the Sandbanks peninsula. He turned off the ignition and looked at me. 'If you keep tying yourself in knots like this, Hunter's going to suspect something. And none of us want that. Look around you,' he said, pointing towards the harbour, the sea. 'No one knows you here. It's a time to switch off. Think about what you want for the future when all of this is behind you and you have your wife by your side again and money to start over.'

He swung out of the car, grabbing my suitcase from the back seat and led me out of the garage so that I could take in the full front of the house.

'The friends we're renting from are away in their little French chateau for the weekend, if you can believe it,' Gabe said. He smiled widely at me, and maybe it was the sea air, the devil-may-care aura that cloaked Gabe, but I felt myself relax. The spectre of Hunter's investigation followed me but I held back on my questions. Honestly, part of me didn't want to know the answers because I knew they wouldn't be good.

Gabe waved me through to the front of the house, put my case down on the patio. 'I'm glad you decided to come down,' he said. 'Personally, I'm not one for trusting in fate. And I think

172

knowing a little of your background you would share that view. What I trust in, is a good plan, well thought out and executed. And that's what I've given you. So, the question remains, do you trust me?'

I let out a long breath. Tried to blow away the tension that held me in its grip. I didn't trust anyone. Least of all myself. But I nodded.

He smiled, and I smiled his smile back to him.

'Let's get you settled,' he said.

He moved off towards the main house, then shouted over his shoulder, 'You're the room on the front left upstairs. In case you didn't have time to pack properly, there are clothes and shoes in the wardrobes. Take what you need,' he said, and bounded through the open glass doors.

On the second floor, there was a wide balcony that went across the front of the house, the balcony framed by glass panels, nothing obscuring the view of sea and sky beyond. At ground level, a large jacuzzi was submerged in the pale stone patio. On either side a shallow set of steps ran down to the lower floor, a neatly kept hedgerow of topiary followed the line. Tiny gold lights lit up the greenery, purple and blue neon lights wobbled beneath the surface of the jacuzzi. Inside, the furniture looked large and expensive. If Gabe's idea was to give me a glimpse of another life, a richer future, then I had to confess, he had set my mouth to water. Not that this would be within reach once the payment came through, but it could be a dream on the horizon. With the right moves across the board, it could be us.

I stood on the patio, inhaled the briny seaweed air, closed my eyes and tried to let the possibility take hold. Inside, Gabe was dropping ice into glasses. I made my way upstairs to the bedroom. The room was spacious, a super-king bed, floor-to-ceiling wardrobes in pale wood. Inside the wardrobes, clothes arranged like I'd seen in exclusive clothing stores. Each item had its own place. A row of thin drawers on one side. The top drawer displayed four rows of cufflinks, the second, sunglasses. I picked up a pair of gold-edged aviators. Went to the mirror. There were new lines on my forehead. The skin around my eyes was pinched. I put the glasses on, pushed my hair up and back at the front, adjusted the line of my parting. Then leaving my own clothes in the suitcase, selected a pair of cream trousers and a fresh shirt from the wardrobe. I could feel sweat already soaking through the fabric at my back.

When I got downstairs, Holly was sitting on a large corner sofa that curved around a low glass coffee table. She was wearing a white summer dress, the straps meeting over her shoulders in two neat bows. She was holding what looked like a cotton tip and cleaning a black circular disc. In front of her was her camera, numerous lenses and various photography paraphernalia laid out as if she were disassembling a rifle. I noticed the band at her wrist was back. The skin around it a smacked pink.

'Myles,' she said. 'You came.'

I walked to her, bent down and kissed her cheek. 'Thanks for having me here.'

She put down the cotton tip, rested a cool hand on my forearm and looked up into my face. Her blue eyes pinned on mine. 'How are you?'

'Still taking it in,' I replied.

She nodded, removed her hand. 'It will be okay.' But she

looked away as she said it. She stood, dusted off her dress. 'It's hot,' she announced. 'I'm just going to change. Excuse me.' She stepped out around me, patting my shoulder as she went, then disappeared swiftly up the stairs.

'Drink?' Gabe said from the kitchen area. I returned to his side and he handed me a mojito. The scent of freshly pressed mint hit my nose.

'Like a different person,' he said, looking over my clothes. 'Suits you.'

I tugged at the cuff of the light blue linen shirt. 'I appreciate this. I'd no time to pack properly. Hunter breathed down my neck the entire time.' Unable to keep my promise not to talk about it, I lowered my voice. 'Who was the woman?'

Gabe took a sip of his drink. 'Woman?'

'The woman,' I said. 'Who was she?'

'Myles,' he said, his tone a patient kind of pleading. 'That was your wife. That's all you need to know.'

My fingers tightened on the glass. 'You're a surgeon, for Christ's sake. You know how these things work. There'll be a post-mortem.'

He was eerily calm about it. He should be panicking, because I was, but then I thought how easy it would be for Gabe and Holly to dust their hands of this entire mess. It wasn't them that Hunter would be waiting for. It was me.

'I do know how these things work,' he said, then took another slow sip of his drink. He rolled his mouth to gather up the sugary residue that coated the top of the glass. 'They will only find what I want them to find.'

'And what is it you want them to find?'

He looked at me, blue eyes steady. At the corner of his jaw, a small muscle flickered beneath the skin. 'Evidence that the remains they have are those of Lana Butler.'

I had again that sense I'd made a mistake at the hospital. Perhaps that had been Lana on that trolley. I saw again the cut down her forehead, the swelling around the eyes. I thought of Lana leaving that night in Mayfair. Saw her again, in profile, her dark hair swept to the side as the taxi drew her away from me. The time not even ten thirty. She would have been home within the hour. Maybe sooner. Gabe must have left shortly after. I remember seeing Holly later that night before the edges of the room began to blur, but now that I thought of it, I'd no memory of Gabe being there towards the end of the night.

The corner of his mouth came up in a half-smile. 'If there's one thing I know about police work it's they don't like spending money where there's no clear reason. They're not going to be searching your entire house. They'll only take what they need.' Another sip of his drink. 'Believe me, everything is going to be fine.'

I tried to tell myself that new beginnings were what I wanted, that money would compensate for walking away from my life, but I think there was part of me already committed to my own plan. I was still hoping for some way out, and it was an itch under my skin that I was trapped on this path now. I tried to ignore the little flare of anger I felt every time I thought about it. And more so, because this was a trait of Lana's she knew I hated. She had a habit of discussing plans with me, only to move on the way she wanted anyway, then to look at me with genuine confusion when I questioned her. 'I got the impression you didn't mind much either way,' she'd say.

A light breeze swept in through the open doors carrying the scent of salt water and seaweed. From somewhere on the beach, the sound of a child's shriek of delight. Away from the house, from the reminder of Lana, I could half believe Gabe. I knew there was a chance that this could all go wrong. Very wrong. But there was also the chance that we'd succeed. And standing in that house, looking out on the Sandbanks peninsula, I allowed myself to imagine what success could look like. By the time we paid our debts, the house sale could still leave us a couple of million at least. Not a bad springboard to begin a new life.

I nodded at Gabe, clinked my glass against his. 'You're right,' I said, realising that if I wanted to find out who this other woman was, I'd have to go about it another way. But I didn't want the answers I sought to lead a trail to my door for the police. Maybe not knowing was for the best. I couldn't be questioned on a crime I knew nothing about. But it was unnerving to be so out of the loop. I guess the real question was, how much did I trust my wife? That was, if she was still alive. 'Could I talk to her?'

'Myles, she's fine.' This struck me as an odd response as I never asked how she was. 'I know the coming weeks are going to be really tough, but put yourself in her shoes. She misses you. Hearing your voice would just make things harder.'

As I said, I was prone to arrogance and therefore a sucker for flattery. The idea that Lana was pining away for me gave me a deep satisfaction.

'At least tell me where she is?'

He brought his drink to his mouth again. 'Soon. I've looked into this Hunter chap. Bit of a stilted career, by the looks of it. You know he has a daughter. Neve, I believe her name is. Cute as a button.' He clapped me on the shoulder. 'Don't look at me like that. I wouldn't hurt a child, for goodness' sake. But dropped into a conversation at the right time, it might just remind Hunter that you're not the only one with something to lose.' He met my eyes but when I didn't respond, gave out a small laugh. 'I'm not serious, obviously. It will all work out. You'll see.' He steered me out into the garden towards a couple of recliners and a suite of rattan chairs.

He pulled out a chair for me and I sat, facing the view of the sea, the horizon trembling in the sun. 'Now, I've invited a few people round this evening,' he said, sitting across from me. 'One or two of them are in health care. There could be an opportunity to –' he shook his head, shrugged – 'see where the ground might lie for you in a few months.'

I laughed. Then realised he was serious. I pulled my shirt away from my back. 'I can't be seen socialising. My wife has just died.'

'No one knows you here. The police have no reason to question anyone you'll meet this evening. You're not under investigation, Myles. Hunter has nothing and he won't be long about finding himself in deep waters with his superiors if he continues on this path. As for the rest of it, they're just following basic protocol. Besides, the people here have money and, in my experience, if they believe you have too, they become supremely talented at looking the other way.'

'Have you spoken to Lana today?' I asked him.

'Not today.' He crossed his legs, giving a little hitch to his trousers at the knee. 'So, I've invited a retired GP who runs a number of surgeries around the country, a few in Spain for expats. He might be a good contact to make. He could be looking for a partner or someone to run a new venture.' He glanced beyond my shoulder, then pushed back from the seat and got up. 'Ah, Holly, you're done. Would you like a drink?'

Holly had changed into a swimsuit and a light see-through kimono in a shimmering shade of turquoise. A wide-brimmed straw sunhat kept her face in shade. 'Please,' she said to her husband.

'Duty calls,' Gabe said to me, went to Holly, delivered a kiss to her mouth.

Holly took Gabe's empty seat and arranged the folds of her kimono over her knees. She gave out a sigh, as if to fill time. Her fingers went to her wrist. 'So how are you?' she asked, then waved her hand through the air. 'Sorry, I've already asked you that.'

'It's okay,' I said. She seemed nervous. I pointed to the band at her wrist. 'Anxiety?' It was a personal question but I thought with what we were all currently embroiled in and what Gabe and Holly clearly knew about me and Lana, this was a rather small invasion of privacy.

If she was offended by the question, she didn't show it. She snapped the band and I winced at the sound. From behind the shade of her glasses, I could sense her watching me.

She grimaced as she answered. 'Not exactly. Would you believe it if I said I have anger issues? According to my shrink anyway.' She lifted the brim of her hat to study my reaction. 'In case that makes me sound scary, it's not what you think. It's to do with my past. You get it,' she said. Was I that easy to read? Then I remembered she'd seen me steal that pen in the shop. I had my own ways of venting my anger.

'Does it help?' I asked.

She was prevented from answering by Gabe's return.

He placed a drink in her hand. 'I'm just heading out to pick up a few items for this evening.'

She tipped her head back, held on to her hat and looked up at him. 'Let's keep it simple, darling.'

'I'm not sure that's in my skill-set,' he said, then turned, walked back up the garden, jogged up the short flight of steps round the jacuzzi and disappeared into the cool shade of the house.

'It's distracting,' she said to me once he'd left. Returning to my question. 'It's either this –' she nodded towards her wrist – 'or this,' she said, lifting up her glass. She took a long slow drink.

I wanted to ask her why she'd been so upset when I'd called in at their house after Lana had disappeared. Had she been left out of the plans like I had? Or had the plan not gone as expected? This was supposed to be a simple matter of exchanging paper-work, but instead I was beginning to suspect there'd been a real flesh-and-blood cost to their offer. I thought it might be easier to get information about the crash victim from Holly. Or rather I felt Gabe's patience might be finite, and some primitive instinct told me not to confront a man who was capable of murder with my ideas on his guilt. With Holly, I could feel around the edges, get a sense of who Gabe really was.

'How are you feeling about everything? You were quite upset when I called around after . . .' I trailed off.

'Oh, was I? I don't remember. I feel fine. I mean it's done now,' she said, as if she were explaining away a bad haircut. She turned up her toes, examined her pedicure.

Any hope of prising information from Holly began to look very meagre indeed. But I had no one else to turn to. I couldn't go to the police. I couldn't speak to my wife. I couldn't explain the situation to her family, her friends. Because behind all of this was the chance to leave our debt behind. My debt behind. And I was holding on to that possibility as if it were a single feather that enabled me to fly. I hadn't quite come round to the idea of leaving my job, our house, and I was already beginning to fantasise of ways by which I could hold on to it all.

If I were to extract anything from Holly, it would have to be between the cracks of what she was willing to talk about. I forced myself to relax into the rattan furniture, gazed out at the cool blue waters of the Channel, the sun twinkling on the surface as if the gods had scattered diamonds all the way to the horizon.

'I never asked, how did you two meet?'

She took a packet of cigarettes from a fold in her kimono, removed one, lit it, then offered one to me. I shook my head. 'University. Feels like yesterday and –' she looked back in the direction of the house – 'a whole other lifetime ago.' She smiled briefly at me, then continued, dishing the words out carefully. 'I was studying History, working in the union bar at the weekend and the occasional evening. He came in for a drink sometime in the first term and we haven't looked back since.'

'History?'

She drew on the cigarette. 'I didn't see the first year out,' she said. 'We were in love, and I let everything else go.' She gave a short laugh. 'Seems like a ridiculously naïve decision now, but Gabriel . . .' Another pause. She looked at me out the side of her glasses, feeling her way forward. 'He's all-consuming.

I'd intended to go back. Finish my studies. It never seemed like the right time. For us, anyway. Maybe I'll return in the future.'

'Gabe knows you'd like to go back. To study?'

While Gabriel made no secret of the type of person he was, Holly, it seemed to me, was not so ready to show her cards. What she was holding back I couldn't say, but there was a tension to how she held herself, as if she were curating her movements, a dancer moving through well-planned steps.

'That part of my life is in the past now.' She reached for her drink. 'Don't misunderstand me. Gabe would be all for it. You want something, you go and get it, that's his view.' She smiled at me.

'I could agree with that,' I said.

A flash of something in her eyes. I'd misread her tone.

'And still,' she said, with firmness, 'I think what Gabe occasionally misunderstands – or maybe it's that he wouldn't want to confront it . . . but often a goal is left unfulfilled, not because anyone has said you're not allowed to go and get it but somehow the message is implicit that you shouldn't. Therefore, you don't broach the subject at all. Ever. You fold it away inside and tell yourself that, because it's never passed your lips, because you've never put it out there, you've agreed with how things stand. Eventually, you accept that this dream, or whatever it was, is only a passing, trivial regret that's barely a regret at all but someone else's path entirely.'

I didn't know how to reply. At the same time, I couldn't help seeing the comparison to what was happening to me. The plans for my own future, tidied away, slipping away.

She glanced at her watch, sighed. 'Ignore me. I've a habit

of getting too self-reflective when I drink. It's marriage. You know what it's like. Gabe,' Holly went on, 'he's amazing. He tolerates a lot, Myles. I'm far from perfect, as you'll no doubt discover.' A tinkle of laughter that I returned with a smile. 'I couldn't believe he was interested in me, you know.' She held up a hand when I went to speak. 'Sometimes I still can't believe it.'

I swallowed. I wasn't sure I wanted to know the mental gymnastics each of them performed in their relationship. To know it stood on the same insecurities as any average marriage. That the same fears ran trembling beneath the foundations. I wanted to believe they were beyond that.

'Why are you helping us?' I asked.

She took her time answering. The cigarette going to her mouth again. A breeze lifted her hair back from her shoulders. 'Does it sound terribly arrogant to say because we could?'

I didn't believe that for a second but I went along with it. 'There's a lot to lose for you both, if it goes wrong.'

She thought on this for a while, then she removed her sunglasses, brought her pale blue gaze to mine and said, 'You don't know Gabe as well as I do. So, I get why you'd doubt this plan. But when you do – get to know him, that is – you'll understand that Gabe doesn't lose.'

There was something about her tone that made me feel this was not offered in the spirit of reassurance. It may have been my own stress about the whole situation but all I heard was a threat.

'Anyway.' She reached out, extinguished her cigarette in the ashtray. 'I need to check on the catering.' She got up, floated off

183

back towards the house. She lifted a hand as she went. 'Enjoy, relax. Try the jacuzzi.'

She left me in the cloud of my thoughts. I looked after her as she stepped through the open doors of the house, the thin kimono drifting out behind her.

CHAPTER 17

Right before I proposed to Lana, we took a trip to the South Coast. We stayed just outside Worth Matravers. The weather was dry, the roads sun-baked and dusty. The sea-blown brittle hedgerows were heavy with rosehip and blackberry blossom. We rented a cottage that could have manifested from a postcard. It had a thatched roof, walls strewn with ivy and red roses.

On our last night there, we went to a pub set high on the cliffs overlooking the sea. The tables were huge slabs of granite, warm from the day's sun. We drank locally brewed cider and ate chips from newspaper. Later, loose-limbed and giggling, we stumbled down the quiet roads towards our cottage. My arm was round Lana's waist, hers looped over my shoulder, her hand clinging to my neck, like she was gripping the mast of a boat on a rocky sea. The sky was so clear, it was as if I could reach up and pluck a star from the darkness. We stopped outside the small blue cottage gate and kissed. I tasted the sweet and sour stickiness of cider on her lips.

'Lie down,' she said, tugging me towards the ground. 'Look.' She tipped her head back.

We lay down. In the middle of the road. And gazed upwards, the tips of our fingers touching. The earth, like a cradle, swayed left then right. It was as if we were floating, up, through the inky night, stars falling, like rain, around us.

'We're going to do great things together,' Lana said. Her voice breathy, happy.

'Take that sushi cookery course,' I replied.

She didn't laugh but even without looking at her, I knew she was smiling. 'How else would we lord our brilliance over our friends?' A pause. 'We'll buy some stylish big house with enough rooms to prove we don't need them but not so much that it's obnoxious.'

The earth swayed.

'You'll make partner at the surgery,' she whispered. 'Everyone in the Village will know who you are. I'll work part-time so that I can finish my master's. Become a real-life psychologist. We'll entertain. Our hosting will be exquisite. We will be the couple everyone thinks of for their parties. And when we're not dining with others, we'll eat out.'

'We'll have a reserved table at the best restaurant in town,' I added.

'They hold it, just in case we turn up,' she said.

'We'll have other properties. A holiday home in Portugal or France.'

'No. Somewhere in the UK, so we can drop into conversation ad nauseam how we'll be nipping down to the coast for a few days.'

'Cornwall,' I said.

'Sandbanks,' she replied.

The couple who dream together, stay together. Or at least until death us do part.

'Vision. That's what one needs.'

I was fenced in along the kitchen counter. The man speaking was the doctor Gabe had told me about. Dr Anthony Chapman. In one hand he held a Pimm's, in the other a cigar, which he waved about like a conductor's baton as he spoke. The blue smoke stung my eyes and made me nauseous. Every time I stepped back, he took it as a sign to move closer, when I could have easily heard him if he'd been on the other side of the room.

'Six surgeries and counting,' he said, lifting a finger from the cigar to point it in the air.

So far, we'd covered his training, his down-and-out background. What a gobshite his father was, his mother a 'hopeless case'. How he'd practically raised his younger siblings. Still bailed them out financially from time to time. He added an affectionate bubble of laughter here. He was from just outside Dublin and once he'd discovered I was half Irish, he'd not let me out from under him.

'We have something, us Irish,' he said. 'Can't keep us down. What's going on over there now, we'll come back. Can't blame the country for wanting to own their own homes, can you? But the Celtic Tiger will roar again. Thankfully, the crisis hasn't affected us too much. The beauty of health care, right?'

The question caught me off guard and I quickly swallowed down a mouthful of water to cover my slowness in answering.

'Right,' I said.

'Where you working now?'

187

'Wimbledon Village.'

'Nice. Good practice, I'd say. You ever thought about opening more?' He prodded my shoulder with his finger. 'Not too many – ha, don't want the competition!' More laughter, more blue smoke.

'Possibly,' I said.

'You need a plan. You need to be certain. State the goal and go after it. And if an opportunity crosses your path that's for you, you fucking take it.'

I nodded.

'GPs are the lifeblood of the medical profession. The rest stand on our fucking shoulders. Don't let these fancy surgeons, like Gabe here, make you feel like you're not at their standard. I could have gone on, could have easily continued training –' another prod – 'as no doubt you could.'

Gabe, on hearing his name, came wandering over. He looked sharp as always. He put an arm around Anthony's shoulder. 'He boring the tits off you yet, Myles?'

'Not at all.' I guessed I should be grateful that I was trapped in the verbal wind tunnel that was Anthony Chapman; it paralysed any other thought, such as worrying about Lana or the maze of lies I was going to have to navigate over the coming weeks.

There was a vibrating in my pocket. I removed my phone, checked the screen. More calls from Fred. I tried to field most of them by text but every time I replied it prompted a whole other flood of phone calls until I was forced to turn the sound off. I wasn't ready to speak to him yet.

'This surgery of yours in Wimbledon,' Chapman said. 'Are you interested in selling up in the future?'

'I'm afraid I'm not the owner. I'm an associate,' I said.

'You mentioned you might be interested in branching out, though?' Gabe said.

I played along. 'It might be nice to know what's out there.'

Chapman seemed disappointed. He reached round me, stubbed the cigar out in an ashtray on the kitchen counter. 'If anything comes up, I'll be in touch.' He removed a card from inside his jacket pocket and handed it to me. 'Your boss ever needs an investor or is looking to sell, send him my way.'

I took the card. Slid it into my back pocket. 'Will do.'

Most of the guests drifted on, back to their own houses after a couple of hours. As the sky turned dark, there remained a couple of men and a woman in her sixties. The woman had a flamboyant air, and the kind of posture adopted early in childhood when you knew your life would be to look down on others. I was shattered. My limbs heavy and my mouth getting careless. I made for the stairs, ready to fall into bed. The woman collared me as I crossed the lawn. She was wearing long, loose-fitting trousers, a silk sleeveless blouse and one, two – no, three – shawls in those jewelled shades of turquoise, burgundy and dark blue, layered over one another so that when she lifted her knuckles to me (I was to kiss her ringed hand), the fabrics fell back from her wrist in a wave of gossamer and satin.

'Genevieve,' she said. 'Neighbour.' She laid down her purse on a low wall beside us, a signal that I wasn't to move on by. The clasp was open and a gold tube of lipstick poked out alongside one of those miniature toolsets that come in Christmas crackers.

I kissed her hand, then she drew it back into the swathes of material.

'Dr. Myles Butler,' I said. 'Guest.'

She lifted her chin. You could tell she'd never been beautiful, but there was a strength around the bone structure of her face, the jaw and forehead, that gave her a regal air.

'Your wife recently passed, I hear?' Straight out.

I was tired enough that I'd momentarily forgotten that Lana was supposed to be dead. It took a while to drag my own reality from the depths of my exhausted brain.

'Oh,' I said. 'Yes.' I glanced across the garden towards Gabe and Holly. Had they told this woman?

'All this must be a welcome distraction for you,' she commented. She looked me straight in the eye as if her gaze could hook the truth from my mind.

I didn't know how to respond. Shame flooded my face.

'Don't fret, Dr Butler. When my husband died, the party went on for three days,' she said, her accent smooth as polished marble. 'Then, one might grieve the sound of a dripping tap if you've had the time enough to grow accustomed to it.' A sigh. 'But I suppose you loved your wife?'

'Very much.' Although since Lana had thrown me into this mess, that love felt like it was diminishing somewhat, sifting away like sand through an hourglass.

She tilted her head like a bird who had spotted a worm. 'Interesting. That does make your presence here more peculiar,' she said. A devilish lift at the corner of her mouth, a flash of pearly white veneers. 'Say, you're not one of those psychopaths, are you?'

I had a sudden flash of my hands round Lana's throat, followed by a bird's-eye view of the back of my head as I looked down on that woman's body, then a new feeling, a slow swelling of relief every time I said Lana was dead.

I met the woman's eyes and whatever expression was on my face, she pulled back a little. For some reason, this gave me a jolt of satisfaction.

I smiled, then said, 'Of course not.'

The next morning, I woke to my phone buzzing across the bedstand. I sat up in bed, disorientated, a stream of startling white sunlight pouring through the floor-to-ceiling windows. I was naked, save for my underwear, and had kicked the sheets off somewhere in the middle of the night. My jaw was clenched shut and I knew I'd been grinding my teeth. My head pounded. Whatever blood vessel needed to burst to grant me release, I wished it would get on with it. I reached out to the bedstand and grasped at a glass of water. I downed it, then grabbed my phone, answering without thinking.

'Hello,' I said. My voice was not my own.

'Myles?' The short, aggressive tone of Lana's dad, Fred.

'Fred.' I coughed. 'Sorry, I was sleeping.'

'At almost noon,' he said. I squinted at my phone. It was eleven but he never liked to let an opportunity to humiliate me slip by. 'Yes, sorry. I haven't been sleeping well.'

'Where the fuck are you? I went round to the house.'

'I needed to get away for a few days.'

Silence. I could almost hear his antennae twitching.

'She should never have married you. I knew this would end badly.'

'It was a car accident, Fred.'

'How? What on earth was she doing out there in the middle of the night?'

'I don't know,' I said. 'I wasn't there. They're looking into it but, Fred, it just seems like it was an accident.' I made a show of a choking cry down the phone. 'I can't seem to accept that she's gone.'

He ignored my grief. 'We want to see her.'

A cold sensation fell over me. 'You can't. They're doing the post-mortem today.'

A stony silence. I could hear every accusatory breath come down the line. 'Have you done anything about the funeral yet?'

'She wanted cremation.'

'You've made the calls?'

'I . . . I . . . was waiting—'

'Just answer the question, Myles.'

'No.'

'Crematoriums are busy places.'

'Yes, sir.'

'Send me the details this evening. Lana was very loved, not least by us, there'll be a lot of people who'll want to be there. She should have the very best of send-offs.' So much for getting away with this quietly.

'We'll have something at our home after,' I said without thinking.

He hung up, leaving me to my head pain and remorse, and now a sulking kind of anger.

I put on a pair of sports shorts, a T-shirt, and grabbed my trainers. As I sat on the edge of the bed to put them on, my eyes caught on the miniature toolset – or was it a glasses repair

192

kit? – that I'd swiped from the old woman's purse the evening before. I picked it up, tucked it into the side pocket of my suit-case, then I left the house and headed for the beach. I needed to run, to sweat off the stress of the last two days, try and work up some energy to do what needed to be done. The beach was well populated with people. Sun-loungers and restaurants were full with lunch-goers, already sipping wine. I clocked up a couple of miles, then turned back on myself, jogging slowly to a walk.

By the time I got back to the house, I'd contacted the cre-matorium. I'd ordered catering to be delivered to our house for after the service and emailed all the details to Fred. I hit the send button with a pathetic kind of aggression, thinking how, when all this was over, I never had to see or talk to Fred Grosvenor ever again. The glee I felt at this was fleeting, eclipsed by growing dread and a wave of self-pity. I paused outside the open glass doors and looked out at the sea to where the mass of water met the horizon in a haze of light blue. I pressed the heel of my hand against my breastbone. I wanted to scream.

Later that evening, Gabe grabbed a bottle of Chardonnay and motioned towards the pontoon where two deckchairs sat facing the sea. We sat, Gabe lit a cigarette and we stared out at the grey-blue waters that surrounded the harbour. The waves slapped against the shoreline. A ledge of cloud was building on the horizon, the air becoming cooler.

I sipped slowly at the wine which had been left out too long and was sticky and warm in my throat. My time down here, away from the looks of pity, sympathy and questions, was nearing an end. Both Gabe and Holly had shut down almost all of my queries about what had taken place. My anger at being kept in the dark was only surpassed by the gnawing anxiety caused by the fact I'd yet to hear from Hunter. A constant reel played in my head of him receiving the DNA comparison between the remains in the hospital and the selection of Lana's possessions he'd retrieved from our house. I could see his odd little mouth, bottom lip rolling over top as his mind offered up theories around what had really happened. One look at my bank statement would point him in my direction. Thinking of Hunter took me back to my last conversation with him.

Gabe was slouched in his chair, a faraway look in his eyes and a tight line of concentration between his brows. He was dressed in a pair of soft blue jeans and a pale grey shirt. His feet were bare. As the evening light reflected from the sea, it cast one half of him in shadow, the lean of his nose to the left making it look like the opposing sides of his face were delineated by a zigzag line.

'Did you tell the police that Lana and I had argued in Mayfair?' I asked.

Gabe drew on his cigarette, then examined the tip as if confused about how it came to be in his hand. I thought he was going to fob me off again or tell me that this too was another piece of the puzzle I'd have to work without. But he didn't, and later I would think he was using that old tactic favoured by those expert in deception. Give your interrogator information, just not the important information.

'I thought it'd be more convincing to say that Lana would leave on an argument and then decide to go to her parents without contacting you,' he said. 'Hunter asked why she left the hotel. Despite what really happened, I felt he wouldn't buy that your wife had a headache and you let her leave alone. I thought this was best.'

'I denied that we'd argued,' I protested. 'Or at least one serious enough for her to leave the dinner.'

'As any husband would. But he knows something happened. He doesn't want loose ends flapping about here. He has a list, he'll check it twice. Are you naughty or nice?' He grinned at me. 'You know what it's like. When you've police sniffing around like this, when you know they know something, it's best to give them a little. No marriage is perfect, Myles. Personally, I wouldn't even attempt to convince them of that.'

I took a swig of wine, kept my eyes on the horizon and pretended to laugh. 'I thought our marriage was pretty perfect. Or at least I knew what to do so that it looked that way. I would have thought you and Holly are pretty close to perfection, no?' I said.

He read the tone in my voice and we were both quiet for a while.

'You asked Holly why we're doing this,' he stated. 'Maybe this will help you relax a little.' He leaned forward in his chair, looked back at the house, as if making sure no one else was in earshot, even though Holly was inside, settled in front of a movie. 'I couldn't say. I didn't want to say because –' he sighed – 'well, Holly wouldn't like it.'

I leaned in too, mirrored his posture, my elbow on my knee, head turned, all ears. This had been the crux of my concern from the moment Lana and I discussed the plan. Now, though, I knew it would only go halfway to eliminating my worries.

'It was my fault. I should have paid more attention really, but I get . . .' He sighed again. 'I'm a selfish bastard, Myles, that's the truth of it, and I don't deserve Holly. She was unhappy and I didn't see it or didn't want to see it.' He paused for a moment, looked out at the water, the cigarette, forgotten in his hand, sent blue tendrils of smoke curling up into the evening air. 'Between us . . .' He stopped, met my eyes.

'Go on.'

'Holly has a gambling problem. And not a small one,' he said. He ran a hand through his hair. 'Despite appearances, because of this problem we also have a cash-flow issue, if I can put it that way.' He sighed. 'Don't get me wrong, she's fine now, or as fine as she can be. I have to be careful, look for the signs and all that, and my wages will, in time, cover the debt –' he stumbled over the last word, as if it were foreign to his tongue – 'but we could certainly do with this money. It would allow us to move forward quickly. It's what she needs.'

At first, the statement stirred up anxiety. Made me question how well our plans had been talked through, hammered out. I worried that our entire scheme was simply another gamble to stoke a dopamine rush. Had my life, our lives, been thrown down on a roulette table where, despite my efforts, the outcome would be decided by a tiny round ball dancing to gravity at the spin of a wheel? But this information went some way to level the playing field between us. They needed this money. Maybe as much as I did. I looked at Gabe. He lifted his drink to his lips, rolling the wine slowly round his mouth before he swallowed. His brow was creased but otherwise he appeared as calm as the sea he gazed out on.

He threw the cigarette to the ground and shuffled down in his chair to stamp on it. 'You'll have the post-mortem results from

Hunter tomorrow,' he said. 'Then perhaps you'll begin to trust that this is going to work.'

I gave a half-shake of my head. The fact that he'd confided such a huge thing to me made me feel like I could be less cagey about my own feelings. 'Honestly, even if this was the perfect plan, I don't know how I'll get through the coming weeks. The barrage of questions, remembering what one person knows against the next. Not to mention the investigation the insurance company will undertake . . .' I wasn't a stranger to lying, which was why I knew this would be extremely difficult. 'And, I can't get the image of that woman out of my head. Tell me who she was.'

'Myles,' he sighed.

'We're doing this. I'm doing this. I don't like getting information after the fact, Gabe.' He leaned back in the chair, crossed his legs. 'Let's say that trust does not come naturally to me,' I said.

'Yet here we are,' he said. 'It's best you don't know.'

'If I'm going to cremate this person, I want to know who they are. Events haven't really gone to the plan we'd discussed.'

He pushed up his bottom lip. Sighed. 'A body came in, female, the right age. She was known to a few of the staff, homeless. Clean, though. Another RTA, so it fit. No one will be looking for her.'

I took a long breath. 'Name?'

He paused. Unsure whether to give me that. 'I don't know.'

'What about the paramedics? Surely they noticed the body was not recently deceased. And how did you make it look that a dead body was driving? I mean, she hit the windscreen, right? I saw the photos of the crash site.'

'Myles.' His voice firm. 'She was pronounced dead at the scene. Why look at what isn't a problem?'

'How did she do it?' I asked him. 'I can't quite work out how Lana got that body out there. How does a dead person crash a car?'

'I took care of it,' he said. 'That's all you need to know.'

'The burns?'

He sighed. 'A well-placed cigarette, helped along a little,' he said. 'With the bruising –' he motioned over his face – 'it was probably enough, but I didn't want to take any risks that the police would ask for a picture of Lana and suspect it wasn't her. The burns served that purpose.' He turned to face me; something in his expression said he was weighing up whether to tell me more. 'She said you'd do this.'

'Do what?'

He shook his head. 'She said you'd have difficulty . . . moving things on. I don't agree,' he said quickly. 'I realise we've not known each other very long, but perhaps I recognise something in you that your wife doesn't. That you can't see yourself.'

'And what is that?'

He stood, put his hand out to mine. I placed my palm in his and he pulled me upright. But he didn't let go of me completely, instead moved his hand to my shoulder and gave it a sharp shake, making me look him in the eye.

He leaned in, 'People like us –' and for a second I thought he meant me and him, and I felt a pathetic surge of pride, but he continued – 'like Lana and me, never fully understand what it really takes to get to our position in life. We believe we've the same drive, the same ambition as the next person, that if we found ourselves truly at the bottom of the ladder, we'd dig in those heels, bite down and begin the long push forward. But

198

we can't really know what we're capable of because even at the lowest point, we're still not touching bottom. But you. You! You have that grit, Myles. I can see it in you. The way you watch others, always assessing the ground under your feet. You are the grain of sand in the shell, Dr Myles Butler. Pearldom awaits.' He finished by turning me so that I was facing the sparkling lights of the harbour.

When I slipped between the fresh sheets that night, I lay on my back and replayed our conversation. I'd left the balcony door open. The wind had picked up, and every now and then the fine floor-length mesh curtains ballooned into the room like the sails of a ghost-ship.

There had been no call from Hunter. And I imagined arriving back to The Court only to be carted away by police. I thought through the crash. How they might have orchestrated it. A concrete brick on the pedal? But that only seemed plausible in movies. And there was the medical assessment to contend with. There's no way paramedics would have been fooled into thinking the victim had only just perished. There would have been a distinct lack of blood on the windscreen for one. Not to mention lividity and blanching of the skin along the woman's back. I thought about Gabe's deduction of me and realised he didn't expect me to believe the story offered, but he had faith I was capable of playing my part. That flush of pride I'd felt on the pontoon rose as swift as shame in me again. If I could suppress my suspicion that murder had been involved, there was part of me that admired the audaciousness of what he'd undertaken.

Lying in that bed, listening to the stir of the sea outside my window, I had to admit that a large part of my struggle with our plan was that I wanted nothing to do with it as well as everything to do with it. I wanted to have been the one alongside Gabe, forever holding to myself the outrageous secrets of that night. I imagined the exhilaration Lana must have felt when they'd pulled this off, knowing she was experiencing one of those events that shaped a life, an event that would stand vivid against the mulch of time and memory as if it had only happened yesterday. But she hadn't trusted me enough to bring me in on their plan, had even expressed her doubts to Gabe. The imposter syndrome I suffered like a chronic infection throughout my teen years erupted anew. I began to see Lana as that person who'd not only rejected me for the team but had taken my place. I was the egg pushed from the nest, the vestigial organ to be cut from the whole. Determined unusable, not capable of twisting my morals. I realised that I understood my wife about as well as she understood me.

CHAPTER 18

I walked down to the beach, morning espresso in hand, and watched the sun rise like a god over the horizon. A dog trotted along the shoreline, a large piece of driftwood in its mouth. The owner strode alongside, bag of shit swinging from his hand. I'd woken in a peculiar mood. Strangely focused and calm, even though everything there was to go through yesterday still waited for me today. But I had that familiar internal quiet that comes with acceptance, when the chips have been chucked into the air and no interference can dictate where they fall. I realised it was a feeling that had kept me company throughout most of my teens and university years, only a fingertip hooked on the reins of my life. And even though I had no right to feel comforted by that, I did.

I met Gabe for a breakfast of baked eggs and avocado. Holly rolled her yoga mat out on the grass and began her sun salutations.

'I thought we could take the RIB up the peninsula, have lunch in Poole,' he said.

I downed my coffee. 'Sure,' I said. 'You spoken with Lana today yet?'

'Not today,' he said. 'I'll check the fuel in the boat.' He bounded off down the garden, pausing only to drop a kiss on Holly's forehead.

I got up, carried my plate and cup to the dishwasher. My phone rang. Fred's calls had stopped, which strangely left me more uneasy. I removed my mobile from my pocket, half hoping it was him. But it was Hunter's number flashing on the screen.

I took a quick breath then pressed answer. 'Myles Butler,' I said.

'Dr Butler,' he said. 'Sorry it's taken me a little longer to get back to you.'

'You have a job to do,' I said, hoping I was striking the right note between weariness and empathy.

'We got what we needed from your house. Thank you for your patience. Everything is as expected,' he said. Did I imagine disappointment in his voice? 'We've also had the post-mortem report.' He paused. 'May I speak plainly? Sometimes, people who've lost a loved one want to know all the . . . um . . . details so if you'd prefer me to—'

'Thank you, Detective. It's hard to hear but yes, any information around how this has happened is helpful.'

'Okay. Well, initially, it had troubled me that it appeared unlikely the impact would have killed your wife,' he said. 'The injuries were extensive but didn't appear to be life-limiting.'

I waited.

'Sorry if this is upsetting—'

'It's okay.'

'Your wife had a mild heart condition. A weakness in one of the valves, so the doc's told me. They can't be certain, but they believe the shock of the impact would have been enough to cause her death,' he said.

A heart condition. Gabe's voice emerged from my memories:

There seems nothing more mechanical, nothing more robust yet fragile, than this soft human machine. We are but complex engineering controlled by nothing more than chemistry and physics.

'We're able to release your wife's remains to you,' Hunter was saying.

'Thank you, Detective,' I mumbled.

'We also found a wedding band. I think I recall that you were wearing yours when we spoke.'

I looked down at my hand. 'Yes.' I flushed the ring, but it mustn't have gone down the drain.

'Your wife's then?' Hunter was asking.

'It must be.'

'Only . . . Linda, is it? Your cleaner. I happened to speak to her and she believes she saw you with it.'

I closed my eyes. Why was he talking to Linda? I tried to keep my voice even. 'That's right. Yes, it was in my back pocket, it probably fell out when I went to the loo.'

'Thought it would be something like that.'

'Thank you again for your call, Detective,' I said, and hung up.

I stood against the glossy kitchen counter and looked out at Holly as she balanced on one leg, the other foot tucked up along her groin, her hands joined in a point above her head. On the counter beside me was her camera. I glanced out at her again, then reached for the Nikon. I turned the playback screen towards me and switched it on. The screen sprang to life with a beep. I scrolled back through her photos. Pictures of houses I recognised from along the harbour. Then more, similar to what I'd seen framed in their home. Desolate, lonely places, neglected and left to the hungry mouth of time. I stopped at one. A small wooden lodge. It was different to the others. Surrounded by tall, dark pine trees, and a small clearing to the side about the width of a car. But this property was cared for, a place of refuge or escape. In the small eye of the front window, there stood a ghostly figure.

I zoomed in. It was Holly. Dressed in white, the baby blonde of her hair giving her an other-worldly appearance. A felt a frisson of excitement in my gut. Did they own this place? Was this where Lana was whiling away the days until all this was over? I clicked on the image, hoping there was an indication on where it was taken. But there was nothing. I took out my phone and took a picture of the image on the screen. Holly was now lying on the yoga mat, her face turned up to the sky, her eyes closed. I knew from Lana's yoga practice that this signalled the end of her session.

I clicked through more of the photos until I came across one of The Court. Again, it was unusual, as it was the only one that didn't capture the front of a house. Instead, she'd taken a picture of the gates that accessed our small residential street. There was a sense of longing about the picture. She'd angled the lens so that the view was at eye-level, peering through the black iron bars of the gates like a child waiting to be let in. I looked out of the window. She was rolling up her mat. I flicked forward through the pictures until I arrived at the one she'd taken most recently, then turned the camera off and returned it to the counter.

★

In the afternoon, we took the RIB across to Poole harbour. Gabe stood at the wheel, his hair blown back, a hand lazily adjusting the boat through the waves. I clung to the seat, feeling increasingly seasick. When we got to the harbour, he killed the engine and let us bob slowly towards the quay. He leapt from the boat, then extended a hand and pulled me out onto the jetty.

It was an odd day but Gabe was good company and it surprised me how many people appeared to know him by name as we walked by restaurants, shops and bars. He insisted we stop at a favourite tailor's; a good suit, he said, is never a poor investment. It wasn't until I was measured up and he'd insisted that the navy did little for my colour and that the black was the better choice, that it dawned on me that this was for the funeral. Next, down a narrow lane, squeezed between old fishermen's cottages, a barber swept a cut-throat razor over my jaw and shaped my hair. The result was impressive. I hadn't realised how worn round the edges I'd become, how jaded I appeared. But as I sat in front of that mirror, it was as if he'd unearthed some previous or unknown version of myself.

By the time we returned to the spit, the sun was high and hot in the sky. I was full on lobster and champagne, my eyelids drooping, the first of a sunburn kissing my forehead. The engine slowed, then jolted to speed again. I sat up and immediately felt queasy. Gabe pulled back on the throttle. Holly was on the pontoon. A man was there with her. Even above the roar of the engine, you could hear her shouting. As we got closer, Gabe slowed to moor.

I looked at the man on the pontoon. He had a worryingly thin physique, a large jaw, wide eyes and sloping nose. Gabe leapt from the boat just as the man grabbed Holly's shoulders; leaving me to scrabble with the rope.

In the short time it took for me to clamber out of the boat and tie it to the pontoon, Gabe had an arm around the man's shoulders and was guiding him through the wooden side gate towards the street and away from the house. He spoke to the man in low, even tones, almost soothing, a patient tutor coaching a disobedient student. All I caught of the conversation was the man's voice, close to tears as he asked, 'Help me find her, please.'

Holly folded her arms, rubbed the bare skin as if to warm herself.

'You okay?' I asked, looking down at her.

A sigh and an attempt at a reassuring smile. 'Yes,' she said, glancing up at me, eyes watering. 'He's an old patient of Gabe's. He gets scared and . . . well . . . only wants to speak to his sur- geon.' She glanced over my shoulder.

Help me find her, please. Once again, I was back in the hospital, Hunter's breath on my neck as the nurse drew back the white sheet from the woman who was to take my wife's place in death.

Charlotte pulled me into a hug. 'I'm so sorry, Myles.'

There were purplish marks under her eyes, a delta of tiny red thread veins over the whites. She'd spared herself her usual mascara and her pale lashes were sparse, spiky and wet. She scrubbed her nose with a tissue. 'What a shock.'

I nodded. An ache in my throat at how many people had turned up for Lana's funeral. It was moving. At times, as I looked back over the congregation, heads bowed in respect, shoulders shaking with emotion, it was not difficult to cry. It was sad. And

206

in many ways, I was grieving. It had been over two weeks since Hunter had knocked on my door in the early morning and I was still finding it impossible to accept that life, as I knew it, was over. In the eyes of these friends and members of family, I was now a widower.

'Thank you, Charlotte.' I held her hand in both of mine, glanced over her shoulder. 'Where's Daniel?'

Her bottom lip did that twisting thing that signalled another wave of emotion.

'He's not here,' she said, her voice a whisper. 'We're taking a break.'

'I'm sorry,' I said.

She pulled herself upright. 'Don't you worry about us, just take care of yourself, and we're ... I'm just across the street if you need anything. And Daniel too, I know he'll want to be there for you,' she said.

Charlotte hooked a loose strand of hair behind her ear, then looked back at the small church at the front of the crematorium. 'I can't believe she's gone.' She brought her hand to her mouth, chewed along the tip of the nail on her index finger. 'What on earth happened?'

She shook her head, put her hand on my forearm and squeezed. 'Sorry,' she said again. 'Don't answer that. Another time maybe.' She looked me over. 'You look nice though. New suit?'

'I thought I should try to clean myself up,' I said. 'For Lana.'

'She would have fancied you rotten in that.'

'Will you come to the wake,' I asked. Hoping she'd say yes. It might be worth having an ally of sorts when Lana's dad began to throw verbal spears at me.

'At the house?'

'Yes,' I said.

'Of course. I'll be there,' she said.

Linda had agreed to meet and greet at the door so there was no need for me to hurry back to the house. There'd be plenty of time to tend to those who wanted to give Lana a send-off worthy of my Irish heritage. My dad, Ambie, would have commandeered the front room already, in easy reach of the spirits. My father had dealt with news of Lana dying in the same way he dealt with any other hour of any other day; he asked for a drink. But for once, I was grateful for my dad's lack of interest or awareness of what was going on in my life. I would have been happier for him to have stayed in Bristol, but it was important that everyone who'd be expected to attend Lana's funeral was there. I'd driven back to Bristol the night before, dreading the visit the entire way. The moment I'd stepped into the house, the old familiar smells caught me right in the throat. Stale booze and damp, the scent of fried onions and liver. My hand had reached for the light switch, turning it down halfway, a knack for the wiring to catch and the walls of my teen years had pressed in around me.

I sat in my car and watched the mourners make their way to theirs. On the other side of the car park, another family was gathering. Death's conveyor belt. I looked towards the crematorium, imagined the body inside. I wasn't religious but I found myself whispering what I could recall of the Prayer for the Dead.

I rubbed tiredness from my eyes and started the car. Just as I pulled free of the car park, I saw the detective, Hunter, propped against his red Escort. I slowed, pulled over.

'Thank you for coming, Detective. I'm sorry I didn't see you inside,' I said.

He leaned both his hands on the open window. 'I didn't want to intrude, so waited here.' He handed me Lana's phone, then held out a clear bag; inside was Lana's wedding band. I took the bag and murmured my thanks.

His fingers tapped one by one on the car door. I knew that he couldn't quite pin me down, but like a dog sensing thunder, he knew there was something. Something wrong with me. 'You know,' he said, ' when we found the ring, it reminded me of a case I worked years ago. A man who killed his wife had sewn her wedding ring into the lining of his pillowcase so he could feel it beneath him when he slept. Some people who . . . How can I put this? . . .' Then he lifted the corner of his mouth briefly in an 'Ah, well' gesture. 'Murderers, they like to take something. They like trophies. It gives them a little buzz to hold it. Takes them back to the thrill of the kill.' My bladder gave a painful squeeze. 'I guess the habit could start out with minor theft. A pen here, a key ring there. Not saying that every thief becomes a killer.' He looked down at the ring in its cellophane bag. 'What I mean is, taking a trophy in any way, theft or otherwise, is simply irresistible to some offenders.'

I wanted to slam my foot against the accelerator and put as much distance between Hunter and myself as possible.

'I don't understand what you're trying to say,' I said. What could I say except that I didn't understand? But I understood, and he knew I understood. I replied how the guilty always reply, with a question. *Why on earth would I try to flush her wedding ring down the toilet if I wanted it for a trophy?* When, clearly, I should have said I'd no idea what he was talking about.

He was quiet for a long moment, his eyes locked on mine. Then, he straightened away from the car. 'It was just a stray thought,' he said.

I made myself pull away slowly. He grew smaller in the rear-view mirror as I went, but his gaze didn't lift from my car until I turned a bend and disappeared from his line of sight.

By the time I got to The Court, most of the guests were there. Fred's obnoxious Ford Ranger was blocking the drive, so I parked on the street, just outside the Wrights' house. I took a moment to compose myself. The onslaught of grief was quite a lot to digest. The guilt attached to putting people through Lana's death had taken me by surprise. I wondered whether Lana had thought that far, how the decision to go down this path affected many more people than ourselves. The further we went down this road of deceit, the more difficult it became to extricate ourselves. For all intents and purposes, however this panned out, if we were discovered or not, this would be the last time our friends and family stood in our home as friends and family.

Two hours, that's all I had to get through, and Linda had been primed to start clearing the food away after the first hour and gathering coats shortly after. I got out of the car and was about to cross the street when I noticed a man outside the Wrights' house. Him. The same man that Holly had struggled with in Sandbanks. *Help me find her, please.*

'Hello,' I said. I walked towards him.

He turned. He was young. Early thirties There was a sprinkle of acne over his lower jaw and a centimetre-wide strip of white in the front of his hair.

He took a few steps away from the house, thumbed the air over his shoulder. 'Wondered if he was in?'

'Who?'

'Gabriel. Mr Wright.'

I looked him up and down. He was wearing a padded jacket, zipped up to the neck, but his blue jeans were stained, mud-flecked along the ankles, dull stains on the knees, a small circular patch of what looked like blood on the toe of one trainer.

'Have you tried his mobile?' I asked.

He shook his head. 'He's not working. I know that,' he said, in a way that made me feel like he shouldn't have that kind of information.

'I saw you. At the harbour. Maybe if you tell me what's going on, I could help?' I asked. 'I'm a doctor.' You'd be surprised how often that one line makes people trust you immediately.

'I don't know,' he said, looking down at his trainer. He bit his lip, thought for a moment. 'My girlfriend, well, my ex, she's missing.' He scratched a hand over the inside of his forearm. His jacket rode up. His skin red raw.

'I don't understand. What's that got to do with Gabe?'

'They worked together. In York,' he said. He made air-quotes around 'worked'.

I swallowed. 'I'll tell him you want to speak to him if I see him.'

He began to shake his head. 'He just lies.' He looked up at me, watery gaze, red-rimmed. 'He knows. She loved him, you see. He told her all sorts, that he was going to leave his wife for her. The usual fucking fairy-tale that never ends in happily ever after. I tried to tell her, tell her that men like Gabriel Wright

211

don't leave their wives for people like us. But he has a way . . .'
He bit down on his lip again, a little bubble of blood appeared.
'He's a way of convincing you. He said he'd help me look for
her, but he lied.'

'I'll tell him,' I said, more firmly this time. The man was
making me nervous. I didn't want him following me inside the
house and creating trouble.

'Wait,' he said. He put his hand in his pocket. For a moment,
I thought he was going to produce a knife. I flinched and took a
step back. 'Here. Maybe you've seen her? Or could keep an eye
out. I'm Pete, Pete Clifford. This is Violet Dryden.'

I glanced down at the photo.

'I haven't seen her. Look, this is my wife's funeral,' I said. 'I'd
really appreciate if you came back another time.' I could hear
the shake in my voice.

'Yeah, I'm sorry, Doc. It was a nice service,' he said. I didn't
like that he'd been at Lana's funeral. 'Sorry.' He returned the
photo to his pocket, then backed away.

I waited until he passed the gates of The Court.

Inside, Fred followed me into the kitchen. I'd hired caterers
but I couldn't quite bring myself to listen to tales of how Lana
had touched individual friends. I tucked my tie into my shirt,
rolled up my sleeves. I opened the dishwasher and began rinsing
plates and loading them into the machine.

'Myles,' he said.

I kept my back to him for a second, then turned. 'Fred.'

'This is a good spread,' he said. It was as close to a 'well done'
as I could expect to get from him. 'Julie's not taking it so well.'

'Understandable,' I said.

'She's our only child. It's not only Lana we've lost,' he said. Meaning the grandchildren he blamed me for not providing.

I washed my hands, dried them on a tea towel. Waited for what he really wanted to say.

'At the service, I spoke to that detective. I came to the house when they were searching it. You'd just left.' Suddenly, Hunter's strange little anecdote about trophies and the like made more sense. Fred could never resist painting me in a bad light. And now he had me to blame for his daughter's death.

Turning away, I made a show of looking for something in one of the cupboards. 'They weren't searching the house. They needed a few things, to formally identify the body.'

'I got the impression he doesn't seem very convinced by your story,' he said.

Closing the cupboard, I faced him. 'My story?'

He looked down at his hand. Fingers stroking the corner of the island, searching for imperfections. 'You were never good enough for her,' he said.

I sighed. 'Fred, please.'

He waited a full ten seconds. This was one of his favourite manipulative tactics. I bit down on the back of my tongue.

'You're going to do quite nicely out of her death, aren't you? The amount of money I sank into this house. I did it for her. And now—'

I felt my nails bite into my palm as I made a fist. He flicked his eyes at my hand. Grinned. 'Don't worry, we're leaving,' he said. He leaned in, lowered his voice. 'You're a wrong 'un. I could smell it on you the first time we met. It was a fault of Lana's, she couldn't resist a rescue case like yours. But I see you,

213

Myles, and you will fuck up, and when you do, I'll be there to make sure you get what you deserve.'

'Myles.' Charlotte's voice. She held out an apple tart, in a foil tin. 'I brought this. I reckon it will go in the freezer.'

I let out a long breath. Fred, his eyes rigid on mine and bulging, stepped back with what appeared to take considerable effort, then turned and strode out of the room.

'Sorry, did I interrupt something?' Charlotte asked, all innocence, but I knew she had sensed the friction and had come to my rescue.

'No,' I said. I reached out to take the apple tart from her, fingers shaking. 'This is thoughtful of you. Thanks.'

She waved that away. 'I'm going to miss her.'

I slid the dessert into the freezer. 'I miss her too.'

'You'll be okay, right?' she asked, her brow creased.

I dragged a long breath in through my nose. 'I don't know,' I said.

She walked towards me and pulled me into a hug. She held me a fraction too long. Her cheek against my neck. When she drew back, she glanced behind her towards the living room. Gabe was in there talking to my dad.

'We had a little drama while you were away,' she said, her voice low. 'Did he tell you about it?'

'Who?'

'Gabe?'

'No.'

'There was an attempted break-in. Or they think there was.'

Immediately, I thought of Pete Clifford. 'The Wrights?'

'The police, but yes, at the Wrights'. The alarm went off in

214

the middle of the night. The security company wouldn't turn it off until the police reached the owner. The landlord,' she raised her eyebrows. 'They're renting,' she whispered.

She waited for my reaction. 'Right,' I said. I turned down my mouth, shrugged. 'So they're renting.'

'Of course. Just first impressions and all that. I thought they owned it, is all. Maybe they're not as well-off as they like to portray. Anyway, you might want to double check your alarms, the locks. The gates don't keep everyone out, it seems, and you've enough to deal with without . . .' She trailed off.

'Thanks, Charlotte,' I said, maybe a little sharper than I intended.

I walked out to the back garden, grabbing a glass and a bottle of brandy as I went. The knowledge that the Wrights were renting shouldn't bother me. It was a snobbish titbit of gossip that Charlotte had typically lighted on, but for some reason it lodged like a splinter in my brain.

I sat down on a bench at the bottom of the garden, poured a glass and took a slow drink.

'How you holding up?' Gabe was coming down the garden.

He sat next to me when he reached the bench.

'I don't know,' I said. 'One day, I think I can do this, the next I'm comforting our friends as they grieve for my wife –' I lowered my voice – 'who is not dead. It's fucked-up.'

He put a hand on my shoulder as he had done on the pontoon that evening, and I stared back at the house and sipped the brandy.

'You know I lived not too far from here when I was a child?' I said.

Gabe sat down beside me. 'I didn't know that.'

'Perhaps a little closer to New Malden.' I swallowed another mouthful. 'Dad owned a series of restaurants. Mum stayed at home, looked after me. It was a great childhood. Perfect, I'd say. Then we lost everything. Everything,' I said. 'It's taken me a whole life to get it back.'

I wasn't sure why I was telling him this. Perhaps there was part of me that hoped to make a silent plea to him not to drag me into something deeper, something darker. Even though, deep down, I knew it was already too late. The appearance of Pete Clifford made me uneasy. When he told me about his missing ex-girlfriend, I was cast back to the night Lana threw me out and I slept in the car. How I'd woken up to see Gabe on the street with that woman. And I'd an unwelcome flash of the remains at the hospital. As devoted as Gabe appeared to be to Holly, he didn't strike me as the monogamous type. Was he having an affair with this woman? And if he was, where was she now?

'Did you know Violet Dryden?' I asked.

He tensed. It was brief, like the transient twitch of muscle beneath a lion's skin before it leaps.

'You spoke to Pete?' he asked, following the question with a weary sigh. He didn't wait for me to reply. 'I had an affair with Violet, his ex, who he can't seem to let go,' he said, then turned to me, looked me in the eye. 'It's been over a long time. Two years now. Then a few weeks ago, she turned up here. She wanted help. She'd got caught up in something and needed money.'

'What did she get caught up in?'

He shook his head. 'I never asked. I didn't want to know. Holly and I had only just moved here. We wanted a clean break.

216

Holly knew about the affair but it was behind us. This was a fresh start for all of us.' He paused. 'Violet said she needed to get out of the country. She said she couldn't tell anyone. Pete stalked her relentlessly. I got the feeling that she was fearful of what he would do and wanted to get away. I gave her enough money to keep her fed and watered for a month, drove her to the station, and I haven't seen her since. Pete, though, won't hear it. He's convinced I'm in touch with her. I don't know what to do about it. Every time he appears, it brings up the affair all over again for Holly.'

Gabe didn't know I'd seen him that evening with Violet. The fact he'd volunteered the information about the affair made me relax, made the bubble of distrust that had expanded inside me, melt away. This was one of the many mistakes I made. Or maybe one of the many he made.

He looked back towards the house. 'Part of me wants to photograph this.' A glance at me. 'For Lana? I think she'd be quite moved by the turnout, no?'

CHAPTER 19

I pushed two paracetamol out of the blister pack, stood over the kitchen sink and washed them down with water. Then, I filled a fresh glass and carried it through to the man sitting at our dining table. Andrew Holstein had arrived as promised at 11 a.m. on the dot, not a moment before or after.

'Thank you, Dr Butler,' he said. Deep, gravelly voice that could have been lifted from a BBC broadcast from the forties. 'I am almost finished here.'

He wore a wool suit that was some mix of moss green and brown. A waistcoat to match. Sturdy, brown leather shoes that had worn around the knuckles of his toes and sagged outward at the heel. He moved swiftly through the papers, occasionally stopping to ask me a question.

'What was the cause of the accident?' he asked. He knew all this. Had spent weeks requesting any medical and financial information that could pertain to Lana's death. I knew the questions were asked over and again to see if I would trip up. It might be easy to lie but it's not so easy to repeat the same lie over and again.

'They're not sure. It had been raining and the roads were greasy. They think she might have been trying to light a cigarette,' I said.

He thought on this, consulted a printout of a roadmap he had at his elbow. As he turned his hand, the light caught on his cufflink. A silver die.

'Hmm.' He returned to the paperwork. Then closed over his folder. 'If you'll just sign here,' he passed a declaration form to me and I pretended to look it over for a few seconds, then scrawled my signature and the date across the bottom.

He slotted the form back in the folder, then put the lot into his open briefcase.

He stuck his arm out. 'Give it five working days, Dr Butler, and it should be in the assigned account.'

I shook his hand, he stood, grasped his briefcase. 'I'm sorry for your loss.' And he was gone.

It had been a week since Lana's funeral. I'd spent it in a blur of sleep and work worrying about this meeting, and now it was over I couldn't quite believe it. It was that easy. Just like Gabe said it would be. As Lana believed it would be.

I went to the kitchen and made myself a coffee. Outside, the Wrights' drive was empty. It was a dull afternoon and there was a light on along the top floor. Another in the living room. I'd not spoken to them since the funeral. Gabe had been away most of the week. A conference or retreat in the Lake District, Holly said. But I sensed there was contact with Lana somewhere along the way. He'd returned sometime late last night. Holly I'd seen from time to time as she moved around their kitchen. Occasionally, I'd catch a glimpse of her blonde hair as she walked their back garden to admire the green foliage and deep red peonies or I'd see her with her camera bag, climbing into her car, off to capture more buildings.

No one had called to visit me. Despite all the promises at Lana's service, people seemed eager to move on, to move away from grief. I admit, I enjoyed the reprieve from having to field the numerous variations of 'Sorry for your loss' and lingering stares where you're forced to trade your grief so others felt like they'd done their duty.

The sky darkened, turning from silver to slate, and along with it the wind stirred, ruffling the heads of the great sycamores, oaks and cedars that crowded the boundaries at the end of The Court. The silver birch that lined the street shivered in the breeze and the first droplets of rain struck the living-room doors. Soon, the rain was coming down hard, bouncing from the pavement. Daniel's BMW snaked by, the wipers scudding across the windscreen. He pulled up at No. 3 and hurried to the porch. He shook out his hair as he waited. The door opened, and a rucksack was passed out. He took it, pointed inside, then out at the car. The door closed. He waited for a moment staring at the door, then turned and hurried back to the car.

I moved away from the window. It could have been my fate. Divorced, sleeping in the surgery or pleading with Nathan to let me take his spare room until I'd paid off some of my debts. This recession could have dropped me right back to where I began. A long curling snake back to the start to scrape the barrel. I'd been wrong to underestimate Lana. I should have trusted she'd pull this off for both of us.

'You don't trust that the ground you walk on will not give way,' she said to me one morning.

It was about a month after Madison had joined the surgery and I confided in Lana that I thought she could be my replacement. From the moment of our meeting, Madison looked at me as if I'd already disappointed her. Her pandering to Nathan trod the line between patronising and nauseating. How she fluttered about him, bringing him tea so that they could have a *chat*, a box of doughnuts from his favourite bakery on a Friday, lighting up when she spoke about all they could do for the surgery going forward.

'You're a brilliant doctor,' Lana had said. 'Nathan knows that. And if he doesn't, you have me. And nothing on this earth could prise me from your side.' She stretched up over my chest, kissed my chin. 'I'm stitched right down the seam of your soul.'

I was lucky. We were lucky. But I felt, not for the first time in our marriage, conflicted. We'd just pulled off insurance fraud, but I couldn't say I was happy. I felt an urgent need to speak with her. She had ways of straightening out the crooked and fractured lines of my thoughts. I sent Gabe a text. *I need to talk to her.* I needed to plan. I wasn't yet ready to give up my practice at the surgery. I had been thinking of ways where I could still work at Willowhaven while simultaneously preparing a move elsewhere. The doctor I'd spoken to during drinks at the beach house, Anthony Chapman, had fleshed out what could be my future, our future. If I could hold on to my place at the practice, if I could hold Madison off, I'd run it one day. And that day might not be too far off. I knew Nathan was itching to retire. From there I could expand, develop multiple practices as Anthony had done, run them from afar. I could be with Lana and not have to let go of what I'd worked a lifetime for. So many years, clawing my way forward, so many times holding on to squeeze out an opportunity in the last moment. But there were ways we could, as they say, have it all.

Outside the rain eased. A temporary break. A patch of blue sky sent streaks of sunshine through the haze and a rainbow shimmered over the gleaming slate roofs of Belvedere Court. I waited for Gabe to reply. Three dots flashed in a slow rhythm beneath my message, then disappeared. Walking into the dining room, I went to the lounge area and sat in one of the deep tub chairs we'd settled in that night. I pictured Gabe, as he was when they made us the offer. In control, calmly laying out how we'd untangle ourselves from our debt. His blue eyes, dark in the low light. The smoke from the cigar swelling out into the room. Holly listening, her feet tucked under her like a child. The boldness of their plan dressed up as if it were a joke. A simple game of what if.

It could be that memory is not to be trusted. That the brain, in its effort to make use of our experiences, repackages them so they follow a sensible narrative. And so, I can't wholly trust my recollections because that night had taken on a relevance, a prominence in my mind, that could only have been awarded in hindsight. But I must have heard the change in the atmosphere, like a dog picking up a high-pitch whistle, soundless to the human ear. The more I think on it, the more fresh details emerge from the memory. The quick flashes of concern that Holly threw my way, which I put down to some other personal anxiety. The meaningful look Gabe sent to Lana, right before he started talking. A feeling that all of it had already been discussed and the entire conversation had been engineered for my benefit.

I got up, found my phone on the table, moved to the sofa and lay down. I opened up a search engine, scrolled through all the many keywords and phrases I'd used since I'd found that picture on Holly's camera. Cabin in woods. Remote cottages for hire. Rentals in the Lake District. New Forest. Brecon. I scanned through the images but it was the needle in the haystack. I closed the search windows then pulled up Lana's old number. I hit DIAL and let it ring until the call clicked through, then talked into her voicemail, all my worries and frustrations. I drifted off to sleep feeling like I had just said goodbye.

CHAPTER 20

I sat at my desk in the surgery and stared at the computer. Violet Dryden's face filled the screen. I had searched for her on social media, eventually landing on Pete Clifford's Facebook page, and there she was. The two of them. Violet, late thirties, dark hair, not so like Lana, too slim, skin a shade too pale. Beside her, Pete, his face pressed up close to hers, nose to nose. He looked better in this picture than any time I'd seen him. His skin clear, hair trimmed, the shadows gone from his cheeks, less of that shifting anxiety in his eyes. He had a hand lifted, index finger pointing in the direction of Violet's ear. The caption read *New Ink*. I stared at the three black stars newly embedded in her skin.

A cold sensation of dread dropped through me. It descended slowly from the top of my skull, down over my face, where it sucked the moisture from my mouth before settling around my throat like an icy hand.

I fell back in my chair. The tattoo was identical to the one Lana had done in the weeks before the accident. I recalled the nurse asking me about identifying marks on my wife's body.

Yes, I heard myself say again, she has a tattoo. The remains I'd cremated had been those of Violet Dryden. I ran a hand over my face, then taking a deep breath opened another tab.

I searched for the number of Gabe's old hospital, then picked up my handset and dialled. I navigated the usual obstacle course of automated attendants until I got to an operator.

'Merryfield switchboard,' a woman's voice said.

'Hello, this is Dr Myles Butler. I'm trying to get in touch with a patient about some blood work. I believe she works there.'

'We can't give out those details, Doctor,' she said. 'You could email the relevant department.'

'Ah, yes, sorry. I will. What department is that?'

'Name?'

'Violet Dryden.'

'Mortuary Services. But it says on our system she finished a few months ago. You need the email address for the department?'

'No thank you. I've found it on your site. Thanks for your help,' I said, and ended the call.

Then I searched for St Anne's Hospital. I navigated to the consultants' page. Scrolled through the departments until I found Cardiology. I opened the page and taking my time rolled down through the team of staff. There was no Gabriel Wright listed. Fissures were opening up in the perfect façade the Wrights had presented to us. I felt foolish. Then angry. I lifted the phone again. Dialled St Anne's Hospital. Once more the operator.

'I'm a GP in Wimbledon, I have a patient on my books who needs an urgent referral to a cardiologist. I had a recommendation for one of your consultants, a Mr Gabriel Wright, but can't see his contact details on your website.'

'Please hold,' the voice said.

Warbling music came down the line. I pulled my mobile forward and read the reply I got from Gabe. He'd sent it close to midnight. *Timing's not right. Soon. G.* I recalled the scratch on his jaw the day I'd gone round to theirs after being at the hospital. I'd assumed it was a shaving cut. I'd noticed a limp as he'd walked through to the kitchen to pour a drink. He limped because he'd been with Violet when the car slammed into that tree. If Violet had been alive at the time of the accident, she had to be the one driving. It had to be her head that hit the windscreen on the driver's side. The scene had to look convincing. The injuries matching impact. An ache started up in my temples and I pinched the bridge of my nose.

'Doctor . . . ?'

'Butler.'

'Thank you. I'm sorry but we don't have a consultant of that name working with us.'

There was a light tap on the door.

'Are you sure?'

'Yes.'

I hung up, changed the browser on my computer just as Nathan stepped in.

'Myles, good, you're in.' He crossed the room, sat down in the chair reserved for patients and rested a cup of tea on the desk.

'Let me say again how sorry I am about Lana,' he said. He removed his glasses, looked at me with those dog-sad eyes, the lids drooping onto his cheeks.

'Thank you,' I replied. 'And for the flowers at the funeral.'

226

His chin drew in, his cheeks grew pink. 'It was a lovely service, Myles. For a very special person. How are you?'

'Not great, to be honest.' I rubbed a hand over my face. The tattoo appeared as a series of red blotches behind my eyes.

Glasses back on. 'I thought perhaps you could do with a little more time off.'

I frowned at him. 'I need to work.'

He cleared his throat. I could see he wanted to say no. I knew Nathan better than my own father at times. He reached into his pocket and removed a card of antacids, pushed four out of the packet and dropped them one by one into his mouth. I waited as he crunched through them, the heel of his hand going to his chest and massaging them down to work their magic.

'Myles, you know I've always backed you. In some ways, you've felt like a son to me,' he said. His face flushed. 'Sofia and I were never blessed with children and there are no other medics in our family so I had imagined that in time, with the right investment, you'd take over here as senior clinician.' He looked up at me over the tops of his glasses. 'Even as owner, if that was the way you had wanted to go. I would have been happy knowing our patients and my legacy was in good hands.'

'Would have?'

'I know about the insurance fraud,' he said.

I blinked. For a second, I imagined that despite fooling the insurance handler and the beady-eyed Hunter, Nathan had somehow uncovered the truth about Lana.

He went on. 'Look, you made a mistake, you are in some financial difficulty – and we can probably smooth things over with the patients.'

The false medical claims. I'd almost forgotten about that.

'It was a cash-flow thing, nothing more,' I said. 'I wasn't thinking. I'm truly sorry. You have to believe me when I say it will never happen again.' When he didn't respond, I gave a short laugh of disbelief. 'Nathan, come on. After everything we've achieved together, you have to give me a second chance. I've been through hell these last weeks, I can't lose my job as well as Lana. It's who I am.'

He closed his eyes briefly, shutting me out. 'I'm sorry,' he said, shaking his head. 'I could almost overlook it as desperation if you'd taken the money from the surgery itself. But you've taken it from patients.'

'Insurance companies,' I corrected, before I could stop myself. He sighed, and I added, 'I know. I know it was wrong.'

He pushed a hand against his chest, then reached for his tea and took a hasty mouthful. 'I'm not sure you do,' he said quietly.

That hurt.

'Nathan,' I said. I didn't have to fake the emotion. There was a chill creeping into his voice. Impatience. He'd made up his mind on something. And Nathan rarely made up his mind on his own.

Madison.

'I can give you a few months,' he said. 'Give you a chance to find another position, which shouldn't be a problem with your credentials.' A brief glance over the top of his glasses. 'I'll give you a good reference. You're a good GP, Myles. The patients like you, but I need to work with people I can trust.'

'Nathan, please—'

He held up a hand. 'I've made up my mind.'

I sat for a moment more, trying to swallow down my anger,

telling myself not to forfeit the good reference. I'd need it in the coming months. Perhaps fate had taken a turn at the wheel, the universe wiping away all my options until all that remained was to leave this life behind. I stood up. Nathan too. He shook my hand.

'Go home. Digest matters.' He looked me over. 'Cool down a bit. Get organised,' he said. He could barely meet my eyes. It wasn't me who needed to cool down.

'Nathan, please. I'm here now, I might as well see out today at least.'

He opened his mouth and I could see the word, 'no' forming on his lips but he hesitated then, 'All right, finish up with the rest of your patients.'

'Thank you,' I said quietly. Madison had managed it, risen to the top as Nathan's golden child. She must be about to spontaneously combust with happiness. She'd be who'd take over here when Nathan retired, which looked like it couldn't happen soon enough for him. It shouldn't have bothered me, given that I was likely going to have to move anyway, but I'd already begun to shape my future in my mind and that future included Willowhaven.

'Would you mind not saying anything yet? To Madison, the staff, the patients. I know I've no right to ask, but if it got out I might struggle to get another position.'

He frowned, but eventually he nodded. 'Of course. I'll keep it between us for the next month.'

I nodded. 'Thank you, Nathan.'

He patted the back of my hand. 'You'll be okay, Myles.'

'I always am,' I returned.

He left and I sat staring at the closed door for a full minute, resentment glowing like a burning ember in the pit of my stomach. I finished the day's clinic then sat at my desk and began clearing the internet search history from my computer, tidying up my notes and updating patient records. Before I left, I stood at the door, my work bag in hand and looked in at my consulting room, a lump swelling in my throat. I walked up the hallway but before I turned the corner into the reception, I heard Madison's voice then Sam's faltering reply. I guessed from Madison's conspiratorial tone that their topic of conversation centred on me.

'I'm just asking should Dr Butler ask you to file any unusual paperwork, let me know. Or if complaints come in, that you notify me,' she said, her voice low and strained.

'Um . . . usually Dr Kingston deals with any that come in.'

'There have been complaints then?'

'Not recently,' a pause, as if he was considering telling her something. 'I'm not comfortable doing this.'

Finally, some loyalty.

'We need to look out for the practice,' Madison pushed. 'If something does come to light, publicly, something serious, all of us suffer.'

'Dr Butler has been under a lot of pressure,' Sam sounding uncertain. 'He's just lost his wife.'

'I know,' her voice softened. 'I get that,' she said, 'and it's very thoughtful of you to think of him. But it's patient care first. And frankly, I'm not sure that has ever been Dr Butler's priority. Even Dr Kingston is worried.'

'He is? He's not said anything to me,' Sam said.

'He's not said so directly,' she gave a little sigh of frustration, 'But you know how Nathan is.'

'I guess.'

Her voice dropped even lower. I held my breath. 'Between you and me, Nathan is preparing to retire. He's implied that I'll be named senior clinician here at Willowhaven. All of us,' she emphasised, 'all of us should be thinking of where we want to be in a few years.'

A mean tactic. She might as well have said you scratch my back and I'll scratch yours. I didn't give Sam a chance to reply.

'Well done today, Sam. It was non-stop,' I said with a smile. I flicked a glance at Madison. 'Dr Lopez.'

'Myles,' she said. She had the decency to blush.

'Sam, those hours you were looking to take off next week are fine,' I said.

'Really?' Sam said, a smile breaking across his face.

'Wait,' Madison said. 'There's no one to cover front desk.'

'We'll manage,' I said, feeling a jab of satisfaction that I wouldn't be the one dealing with the upheaval.

I drove back, a foul humour stinking up the air around me. All the threads I'd held in my hand were slipping from my grasp. Dealing with Madison and Nathan was one thing but in some ways, the work politics had proved a welcome distraction. Now, its potential removal left only the twisted reality of my personal life and the image of Peter Clifford and Violet Dryden loomed in my head.

It was another grey day but the heat swelled beneath the cloud and despite the air con in my car, there were sweat patches beneath my arms. I waited at the entrance to Belvedere Court, fingers tapping impatiently on the steering wheel as the gate pulled back.

I needed to know what happened. I needed to know what relationship Violet had with Gabe and Holly. I couldn't believe Lana had known about the woman's death. Her murder. Then straight on the heels of that thought was the fear that Lana could be in danger, just how precarious our situation was. I'd no idea where she was, no means to contact her. I couldn't go to the police. I'd helped commit fraud. I'd knowingly identified another woman as my wife.

I parked and went straight to the Wright house. Gabe answered the door in green scrub trousers and a white T-shirt, a half-eaten apple in his hand. I glanced at the scrubs, appalled and impressed in equal measure at the lengths he was going to preserve his lies.

He bit into the apple and said from the corner of his mouth, 'Myles, excuse the attire, I've just got in from a shift.' Then, swallowing quickly, 'Oh, is something wrong?'

'I need to speak to Lana. Now,' I said, trying to keep the anger out of my voice and not quite succeeding.

'Let's talk,' he said, stepping aside.

If Lana was in danger, I needed to tread carefully. I clung to the hypothesis that the Wrights might need this payout almost as much as I did. If Gabe truly hadn't worked since he moved here, if they were only renting the house, then their financial position was definitely looking shaky. Their need for money might keep Lana alive. Or was it that they only needed me to believe she was still alive?

I pushed by Gabe, down the hall and into their dining room.

Through the French doors that led to the garden, I could see Holly sitting at a table, her laptop and her camera in front of her; a stray beam of sunlight cresting around the white gold of her head like a halo.

Gabe lingered at the door to the room. 'Coffee?' He looked uncomfortable. It didn't take a genius to know that I'd reached some kind of breaking point. It gave me a mean sort of pleasure that I'd made him uneasy. Even in this small way. *See how you like it.*

'No,' I said.

His shoulders fell. 'Look, we're not trying to torture you. The quietude, it stops all of us from making mistakes.'

I took a step towards him. 'Yet, you're able to speak to her. Why is that?'

'I keep any contact to a minimum, Myles. It's literally a text here or there to make sure she has enough food. We're all waiting and wanting to get to the other side of this.' He laid the apple core down on a white gloss sideboard. 'And, truth be told, I'm taking a big risk here. You must see that.'

I swiped my tongue across my bottom lip. 'No. I don't see that. I don't see anything. I want to know where the fuck my wife is. And I want to know it now.'

He sighed; an infuriating little puff of an exhale, as if I were the one who was trying patience here. 'I realise the temptation you both have to see each other is unbearable. But you must hold your nerve, Myles. You have to trust me.'

My fingers bit into my palm. 'Trust you?'

He frowned. I saw the quick glance to my clenched hands. 'What's changed? Has something happened?'

233

'Other than not seeing or hearing from my wife for weeks? I've no idea what she's thinking, how she is. Is she even alive?'

He swallowed. Shook his head. 'Why would you even ask that? Lana is safe. This is what she wants.'

'Stop lying,' I said. I took a step towards him. 'I don't want to go to the police, Gabe, but that doesn't mean I won't.'

A shadow fell across the glass doors and Holly stepped inside, her laptop tucked under her arm. She left it on the dining table, swept off her sunglasses leaving them nestled in her fine hair.

'Hello, Myles,' she said. 'I didn't know you were here.' She made to move towards me, then stopped halfway; her lips, which had drawn into a smile, pulled flat as she took in my expression, then her husband's. 'What's happening?'

There was a long pause. I stared at Gabe. The anger I'd been feeling, all of it pushed up inside me. Anger at him, at Holly, myself and even Lana, for going along with this, for lying. For putting herself in the hands of strangers. And I hated myself. That part of me that even now, as I stood between them, wanted to believe whatever they told me, wanted to continue on this helter-skelter plan so that we could succeed. All so I could stick it to my past, to the present. I wanted them to be who I thought they were. These people I wanted to be. Strangers.

'Did you kill someone?' I said, my voice was surprisingly steady. The words rolled out low and deep, falling into the silence like stones down a well.

I caught the look that passed between them. Not quite panic, but something between frustration and resignation. The truth of Violet's murder felt like it was burning a hole in my throat.

'The woman,' I said. 'The one I just cremated. You knew her. She knew you. You killed her.'

Gabe shook his head. 'We've done the hard bit. Okay? Let's just—'

'Violet Dryden,' I said. 'She worked in the Mortuary Services at your last hospital. Ever since we embarked on this madness, I've had the sense you've done this before. That's right, isn't it? Had she helped you in the past with similar schemes? Took payment to adjust paperwork? Or to look the other way? What was it? And then everything went sour. Because you started an affair with her?'

I saw Holly wince.

'Was she blackmailing you?' I pressed on.

No answer. Gabe looked at the ground. A flush of pink rose over the collar of his shirt and into his face. I wasn't sure whether it signalled anger or guilt.

I pushed on, half of me wanting to run from the house and put as much distance between myself and the Wrights as possible, the other half needing to unearth as many answers as I could. Needing to know exactly how far my wife was willing to go for money.

'How did you get her in the car? She was driving, right? Why? Why would she go with you?' I glanced between them.

Holly stiffened. Pink blotches spread up her neck and into her face.

I turned back to Gabe. 'She went with you because she trusted you. She drove because you told her you'd been out at the Mayfair dinner. That you'd been drinking. Only you hadn't. You didn't touch a drop all evening. Did she know? Did Lana know?'

235

Out of the corner of my eye, I saw the small nod of Holly's chin, not a nod of agreement but as if she were giving Gabe permission to speak.

'I didn't talk all the details through with Lana but she probably put some things together,' Gabe said. 'She picked me up in my car after . . . it was done and I drove her to a secluded location.'

She'd known. I couldn't make the thought fit with what I knew of my wife, and yet . . . and yet somehow it slid alongside everything I knew about her. I put my hands on my hips, tried to keep my thoughts straight in my head. Violet Dryden's body rose in my mind's eye. I pressed my fingers to my eyes.

They remained. Silent. Watching. Waiting to see whether Myles Butler could hold it together. Who knew what silent messages were behind the many glances between them. Was I the problem now too? Was I the next Violet Dryden? I had so much anger in me, I almost wanted someone to hit me, to try it on. I remembered what Hunter had said about the post-mortem results about Violet's cardiac problems and whatever veil had been shielding me from the Wrights' true characters dropped.

'You knew about Violet's heart condition,' I said quietly. This to Gabe. 'You knew because she'd told you, or maybe you looked up her notes. You knew they'd likely put it down as cause of death.' I lifted my chin. 'That crash wasn't enough to kill her. What did you do?' I stepped closer. Holly followed as if to protect him, but he gave her a small shake of his head. The evening of our first dinner came flooding back again as it did when Hunter first relayed the post-mortem results to me. The seemingly friendly banter between a husband and wife. Between Gabe and Holly.

'*A person is more than a muscle beating in their chest*,' Holly had said.

Gabe's laugh as he replied, '*A dose of potassium chloride would argue differently.*'

'Potassium chloride,' I said. I saw the truth widen in his eyes. The drug would've been absorbed quickly. The pathologist wouldn't think to look for it. The injection site, concealed in the armpit, maybe, between the fingers, along a nailbed, administered directly after the crash when Violet would have been incapacitated or confused.

He pulled himself to his full height, looked down on me, an expression of self-righteousness on his face. 'You knew too,' he replied. 'Not all the details, granted, but you knew the line you were crossing. When you saw that body, you knew.' He kept his eyes on mine.

I swallowed. I thought about standing in that miserable little hospital room, the trolley, the sheet drawing back, and Violet. I had thought there could have been some internal bleed perhaps. Some unseen vascular wound caused by the recoil of her head against the seat that had caused her death; a swift torsion of an artery, or maybe the impact had ripped through one of the cerebral vessels resulting in a severe subdural haematoma. But he was right. When I stood in that hospital, there was some part of me that understood what had happened. I sensed foul play before I could name it. And still when the nurse asked if I was looking upon my wife's remains, I'd answered yes.

As if reading my thoughts, Gabe continued, 'You identified that woman as your wife and you knew exactly what you were signing up for.'

Gabe had mentioned a few times how we all needed something to lose. For us, we'd committed fraud. A lengthy enough sentence waited for us if we got caught. But nothing in comparison to murder. We couldn't be part of this. I couldn't be part of this.

'Tell me where my wife is or I go to the police,' I said.

'We can't do that,' he replied.

I turned to leave but Holly gripped my sleeve and pulled me back round. Her nails bit into my forearm.

'Enough,' she said. Her voice barely more than a whisper. 'Sit down.'

I looked at Gabe. He was sickeningly calm. I went to the dining table, pulled out a chair and sat.

Holly walked to the sideboard, removed a notepad and a pencil. She wrote something on a sheet of paper, tore it free, crossed the room and held it out.

'This is the account you'll transfer the money to when it comes in,' she said.

I raised my palms. 'I won't do anything until I have Lana far away from both of you.'

'You will,' she replied, and I didn't like the ring of promise in her voice. 'You're not going to see or speak to your wife until we have our money. All of it.'

'All of it?'

'Every penny you get from that payout. We were happy to take a cut but now we're going to need more. We need enough to start over.'

I laughed. Stood. 'I'm not giving you anything.' I was halfway to the door when she spoke again.

'We'll kill her,' she said.

I stopped, turned.

'We'll kill her,' she repeated. Her fingers picked at the band on her wrist. 'Her body will be found along the banks of the Thames among the shopping trolleys, discarded bikes and traffic cones,' she said. She walked towards me, reached out and tucked the piece of paper into my shirt pocket. 'As you say, you're the one who identified and cremated a woman who wasn't your wife. Who do you think would be done for her murder?' She threw a smile in Gabe's direction. 'Her friendly neighbours who barely knew her and had no reason, no motive, to touch a hair on her head. Or her broke, desperate and soon-to-be homeless husband who knew all about her big juicy life insurance?'

CHAPTER 21

Daniel finished off the last of his pint and smacked the glass down on the table. I plucked the shell from a pistachio, then dropped it in my mouth.

'It's all I can do not to sit outside the house and watch her coming and going,' he said. 'Have you talked to her?'

I nodded along. Half irritated, half grateful for the distraction. I'd avoided all interaction with the Wrights since our last conversation. It was as if I were trapped in one of those dreams where you want to run, you're acting out the movements, but your limbs are sluggish, heavy and you can't get away. Numerous scenarios cycled through my head. I could try and talk to the police, tell them everything. They must know how to deal with these situations. Maybe Hunter could be trusted, although his strange little monologue on trophies and murderers suggested he wasn't one to give me the benefit of the doubt. And I couldn't be sure that Gabe and Holly were working alone. If I disclosed what had really happened to the police, Lana would graduate from wife to evidence, the lynchpin to our schemes. Lana was already dead on paper; in order to maintain their innocence, she'd need to remain dead, and there was only one way of ensuring that.

I could threaten Gabe, catch him off guard, pin him against a wall and demand he tell me where my wife was. However, I knew I wouldn't come close to winning in a fight with Gabe. I could hire a private investigator. But we had almost as many secrets as the Wrights and as much to lose.

My head hurt, I hurt; I'd thought our friendship had been genuine. Holly's voice circled in my mind, sharp as spinning blades and cold as ice. Out of the two, I had thought, she was the one I'd more hope of influencing. Gabe, once he'd set his eye on a goal, his focus wouldn't be broken. But I had been wrong about Holly. I realised I'd fallen for her sugary presence, the soft flyaway hair and heart-shaped face. The clear blue eyes that I now knew concealed a bitter darkness.

'Myles?' Dan drew my attention back to him.

'Sorry,' I said.

'You seen her?' For a second I thought he meant Lana. 'Charlotte,' he said.

I peeled another pistachio. 'Only at the funeral.'

'I should have been there. I'm really sorry.'

'It was a tough day,' I said.

'You're holding up well, I have to say.'

'It doesn't feel like it.'

'You're working, you're keeping busy, holding down the house . . .' He gave a series of small nods. 'Trust me, you're doing well. I've spent the last two nights in my car. I'm a mess.'

He was a mess. At least three days' beard grew along his jaw. And Daniel didn't really do beards well; he had two patches along the right side of his face where growth was sparse or non-existent. His hair was brown, grey at the temples, but along his jaw it manifested as a dirty white.

He waited. I suspected he was hoping I'd invite him to stay at mine, but even without everything that was going on, I didn't want Daniel in my house. He was a friend. But one with whom time was best spent in small doses.

'I'm looking to put the house up,' I said.

'You're moving? Why? I thought you were set with the insurance and all.'

I shrugged a shoulder. Took a drink. 'There's nothing here for me anymore,' I said.

I forced a brightness into my voice, my face. 'I need a fresh start. Somewhere I'm not haunted with all the places Lana and I visited together. It might be a good idea for you too,' I said.

He frowned. 'Maybe. I've lost everything. Marriage, business . . .' He paused. 'The will to fucking live. But I can't leave. If I don't get her back, what's the point in anything.'

'Don't say that.'

'We were up there,' he said, bringing his hand high above his head. 'Up there. Fucking recession.'

'Charlotte will come round.'

He laughed. 'Not a chance. Got papers through today. And she threatened a restraining order.'

'A restraining order?'

He shrugged. 'She won't talk to me. How are we to work things out if she won't speak to me? I just need an hour to explain the situation.'

'You lost a lot of money,' I pointed out.

'I don't think it was the money. It was what having no money did to me,' he muttered. 'Or what I failed to do with no money. She couldn't take the sitting around. I couldn't sleep so would stay up half the night playing video games. You don't know what it's like living with Charlotte. She has her shit together and she expects everyone to be at that level of control. All the fucking time. She used to tell me she loved that I was laid back. That it was why we were so good as a couple. Now, I disgust her.'

'She's hurting.'

'How did she seem to you? At the funeral?'

I sighed. 'Daniel.'

He held up his palms. 'Sorry. That was insensitive of me. Sorry, mate,' he said.

I thought back to the evening when Lana realised just how badly I'd fucked up financially. The horror on her face, how it turned to revulsion when I tried to explain my side of things. Watching Daniel wave at the barman for another pint, the dejection in his shoulders, the wild look in his eye, his hair matted at the back and standing out like he'd just got up from napping on a sofa, I should have felt deep pity, but all I felt was grateful. That it wasn't me. It couldn't be me. I wouldn't become that.

The barman delivered his pint and Daniel lit on it like a fly on sugar. When he came up for air, a third of the lager was gone, leaving frothy streaks down the inside of the glass.

Daniel nodded to my wine. 'You want another?'

'I'm okay,' I said.

He turned the glass on the beer mat, glanced at me in a conspiratorial manner. 'Don't say anything to anyone but I put an app on her phone. One of those tracking apps.' He looked pained. I'd never heard of such a thing and when I didn't say anything, he went on, 'I know what you're thinking. I think it about me too. I've become one of those people. Possessive and controlling. But I don't know how she can be so sure that it's over. We were fine a year ago. She loved me. You can't just switch that off. Not by yourself anyway.'

'You think there's someone else?' I asked.

'There has to be,' he said.

Of course Daniel thought it was impossible that someone could leave him of their own volition. Even at his lowest point, he unearthed confidence from somewhere.

'Daniel, you need to remove it,' I said. 'It's morally questionable, not to mention probably illegal.' As I spoke I heard myself, and a twisted sensation of laughter threatened to bubble up my throat. The hypocrisy. But I was protecting my friend. It was the intention that mattered.

'I can't. I can't get near her phone. She won't let me in the house,' he said.

'If she discovers it, she'll have you arrested. She'll never speak to you again,' I said.

'I was desperate,' he said. 'I couldn't stand not knowing what she was doing, where she was. I thought if I could, you know, accidentally bump into her, she might . . .'

I put a hand on his back. 'Dan, that's stalking.'

He dropped his head in his hands. 'She'll hate me.'

An idea was forming. I thought about the picture I'd found on Holly's camera. The one of the wooden lodge surrounded by trees. I'd attempted a Google image search but nothing had come up. The location could be any number of isolated woodland areas in the UK and I'd almost given up on trying to find it. But the more I thought on it, the more sure I was that this cabin was where Lana was being kept.

'How does it work?' I asked, trying to hide the intrigue from my voice.

He misinterpreted my question. 'She must be seeing someone during work hours or they're going to ours—'

'The app?' I asked.

'Oh, um, I downloaded it onto my phone. Had to enable it on hers though. That was more tricky but she agreed to a coffee when we heard about . . .' He stopped himself referring to Lana's death, then, 'And I installed it then.' Removing his phone, he flicked the screen awake and leaned towards me. 'Here's the app. Look.'

He tapped the screen and a map appeared; a blue dot pulsed over The Court. 'She's home.'

I knew that Gabe wasn't working and I knew he was occasionally away for long periods of the day. I felt sure, at least on some of those days, he was likely visiting Lana to bring food, clothing and other essentials. That is, if she was still alive.

'Daniel,' I said. 'Be careful. Charlotte, she wouldn't do anything to hurt you, but she is a divorce lawyer. If she finds out about this, it won't be good.'

He closed the app. Slid his phone back into his pocket and sighed. 'I know. I know. I'll sort it.'

I left a fifty at the bar with Daniel and made my way home.

I went to the kitchen, took a beer out of the fridge, then, grabbing my laptop, I stepped out into the front garden and sat down on the love seat. The pressures of the last few weeks stretched against the inside of my skull. My chief worry was how I'd get to Lana. I'd received notification from the insurance company that payment had been sent and I could expect to see the amount in my account in the next twenty-four hours. It wouldn't be long before the Wrights would be pressing me for the money and I had not gone through all I'd gone through to hand over every penny to the Wrights. Then there was Hunter, a shadowy figure that hovered on the periphery of my mind.

They say a good detective relies more on their instinct than on solid leads. And I knew Hunter's instincts were pointing him in my direction. I lay in bed each night, crossing through a mental checklist. The body had been cremated. He couldn't exhume it. He couldn't mine it for more evidence. It was ash. The wedding ring. Proof that we fought. But not proof of murder. And he knew it. And even if he made a connection between Violet Dryden and Lana, again, without finding Lana herself, there was nothing to prove. I felt relatively confident that, as things stood, Hunter couldn't open an investigation, but I felt equally confident that the moment anything concrete came his way, he'd be on me like a cat on a bird.

I sipped my beer and, half watching for activity in the Wrights' house, opened up a search engine on my laptop. I spent some time looking through various sites on spyware apps, the idea inspired by Daniel's desperation, but one that could help me pin down Lana's location. All claimed easy installation, but there would be nothing easy installing this on Gabe's phone. I got the impression he'd have added security or a fail-safe in place that would alert him to such a thing. I couldn't risk it. I scrolled through anyway, clicking on a few forums that discussed the pros and cons of spyware applications. There were some very worrying people out there, I thought. I clicked on a website selling magnetic tracking devices. A simple palm-sized tracker that I could fix to a car. The device synched to the GPS on my phone. It boasted a strong magnetic connection to the vehicle, which would be needed if Lana was in an isolated location. And better yet, the company could deliver in a couple of days.

The next morning, I drove to the surgery. The day ahead looked set to be warm if not bright, but when I stepped out of the car, I felt a chill in the air that hinted at autumn days, time moving on, moving away from those dawn hours when I opened the door to Hunter and Davies. I needed to speak to Nathan. I wanted to secure that reference before he'd a change of heart. Wherever we were to go next, it would help if I could start on a similar salary, and that would be much easier if I had a glowing reference from Nathan in hand. I stepped through the front entrance, already feeling a stranger in the place I'd believed would one day be mine. Sam was just getting off the phone when I entered.

He looked at me, stricken. At first, I thought Nathan had told him what I'd done. 'Everything okay, Sam?' I asked.

Vera appeared in the hallway behind the desk, tea in hand and a single stick of KitKat in the other.

'Dr Butler,' Sam said, getting up from the chair. 'I'm so glad you're here.' He looked on the verge of tears.

'What is it?'

'It's Dr Kingston. He's had a heart attack.' He pressed a hand to his chest.

'Nathan?'

'That was Sofia. He's in a really bad way. He's at the hospital now.'

I digested this information slowly while Sam watched my face, waiting for instruction. 'Reschedule his patients. Whatever happens, he'll need time to recover without worrying about the surgery.'

'Should we not just call Dr Lopez?' Vera asked. The tea threatened to fall from her hand.

I sighed. I had no desire to bring in Madison on this. I wanted to show Nathan that I was the one who could be relied upon in a crisis, however things were coming to a head with the Wrights and I needed to be free to make my move should the time come.

I had to force the words from my mouth. 'Yes, let Dr Lopez know. I need to be there to help Dr Kingston and Sofia over the coming days but move his patients to me where possible.'

'Yes, Dr Butler,' Sam said.

'I'm on my mobile if there are any problems.'

'Yes, Dr Butler,' Sam repeated.

At the hospital, in the hallway outside Nathan's room, I found Sofia pale and borderline hysterical.

'He's dead,' she said, flatly. 'Just now, they told me. How can he be dead? Myles, I'm sorry, you've only just gone through this and now, Nathan. Oh God, oh God.'

She collapsed against my chest. I tried not to think about the smear of make-up, tears and snot now pressing itself into my suit.

I brought my hand up, stroked the back of her head, her hair coarse as a horse's mane. 'Sofia, I'm so sorry.'

248

She sobbed for a moment or two more, then peeled herself away and made for a seat along the wall. 'They said I could have a moment with him but I can't bring myself to go in.'

I took her hand. 'I can go in with you, if you like.'

She gave me a wobbly smile, pulled a tissue from her sleeve and dabbed at her eyes. 'Oh, look at your suit, I'm sorry.'

'Don't worry about that.'

'He got up to spend a penny and that's when I heard the crash. Heart attack, they said.' I had a flashback to Nathan taking those antacids at our last meeting.

Sofia sniffed. 'They tried to save him but . . . how has this happened?' Her face cleared. 'He'd been suffering a lot of indigestion. The consultant said he'd probably been having symptoms for days. It's stress, I know it. He'd something on his mind, but so like Nathan, he wouldn't burden me by talking about it. That surgery,' she said, bitterness turning her voice hard. 'He worked too hard. I've been trying to get him to retire for years but you know him, life changes around Nathan, he doesn't change with it.' Her lip came up, tears tipped onto her face.

I waited until she indicated she was ready, then helped her up and walked her towards the room. She clung to my arm like she was approaching a cliff edge.

The bed was behind a screen. The room was quiet, semi-dark, blinds drawn. I pulled the screen back and heard the soft cry from Sofia beside me; she went straight to her husband. The nurses had pulled the sheets high up on his chest, his hands were by his side. I'd never seen Nathan unwell, not so much as a cold. It was odd to view him in such a vulnerable state, but strangely and perversely, perhaps because of our final discussion,

I felt nothing but the vaguest sensation of excitement. As Sofia said, this was a change.

Sofia sat beside him, put her hand over his, rubbed across the skin as if she could warm life back into him. 'I'm so glad to have you here, Myles,' she said, glancing back at me.

I reached out and squeezed her shoulder. 'There's no need to worry about Willowhaven. I'll keep things going until you decide what you want to do.'

'I realise you've a lot on your plate right now. I don't know if you were planning on staying around, after Lana, but if you felt up to it, I know Nathan would've wanted you to take over. I'm sure I could sell but I know he wanted the surgery to endure as Willowhaven.'

I stared down at Nathan's face, the round bulbs of his closed eyes, the dragging mouth now tinged blue. The greying nose hair and the large mole on the right side of his forehead. I should tell her about our conversation but part of me felt like I was owed this. It was sad that it meant Nathan was dead, but he was dead. Whatever his desires a few days ago, they did not matter. What mattered was that I took the opportunity that was now being offered to me. I could work something out with Lana. Or once I got the surgery on track, run it from a distance. Pull Madison out like a bad tooth and replace her with an experienced associate who would respect me.

'It would be an honour to continue on his legacy,' I said. 'I'll check in with you soon.'

I left Sofia to her grief, returned to the surgery.

Sam was red-eyed on the front desk. The waiting room was empty. But I could hear voices down the hall.

'Is Dr Lopez in?' I asked.

'She's just got here,' he said.

'Mrs Kingston has asked me to collect some of Nathan's things from his office, do you have the keys?'

'She didn't give you his set?'

'I didn't think to ask. She's devastated.'

'Oh okay, hang on, I think there's a spare set somewhere here.' He got up and I followed him to the staff room. He opened a cupboard over the coffee machine and took down a tin. He tipped it out, looked through the contents, paperclips, a pencil, three different-sized Allen keys and numerous other door keys. After a while, he selected a thick room key that had a yellow piece of thread looped around the end.

'I think this is the master,' he said, and handed it over.

'Thanks,' I said. 'I'll clear urgent appointments tomorrow morning. Out of respect to Nathan, of course, but we should try to keep up our usual diary. Nathan's entire list is to come to me. I'm familiar with most of his patients and I don't think it's the right time for them to acquaint themselves with someone new.'

'Yes, Dr Butler,' he said.

I went to Nathan's office and locked the door behind me. I knew the moment Madison discovered I was on the premises and going through Nathan's files, she'd realise what I was doing. I opened his computer, my palms growing hot and sweaty as I searched his desktop. It didn't take me long. There: a file titled 'Myles'. This was Nathan. Too trusting. He knew I'd the passwords to his computer and yet every piece of evidence against me was stored in these files. I opened it, saw he'd already sent letters to each of the insurers explaining

251

that there'd been a technical error with our reference system, promising to correct and return any funds the surgery had inadvertently claimed.

Counting up the amount, it seems paltry now in comparison to what I had. A mere five thousand. A sum that wouldn't have even touched the sides of my debt. For the first time, I really understood how desperate I'd been in those weeks. Among the documents was my reference. I opened it but Nathan had yet to write anything. Bitterness flooded my mouth. I dragged all the files to the trash can. Then emptied that too.

By the time I left the surgery, I'd cleared all incriminating records from the surgery's records. I stepped out into the car park, closed the door behind me and looked back on the building. Nathan's life work. It was unfortunate that our last exchange had been less than good, but the surgery had stagnated under Nathan's care and I told myself that I could take this on and run it how it should be run; reignite Nathan's initial vision. Lana would wait, like I had, until I'd steadied the ship, so to speak, then with the right people in place, I could run it from a distance, or set up some satellite clinics.

The wind had picked up, warm but strong. I pulled my jacket closed and made my way to the car. My phone vibrated in my pocket as I sat into the driver's seat.

'Myles? You remember dinner at mine on Saturday? I wondered if we could do tomorrow night instead?'

Charlotte.

'Ah I'd completely forgotten. I'm afraid—'

'Please,' she chirped, but there was a serious note of pleading

252

in her voice. 'I know it's a last minute change but Daniel's . . . not here, and the Wrights are coming. It would be awkward if it were just the three of us.'

I turned the car out of the surgery car park. 'The Wrights will be there?'

'Gabe has some fancy medical retreat and will be away Saturday evening, hence the date change. Who chooses a medical retreat over my hospitality?' she said, with a laugh.

Someone who's not going on a medical retreat. Lana.

'No problem,' I said. 'I'm looking forward to it.'

I drove out of the village, turned toward Sofia's house. I promised I'd take her some of Nathan's personal effects from the surgery. A watch she'd given him when he'd first qualified; it was gold plate and worn around the bezel where he held it while his other hand rested on the radial pulse of his patient. I picked up Sofia's favourite flowers on the way, a large bunch of deep red roses and a bottle of her preferred gin. When I arrived, she pulled me into their home and immediately I was back in those early days of returning to Wimbledon. The house smelled like it always had, a mix of lavender, cat and Chanel No. 5. She had friends around. They were chatting in low, respectful whispers around a large AGA in the kitchen.

I stayed for half an hour, while Sofia found a vase, trimmed the stems of the roses.

'Thank you for bringing these round,' she said to me, resting her hand on the watch. 'Did you manage to find his reading glasses?'

I shook my head. 'Sorry, I'll keep looking.'

Her friends talked about their memories of Nathan; his

253

passion for cooking, how he loved nothing more than to spend his evening attempting impossible dishes he always overcooked or over-salted. I left feeling a deep sadness and regret. I drove slowly back to The Court. The sun was low in the sky and flashed through the treeline like strobe lights. I re-imagined my last few months with Nathan. Made it so he'd never discovered those insurance claims. Madison and I would continue our hair tugging, but it was always me he cast a proud paternal eye upon. I was disgusted at every cynical thought I had about him, every manoeuvre that made me unworthy of his trust, his belief. But knowing myself as I did, and knowing the outcome as it was, I also understood that given the time back, I wouldn't have changed a thing, other than hide my true self better.

CHAPTER 22

The following afternoon my list was crammed with patients disguising morbid curiosity with minor ailments. I didn't get back from the surgery until close to seven. Madison had barely spoken to me throughout the course of the day. I knew she'd already scoured the surgery's system for information against me that she could take to Sofia or even the General Medical Council. It made me itch with frustration that there was a possibility I'd soon be in Madison's rear-view mirror. That in time she'd get to view me as just some irritating man she used to work with. That no matter how things panned out, where I should have been the one to feel victorious, in effect she'd won.

Dinner at Charlotte's was at seven thirty. I texted her, apologising that I'd be a few minutes late, to not to hold back on serving up and I'd join as soon as I could.

'*No worries*,' she replied. I smiled. Her attempt at easy-going. I knew she wouldn't serve until I was there, and right now was probably re-setting timers on her state-of-the-art oven.

There was a package just inside my porch. I carried it through to the kitchen, removed a knife from the long magnetic bar to the side of the oven and cut the package open. I removed the magnetic tracking device. It was no bigger than my palm, and in moments I had the corresponding program downloaded onto my laptop. I cleared away the packaging, then went upstairs to shower and change. Returning to the kitchen, I saw that the Wrights were just leaving their house. I watched Gabe, his hair slicked back, dressed in a deep blue suit, a pair of tan soft-leather loafers on his feet. The watch on his wrist caught the last of the yellow light from the sky as he lifted his arm and curled it around Holly's slim waist. She was dressed in a lilac summer dress, a white cashmere sweater tied prep-school style around her shoulders. She carried a bottle of champagne in her arms like it was a baby.

I went through to the living room and waited by the double doors, and watched as they reached the Preston home and were welcomed inside. I could hear the Foresters' kids screeching in their back garden but only Mrs Shelton occupied the front of her home, continuing the perpetual war she waged against vine weevils and weeds. I sent a text to Daniel telling him that if he still needed a place to crash, he was welcome at mine.

He replied in moments: '*Tonight?*'

'*How's tomorrow and however long you need,*' I answered. '*I'll be in from 6.*'

'*Thanks, mate. See you then.*'

I had to hope that Charlotte had it right and Gabe was not leaving until the evening. I wanted Daniel here. I wanted the house to look occupied. To appear as if I was home and Daniel was not likely to ask too many questions about where I was going. I slid a bottle of Shiraz from the wine rack, collected up the tracking device and left my home. There was a light on somewhere at the back of the Wright house even though it wasn't dark, and I took this as a signal that the property was empty and they'd left it on for security. I gave a final glance up the street to ensure neither Gabe nor Holly had re-emerged from Charlotte's, then crossed the street towards their house to where Gabe's Mercedes was parked in the drive.

As advertised, the moment I placed the tracker on the inside of the passenger side wheel arch, it clung to the panel with a firm click. I walked down the street, then made my way up the short path and pushed on the doorbell of the Preston house.

Charlotte opened the door with a smile. 'Lovely to see you, Myles.'

'Clinic ran over. Sorry,' I said. 'For you.' I handed her the wine.

She lowered her chin. 'You shouldn't be working so hard. You need to take care of yourself,' she said. She stepped back and I followed her inside, closing the door behind me.

'It's easier to keep busy. Don't worry, I've the day off tomorrow,' I said.

She led me into the kitchen. 'What would you like to drink?'

'Red, please,' I said.

She reached for a bottle of Rioja, uncorked it, then poured a glass. 'I heard about Nathan. I'm sorry,' she said, and handed me the wine.

I thanked her. 'It was a shock. But, honestly, Charlotte, I just want to relax this evening and forget about the last few months.'

She made an expression of sympathy, raised a glass to mine. 'Well, we certainly have enough alcohol for that to happen.'

I drew in a breath. 'Just the one for me this evening. I'm expecting a call from a patient early in the morning and want to be clear-headed,' I lied.

'In that case, we'll leave you sleepy and full on a carbohydrates. Beef Welly tonight.'

As soon as Charlotte and Daniel had moved into The Court, she'd begun her renovations. For us, the attraction of Belvedere Court was that the houses were a turn-key purchase. Neither of us had the time nor inclination to begin interior decoration. But Charlotte liked to make things fit her own particular tastes. The world according to Charlotte, Lana used to say, only worked if it was *between the lines and on her terms.*

'Surely,' Lana had said, peering out of the kitchen window at the skip on the Preston driveway. 'The entire point of buying a place like this, on a street like this, is that you don't have to rely on your own crappy taste.'

'Some people don't know when they're looking at perfection,' I'd said, coming up behind her and slipping my arms around her waist. I'd kissed her neck, then rested my chin on her shoulder, following her gaze down the street.

Daniel had been shuffling out through the front door, a long strip of wood that I'd recognised as the panelling around his fireplace under his arm. He'd swung it upwards, then had let it drop into the skip. A cloud of dust had risen up and enveloped him.

'Bet everything will be varying shades of beige,' I'd said.

Lana had laughed, pushed against me. 'Beige walls, beige flooring, sofas in mocha maybe?'

'There'll be feature walls.'

'But of course, how else would we show our personality?'

I'd grinned against her shoulder. 'Oh, but wouldn't we achieve that with some quirky light fittings?'

It wasn't beige. They'd gone for silvers and greys. The hallway was carpeted with a thick pile carpet. Along the door, a metal rack for shoes. The kitchen was industrial chic but they'd tipped the theme slightly too far. The cooker and backsplash were stainless steel, coffee machine too. The effect was that it had the feel of a mortuary. When I'd first seen it, Daniel had pointed to the red brick wall running along the length of one side of the room. 'Tiles, can you believe it? Not real brick,' he'd said.

I'd put an arm around Lana. 'What an impressive feature wall,' I'd whispered into her ear. She'd curled her fingers into my forearm in response, a hint of a smile at the corner of her mouth.

Gabe and Holly were already seated on the stone-grey leather sofa, at the far end of the dining room. Charlotte had brought out the good tableware, four tapered white candles arranged down the middle of the table. The candleholders were of a contemporary design, asymmetric lines and sharp angles. Red wine had already been decanted into a wide-bottomed crystal decanter. Six silver pots divided the table setting in two. Each one contained a blood-red rose.

Gabe got up when he saw me. 'Myles,' he bellowed. He crossed the room, clapped his arms around me, patted my shoulder. 'Good to see you, friend.'

Tension crept down my spine, I made myself relax into his embrace. 'How've you been?'

'Busy,' he said.

'Too busy,' Holly chided. 'He's off again tomorrow.'

Gabe put his hand over hers. 'I'll only be gone the one night. Back Sunday, I promise. Besides, you know what they say about idle hands, darling.'

Devil's work, I thought. 'Hello, Holly,' I said. I leaned down and kissed her cheek.

'I'm just going to serve up,' Charlotte said. She gestured towards the table. 'Feel free to sit anywhere. It's just us tonight.' She turned towards the kitchen and Holly took the opportunity to raise an eyebrow at me.

We sat, Holly next to me, leaving the seat free next to Gabe for Charlotte. The last thing I wanted to do was sit through an evening meal with Gabe and Holly, but I felt more comfortable in their presence than not. At least when they were in front of me, I worried less about what they could be doing to Lana.

'I was sorry to hear about Nathan,' Holly said; she slid her hand over mine.

I nodded, not trusting myself to speak. I counted down the seconds to when it was polite to remove my hand, then drew it away and lifted my drink.

'The money must be due soon, then all of this will be over,' she said, mistaking my silence for fear.

Charlotte returned with the first course. Cold roasted peppers, olive oil and burrata. She sat down, lifted her glass for a toast.

'Thank you all for coming this evening. There've been a few . . . adjustments in my life lately and it's wonderful to have friends come by. Cheers.'

'Cheers,' I said. I touched my glass to hers, then to Holly's, then met Gabe's eyes as we clinked glasses.

The glass tipped and red wine dropped onto the white table runner.

'Sorry,' I said.

Holly reached across and dabbed at the stain with a napkin. 'Historical anecdote for you. In medieval times, it was polite for the host to clink glasses so that some of the guest's wine would tip into their glass. This was to reassure guests that their wine was not poisoned,' she said. She gave me little flash of her teeth.

'Really?' Charlotte said, examining the pale gold of her champagne. 'I don't think we have any poisoning going on here. Let's keep our drinks in our glasses and off the linen, thank you very much!' She laughed.

The first course went by with gentle chat and small talk but soon silences appeared like black holes around the dinner table, the only sound the ring of cutlery on plates and the odd appreciative noise or comment on how good the food was. Charlotte cleared the plates but just before she returned with the main course she went to a cupboard in the corner of the room and produced a small box of cards. 'I thought these would be fun,' she said, lightly. The box was titled *Conversation Starters for Dinner Parties*. She set the cards down on the table with a wide grin.

'Are we that bad?' Gabe asked, his eyes glinting against the candlelight.

Charlotte flushed. 'No. No. Of course not. I'd got them before and just forgot to put—'

'He's teasing,' I said.

'Oh, God.' Charlotte put her hand to her mouth. 'I just got so used to Daniel being here,' she said. Tears gathered in the corners of her eyes. 'He likes to talk, and I was nervous about hosting without him. I'll take them away.' She reached for the box.

'You will not,' Holly said, putting her hand on the cards. 'If this saves me having to sit through another one of my husband's surgery stories, then this may be the best dinner party I've attended since meeting him.'

'I'll get the next course,' Charlotte said, eager to escape.

She returned a few moments later with the main. The beef was perfectly cooked, a side of green beans and a generous jug of gravy.

'This looks exquisite,' Holly said. Charlotte beamed.

Gabe took up his fork, speared the centre of the meat, cut through it once, twice, then across again, until it was dissected into small pieces on his plate. 'We're planning a bit of a thing for my forty-fifth. A party, I guess,' he said, glancing at Holly.

'Oh yes, you must clear your diaries,' Holly said.

'We never really got round to a proper house-warming.' He dropped a piece of meat in his mouth, chewed briefly, then swallowed. He paused, looked across the table towards me. 'Would you be up for it?'

I glared at him. 'I don't know. I've a lot on.'

A brief frown. His smile remained but there was a look in his eyes, like he'd caught a peek at what was really happening in my mind. I put down my cutlery, took another sip of wine. I turned away from him, looked at Charlotte. 'Maybe time for those cards of yours, Charlotte?'

'Yes,' she said and dabbed the corners of her mouth with her napkin. Picked up her card and read, '*Which famous person would you like to have dinner with? Alive or dead?'* She shrugged. 'Easy. George Clooney. Sorry, I know I'm shallow, but there you go.'

Holly laughed, a forkful of beans on the way to her mouth. 'Circa his *ER* years. I think I'd like to join you at that dinner, please.'

'I don't share,' Charlotte grinned.

'And what does George Clooney have that I don't?' Gabe asked. 'An actual surgeon?'

'A lady would never answer that.' She grinned at him, but there was a flash of something in her eye and I saw his brief frown in response.

By the time the main and cheese course were finished, we'd suffered through *What era in history would you most like to live in for a week?* and *What is your most significant childhood memory?* That one I evaded by skipping straight to my card.

I turned the card over and immediately contemplated returning it to the box and choosing another.

'Come on, Myles.' Charlotte nudged my elbow.

I cleared my throat. '*What would you kill for?*'

Holly met my eyes, rubbed her palms together. 'My kind of question.'

'I don't think I could imagine a circumstance where I could take a human life,' Charlotte said.

'I spend all day trying to keep people alive, but –' Gabe held up a finger – 'I think I would kill for love.' He looked at Holly.

'You softie,' she said. 'Well, now I have to say the same. Although, really, would it be worth it? The clean-up . . .' She shuddered.

263

Charlotte laughed. 'Myles? Are you killing for love too?' Then she flushed, remembered. 'Oh, I'm sorry—'

'That's okay,' I said. I turned my water glass between my fingers. The image of that body in the hospital. Violet's body. How Gabe had put it there and how he wouldn't get away with it again.

I looked up. 'Survival. I'd kill to survive.'

CHAPTER 23

The following evening, Daniel sent a text saying he was on the way. I replied, asking him to leave his car outside The Court and walk through. I knew he'd assume this request was to avoid any conflict Charlotte would have with me if she discovered I let him stay. But my hope was that he'd let me use his car tonight. I worried Holly might be watching my house for any movement and my car in the drive would serve as a temporary decoy.

The night before, I'd left Charlotte's at quarter to ten, getting up as soon as Gabe expressed a wish to leave. We'd walked back down the street together, Holly between Gabe and I, her thin arms looped through ours. She was drunk and complained about how Gabe was heading off again. He'd reassured her that it was for the one night, but she pouted like a schoolchild, and I knew, like me, whatever magic Gabe dusted over his lies was fast losing its effectiveness. I had turned to cross to my house and he called me back.

'The money? When's it through?'

'Next week sometime,' I'd said.

He'd held Holly up with one arm but gripped my sleeve with the other. 'Show me.'

'Pardon?'

'Lana gave me the account number the payment was set to go to. Take out your phone and show me the account now.'

I had tried to think of a reply but I knew my hesitation was signal enough to him that I was lying.

'Don't fuck with us, Myles. You have until end of play Monday.' His hand had tightened on my sleeve pulling me closer. 'Do you understand?'

'Come on,' Holly had moaned, tugging Gabe towards the house.

Nodding quickly, I'd said, 'Yes. I get it.'

I had tripped towards my front door, looking back when I'd turned the key. Gabe was helping Holly inside. He placed a supportive hand beneath her elbow but she'd jerked away, losing balance briefly, before finding the wall. I was sure I'd heard her say, 'Don't touch me.'

The next evening I sat at the island and I pulled my laptop towards me. Through the kitchen window, I kept an eye out for the lights of Gabe's car. Or the sight of him readying to leave. Then checked that the tracker was still communicating with the app on my laptop. Once I was sure it was working correctly, I synched the lot to my phone. Wherever Gabe was headed this evening, I'd be following. At five past six, he emerged. He loaded a case into the back seat, then threw a backpack into the passenger seat. A silhouette appeared in the top room of their home, the blinds flicked open and Holly looked down on him.

He walked round to the driver's side of the Mercedes, got in, reversed away from the house, then drove out and away from Belvedere Court, pausing only for the gate to open.

Daniel rang the doorbell shortly after and I opened the door to him.

'I appreciate this, mate,' he said.

I pulled him into a hug. 'You stink.'

He grinned. 'That scent is Eau de Real Man. You wouldn't recognise it, of course,' he said. 'All the same, wouldn't mind a shower?' He lifted up a holdall. Fresh clothing.

'Anything you need. Come in. Beer, wine, champagne?'

'I'd murder a beer,' he said. 'Been out most of the day, trying to scrape together a few jobs. There's a loft conversion company looking for a foreman. Bit of a step down from hotels and shopping malls, but it'd be a good bit of work if I could get it. Part of me is looking forward to something that could be a little more hands-on. Get out of the corporate suit with the hard-hat club and into some proper manual labour. Like old times.' He let out a long shaky sigh. 'Yeah, would be good, would be good all right, if I could get it.'

I opened the fridge, removed a six-pack of bottled beer, handed one to Daniel, then we went through to the lounge. All I wanted to do was check which direction Gabe was headed but I needed to see Daniel settled first. Some instinct told me I may well need an alibi for the night.

'I was thinking of putting on a pizza,' I said to him.

'You haven't eaten?' he asked, leaving his holdall down by the door.

'The odd snack here and there but nothing substantial,' I said.

267

'If you're putting it on anyway, I could do with a bite.'

I pressed a remote and the bookshelves drew back to reveal the wide screen TV Lana and I had had mounted on the wall.

Daniel put down his beer. 'Would you mind if I had that shower now? Wash off the day before we eat.'

'Of course, you're in the room next to the study upstairs on the right,' I said.

He left quickly, returning to the hall to grab his bag. A few moments later, I heard the door of the guest room close. I hurried to the kitchen, looked down at the app on my phone. The blue dot was moving slowly southwest towards the M25. I closed down the application, went upstairs. The shower was still running in Daniel's room. Making my way quickly to my own, I drew a backpack from the bottom of the wardrobe and packed another pair of trousers, a fresh shirt and my phone charger. Then, at the last minute, pulled open the top drawer of my bedside cabinet and found the Sod Buster pocket knife I'd kept there since moving in. I threw it into the bag, then, running a hand over my jaw, I went to the en-suite to shave. If I was to see Lana for the first time in over a month, I wanted to look good.

When Daniel came downstairs, I was waiting by the front door, ready to get on the road. The pizza was in the lounge on the coffee table. Some football match was playing on the TV and there was an ice-bucket filled with bottles of beer within arm's reach of the sofa.

'You're going out?'

'Sorry, I've just had a call. I need to go out to see a patient. Shouldn't be too long.'

'On a Saturday evening?'

'Who wants to be a doctor, eh?'

'Probably wouldn't turn down work either, no matter when it came in. Okay, mate, you want me to save you some pizza?'

'No, I'll pick something up,' I said. 'But I wondered if I could borrow your car? Third gear keeps slipping in mine and I shouldn't drive it until I can get it fixed.'

'You might need to top it up with fuel to get you there, but no problem. Keys are on the sideboard.'

I left him on the sofa, eating pepperoni pizza and slugging happily on beer. I reminded him not to answer the door. Even if someone was persistent.

'It would be awkward for me, if Charlotte discovered you stayed here. Obviously, no reason you shouldn't but, you know . . .' I said.

'Women,' he answered for me.

'Right. It's just easier,' I said. I left through the back garden, moving carefully round the side of the house so as to stay out of sight.

I found Daniel's car a little way up the street. A navy Beemer with a new dent in the passenger door. Tax was up to date and the tyres were good. I couldn't risk being stopped by police. I got into the car, clipped my phone to the dash and turned on the app. Behind me, the gate to The Court slid open. I shrank down into the seat and watched in the rear view as Rachel Shelton followed her springer spaniel out, across the road and down the lane towards the Common. The evening was clear and dry, the sky only just dipping into twilight. Gabe was now clockwise on the M25. I turned on the ignition. The fuel tank was almost empty. I sighed, pulled away from the kerb and out towards the nearest station; two miles south of the Village.

By the time I'd filled up Daniel's car, Gabe had exited the M25 via the M40. I watched the blue dot blink away from me. I got back into the car and sped away in the direction of the motorway. He had a good head start, an hour or so, and from his progress I wagered he was doing between eighty and ninety, while, fearful I'd be pulled over for speeding and it would further delay me from getting to Lana, I stuck to the speed limit as much as I could.

After three and a half hours of driving, I left the A5 and crossed into Wales. Tiredness had crept into my limbs. On the radio, Linkin Park's 'New Divide' played. I turned it up, wound down the window to keep myself awake. In my mind's eye, I saw Gabe coasting smoothly through the narrow Welsh roads ahead, ears popping as he gained then lost height over the hills and down into the dark valleys; the headlights sweeping through a tunnel of pine or fir. I could see him as he turned down an isolated lane, the glow of light on his face from the sleek dashboard, a lodge high up on the side of the hill, a view of the slate-grey sea in the distance. Warm light coming from the front window of the lodge, a single bulb on over the porch. Perhaps a thread of dark smoke coming from a stone chimney.

Lana may well have agreed to hiding away at the start of all this, but perhaps her background was finally going to demand a price. She had that gift of always believing she'd be the one who slipped through the net. With the smallest of efforts, she tended to elude what fell on others. There'd been no precedent to suggest otherwise, so why would life make her feel any consequence now? But neither of us had anticipated Gabriel Wright's true nature.

CHAPTER 24

It was nearing midnight when I passed through the village of Arthog. Gabe's car had stopped moving some time ago and was located some ten miles outside the village. The moon was a soft-grey glow behind the night clouds. It felt like I was driving into nothing, the world opening up like sliding doors until I passed through. The headlamps swept over the tree-lined hills that spread over the sides of the valleys.

I watched for access to a property somewhere through the trees. The map was telling me his car was somewhere above me, on the hillside. I passed by a huddle of rental properties. Three small wooden cabins, each roughly the size of a standard caravan. I couldn't see a car, but then spotted a simple hand-drawn sign with an arrow pointing to a track to the side of the cabins. As I got closer, I could see the track led only to a gravel car park which contained one car, a silver Nissan, and no sign of the black Mercedes. I drove a little further, then caught a glimpse of yellow light between the trees, high on my left.

I pulled over, wound down the window and peered up into

the darkness. The light could have been coming from a shed. I'd passed a lot of farm outbuildings on the passage around and through the Welsh hills. It could be a car, pausing, like me, to assess their location.

I looked up at the trees. The light above was unmoving, so not a bonfire from a camp. There was another property up there. I checked my phone. This was it. I turned the car around, drove back towards the cabins and parked quietly in the car park behind the rentals. I lifted my bag onto my lap, removed the fresh shirt, pulled on my jacket and slid my phone into the pocket. Then I smoothed a hand over my hair before getting out of the car.

If anyone noticed the Beemer's arrival, they'd assume I was a new tenant for a few days, or a guest of an existing one. I wasn't planning on being here long enough to attract more attention than that. After all, the endgame was paramount, and I'd no intention, after everything I had been through, of giving up on Lana now.

I walked out of the park, not bothering to lock the car; I didn't want the obnoxious beep and orange flash of Daniel's Beemer to draw attention. Crossing the road, I set off towards the bank of trees and up the steep incline. I waited until I was beyond the rental cabins before turning on the torch on my phone. I was a few feet in when I spotted a narrow pathway through the trees. I pulled my trousers through the briars. Just as I broke free onto the path, a stray branch caught me on the side of the neck. I reached up, touched the scratch but I couldn't see if I was bleeding. So much for the fresh shirt, I thought. I was half frightened, half angry that I was the one crawling through brush in the middle of nowhere and in the dead of night to see my wife – when Gabe had been able to drive right up to the door.

By the time I ascended the bank, I was out of breath, and sweat was soaking through the back of my shirt. I stood in the shadow of a couple of firs and looked into the clearing. The lodge was well camouflaged. I kept to the periphery and moved along the side property, wanting to get a sense of Gabe's position inside before I went in. The Mercedes was round the back. Black and sleek as a panther. There were no other vehicles. I crouched down and shuffled towards the window.

I questioned why I didn't just walk up to the door, knock and take it from there. But if I was wrong and Gabe wasn't visiting Lana but someone else, then how could I explain my presence? And I would have blown my chance of finding her. Then I heard her voice. That laugh. Didn't she realise the danger she was in? My stomach tightened. Breath held, I straightened, peered into what was a small dining-kitchen area. Even though I was expecting it, the shock of seeing her, well and whole, almost made me cry out. She was wearing a white robe, a towel twisted, turban-style, around her hair. She tipped her head forward, rubbed the towel over her head, then ran fingers through the damp, dark strands.

The sink was full of white dinner plates. A couple of saucepans sat on the side. A male voice rumbled from somewhere out of view, then Gabe appeared. He held two glasses of red wine, passed one to her, and that's when it really started to go wrong. She took the glass but he didn't let go, forcing her to turn in towards him. His glass went down on the table, his hand curled around her waist.

The blood drained from my face, I felt it drop like I'd had my throat cut. She was up on her toes, glass held out, her body closing the gap between them. His hand slid up, cupped the back of her head. Her face tipped upwards. His mouth was on hers, then the hand was on the move again, down over her left shoulder, the dressing gown peeled back.

The breath seized in my throat, blood rushed back to my face, my head. I'd heard people describe a red mist descending but could never have anticipated the rigid, trembling rage that consumed my body. I had to grip the window ledge to stop myself from driving my fist through it. I couldn't move. I was both revolted and transfixed by what I was seeing. The hunger in their movements. The gown fell to the floor. Their mouths moved desperately over one another, Gabe devouring her neck, her shoulder, then back to her mouth again. Her eyes closed, her fingers clawed at his back, pulling him closer. They were moving backwards, into the other room. I couldn't see, and using the house as guide, navigated my way round the back to another window.

The light remained off, but in the glow of the fire I could make out the smooth satin sheen of her skin. She was lying on a sofa. Her arms wrapped possessively around the shape on top of her. Her leg hooked around his hips. My eyes adjusted to the darkness and I could see him. Now thrusting. Fucking my wife. Lana. I became aware of moaning, deep groans of pleasure that used to emanate from her throat when we made love. Then it was over. He collapsed on top of her and they shuffled round until she was lying like a starfish in the sun on top of him, his hand absent-mindedly stroking her still-damp hair.

I staggered back from the window. Sweat across my brow. Nauseous. Angry. Furious, then nauseous again. I looked back through the window. Half disbelieving what I'd just witnessed. Lana was pulling her robe back on, saying something, that lift to her lips. Gabe hooked his hands behind his head. I couldn't make it out but I knew he was enjoying the slow close of the gown, the flick of her hair. The scent of her filling the room. I stumbled back towards the treeline. Sat down in the dirt. I should confront them. Shouldn't I? The betrayal was like a knife between the ribs, and before I knew it, I was on my feet again and storming round to the front of the lodge. I made a fist, raised my hand and prepared to rap on the front door. What would I say?

'I was passing.' Or, 'There's a family emergency.' Or, 'Yes, I did track your car. I was desperate to see my wife. To hold her in my arms. You fucked her. You bastard.'

I could actually see my hands around his throat. Around hers. I stepped away from the door, moved back towards the line of trees. I half ran, half slid down the steep bank towards the row of little cabins. I broke free onto the road, breathing heavily. Flashes of their love-making beat through my head, each one blowing air on the coals of my anger until I was trembling and stiff with it. I reached the car and a man's voice called out.

'Bit late for a walk.'

I turned. Confused.

Pete Clifford was leaning against the open door of one of the cottages. 'Think we should have a chat.'

'I have to go,' I said. I put my hand on the handle of the car door.

'You probably want to know what I know,' he said. 'Thought

I'd catch him at least once with Violet.' He stepped inside the cabin door, waited for me to follow.

I took my hand away from the car. Walked towards him. My movement was stiff, jagged. I didn't feel part of my own body like I was trailing after myself, a balloon on a string. What had their plan been? Was it Gabe Lana planned to set up her future with? Where did Holly feature in all of this? She couldn't know. But when I transferred the money, it would be easy for Gabe to hightail it with all the funds. Lana with him. But Gabe wouldn't leave a loose end behind like that. Once he'd left with Lana, once they had that money, like a limping animal cut from the herd I'd be killed, like he had killed Violet.

I hesitated at the doorstep. The wood along the frame near the door handle was splintered and broken.

'Come in,' Pete said.

The acne on his jaw was an angry red. His eyes were bloodshot, and when he spoke, his lips had that looseness that told me he was drunk. If Pete wanted to speak with Gabe, why wasn't he up at the lodge right now confronting him? Maybe, like me, he was thinking about next moves. Weighing up repercussions. Choosing paths. Then I remembered he'd been at the funeral, where the large framed photograph of Lana greeted mourners as they entered the service. If he'd seen her up there in the lodge, he knew. He knew Lana was still alive. And if he'd seen what I had, he'd already worked out who we'd really cremated that day.

I stepped over the threshold of the cabin. The walls of pine seemed to close in on me so it felt like I was navigating my way down the aisle of an aeroplane. He led me into the kitchen, and with some relief I moved into the wider room. The shock of seeing him had temporarily put a stopper on the neck of my anger. The kitchen was split in two, a breakfast bar on one side with the usual occupants – sink, four-hob gas cooker, cupboards (all pine) – a half-fridge on the other side; a round dining table in the middle of the room that would fit four at a squeeze. The windows were covered by a skirt of gingham cloth that gave the entire room the feel of a camper van.

'How are you here?' I asked. I pulled a chair away from the table to sit, but then thought better of it and leaned up against the wall instead.

'Drink?'

I cleared my throat. 'Sure.'

He jerked open the fridge, plucked a bottle of beer from inside. There was something in his movements, drunken as they were, that warned violence was a misjudged glance away. I thought about the pocket knife lying redundant in the bottom of my backpack and cursed myself.

Pete held the bottle out towards me and I took it. I tried to twist the top off.

'Here,' he said and threw me a corkscrew.

'Thanks,' I said. I levered the top off the bottle and placed the corkscrew on the table.

He came round the breakfast bar, stood wide-legged in front of me; one hand in his pocket, the other clutching the beer to his chest. 'I should be asking you,' he said, in reply to my question. 'I mean, I take it you're not invited, otherwise you'd be up there, kicking your feet up and drinking whatever fifty-quid bottle of shite he's brought.'

277

I waited for him to answer the question. I could tell from the smug look on his face that he wanted to.

He chinned the air. 'She messaged me. Told me that I'd find Gabe here and she thought Violet would be with him. Gave me the address last night, said he'd be here today. So this morning, I borrowed a car, stocked up on some beers and a few other essentials and been waiting all evening. You get that I wasn't sure I could trust her at first. But I guess she's pissed at something.'

Holly.

He took a slug of his beer and looked at me, waited for me to tell him why I was there. 'And you?' he prompted. He blew across the top of the bottle so that it let out a low whine.

'Just a friend visiting,' I said.

He grinned. 'So, you're not here because he's fucking your wife? I mean, I figured he is. From the moment he got here. She opened that door and there was no chit-chat. The first thing your wife did was slide her hand beneath his waistband and down . . .' As he spoke he mimicked the action.

'Shut up,' I said.

'When I saw your dead wife here – I mean she knows how to move, for a corpse, right? – I sat in the ditch, thinking over what it all meant.' His eyes seemed to swell in his head, he lifted his fingers to his temples, then brought them sharply away, hands spreading outwards in the way of an explosion. 'It was a lot to take in, right? Here was your wife. Alive. Isn't that crazy?'

I didn't say anything. I was having flashes of Gabe on top of Lana, her writhing body beneath him. Even the intimacy of their movements before that, the way he'd slipped the gown from her shoulder with ease, confidence. No fear he'd be rejected.

'You must be so relieved, man. What a thing for a bloke to be through, right? Thinking you'd cremated your wife, but here she is, not one hair on her head harmed,' he said, then took a step forward, his expression darkening, eyes spitting a hatred so pure, I could feel it pour over my skin like liquid. 'Here's my confusion. Who was in that coffin, if your wife was here spreading her legs for that prick?'

I don't know how it happened. One minute I was standing there, the next the corkscrew was in my hand and my hand was pushed up against his abdomen.

He looked down, then back up at me, confused, then a smile, wickedly gleeful. He staggered back, the corkscrew projecting from his gut like an alien limb. He gasped a couple of times. I stared down at my hand.

'You shouldn't have said that,' I muttered.

CHAPTER 25

Pete gripped his side, but laughed.

When my dad was early in his descent into alcoholism, he'd have the odd day of striking motivation. Even though it wasn't his nature, he'd head out looking for work like a man desperate to take revenge on the world by surviving. 'You watch,' he'd say, a wild look in his eye. 'You watch me take it all back. They don't know, Myles kid, there's nothing quite so dangerous as a man with nothing to lose.'

That's what I could see in Pete's face.

'As I sat in that ditch,' he panted, 'not even sure if I was hallucinating, I began to understand what was going on. He killed her. He killed Violet. That's who you really burned, wasn't it?' He moved towards me, nostrils flaring. 'See that?' he said, pointing his chin to a jerrycan behind the door. 'Was going to torch the two of them, it's what they deserve. Was just building up to it too when you arrived. Couldn't believe my luck. All of you here. Why kill two birds with one stone when you can burn all three?'

Another step forward. I glanced at the corkscrew. I was angry enough to go for it. All I'd have to do was pull it free, he'd bleed out eventually. But some messed-up part of me wanted to wait to eke out more information from what he'd gleaned. But Pete would have to die. He knew. He'd worked out in hours what had taken me weeks. And not only that, he knew before I did that my wife had been in on it from the start. I thought of the tattoo, the three sisters, lined up like a sword behind Lana's ear. I didn't know my wife at all.

'That's not true. I've never met Violet in my life,' I said. Even I could hear the pathetic bleat in my voice.

Pete launched his beer across the room. It skimmed my ear and crashed into pieces on the wall behind my shoulder. 'Don't fucking lie to me. What? Let me guess. Insurance, right? It won't take me long to convince authorities to look a little deeper.'

'Don't say that,' I said.

'You didn't know about their affair?' He didn't wait for me to answer. 'No. I don't think you did. I saw the pasty, green look on your face when you came stumbling back down that hill. Are they planning on running off into the sunset with all your new money?' He laughed. Pretended to wipe a tear from his eye, then groaned and gripped his stomach.

I looked around for another weapon. He was thin, Pete, but his jaw suggested some underlying strength, like a coil ready to spring, so a full-on frontal attack without a weapon might not be the brightest idea.

He shook his head as if trying to shake away some distraction. 'You know when you know you're not getting the truth. When someone looks you in the eyes and lies straight to your face. And you know they're lying, and they know you know they're lying,

281

and there's not a jot you can do about it but be sure in your gut. God –' he punched the wall to his right, barely flinched – 'that feeling!' He extended his head back as if he were about to howl.

I was moving before I realised. My hand landed on the cork-screw in his abdomen. The veins at Pete's temple swelled. I pushed hard, intending to wind him against the breakfast bar. I wasn't expecting him to fall straight back onto it. His head made a sickening clunk on the corner of the breakfast bar. He went limp as a rag, then dropped to the floor. The movement was so quick that I went down with him, my hand still around the corkscrew. As he hit the floor, his sour, warm breath burst into my face. His eyes focused on mine for a brief moment, then closed.

I peeled myself away slowly. Breathing hard. Stood up and took a step back. Chest heaving. I expected to feel sick. I'd have thought I'd piss myself. But I didn't. As soon as Pete worked out what was going on, especially a link to Violet, there was no choice. I had to kill him. *Fuck Gabe*, I thought. Anger building again. This was his fault. I went to the cupboard under the sink, found a roll of black bags.

I tied one over Pete's head to capture the blood flow. I searched his pockets, found his phone and turned it off. With a grimace, I removed the corkscrew, dropped it and the phone into a smaller bag then tied another black bag around his lower half and abdomen. When I was done, I collapsed onto a chair, picked up my beer and thought about what to do next. The longer I sat, the angrier I got, the betrayal was like acid in my throat. Pressing the heels of my hands against my eyes, I tried to push away the memory of Lana and Gabe together, but the image of her leg hooked round him, the curve of her shoulder, the drive of his hips towards hers, was burned into my mind. I got up, paced, taking swigs of the beer. It struck me that if I stayed here long enough, stayed in this swirl of circular thoughts, pacing, drinking, I'd be as mad as Pete come morning. I looked down at his still body. I didn't feel remorse. I felt pity. I wasn't going to end up like that. There would be no more pleading for answers. I was now the one who knew too much, and that made me a problem.

My eyes lighted on the jerrycan. I finished the beer, then rinsed the bottle under the tap. I cleaned up the broken glass in the far corner of the room. Wiped down every surface I recalled touching, then I reached for Pete's hands and hauled him into sitting position. I got behind him, put my arms under his arm-pits and began to drag him outside. For a thin man, he was surprisingly heavy.

Up above, the light had dimmed or gone out in the lodge. I stopped for a moment, caught my breath, then continued to drag the body round the side of the cabin until he was out of view. I looked at my watch. It was almost three in the morning. Down the valley there were only a couple of lights visible in the darkness and no vehicles moving in this direction. It was eerily silent apart from the odd hoot from an owl. Retrieving the knife from the car, I slid it into my back pocket, then dusted off my hands and headed for the bank of trees again. I found the path in the darkness and crept slowly upwards. I was hoping Lana and Gabe felt safe enough in their hidey-hole that they'd not thought to lock the back door.

I approached the side window again. Peered inside. The fire

had reduced to embers, the fireguard in place. Other than above the door, there were no other lights on. There was no sign of Lana, or Gabe. My heart was pounding in my chest. Part of me wanted to burst into the house and head straight to the heat of the bedroom. I wanted them to see that I knew, to know that they wouldn't get away with it. But I wasn't about to let my desire for revenge land me in trouble. What revenge I took would have to be carefully planned out.

The door was locked but the spare key was easily found in a small ornamental owl on the windowsill. When I lifted it, the owl's body split in two revealing a key hideaway. I slipped the key into the lock and turned it slowly. The lock gave and I pushed the door inwards.

The room was warm. The scent of garlic and cooked meat lingered in the air, accompanied by the lower musky tang of sex. I curled my fingers into my palm. Clenched and unclenched my hands, counting down from ten. The house was not quite silent, the air shifting just enough to give the sense of the two bodies slumbering through the wall. I stared at the wall, imagining Lana entwined in Gabe's arms. Lana's head tucked just below his chin, her arm slung possessively across his chest, like it was once across mine. I suppressed the urge to burst into the room. I'd be back soon enough, but first I had to find his car keys. Slowly, my eyes adjusted to the darkness. His trousers were still on the floor of the tiny living room. The legs tunnelled, fireman style, where he'd stepped out of them so quickly. Trying not to disturb them too much, I slid my hand into the one pocket and, not finding anything, tried the other side, then the back pockets. Nothing. I stood, looked around.

On the counter, near the sink, I could make out a large brown paper bag. Groceries. I crept across the room. His wallet, watch and keys sat in the bundle next to it. I saw Lana, welcoming him inside. Imagined how he'd shifted the weight of the groceries to one arm so he could reach for her with the other. In the kitchen, he'd dumped everything on the counter, bag, then keys and wallet. I grabbed the keys and went to slip back outside but I stopped, spotting the corkscrew next to an empty wine bottle. I saw Gabe again, approaching my wife, the two glasses of wine in his hands. I picked up the corkscrew with the cuff of my sleeve and dropped it into my shirt pocket.

I didn't dare look over my shoulder as I pressed the central locking of the Mercedes and got into the driver's seat. I pushed the ignition and the dash lit up. The headlights flooded the back of the lodge with white light. I reached for them quickly and turned them off. I put the car in drive, released the handbrake and rolled round the front of the lodge. A glance behind showed the lodge still in darkness. I edged the vehicle down and round the short hill through the trees, and stopped just before Pete's cabin. I got out and opened the boot. Golf clubs. I levered them out, shoved them into the footwell of the back seat. Then I went back to where I'd left Pete's body.

A small part of me hoped he wouldn't be there. That I'd imagined the entire episode. A side effect of seeing Lana and Gabe together. But there he was, his feet extended between the cabins, toes turned out. I loosened the plastic bag I'd tied round his abdomen and searched for the wound then I pulled my shirtsleeve over my hand, took the corkscrew Gabe had used from my pocket and drove it into Pete's abdomen. Then I dragged him towards me. Again, under the arms. Towards the open trunk of the Merc. I sat on the edge of the open boot and heaved him up into the car. It was awkward. My foot slipped a couple of times and he broke free, his head whacking the bumper before his body slipped to the ground. But eventually his top half tumbled into the boot, head-first. I lifted his legs up and folded them into the dark space. I went back into the cabin. Gave it a once-over. I couldn't see any evidence that I'd been there. Then I picked up the bag with the corkscrew, and the jerrycan, and pulled the door behind me, wiping the broken handle once it closed.

I placed the jerrycan and the bag into the back of Daniel's Beemer, then returned to the Mercedes. I got back into the driver's seat and slowly – which was difficult, as I just wanted it over with now – drove back up towards the lodge, parking silently round the back. I turned the steering fully round to the left, got out of the car, turned on the torch on my phone and lay down on the ground. Pointing the light towards the inside of the wheel, I found the brake line. Reaching for my knife, I flicked open the blade, then placed it against the brake line and began to cut, carefully, not all the way through, just enough to create a point of weakness.

I wanted to give Gabe a scare, send a signal from the universe that maybe his luck was about to run out. Worst case, he'd have to slow to a stop and someone would discover the body in the trunk. I stood, slid the knife into my pocket and turned off the torch. I straightened the steering, then before locking the car, I reached under the wheel arch and removed the tracking device.

Letting myself back into the lodge, I wiped the keys, then left them back where I'd found them. My eyes lingered on Gabe's watch. The fire had died down to a glowing orange. The occupants still slept. I closed the back door. Locked it and left the key in its hideaway. Then I scrambled back down the hill, got into the back of Daniel's car and waited for morning. I lay awake the rest of the night.

CHAPTER 26

The crunch of gravel alerted me to the approach of the Mercedes. I edged upwards, not daring to sit up fully, even though both the car and myself were out of his eyeline. I was gritty-eyed and exhausted, but anger is a great motivator. And it came flooding back with surprising ferocity. The sting of betrayal. The realisation that all of this was so that Lana and Gabe could leave with my money. Yes, it was Lana's insurance, but it was me who'd taken all the hits. The injustice of it rose in my throat. Made me sweat. The indignity of having that Hunter detective bloke traipse through my home. The lies that spilled from my tongue to protect her. And all the while Gabe picked up each one as if they were feathers to line his nest.

From where I was sitting, I could make out the top of the Mercedes as it curved round the bend, and once I was sure it was far enough away, I sat up straighter and watched it disappear into early morning mist. I began to sweat profusely. My mouth was dry. I needed to act quickly. Get home before anyone realised I was missing. It was very early. She'd still be in bed. I was sure.

Could I do this? I had to. It was the perfect murder. She'd seen to that herself. You can't kill someone who's already dead.

But even as I thought it, I knew, deep down, that I couldn't hurt her. I hoped that once she saw me, she'd forget him. Forget their plans. I got out of the car and hurried up to the lodge. I stood in the doorway for what seemed like a full ten minutes. I couldn't delay too much, but the events of the night were beginning to take their toll. Events of the last couple of months. I'd killed a person. I had the sensation that I wanted to cry. My throat ached, there was a stinging pain at the back of my eyes. In the trees beyond the lodge, the sky was turning from the milky hues of dawn to a flat grey. The birdsong was raucous. I ran a hand over my hair, straightened my shoulders. I pushed all images of her with him out of my mind, conjured up her face as she tipped it upwards to mine. The way her dark lashes would flutter closed when I kissed her. The feel of her palm on my cheek.

I knocked. I thought it would take longer for her to answer. Part of me wished that she was still sleeping and wouldn't hear the door. Then I could still walk away. But I heard the creak of a floorboard, then the door was swinging inward. The expression on her face was glowing. Her eyes glittered with excitement. For a moment, I thought the look was for me and my heart lifted. But then I saw the falter in her expression, the quick blink of her eyes. I think that was almost worse than seeing her and Gabe together. She attempted to recover quickly but although I knew there was lots I didn't know about Lana, I was well trained in spotting the glimpses of her true emotion, like air bubbles on a still pond rising to the surface before swiftly dispersing.

'Myles,' she breathed. She gathered the edges of her dressing gown together in her fist. Then, catching herself, took a step towards me and flung herself into my arms. 'Oh my God. You're here,' she said against my neck. 'I've missed you so much.'

My own arms went around her, my hand gripped the back of her head and I held her to my chest. I inhaled the scent of her hair, the scent of her skin, and felt peace wash over me.

When she pulled back, I released her. 'How did you . . . ?' She moved back into the hallway. 'You should come in,' she said, looking out beyond my shoulder.

I told myself she was searching for walkers, tourists, rather than for the return of the Mercedes.

'Thank you,' I said.

I followed her indoors and I heard the door click behind me.

We went to the kitchen. I took the seat with my back to the living room. To the sofa.

She sat carefully beside me, gripped my hands. 'You found me. I knew you'd come.' Her eyes met mine. 'How did you do it?'

'Gabe told me.' The lie slipped out easily. I enjoyed the look of confusion that crossed her face. I wondered what series of thoughts it triggered in her mind. A zoetrope of betrayal. Could she trust him? Was he hoping she'd be discovered? About to ditch her like she'd ditched me? How would this piece of information fit in with her planned future? 'It doesn't matter, does it? You're happy to see me?' I asked.

Her grip tightened. 'Of course,' she said. She kissed me, her mouth sour from morning coffee. 'I've missed you so much,' she said again. She got up. 'Coffee?'

'Please,' I said. 'Have you spoken to Gabe recently?'

She kept her back to me when she answered but I could see the stiffening of her shoulders, the small hitch of them up her neck. 'He called yesterday. We were just saying how all this is almost over. The money's all in?'

'Yes,' I said, wanting to know what her next move would be.

She glanced over her shoulder towards me. 'You did it. You really did it.' A flicker of a frown. 'Are you hurt?'

I looked quickly down at my shirt, then realised the scratch I'd sustained on my face when I got here had been bleeding. 'A vengeful briar.'

'You should clean it. They can get infected,' she said. Her fake concern was beginning to grate.

'How are you getting food and such?'

'Gabe came up a couple of weeks ago. Stocked the freezer. I couldn't risk going out or deliveries. I'm so glad you're here. It's been really grim. Here alone,' she said with astounding selfishness.

'Not as grim as cremating your wife.'

She flicked me a look, and in it I could see something of the Lana I knew. She'd normally tell me off for that. Give me some psychology twaddle to put me in my place. I don't think I ever won an argument with Lana. And the times I did, it always had the taste of loss, as if she'd let me get away with something, given me permission to win, rather than feeling justified that what I was saying was right. But this Lana was different, this Lana was on guard.

'I'm sorry,' she said. 'Jesus, that was insensitive of me. I know you've been through hell. And Gabe told me all about the detective and poor Nathan.'

291

'Sounds like you and Gabe are in touch a lot?'

She turned, a cafetière in her hand and two mugs in her other hand. 'No milk, I'm afraid.' She put the mugs in the centre of the table and I pulled one towards me.

I waited until she'd sat down, then asked, 'Sugar?'

She got up again. I noticed how she'd dodged my question. She opened a cupboard, withdrew a heavy glass bowl and put it in front of me, then jerked open a nearby drawer, took out a teaspoon and sent it sliding across the table. 'Myles, is everything okay? You seem . . . angry?'

I spooned a half into my coffee. 'I'm fine. Just tired. Driving at night always leaves me exhausted.'

'At night?'

'I had to sleep in my car when I got here. Didn't want to disturb you until morning.' I took a sip of the coffee. 'It's been an interesting night.'

She stiffened. A beat of silence, then, 'You know,' she said. Her voice turned painfully cold.

I didn't answer. I let the silence grow for a half-minute. But knew that Lana would win any game of silences. It's what she did all day with her clients, waited, waited for them to offer themselves up.

'How long?' I asked.

'Does it matter?'

'Yes, it matters.' I found myself giving a short, outraged laugh. 'It matters.'

'Myles . . .' In that grating tone like she was trying to reason with a stubborn child.

I reached for her hand, a desperate act that contained whatever hope I had that I'd got this all wrong. She pulled away. I expected an apology. Some remorse. I took in a breath.

But she couldn't even look at me.

'Do you love him?' I asked.

Finally, she looked at me, tears in her eyes, but I didn't trust them. 'I'm sorry, Myles. I was confused. Lonely.'

'So, you don't love him?'

'I barely know him. Not really. Everything felt out of control. And he just made me feel safe in that moment.'

It was like my skin was growing thorns, like they were pushing through my body, a sensation of prickling hatred ran over me. 'I couldn't be here. Remember? You made sure of that.'

She began to walk over and back, her thumbnail between her teeth. 'How has this happened?'

She hadn't answered the love question.

'Did you sleep with him before or after your "death"?' I hooked my fingers in the air at the word 'death'.

She stopped walking, frowned at me. 'Myles, we can get through this. This can't all be for nothing.'

'I could walk away,' I said. 'You'd get nothing.'

'You wouldn't do that to me,' she said.

'You were about to do it to me.'

She touched her tongue to her top lip, approached slowly. 'No. You've got that wrong.' I knew she was lying.

The image of her on the sofa, Gabe on top of her, flashed in my mind. 'Where were you thinking of going?' I asked. 'I assume you have plans for . . . after you've managed to screw me out of my money.'

'My future is with you,' she said. Tears gathered along the bottom of her eyes.

'How could you do it to me, Lana?' I said. 'We were a team.' I needed her to feel the full force of her mistake. 'And that woman. Violet. He murdered her. How could you be with someone like that?'

'She was blackmailing him. About to tell the police all about his last scheme, which would have jeopardised ours. Don't you see that?' She shook her head, wanting to get away from the topic of Violet's murder. 'How can I make this right?'

I tipped my head, tapped a finger against my lips. 'How to make right an innocent woman's murder?'

'No one is wholly innocent,' she snapped.

It hit me again that I'd just killed a man. That his body was slowly stiffening in the boot of Gabe's car. But that was to protect her, us, the entire crazy enterprise we'd embarked on. Pete should have stayed away, and Gabe should not have dirtied our plan with his past mistakes. But deep down I knew I hadn't done it to protect Lana, or Gabe, or any of it, but I'd acted against Pete so swiftly and without equivocation because he threatened *my* future.

'I guess not,' I said. I pressed my fingers against my temple, squeezed my eyes shut and willed the last twenty-four hours to rewind. The more I thought on it, the more I felt Gabe deserved what was coming to him. He had wooed us all and then fucked us over.

I lifted my head to ask her if she planned on seeing him again. 'What about—'

But I never got to finish the question. A bright burst of white sparks exploded across my vision accompanied by a short sharp pain behind my eyes. I had just enough time to look up and see Lana's tear-streaked face, a cast-iron poker in her hand, before I rolled off the chair.

CHAPTER 27

Can you call it luck when your wife tries to kill you but you survive? Luck would have been bestowed had I'd been deleted by the swing of that poker. Had I sunk into oblivion. Over. That last memory of life, that short, sharp pain; it would have been nothing at all to what followed. Instead, I was slumped against the wall of the kitchen. There was a dull pain thumping with a steady beat through my head. My eyes ached but I tried to force them open a fraction. Ahead of me, the legs of the table stood like fuzzy pillars. Beyond that, the room was a watercolour mix of beige and white. There was a high-pitched screech in my left ear. Under my right eye, something warm, wet. Blood. My right arm was twisted behind me. There was a tingling in my fingers. I wanted to wiggle them. Stretch my arm out but I didn't know where Lana was.

I slowed my breath and the din in my ear lowered enough for me to make out her voice. I felt as though I were at the end of a long tunnel, like I'd been submerged underwater. You don't trust sound underwater. The sound got louder. I kept my eyelids lowered just enough and peered through a murky slit of vision.

'What did you expect me to do? Please, you have to come back,' she was saying. Her bare feet appeared. 'Not quite. Oh God, he's really groaning.'

Was I?

'Can't you come back?' A shaky breath. She still held the poker. I could make out a few spiky strands of my hair stuck to the end.

Her feet turned and walked away.

I was pretty sure she'd moved into the hallway. Now that I wasn't dead – that I had been denied that descent into oblivion, forced to witness how little my wife cared for me – a familiar bitter anger curdled in my stomach. Anger at how I was here again. With nothing. That I'd been betrayed by my wife. That Gabe had, most likely, from the moment of our first meeting seen me as less than. At least I could go with the knowledge that he wasn't escaping from this mess clean. When Pete's body was found in his boot, if there was a God, he'd lose his surgical licence pronto, if he hadn't already. A man like Gabe wouldn't do well with that loss. Even though he wasn't working at the moment, I knew that being a surgeon was integral to who he was, how he held himself, how he moved through his world. I derived a twisted pleasure in knowing that I would be taking that from him, from Lana.

My vision sharpened in correlation with my head pain, now less of a dull ache and more the stabbing pain of a nervous system finally catching on to what's happening. I could hear that I had indeed been groaning and took a few shaky breaths to loosen my throat. I clenched and unclenched my fingers. All working. Then my toes. Ditto there. Head wounds bleed a lot. Even ones that do no more damage than just puncturing the scalp. I had no double vision. Didn't feel sick. But then I hadn't attempted to stand yet. Every few breaths I paused, listened for the sound of Lana's voice. Lana, I sensed, despite her penchant for passive aggression, was more likely to clobber me to death when I was upright and looking her in the face than when I was vulnerable and out cold.

I began to sweat. Not just a little warmth, but a cool eruption of moisture across my forehead, the soles of my feet and the palms of my hands. I pushed into sitting position. The room swam and I pitched both hands out to the side to maintain my balance. She was still on the phone. Fuck his fucking car. He should have had more trouble on those hills and bends by now. There was no doubt in my mind that if Gabe managed to get back here, I would be lining the bottom of a ditch within the hour. I forced myself up the wall. I was surprised by how much strength I had in my legs. Adrenaline caused my heart to race. I lurched towards the back door.

'No. No. He's up,' I heard her say.

I reached for the door handle. I couldn't quite understand why I wasn't grabbing it faster. Staggering a little more, tears of frustration burned my eyes, a droplet of bloody spittle flew from my mouth and landed on the back of my outstretched hand. The green surroundings beyond the door wobbled and waved. A short grunt came from behind me and something whistled by my left ear.

'Fuck,' she said. 'Myles, I'm sorry but I can't let you leave.'

She'd missed; just as she took aim I'd misstepped and stumbled further into the kitchen. I stopped against the fridge. She swung again, I put my arms up and caught the poker in both hands, the metal ringing against my thumb. Her leg came up and her neat, toenail-painted foot slammed into my groin. I let go of the poker and fell backwards, the edge of the counter matching her attack across my back. *Fucking hell*, I thought. If it had been happening to someone else, I might find the situation amusing. How had I ended up here? And at a disadvantage? I looked at her with confusion. The deep brown of her eyes were dark and glittering as the night. She was focused on me, like a tennis finalist preparing to serve. I was not so much immobilised by pain and weakness as with a strange kind of fascination at her transformation. And yet, it wasn't a transformation at all. I realised it was glimpses of this very Lana, small flashes of some dark reservoir within her, that held me captive in her love. I had thought I'd tamed something.

However, time stretches out in these moments, my mind swept me back to a dinner at the Wrights' house. I held up a glass of Rioja, twirled the glossy red within the bowl. The conversation had turned, as it did sometimes when we'd not yet had our fill of our own pretentiousness. Gabe, who was contemplating the existence of a higher being, of God, had told us how he was confronted daily with unexplainable wonders, elbow deep in the chest cavities of his patients.

'It's an indifferent god who allows those patients to be on your table in the first place,' I said, scrambling to get the Epicurean Paradox right, and failing. 'So much suffering. Who can look with equal favour on those upon whom cruelty is inflicted as those who dish it out?'

'Right!' Holly had exclaimed, banging her hand against the

table, emphasising her agreement with me and parsing what I wanted to say with an eloquence only somewhat marred by her slurring of the word 'wishes'. 'He either wishes to take away evils and is unable, which makes him a feeble god, or he doesn't wish to remove evil, which makes him complicit at best. If neither able nor willing, then he's not worthy of the status.'

Lana had reached towards a bowl of edamame on the table, pulled the bean through her teeth, then dropped the empty shell on her plate. 'But evil implies some entity to be fought, like it could be plucked up and erased, but it's a human affliction. I would say, if there is a higher being, then perhaps their hesitancy in erasing evil is one of mercy. We are the evil.'

Gabe had given two loud claps of his hands. Laughed.

I extended my hand to Lana, my smile widening. 'My wife has an answer for everything.'

We are the evil. We are the evil. Seeing the determination in Lana's eyes now, the braced stance, the willingness to end me, I could believe that. In the moments before the poker came down, I reached back to the knife in my pocket. She struck, and I twisted out from beneath her, the metal clanging against the countertop. I didn't wait. Or hold back. She didn't make a sound. Just turned to face me, an expression of bewilderment on her face that haunts me still. The poker slipped from her hand. Hit the tile point first, then fell onto its side. I kicked it away. I pulled the knife free and she grasped at the wound. There was blood in her mouth. Her breathing rattled. I struck again. Not wanting her to suffer. And wanting it over.

I carried her into the living room. I couldn't look down at her face. There was a sick clammy sweat on my forehead, behind my ears and settling cold over my top lip, but otherwise I felt surprisingly calm. It wasn't that I wasn't upset, that I didn't want to cry, to cry out, but there was a strange feeling of inevitability to what had happened, to what was happening. I could hear her voice, clear as a bell, in my mind. *The idea of choice is an illusion. All our actions are decided for us long before we carry them out.* I laid her on the sofa in front of the cold hearth. Then I knelt by the fireplace, balled up a few sheets of the newspaper, found the firelighters. Once the fire leapt to life, I washed my hands. Then the knife; dried it and placed it back in my pocket.

I knew enough about what science could reap from a crime scene. I couldn't risk them finding evidence that I was here. I went to the kitchen sink, ran the tap and soaked a tea towel, then gingerly held it against the back of my head. It stung, awakened the dull pain at my temples. The bleeding had eased but not enough. There was a roll of tape in one of the drawers. I made a makeshift pad with a fresh tea towel, then ran the tape around my head. I felt strangely energised, like the feeling I got when I stole. And my thoughts were clear, my actions efficient.

I went into the hall, found the mobile she'd been using. It was a basic analogue. No password. No need when you're on your own, I guess. I opened the contacts. There was only one number. Gabe's. That was it. There were a few text messages. Most written in a kind of shorthand code. *SUS.* Which I translated as *See you soon.* Or *C @ 24 hrs,* meaning *call at 7 p.m.* I found an accompanying call at 7 p.m. in her phone log. The record went back to the morning I was brought to the hospital to identify her remains. I put the phone in my pocket. I cleaned the door handle, the table, washed my coffee mug in hot soapy water and placed it back in the cupboard. Then I carried the damp tea towel to the fireplace and threw it into the long tongues of flame.

I went to the car, drove it up to the lodge and parked round the back where the Mercedes had been. I opened the boot and removed the jerrycan. Then I set about dousing the lodge with petrol. There was no better way to get rid of evidence than fire. The lodge was ideal for burning, sheltered by trees, and the ground around it was dry. With the right fuel, it would go up in minutes and destroy everything inside. I knew there was a possibility police would be able to retrieve DNA samples from Lana's remains. But they would have nothing to compare them to. She was a ghost on their system.

When I was done, I drove downhill and waited in the car park until the first tendrils of smoke began to lift from the trees above me. I thought of Mr Hartigan from all those years ago. It's strange how some events echo down through a person's life. As I've said before, the problem with living with murder as the limit to one's morality is that you tell yourself that as long as you didn't cross that line, you're good. But I'd lived so close to that line for so long that murder didn't look so bad at all. And for me, it didn't seem such a leap. It seemed like the smallest of steps.

I hung on for as long as I could, to see whether Gabe would return. Ten minutes. Fifteen minutes. The smoke was now black, twisting like a dark ribbon into the sky. I reeked of petrol. My head hurt and I was aware that I needed to get home, shower and dress before anyone noticed I was missing. A final glance up through the trees and I got into Daniel's car, turned the ignition and drove out of the car park, away from the lodge, away from last night, away from this morning.

CHAPTER 28

My only stop was at a viewing point next to a lake, where I launched both Pete's and Lana's analogue phone as far as I could into its cold depths. Two hours' drive saw me leave the peaks and valleys of Mid Wales in my rear-view. I was aware I was driving too fast, but once I got to the motorways, the desire to put as much distance, if not time, between what I'd done and what lay ahead became all I could think about. I wanted to drive until that entire dark period was far behind me, so far I could tell myself that those memories belonged to another person, another Myles. I wondered whether Gabe was doing the same. Hurrying home to Holly. Or had he returned to the lodge? Was he at this moment attempting to put out the fire?

The rest of the journey I remember only as a blur of white lines and tarmac, the other cars on the road, toys, pixelated images to move around. I arrived at the kerbside outside Belvedere Court with a stunned realisation that I was home and not entirely sure how I got there. The fuel tank was once again empty as if the last nineteen hours had not happened, all chess pieces returned to starting positions. I reached into the back seat, collected my bag, removed my phone from the dash and got out of the car. I pressed the fob for the gates and headed quickly for my house, slipping down the side passage and letting myself in through the sliding back doors.

Standing inside the door, I listened for sounds of Daniel. It was after midday, but I knew his pattern was late to bed, late to rise. I hurried to the utility room, took off my shirt, trousers, socks, and pushed the lot into the washing machine. I added powder and selected a hot wash, not caring what state the clothes came out as long as every trace of Lana and Pete Clifford had disappeared from them. Then, taking a pair of trousers and a T-shirt from the laundry basket, I shrugged them on quickly. I crept upstairs, clutching my bag. When I got to the landing, I could hear the soft rhythms of Daniel's snores and felt some of the tension leave my body. In my room, I locked the door, went to the en-suite, dropped the bag in the corner, then leaned against the sink and looked into the mirror.

I should have been shocked by what looked back at me. There was a pale yellowish tinge to my skin, still that slick of sweat over my brow. A bluish shadow around my right eye, a small purple lump beneath the skin over my cheekbone. Bright red abrasions on the heel of my right hand. The tape that held the black-and-white tea towel to the back of my head dug into the top of my left ear. My hair stuck out in tufts over the top of the makeshift bandage, matted, clumps held together with dried blood. But the look in my eye I'd seen before. A steady gleam, even as my hands and limbs shook. I found the corner of the tape and gingerly peeled it away from my skin. I prised the tea towel from the back of my head, touched a finger to the wound.

I located a hand mirror in one of the drawers and held it out from the injury, studying the extent of the damage in the reflection in front of me. It had stopped bleeding for now and despite how profusely it had bled, it didn't look like it would need stitches. I stood in the shower, let the cold jets of water hit my closed eyes. I scrubbed my arms, my abdomen, my face, until I was shivering and awake. Then I stepped out, returned to the sink and shaved. I was surprised by how well I looked. Under the sink, I found our first-aid kit. I opened it, found a sachet of haemostatic powder. Not your standard first-aid stock, unless you are a doctor.

I put a towel around my shoulders, opened the sachet and tipped the granules into my hand. I pinched some between my fingers and pushed them into the wound at the back of my head, pressing against the injury for a minute before applying some more. I lifted the hand mirror again. The powder had done its work and stopped any further bleeding. Content, I combed my hair and got dressed.

In the bedroom, I sat on the edge of the bed, my backpack at my side and looked out on The Court. There'd been rain in the morning and the street glistened in the sunshine that followed. The silver birch that lined the street fluttered in a light breeze. There was no sign of the Mercedes in the Wrights' drive. But I could see Holly in the back garden, working through a series of yoga poses. I emptied the last items from my bag. The corkscrew I'd buried in Pete's stomach and Gabe's watch which I hadn't been able to resist taking.

305

I held the watch in my palm – it was an Omega, silver with a classic blue face – and opened the locker by my bed. Inside was Lana's funeral urn. I'd long since emptied it of Violet's ashes. They were buried at the foot of an acer in the garden. I dragged the urn out onto the floor. It was a heavy thing, made of recycled stainless steel with a simple pattern of criss-crossing lines over its surface. Lifting the lid, I removed a plastic bag from inside. I opened it, dropped the watch and corkscrew inside, where they clinked against the other items; Lana's old mobile, Nathan's reading glasses, a pen where, when you tipped it up and down, a miniature tennis ball travelled across a green court, a wedding band, a tiny toolset of the sort you get in a Christmas cracker, and now a watch that had an inscription on the back: *I'll love you until the end of us.*

Downstairs, I switched on the coffee machine and needing to get some foothold in normality, phoned Sam. The call rang out and I was just about to hang up when I heard his voice.

'Dr Butler? Is everything okay?'

'Sorry for phoning on a Sunday, Sam. But with all the upheaval with Nathan's passing, I wanted to make sure we're all set for tomorrow. How was the diary looking yesterday?'

There was a brief pause of confusion then, 'Good, I think. Full. Mrs Kingston phoned to let us know that the funeral for Dr Kingston is a week next Thursday.'

'Okay. Let the patients know first thing. Many of them will want to attend. We should close. Out of respect,' I said.

'Okay,' he said tightly. I could hear another voice, close to him, telling him to get off the phone. 'Also, Sofia – I mean, Mrs Kingston – said she had the papers for you. She didn't say which ones, only that you would know about it.'

I opened my wallet, searched through the pockets until I located Anthony Chapman's business card. He'd said he was interested in investing in the surgery and now seemed as good a time as any to bring him on board. The surgery needed expansion. Renovation. A fresh look for Willowhaven that people would recognise as mine.

'Thank you. Who is my first tomorrow?'

'New patient. She wanted the senior clinician, I wasn't sure—'

'That's me,' I said.

'Hip pain,' he said. 'She sounded bad.'

There was a shuffling noise behind me and I turned, raised a mug at Daniel and pointed towards the coffee machine. He was wearing a pair of Bermuda shorts and a loose-fitting vest, sleep still pressed against his eyes.

'Thanks, Sam,' I said into the phone then finished the call.

Daniel made a coffee then turned to me with a smile. 'Slept like a baby,' he said. 'Listen, I just wanted to thank you for putting me up and, you know, if there's anything you want doing, around the house or the garden I'd be happy to . . .' He stopped. 'Hey, what happened?'

'Nothing. I fell. Running,' I said.

He shook his head, lifted his hands and waved his fingers at me. 'That's what these are for,' he said. 'You're not supposed to use your head to break a fall.'

'Funny,' I said.

'You okay though?'

'Surface wounds only,' I replied. 'There's a spare key in the sideboard by the hall and a spare fob for the gates there too.

I'll find a way to let Charlotte know you're here so you're not having to creep around.'

He winced. 'Actually . . .'

I reached out for my jacket, which was resting over the kitchen island.

'She called round last night,' he said. 'Not long after you went to see that patient. She was a little worried about you, but we got talking—'

I pointed to the floor. 'Here?'

He took a breath. 'I know you said not to answer the door, but I thought it might be you, you'd forgotten your key or something. Don't worry, she was okay. Not mad or anything, mate. And I took your advice. Came completely clean about the app I put on her phone. I mean, it was excruciating admitting that.' He wiped a hand across his brow. 'The shame of it . . . but you know, she was silent about it for a while, then accepted my apology. I can't quite believe it really.'

Charlotte knew I hadn't been there last night. My chest tightened. But, I told myself, there was no reason for Charlotte to doubt anything other than what Daniel had told her: that I was out dealing with urgent work.

'Okay, that's good then,' I said.

He couldn't keep the smile from his face, his eyes. 'I'm meeting her shortly, in the Village for a bite. Any advice?'

Against the odds, despite all of Lana's sneers and the patronising lens through which I often viewed Daniel and Charlotte's relationship, here they were, still surviving.

'I don't think you need any advice from me,' I said. 'Tell her I said hi.'

'Things are looking up.'

I glanced at the time, took up my work bag. Pulled my chest high. 'They are.'

He eyed my bag. 'You going into work again? On a Sunday?'

I didn't want to stay in the house. I was restless. Half of me was still in that carpark in Wales, replaying all that I'd witnessed, all that I'd done the night before. 'No,' I said then remembering the lie I'd told him about my car, said, 'I found a garage nearby that will sort my gearbox. Going to grab a newspaper and a coffee and kill some time while they fix it.'

Driving out of The Court, there was still no Mercedes in the Wrights' drive. There was no way the damage I did to Gabe's car would have done more than stalled him for a couple of hours, so his absence meant one of two things. Either his car had been taken to a garage, the body discovered, and Gabriel Wright was now cuffed and explaining himself in a police station, or – as seemed to be written in his fate – he had escaped, driven away from his crimes, with Pete's body still in the trunk of the Mercedes. I waited for the gates, then pulled away from The Court. A flash of white and blue from my left caused my foot to briefly touch the brakes. A police car was parked along the narrow road that edged the park.

I drove on, eyes on the rear-view. A young officer in high-vis stepped out of the vehicle and made his way towards an older woman who held out an empty dog lead and pointed off in the direction of the treeline. I blinked hard. It was fine. It would all be fine, I told myself. I just needed to get through the day. Errors would be made if I allowed myself to panic. I could hold my nerve. Hadn't I been doing that my entire life?

★

'Good afternoon, Dr Butler,' Sam said when I opened the surgery door the next morning.

'Could I get a pot of coffee, Sam, when you're ready,' I asked.

'You okay?' Sam asked, making a circular motion over his face.

I feigned confusion for a second then, 'Oh, this.' I pointed to just beneath my eye. 'Caught my toe on a tree root when running. Got my hands out, but not quick enough.' I showed him the abrasions on my palm.

'Oof,' he said, gathering up some papers to the side of his desk. 'This is why I don't exercise.'

Madison appeared briefly down the hall, then, seeing me, disappeared into the storeroom.

'Dr Lopez,' I called out, throwing a quick thank you to Sam as I chased down the hall. 'Madison.'

She stiffened. 'Myles.'

I stopped in front of her. She looked gaunt, red-eyed, and for some reason this irked me, like she was grieving for Nathan better than I was, when I'd been the one who'd worked with him the longest.

But I gave her a sympathetic smile. 'How are you?'

'You've heard from Sofia?' Each syllable punched out through gritted teeth.

'Yes.'

'She's giving you the surgery.'

'Not exactly giving. But some arrangement, yes. A percentage of profits will continue to go to her for her lifetime. It had always been Nathan's intention.'

She tipped her head. 'Was it?'

'Yes,' I said.

She met my eyes. 'We both know he wouldn't have wanted that.'

'I'm not sure why you'd think that,' I said.

'He told me he was planning on giving you notice.'

I pulled back, lifted my chest, looked down on her. 'Nathan valued my work here.'

'He wanted you gone,' she said, leaning in and bringing herself up to my height.

I tightened my hand on my bag. Nathan had told her he'd intended to fire me. He'd promised me discretion.

'If that was the case, then he should have put his house in order before he croaked it.'

Her eyes widened.

I let out a breath. 'Look, we're all upset. This has been a huge shock. Nathan . . . he was like a father to me, and I guess I feel angry that he's left me like this.'

Her expression was unmoving.

'But,' I continued, 'now's the time to focus on your performance here, Madison. Frankly, I think Nathan could've kept on top of his staff reviews a little better. That won't be a mistake I'll be making.'

I left her standing there in the doorway and strode to my consulting room. The afternoon dragged on. In between patients, I searched the internet for news of a man's body found in the trunk of a car. Remains discovered in a hillside lodge. Surgeon arrested for murder.

'It's beginning to blister, I think.' Miss McKee, a twenty-three-year-old woman, turned her face to the side. She reached for the box of tissues on my desk, pulled one free, dabbed her eyes. 'I don't want to be scarred, Doctor.'

311

Miss McKee had booked an emergency appointment and I'd squeezed her on to the end of my list. Both her parents had been patients of mine since I began at the surgery, and they weren't the type of people you said no to. Their daughter had a habit of phoning late in the afternoon and demanding to be seen immediately from anything to an inflamed zit to muscle pain after a workout. There was a patch of skin along her jawline, about the size of a twopence piece, that was slightly pinker than the rest of her face, which was flushed with anxiety.

Pulling on gloves, I brought the lamp round and pointed it in her direction. 'How did you do it?'

'Filling a hot-water bottle. It slipped through my arms before I could put the top on and it splashed upwards,' she said, eyes watering again. 'We have insurance. Could you refer me to a plastic surgeon? The wedding is in a month.'

I turned the light off. 'You're going to be fine,' I said. 'I can't see any blistering. Are you in pain?'

'A little, but you know me, Doctor.'

'Let me prescribe you some antiseptic cream.'

'Do you think I could do with antibiotics? As a precaution. I've seen pictures of what can happen if it gets infected,' she said, her eyes wide with worry.

Normally, I'd go through the many reasons why we don't prescribe antibiotics as a precaution. I should ask her about her stress. About wedding anxiety. But the pressure and exhaustion from the last forty-eight hours and the uncertainty about what the next forty-eight would hold were more than beginning to wear. I filled out a prescription, tore it away from the pad and held it out.

312

She took it. 'Thank you, Doctor.' She closed her eyes. Relieved.

I stayed on at the surgery for as long as I could stand. Filing abnormal blood tests, chasing up results and booking referrals. There was still nothing on the news. A text from Daniel, saying he'd dinner organised and could I pick up wine. I left at seven, the rest of the staff already gone home. I locked up, tension building under my skin. I got to the car, drove to the nearest superstore, grabbed a basket and headed to the wine aisle. I stared unseeingly at the selection before taking a South African red from the shelf. It wasn't until I got to the checkout I realised I'd selected Lana's favourite label.

I couldn't understand how things were so quiet at the Wright house when I got back. Where were the police cars? Those officials in forensic suits should be roaming their home, combing it for clues as to why Gabe had murdered Pete? Again, I checked my phone. Looked for a message from Holly. My mind raced with possibilities around why shit was not hitting the fan. Part of me worried that Gabe had done a U-turn, tried to make it back to the cabin. Discovered the fire and disappeared himself. I'd removed the tracker from his car so I'd no way of knowing where he was. I sat in the driver's seat and watched the house through the rear-view. The light in the kitchen was on, as was the corner light in the living room. The blinds were drawn.

A text from Daniel, that dinner was ready, summoned me from the car. I tucked the wine under my arm, grabbed my bag and let myself into the house. I could hear two sets of voices coming from the kitchen. The scent of roast chicken enveloped me, but I had little appetite. Suddenly, it struck me – the tiredness, the dull ache at the back of my head where Lana had hit me.

The ache spawned a series of images, flashes, memories. Her gasp as the knife went in, her gasp on our honeymoon as she waded into the cool sea for an afternoon dip. The sight of her bare feet pacing in front of my crumpled body, those same feet on my lap, my hands pressing into the sore points along the arch; her toes curling with pleasure. The smell of her, the weight of her, the warmth of her. I stopped in the hall, leaned against the wall and took a series of long, slow breaths, then walked through to the kitchen.

Charlotte got up from a bar stool, a glass of white wine in her hand. 'Myles, hi, hope you don't mind . . . My goodness, what happened to your face?'

I touched a hand to my cheekbone. 'It's not that bad, is it? Running injury yesterday. I fell,' I said. I was almost beginning to believe the lie.

I put down my bag, carried the wine to the counter. 'Are you staying for dinner, Charlotte?'

She glanced at Daniel. 'Not tonight. I've an early start.'

Daniel reached across the island and touched his hand to hers.

She smiled, finished her wine. 'How are you, Myles?'

'Work. It's busy,' I said. I opened the red, set it on the island.

Daniel opened the oven door and stirred a fish slice through a tray of roast potatoes.

Charlotte stood and went to Daniel. 'Talk tomorrow?'

He straightened, nodded. She kissed his cheek and he flushed to the tips of his ears.

She squeezed my shoulder as she passed. 'Don't push yourself too hard,' she said.

Daniel took a couple of plates from the warming drawer beneath the oven then removed the chicken from the oven and went about serving up. 'Nothing like a home-cooked roast, is there?'

'No,' I said.

He slid a plate towards me, dished up his own, then sat down. 'Thank you. For everything,' he said. He raised his glass and took a sip.

'I'm glad to see you and Charlotte working things through.'

I picked up my cutlery, cut through the crisped skin of a roast potato. 'This looks delicious. Thank you.'

'No worries, mate. Glad to do it.'

I chewed slowly through the meal. Even though I'd acid in my throat from hunger, my stomach had tightened into a knot and I only managed half. I laid my cutlery down. I was tired of thinking about Gabe, of Lana. Of what Holly would do when Gabe returned, if he returned. The longer time went on, the more I was sure Gabe had been caught. I should be worried about what he might be persuaded to tell the police. But I had no connection with Pete Clifford. I had no obvious connection with Violet Dryden. The only person who would come out looking guilty after this was Gabe. Gabe wouldn't want to add to whatever sentence was coming his way by telling police he'd also helped me commit fraud. That he'd used his own murder victim as a substitute for my wife in order to receive a slice of an insurance claim.

'What's the plan with Charlotte then? Are you getting back together?' I asked Daniel.

'I don't want to say too much,' he said, sounding like Hunter.

'But things are looking good. I think . . .' He paused. 'For the first time in our relationship we're being really honest with one another. No more pandering, no pretending we're okay when we're not. It's like we've nothing to lose. It's freeing.'

I poured a glass of wine, lifted it to my mouth.

'You know we'd . . . well, Charlotte in particular, we've always wanted kids, right?'

I nodded.

'I thought she didn't want to start a family yet because of my job –' he laughed – 'or lack of it. We can be truthful here, right?'

A sympathetic smile from me.

'It turns out she was scared she'd lose her foothold at work. She's about to get a huge promotion, you know,' he said, a lift of pride in his chest. 'I'd no idea that was holding her back. I told her I'd stay at home. I'd look after the kids. I couldn't imagine a better existence.'

'That's really great,' I said. I reached round, touched the back of my head; the wound flared to life, sent tendrils of pain shooting over my scalp.

Daniel stopped talking. 'You okay? You've gone a bit pale round the gills.'

I got up slowly. 'I have to call it a night.'

'You get some rest, mate. I'll clean up here.'

He was a good friend.

I was in the hallway when the doorbell rang. Daniel put his head round the corner.

'I got it,' I said.

Hunter waited in the porch.

'Detective,' I said. 'Everything okay?'

I watched him taking in the injury on my face. 'There's been a bit of an incident involving your neighbour. Gabriel Wright. I wondered if I could ask you a few questions?'

CHAPTER 29

I cleared my throat. 'Come in.' I opened the door wide.

He stepped inside and motioned towards his eye. 'You okay?'

'Oh, this,' I mirrored his action. 'Running. Turns out you're not supposed to use your face.'

He frowned and I mentally kicked myself. Too light-hearted. 'Come through to the lounge.' I led him inside to the tub chairs at the French windows. I motioned for him to sit, but he shook his head. No thanks.

'Gabriel Wright's car was found this morning by Welsh police,' he said, pitching his hands against the back of one of the chairs. 'It looked like he came off the road at a particularly high part of the hills and rolled. They found some blood on the left bumper, deer hair. We believe he swerved to avoid the animal, went over and . . .' He adjusted his tie, smoothed it down his front.

I swallowed, attempted to moisten the desert on my tongue. I could feel heat creeping around the neck of my shirt.

'Is he okay?'

'Sadly, he was dead before anyone found him. It's believed he was there for some hours.'

Instead of the room closing in on me, I felt as though it were expanding, the walls fading, melting, like wet tissue, and me, head huge, the size of a planet, drifting back like I was being pulled through the universe of our home, where Hunter was a small dark lump on the edge of a solar system. I swallowed, just to bring myself back, to fix on the tinny, distant warble of his voice.

I made myself respond. 'That can't be.'

'I'm sorry, Dr Butler. I know you two had become friends,' he said.

Despite how it looked, I hadn't intended for Gabe to die. I'm not sure what I'd wanted. For him to be hurt, to be taught some kind of lesson. To remove him from Lana. I think the latter is closest to the truth. I wanted him to feel the pain I felt when I knew she was gone from me for good. But then, with Gabe's death, I'd be home and dry. Gabe wouldn't be able to defend himself.

'How was he when you last saw him?' Hunter asked.

I shifted on my feet. The back of my head began to throb. 'What do you mean?'

'Was he stressed? Distracted? How did he seem?'

'Fine. We had dinner together on Friday night. At Charlotte's,' I said, feeling my feet touch the floor finally, 'Charlotte Preston. Our neighbour.'

'So, nothing out of the ordinary? Anything at all. Even if it doesn't seem important.'

'He appeared his usual self. Gabe was always upbeat when I saw him.'

He made a note. 'Okay.' He had surprisingly neat nails, trimmed square at the top.

'He left the dinner early though, which I guess might be unusual for him. He was often one for kicking back after a meal. Liked a brandy and to talk,' I said. 'But he mentioned he had a work thing some distance away the following evening, said he needed rest. The dinner party wrapped up shortly before ten.'

If Hunter thought anything I said was significant, he didn't show it.

'He never spoke about or mentioned a man called Peter Clifford?'

I paused. I could tell them all about Gabe's affair with Violet, give the police a motive for him killing Pete, but I sensed that Hunter had already done his homework and I wasn't about to draw lines between Gabe, Pete, Lana and me.

I said, 'I don't think so.'

'Another neighbour said they witnessed a man of a similar description around The Court.' He put his hand inside his jacket pocket and produced a photograph. 'Do you recognise him?'

It was Pete all right. He was sitting in a beer garden. There was someone sitting next to him who had been cropped out. Violet maybe. Pete's face was half turned. Like in the Facebook photo, he wasn't as thin. The jaw was still substantial, the underbite, but his skin was clear, apart from a light spread of stubble. His hair was shorter and seemed lighter, not the curling greasy waves that I'd seen.

I gazed down at the photo. 'Oh yes, now I recognise him. I saw him once or twice around here. I thought he might be lost or something, so asked him if he needed help. He said he was waiting to talk to Mr Wright, to Gabe. About a week earlier, he'd turned up in Sandbanks when I was staying with the Wrights.'

'You talked to him?'

'Not then. After Lana's funeral we . . . I had a wake here at the house.' I pointed towards the picture. 'He was hanging around outside the Wrights' house. He never told me his name, just said he needed to talk to Gabe. Sorry, any other day it'd probably have made more of an impression. But it was my wife's funeral.'

'I understand. Of course. You didn't feel the need to phone the police?'

'No. As I said, I'd a lot on my mind. I told Gabe, though. He didn't seem worried.'

'What date did he show up at Sandbanks?'

I drew in a long breath. 'I couldn't be sure of the exact date. Perhaps the fifth or sixth of August. It was before the funeral. Sorry, the days, they all blur into one another. But Gabe and I had taken a boat to Poole harbour, we returned a few hours later and this man, Pete, was in the back garden.'

'On his own?'

'No. Holly, Gabe's wife, appeared to be asking him to leave.'

'Asking?'

'It was clear he wasn't welcome.'

'Did you get the impression she knew who he was.'

'No. When Gabe and I got off the boat, it all de-escalated rather quickly and Gabe escorted him from the property. Holly told me he was an old patient who'd become a little too attached. What's going on, Detective? Is this man dangerous?'

'You can rest assured you're quite safe here.'

I let out a cold laugh. I wanted to know what Hunter knew. What his view was on Gabe and Pete's connection. I said, 'For some reason, the need for you to utter that statement makes me feel less so.'

'Peter Clifford is not a risk to you or anyone,' he said. 'We're simply pursuing a few lines of inquiry.'

'Inquiry? As in investigation? Should I phone you if this man comes about again?'

'There's no need,' he said.

'No need? It sounds like you think he could be dangerous?'

He sighed, put down his pen. 'There's no need, Doctor, because Peter Clifford is dead. He was found in the boot of Gabriel Wright's car when it was discovered this morning.'

'My God.'

'So, you see, you can relax,' he said.

I wiped a hand over my face. 'This is a lot to take in. Gabe killed that man?'

'We don't know that he killed him. All we know is that Peter Clifford's remains were found in Gabriel Wright's car.'

I blinked. Walked to the French doors. Peered out between an opening in the curtains. Across the street, the lights were on in the Wright house. A police car was pulled up in the drive.

I heard Hunter turn the page of his notepad. 'I've a few more questions, Doctor, then I'll leave you in peace.'

Tension creeped across my shoulders.

'Did you ever see Mr Wright – Gabriel – with another woman?' he asked.

The image of Gabe in the street with Violet, their silhouette in the darkness. How I'd thought in that first instance it was Lana.

'No,' I said.

'Never?'

I shook my head. 'He was a devoted husband, as far as I could see.'

'My twice divorced mother would have told you there's no such thing,' he said with a laugh. When I didn't join in, he said, 'She was a cynical sort, maybe why it never worked out for her.' He forced a smile. 'Did Gabriel talk about anyone called Violet?'

'He never mentioned anyone of that name to me.'

And then it was over. Hunter snapped his notebook shut, stood and put out his hand. 'Thank you for your time, Doctor.'

I shook his hand and followed him out to the door. 'Is he really dead?' I asked.

He stopped. Looked back. 'Yes.'

Daniel was finished eating by the time Hunter left. He rinsed his plate, opened the door of the dishwasher and placed it neatly inside. He'd already cleared away leftovers into Tupperware, wiped down all the surfaces.

'Everything okay?' he asked. He poured another Rioja and handed it to me. 'What did the fuzz want?'

'Gabriel Wright is dead,' I said.

'Fuck off.'

I couldn't look at him. 'His car came off a road in Wales, he was killed.'

'Jesus.'

'They found a body in the boot of his car.'

'What? Like dead?'

No fear of Daniel cracking this case. I didn't answer.

'Whose?' he asked.

'A man called Peter Clifford?'

He stuck out his bottom lip, shook his head as if he should recognise the name. 'What did the detective say?'

'Just mentioned something about an investigation and that they didn't know if Gabe had killed this guy but it sounded like they were known to one another.' I glanced up, winced. 'He asked about a woman too?'

'Dead also?'

I shook my head. 'He didn't say. He implied that Gabe had been having an affair.' I drank down a good portion of my wine. The dull ache in my head was developing to an excruciatingly sharp point that appeared to increase in intensity with every blink and breath.

'Thought he was off from the moment I met him,' Daniel said.

I surprised myself by coming to Gabe's defence. 'So he deserved to die?'

Daniel pulled back, held up his palms. 'Relax. I'm sorry. I know you two were friends. Charlotte's always on at me for putting my foot in it.'

I threw back the wine. 'No, I'm sorry. I'm tired and this is a shock.'

'You've had so much loss to deal with lately,' he said, putting his hand on my shoulder. 'None of it is fair. You don't deserve any of it, Myles. You're a good person.'

I nodded, muttered my thanks. But Daniel was wrong. I wasn't a good person. I'm not sure I ever was.

CHAPTER 30

I'd spent the whole of the next day at work waiting for the hammer to fall, for Hunter or someone to uncover my guilt. Then later, waiting for Holly to appear on my doorstep. By Wednesday morning, I was a tight knot of anxiety. The rain fell thick and heavy. It drove against the windows, gathered and ran in rivulets along the pathways of Belvedere Court. I looked out of my bedroom window, watched the deluge charge downwards. It thrummed on the roof, dripped from the eaves of the house. Wide skirts of water flew up from beneath the wheels of the police car that pulled up outside the Wright house. My view was obscured, the world a wet blur, the window fogged under my breath, but still I recognised Hunter's slightly hunched posture as he ducked out from beneath his car and hurried towards the door. It opened and Holly's blonde hair was just discernible before Hunter stepped inside and the door closed again.

I'd started the morning with an espresso and paracetamol to get ahead of the pain. The wound had closed over nicely, the soreness reduced to its origin and even then only when I touched it. The bruise around my eye was already turning yellow. I headed for the shower, got ready for work. I had a morning session and expected to finish by lunchtime. The idea of having an entire afternoon stretch out before me filled me with terror. A Welsh online newspaper had run a story on a fire in a lodge near Arthog. I'd already read through the short piece four times, each line burned in my brain. *Police are seeking to talk to . . . Anything suspicious in the days . . . Looking for . . .*

It was clear that the lodge had done what I'd thought it would when I left that morning. The fire had consumed it wholly, the article said. They presumed the body was that of a woman. No age, no name. And even with DNA retrieval there wouldn't be, unless Hunter unearthed some fragment of evidence that caused him to look a little closer at my home. There was a not insignificant part of me worried that Holly in her grief might confess everything to him. But there was a dark hardness in her that I sensed would not be easy to crack. Gabe had come off the road a good hour's drive from Arthog. Clearly, he hadn't been on his way back to Lana but had decided to drive on, away from the mess of their affair. And from what I could read in the papers, the police had yet to connect the fire at the lodge to Gabe's accident. I'd only discovered the articles about the lodge in the media because I'd searched for them. I expected they would connect the two soon, seeing as Pete's borrowed car remained near the site. That was, if borrowed didn't mean stolen. But there was a good chance Holly was not aware of the lodge fire yet and so would stick to her story about her husband attending some medical meet-up.

Daniel was at Charlotte's for a quick breakfast before she'd to leave for work. I took my time leaving, half of me waiting for the knock on my door I felt sure would come from Hunter. But it didn't and I gathered up my work bag and stepped out into the rain. I got into my car, shook droplets from my fingers and hair and left The Court behind and all that was unfolding there.

Clinic churned by, too fast and too slow. Not quite enough to keep my mind occupied. Brian Lovett had saved himself for last.

'What happened to your face,' he said, half mesmerised by the residual swelling and yellow bruises around my eye.

'Running,' I said.

'Gosh. Are you sure you haven't fractured the maxillary process?'

I indicated that he should sit. 'Quite sure.'

He considered me carefully. 'I read that that surgeon neighbour of yours had died. Are you feeling okay?'

'I'm fine, thank you, Brian. What can I do for you?'

'Only, if you're not quite yourself, I could wait, see one of the other doctors.' Clearly he was worried I was going to miss some subtle signal that, yes, after all this time, Brian did have something wrong other than his own hypochondria.

'I'm fine,' I said and added a reassuring smile. 'You look well, Brian.'

I'd a brief flash of Lana's phone leaving my hand, the light plopping sound it made when it hit the water. They wouldn't look for that. Would they?

'I do?' Brian put a finger on his pulse. 'I can still feel it.'

I drove home through the rain, slowing gradually the nearer I got to The Court. I tried to put the growing nausea I was experiencing down to anxiety. Sweat moistened my palms, stung

327

the cut on my hand. I was worried about what the afternoon was going to bring. Hunter asking more questions. Having to keep all the lies I told him yesterday at the front of my mind, clear and easy so that he didn't trip me up. I was practised enough at that but no one really appreciates how exhausting it is to affect ease while pedalling madly in your head in order to conjure up the exact same throwaway comment you made the day before. *Did I say I saw Pete Clifford once or twice, or three or four times?*

Daniel was still out. The police car that had pulled up at the Wrights early this morning was gone. I went upstairs, showered, put on a pair of joggers and fished my mac out of the wardrobe.

I was putting on my trainers when the doorbell rang. I froze; then, left shoe still untied, I went to the door and opened it.

Holly stood in the doorway.

'Can I come in?'

'Of course,' I said and stepped aside.

She walked past me and into the kitchen. She was dressed well, a white shirt and pale blue slacks that were gathered round her waist with a white belt. But I could see the creases in the fabric, the hasty application of make-up that attempted to cover the dark hollows beneath her eyes. Her lashes clumped together into stiff, sharp points.

I stood on the other side of the island and faced her. 'Sorry to hear about Gabe.'

Her chin dimpled as she attempted to suppress her emotion. 'I hope you realise, this changes nothing between us. Where is my money? I expect it in that bank account. By tomorrow evening. Latest. Don't forget, I'm the only one who has Lana's whereabouts. She knows nothing of Gabe's . . . death. But I hold her life in my hands, Myles. A word from me and she's gone. Things have to move swiftly now. I can't have her thinking something is wrong.'

I stared down at her; she was such a slight woman, Holly. Fine hair, that if you were to take a fistful and hold it up to the light it would almost disappear. It was natural to suppose of the two of them, her and Gabe, Holly would be the weaker opponent. But now, as I looked at her, I could see determination vibrating from the very core of her being. All along, I guess she had the measure of me and Lana, could see the cracks, the faults in our marriage, running like fractures through glass.

'Are you hearing me?' she pressed. 'Myles?' Again, that strength barking at the back of her voice. And the merest hint of impatience.

I removed my phone from my pocket and found again the article from the Welsh newspaper. I enlarged the image of the burnt-out lodge. I laid the phone on the island between us and spun it round so that it was facing her.

'What is this?' She picked up the mobile and looked down at the screen. I saw the moment when she realised what she was seeing. Small pinches of colour developed high on her cheeks. I saw the muscles in her narrow throat convulse. She scanned through the article, then placed the phone down. 'What is this?' she asked again.

'It's over,' I said. 'You won't be seeing a penny from me. Lana's dead.'

Her mouth opened, then she closed it again. She looked down at the phone again, fully registering what it meant.

'Why did you send Pete Clifford after your husband?' I asked.

She lifted her eyes to mine. Her eyebrows pulled down. 'I don't know what you're talking about.'

'He told me it was you,' I said.

Her hand rested on the edge of the island, fingers curled in on themselves. A flicker of the muscle at the corner of her jaw. Finally, the dots lined up. 'You were there,' she murmured.

I didn't answer. 'You knew they were sleeping together.'

Her voice took on a sharpness when she answered. 'I heard them talking on the phone. All their plans. How they were going to leave together. To leave me. You.'

'Gabe and Lana?'

'Yes.'

'So you thought you'd send Pete after him. What did you think would happen? The moment Pete saw Lana? Not only would he put together what had happened to Violet, but there would be no choice, Pete would have to die.'

Tears gathered at the corners of her eyes. 'I was drunk. Angry. Or maybe both. I only meant for him to feel . . .' She paused, teeth gritted. 'Some consequence. To pay in some way. There should be consequences when you've done what he has, no?'

I tried to remove Pete from the equation. Tried to imagine what the outcome would have been had he not been there. I'd been angry to the point of violence on seeing Gabe and Lana together, but Pete's murder had flicked a switch, set in motion a chain of events, pushed me across a line from which there was no going back. I glared at Holly. Wanting to shove down her throat her slice of consequence.

330

Silence spread out between us and Holly took a rumpled tissue from her back pocket and rubbed her nose. When she spoke, all sharpness had left her voice, 'Gabe didn't kill Pete, did he?'

I looked down and enjoyed the small step she took backwards when I finally met her eyes. I shook my head.

'Lana?' she whispered.

'I don't think I have to answer any more of your questions, Holly, do you?'

She wiped a palm along her hip. 'I'm moving. In a few days. This whole . . . enterprise, I have as much to lose as you,' she said. 'You know that, right? There's no need to worry about police or . . . anything coming down the line.'

'I'd hope not,' I said.

She left, a backward glance over her shoulder as she entered the hallway to make sure I wasn't following.

Hunter called round that evening. Daniel opened the door. Left him in the lounge and came to fetch me from my study.

'Dr Butler,' he said when I entered.

'Detective Hunter. Can I get you a coffee? Tea?'

'No thank you.'

'Please.' I pointed towards a seat.

As before, he remained standing. 'Can you tell me where you were on Friday the fourth of September through Sunday the sixth?'

Heat gathered at the base of my back. 'Here mostly. At work. Friday evening, as I believe I've told you, I had dinner at Charlotte Preston's. Daniel has been here since Saturday evening. He's through the kitchen there if you need to talk to him.'

331

'And Sunday?'

I shook my head, frowned. 'Again, here.'

'Did you talk to anyone? Someone who could verify your whereabouts?'

'Only Daniel. He went out for a few hours on Sunday. As did I, but otherwise, I was here. Detective, what's this about?' I moved to one of the armchairs, sat down, not trusting my knees to keep me upright.

'We found Gabriel Wright's phone in the wreckage of his car. We retrieved a couple of interesting text exchanges, among them a message from you.'

I scrambled through my memories, tried to get ahead of what he was about to ask me but came up blank. I smiled, shrugged. 'We did text occasionally. We were neighbours. Friends.'

'One from early August caught my eye. You sent a text saying,' he flicked back through his notebook, "I need to talk to her." Then Mr Wright's reply, "Timing's not right. Soon. G." Who did you need to talk to?'

I shook my head, blew out a mouthful of air. 'I'm not sure,' I said.

'Sounds like it was urgent,' Hunter persisted.

'Oh that's right. It was shortly after my stay with them. After Lana . . .' I trailed off here, swallowed. 'Anyway, I'd mentioned to Gabe that I wanted to move, escape in a way, I guess, and he'd said he might know someone who had an opening at a surgery in York. I can't recall her name now and,' I pursed my lips, another shrug, 'In the end, I decided not to pursue it.'

He lifted his chin, his tongue pressed against the inside of his cheek. I could feel the frustration coming from him in waves. 'I remembered our chat, about how you'd spent your student years in Bristol and I thought I'd look up one of my old colleagues there. See if he'd heard of you.'

Mouth dry. 'And?'

'He did.'

'I studied there. I knew a lot of people.'

'Does the name Hartigan mean anything to you?'

I tried to control my breathing. Shrugged, then feigned realisation. 'Yes, he taught at my old school.'

'That's correct. Right up until a car accident left him unable to work.'

'I don't understand what this has to do with me.'

He ignored my comment.

'Mr Hartigan believed you tampered with his car and that was what caused his accident. He believed you had a thing for his wife.'

'From what I recall, Hartigan was a controlling drunk who'd a chip on his shoulder. That's what caused his accident.' I stood. Pulled myself up. 'Despite his spurious claims, everyone he pointed a finger at was investigated and cleared.'

He met my eyes and I saw a dark, determined gleam of hatred in them. 'Strange though that your wife meets her death in a car accident, you collect a very substantial insurance payout, then Mr Wright meets a similar fate. I understand you worked in a garage for a few years?'

'I'm not sure I like what you're implying, Detective. For the record, I would never have wanted to harm my wife, and why on earth would I have wanted to harm Gabe?' Then added, 'Or anyone for that matter.'

He blinked slowly. Eyes still on me, tracking my face, my emotions. 'Hartigan's brake line was cut. Not a great job either. Sliced all the way through. Mr Wright's vehicle, however, the lines blew when he slammed on that pedal. Nicely disguised, I reckon.'

I knew he had no way of knowing they were cut. I knew I'd been careful, just enough to cause a fault if the brakes were used at speed or with force, the pressure within the tube would have done the rest.

I met his gaze. Didn't give him the reply he wanted. He knew something, but he was feeling around in the dark and some perverse part of me wanted him to understand that I knew that.

He lifted a hand, rubbed the stubble along his jaw. A flash of uncertainty crossed his face. 'The marks on the road were almost non-existent. That deer leapt out in front of him and it appeared that instead of braking, he drove right over the edge. Hardly the best decision, even on an instinctive level. My reckoning is he tried to brake and there was nothing there.'

I took a step towards him. 'This is bordering on harassment,' I said. 'Am I under arrest for something, Detective?'

His gaze faltered again. 'No.'

'Then, I think we're done here.'

A ruddy pink rose along the tops of his cheeks. Nostrils flared. Out of the corner of my eye, I could see the slow movement of his hand at his side, fingers curling, and for a second I thought he was going to hit me.

Instead, he pulled his shoulders back, drew in his chin. 'I wouldn't make any plans to go anywhere, Dr Butler. There's something here and I've all the time in the world to find it.' He pushed by me. He was at the door when I spoke.

'I keep meaning to ask you. How's your daughter doing? Neve, is it?'

He froze. Turned.

I put my hands in my pocket. Smiled. 'Goodbye, Detective.'

I got out of the car, took a moment to check the gleam on the toes of my shoes. I had that first-day-at-school feeling. I'd taken care to dress well that morning. Unfolding a new white shirt from its packaging and putting on a fresh dry-cleaned suit. I bounded up the steps of the bank and swept through the revolving doors.

'Good morning, Dr Butler,' the receptionist beamed. I beamed back. 'Eric will be with you shortly.'

I flicked a pointed glance at my watch. 'If you wouldn't mind fetching him. I'm very busy this morning.'

She flushed. Unsure what to do. But I didn't break my gaze until she pushed out the seat. 'Certainly, I'll see if I can locate him.' She hurried off up the hall, chewing the tip of a pencil as she went.

I pushed my suit jacket back and put my hands in my pockets. The suit was the new one I'd bought in Sandbanks with Gabe. The one I wore for Lana's funeral. It looked well on me, Gabe had been right about that. I felt a certain thrill wearing it; maybe that detective was on to something when he talked of trophies. The suit was a reminder of what I'd got away with, what I was about to get away with. The insurance money had come through and now I was only a few signed papers away from freeing myself of debt. Over the reception, the round eye of a camera looked down on me. I smiled up. I knew Eric would be watching.

Eric greeted me in the reception with a cool smile. 'I was sorry to hear about Lana.'

'Yes, it's been a strange few months,' I said. 'I just want to settle some affairs here.'

'Of course. Of course,' he said. Fake bastard.

He brought me into one of the side rooms and closed the door quietly behind us. Walking to a water cooler in the corner, he asked if I'd like one.

'Please,' I said.

'Shit, sorry,' he said. 'No cups. 'I'll get a glass, hang on.'

He left and I sat with the four walls peering down on me. When he returned he handed me the water. The glass was scratched, run through a dishwasher too many times, the water trickling down the side.

'What can I do for you?' Eric asked. He shuffled his chair back from the desk so he'd room to cross his foot over his knee, rested his hands over his stomach and appraised me with a sympathetic expression.

'The funeral costs were a shock, as you can expect,' I said.

He nodded.

'But you'll be pleased to hear that I'm able to make good on the mortgage.'

Legs unfolded, he pulled his chair in. 'Right. We've had details from your insurance company. Or should I say, Lana's insurance company.'

'I was surprised they came through so quickly,' I said.

'As was I, considering the debts you have,' he said. 'Thought you'd be defending red flags for months. You understand we had an obligation to disclose your records to them.'

And I'm sure you sent them off with delight, I thought. 'I signed the release forms, remember? They appreciated that, I think. I'd nothing to hide,' I replied.

He coughed into his hand.

I placed my bag on the table, removed a folder. 'These are the companies to whom I owe money, I need to set up payment to clear all debts and pay off what's owed to date on the mortgage.'

'With interest?'

'With interest.'

He raised an eyebrow. 'What a stroke of luck she had insurance,' he said, then held up his palms. 'Sorry, that's horrendous wording. What I meant was—'

'I know what you meant,' I said, calmly. I leaned back in the chair, put my hands in my pockets.

He swallowed. But he had the nerve to shrug.

I let a short silence string out between us before I spoke, 'This was very Lana. Just when I thought she couldn't get any more disorganised, she produces next-level preparation. But not only has she given me this but she's taught me something.' I paused. 'When tragedy tears through your life, there'll always be some loose end left flapping in the wind for you to hold on to.'

'I'm not sure I'd refer to life insurance as a loose end,' he said.

'Oh, I wasn't talking about that,' I said. 'I was talking about you.'

He ran his tongue along his bottom lip, reached for his water.

'I was talking to a friend of mine,' I said. 'You know him actually. Daniel Preston. He went in on that investment you suggested. Lost a lot of money.'

He ran his fingers along his hairline. 'I don't think I can be blamed for that.'

'Oh, I realise it's not solely your fault. But with the current climate and banks getting such a beating in the press, word could get out. I understand you have some pretty wealthy clients on your books.'

He glared at me for a few moments, then gathered up the folder on the table. 'I'll take care of this for you.'

I nodded. 'Thank you. I knew you'd be happy to help, and I'm looking forward to working together in the future.'

'Indeed.'

I smiled, stood and put out my hand.

He shook it.

'Glad we're back on the same page, Eric,' I said.

CHAPTER 31

Three Months Later

I finish my run with a sprint along the golf course before slowing to a jog and passing down the avenue of frozen trees towards the park. The air is sharp as needles on my face, my breath billows of white. I break free of the trees, a few walkers call out for their dogs, barks circling from somewhere in the mist. I wait for the gates to open, then walk into The Court. I stand for a moment, roll out my shoulders and look over the six houses, quiet, their occupants not yet awake or lingering over breakfast in warm state-of-the-art kitchens. The dim shimmer of dawn glitters on the icy rooftops. What cars have been left on drives are dressed in winter white.

I walk to my house, step inside and go to the kitchen to make coffee. Across the street, the porchlight clicks on. A man appears. He peels back a blue car cover to reveal a gleaming black Audi. I know that in the garage there is a crimson red Audi. It belongs to the man's wife. New neighbours. Hugo and Xanthe Cargill. He's a celebrity. A TV chef. He owns a chain of fancy restaurants called Palate, where you get what you're served rather than what you ask for, in the name of sustainability. I've eaten in them twice. The food is exquisite.

I like him. He is forward, in charge, prides himself on his straight talk. *Myles, I've always believed if you want something, you'll find a way to get it.* His wife is a vet. She carries her substantial family fortune like a shameful sin that she explains carefully and apologetically to anyone who is cruel enough to enquire. Every few days, I see her carry another poorly animal into her home to nurse to health. Pets whose owners can't afford care. Her husband is not a fan of animals.

I have a couple of days off. I'm to visit Anthony Chapman at a prospective premises for a new Willowhaven surgery in Sandbanks. I've packed two suits. One for our meeting, a second for cocktails at Genevieve Scott-Baker's house along the coast. She reached out as soon as she heard about Gabe and insisted I visit when I was next in the area. I pour my espresso, pick up a banana and head upstairs. The doorbell goes. I leave my coffee on the bottom step, jog down the hall.

Charlotte stands in the porch, a wide smile on her face. Her red hair is scooped back into a sleek bun. She's dressed for work, in a black trouser suit. Daniel moved out of my house a few days after the news of Gabe spread through The Court. He and Charlotte had an emotional talk that included many phrases along the lines of *life being too short*. They are planning for their family and Charlotte is on her first round of IVF shots.

'Charlotte, come in,' I say. 'How's Daniel?'

'Hello, darling.' She clasps my hand, leans in and kisses my cheek. 'Sleeping like a baby.'

'I've just made coffee, the machine is on.'

'I'm hurrying as I don't want to get caught in the traffic. I just wanted to drop this off. If you could take care of it, Dan would appreciate it. He said you had the car the night before for work, that you must have been coming back from somewhere.' She put a speeding ticket on the island. 'The M6? A little far out for a patient run, wasn't it?'

I pick it up, a hit of bile creeps up my throat.

'Yes. I'd car trouble that evening, I think,' I say. 'I ended up going to a clinic outside Birmingham, a colleague had a piece of specialist equipment I needed. He put me up for the night so I wouldn't have to drive back tired.'

She smiles but there is a stiffness to it.

'I don't know if I said how happy I am for you both,' I say, trying to push the subject on.

'I feel so lucky. I was so angry with him but, truthfully, I was lost when he moved out,' she says. 'Between us, I couldn't stand the idea that he'd meet someone else and he'd be gone from me forever.'

'I can assure you he had the same worry.' I laugh, trying to break up this strange tension that's snaked into the room.

'I know,' she says. 'He told me all about the app on my phone. I mean, I'm a divorce lawyer, I found it within days. But I couldn't be mad about it as I'd done similar.'

I busy myself at the coffee machine, set another cup under the portafilter, clean out the used grains. 'You did?'

'Worse, probably. Put one of those trackers on his car,' she says, and my heart slows. 'He still doesn't know I did that.' She pauses, waiting for a reply. Then I remember how she told us way back at

341

our first dinner with the Wrights that it was something her clients did to win legal points against their soon-to-be ex-spouses. I turn on the machine and it churns out another espresso. She waits until it stops. 'That's what I thought was odd about this ticket. At first, I thought it was Dan's, then I remembered he was in your house that morning so it couldn't have been him.'

I turn. 'Charlotte.' I hope she hears the note of pleading in my voice. 'I'll pay the ticket.'

But she doesn't let go. 'So I looked up the journey on my app. The route went all the way to Wales. Right out into the hills.' She comes round the island, looks up at me, eyes beseeching. 'Myles, where were you?'

'I told you, it was work.'

'That was when they said Gabe died. And where that other man was killed. The location was close. Practically matched,' she says. 'Were you with him? Gabe? Trying to help?'

I sigh. 'Okay. Gabe asked me to help him. Said he was going to teach this guy a lesson. Lure him out to the sticks and . . . I didn't know what his intentions were at the time. I barely paid any heed until the night of your dinner and he said he was leaving the following evening for some medical retreat. I was worried about what he could be planning so I went after him, to stop him. It all seemed fine when I got there. No shouting. No sign of any violence. Gabe was with some woman and . . . I just wanted to get home. On the way back, I was practically falling asleep at the wheel so I pulled into a lay-by and slept until morning. I must have got the ticket in the rush home.'

She sags with relief. 'Thank God. I thought . . .' She couldn't bring herself to finish the sentence.

'You thought I'd helped murder someone?'

She blushes, blotches of bright pink up her throat. 'I'm sorry. You know what my mind is like. Too many true crime documentaries.'

I smile. 'It's okay. To be honest, it's a relief to tell someone. You haven't told Daniel? I wouldn't want him to think—'

'No,' she says. 'But Myles, you should inform the police. They must want the full picture.'

'I will,' I lie. 'I'll call them today.'

She gives a nod but I know Charlotte and I can see that she won't let this go.

I have to force a smile. 'Thanks for calling. I'll get on to this.' I tap the speeding ticket.

'Great,' she says. 'Dinner this week?'

There's a dull tug in my chest, my mouth dries. 'At mine,' I say. 'Friday?'

'Perfect,' she says. 'See you then.'

She turns, walks out into the hall. She has her hand on the latch when I stop her.

ACKNOWLEDGEMENTS

Thank you to my brilliant publishers. To Stefanie Bierwerth and Jon Riley who, from the earliest stages of this book, gave generously of their expertise, provided encouragement and whose insightful editorial notes were invaluable. This novel wouldn't be what it is without them. Thank you to Jasmine Palmer for reading and for her stellar work in preparing the manuscript for proof reading. Thank you to my copyeditor, Nick de Somogyi and proof-reader, Patrick McConnell. I'm very fortunate to have such a dedicated editorial team.

Thank you to Ana McLaughlin, Lisa Gooding and Lipfon Tang for their work in getting this novel out to readers. I'm so grateful for all your enthusiasm and support for this book.

Thank you to C&W literary agency and special thanks to my literary agent, Susan Armstrong, for her advice, support and excitement for this book. With every step of my publishing journey, I thank my lucky stars that you are at my side.

Thank you to all my friends who have listened, read or given advice on my writing over the years. Thank you to Mariusz for his advice on car mechanics and to Neil Lancaster for his advice on law enforcement. I'm really grateful to those professionals who have given their time and expertise on the medical aspects of this plot with special thanks to Professor Neil Mortensen.

Finally, huge thanks to Matthew and Grace for their unwavering belief, love, inspiration and support.